SUMMER HEARTS

JOSIE RIVIERA

PRAISE AND AWARDS

USA TODAY bestselling author

#1 Amazon Bestseller New Release Religious Romance
#15 Amazon Bestseller Religious Anthologies
#16 Amazon Bestseller Inspirational Religious Fiction

INTRODUCTION

To keep up on newly released ebooks, paperbacks, Large Print Paperbacks, audiobooks, as well as exclusive sales, sign up for Josie's Newsletter today.

As a thank you, I'll send you a Free PDF … The Beauty Of …

Josie's Newsletter

Did you know that according to a Yale University study, people who read books live longer?

5 STAR READER REVIEWS

Amazon Review by Belinda:
A Chocolate-Box Summer Breeze
"I am in love with this series. A short clean story of two widowers in their 70's who meet and start a friendship that develops over time. Who says you are too old to find love again?"

Amazon Review by Mary:
A Chocolate-Box Irish Wedding
"This beautifully written romance whisks the reader off to the Irish town of Wexford. High school sweethearts who had gone off to pursue their individual dreams after graduation are there to attend the wedding of her mother to his father. She is divorced and he has never married.

Is there any chance that the old spark between them can be rekindled or will the physical distance between them keep them apart despite their obvious attraction to each other? While Kiera has returned to live in Wexford, Colum teaches dance in another city.

I loved learning about some of the Irish traditions which Josie Riviera intricately weaves into this story.

This novella can easily be read in one sitting, but once again the author has found a way to make the major characters come alive within the limited number of pages.

Remember to check out the included recipe for Irish Soda Bread."

Amazon Review by Teresa:

A Summer To Cherish

"Sweet romance with a happily ever after. Obstacles can be overcome, and past troubles forgiven. Wonderful read."

This book is dedicated to all my wonderful readers who have supported me every inch of the way.
THANK YOU!

CONTENTS

A SUMMER TO CHERISH

DEAR FRIENDS

Savor the magic of my Summer Romances—exclusively in one collection!

This set includes three sweet and inspirational romances:

1-800-SUMMER
The last thing she can fix is her own life. Until one man's offer changes everything.

A Chocolate-Box Summer Breeze
Will Emily and Joe find their happily-ever-after in a forgotten summer breeze?

A Summer To Cherish (Inspirational)
Faith is fragile. Faith takes time. And the best solutions are always painted with love.

Now, or anytime, I hope you enjoy the promise of new beginnings and beautiful summers with me.

JOSIE RIVIERA

1 * 800 * SUMMER

A SWEET CONTEMPORARY NOVELLA

IND'TALE MAGAZINE REVIEW

CONTEMPORARY ROMANCE:

"Belle Boots loves horses. So much so that she has made them her life's work by running an equine therapy practice. Looking for a change in scenery, she takes on a fixer-upper and goes against the norm of her nomadic ways in exchange for something more stable.

She returns to her childhood home, Wilmington, and it's there she meets Andrew Bransfield. Unfortunately, it doesn't seem as though she can stay.

Determined to keep Belle in town to help his daughter, Andrew sets out to build her the perfect barn for her horses. In doing so, he may just end up building something more.

Ms. Riviera has created a beautiful, moving sweet romance that will resonate with readers long after the book ends! Belle is a heroine that can be admired and loved right off the bat. Her passion for her patients and her drive for adventure give her a beautiful heart mixed with a fun energy.

Andrew is a driven man who has a fear of animals. He is

strong and steady, and when the two of them get together, their chemistry is natural and believable.

This book is part of a series, but it stands alone nicely. There are a few moments when the conflict doesn't feel quite believable, but overall the book is smooth and a joy to read that will fill many with hope. This is a great book for lovers of sweet romance and small town settings!"

PRAISE AND AWARDS

USA TODAY bestselling author

#21 Amazon Bestseller Contemporary Western Fiction

#37 Amazon Bestseller Scottish Historical Romance

#21 Amazon Bestseller Contemporary Western Fiction

CHAPTER 1

*B*elle Boots breathed in the comforting smell of hay and leather and peered around at her beloved stable—the weathered wooden planks, the plastic buckets of water, the wide mirror propped in the corner of the stall ...

And, most notably, at Jenkins—her sweet, colorful appaloosa—all one thousand pounds of quirky loyalty and claustrophobia.

"We're leaving, handsome." She fished in her pocket for a carrot. "Off we trot to greener pastures."

Jenkins whinnied and poked his nose through the stall, noisily accepting the carrot and ignoring her quip.

"Why is the pasture greener?" She rubbed his ears. "Because the new landlord of my sorry excuse for an apartment raised the rent." Which meant fewer than five weeks to find another place. She grabbed a water bucket and brush, scrubbing and refilling the bucket. "Maybe this is the ideal opportunity for us to return to Wilmington."

Another crunch of the carrot, and Jenkins pawed the stable floor.

"I can't play right now. I'm sorry. My therapy sessions begin in an hour."

In the past two years, she'd grown fond of the postcard-perfect community of Roses. In fact, she regarded Roses as her hometown.

She blew out a pensive sigh. Or did she?

Sometimes a person needed to leave a place to discover where home truly was. The sense of adventure that had surged through her when she had decided on Roses—the thrill of a different town and untried places—had worn thin. Despite her efforts to stay busy, Belle had never gotten over her loneliness since she had left Wilmington.

Perhaps she was simply homesick. She missed Aunt Lucinda, her mother's older sister and Belle's only living relative. Plus, she missed the ocean—the bracing waves, the salty air rushing across her face, and the sunbeams flashing off the water like silent jewels.

Jenkins stamped his hoof, bringing Belle back to the present.

"I only brought one carrot with me," she said. "I'll return later this afternoon with more."

In the pale-yellow light streaming through the slats, the echoes of a late May morning drifted, and promised a typical North Carolina day. Sunrises were cool and bearable before the humidity and oppressive heat kicked in.

After she mucked the stall and turned out Jenkins to the pasture, Belle's attentions swung back to her dilemma. Wilmington beckoned. Or perhaps Florida or California.

Only one thing was certain. She was moving. Somewhere.

She glanced at her watch. Swiftly, she washed up and sprinted to her pickup truck. In the tangle of the confusing morning, she'd lost track of time.

Her first equine therapy session was with Joseph, a dark-eyed boy whose lean legs raced so quickly he reminded her of a clockwork figure. His adoptive parents, Candee and Teddy, owned a large Victorian home on Thompson Lane and had built a riding ring on their acreage.

The second session was with Megan Bransfield, a chubby, pale girl who wore a bright pink patch over her right eye and rarely smiled.

How could she desert these precious children? Belle's sentiments wrestled between anguish and indecision. At the other side of the spectrum, anticipation welled.

THE DRIVE into Roses went slower than expected, which invariably happened whenever she was in a hurry. When she neared the Thompson Lane turn-off, she took in the scene in front of her—red, white, and blue balloons; the local marching band; and a banner stretching across the main street announcing the Memorial Day parade.

Quietly groaning, she clicked on her right signal, pulled to the curb, and phoned Candee.

"Hi, Belle," came Candee's cheerful response.

"Candee, I apologize." Belle rolled down her window, and a welcoming breeze gusted in, tousling her ponytail. "I'm running late, and traffic is at a standstill."

"No worries," Candee replied. "We'll wait for you."

"If you and your family prefer to attend the parade, it's fine. We can reschedule."

"Joseph wouldn't miss his session with you for anything in the world. Teddy and I appreciate all you've done, because Joseph's transformation is remarkable. He's considerably more outgoing and upbeat."

Belle's compassion squeezed. *Tell Candee gently.*

Belle and Candee had engaged in numerous coffee chats, most of which had centered around Belle's ex-husband, Tyler.

She'd married him at twenty-three years old. He was stoic and impassive and a suitable complement to Belle's over-the-top eagerness to please. And, they had hoped for a large family.

Or so she'd thought.

She yanked her mind back to Candee's enthusiastic, one-sided dialogue regarding her barbecue that evening.

"I have news," Belle blurted.

"What?"

"This session will be Joseph's last, at least with me." Belle fiddled with her truck's side-view mirror as an emptiness hollowed out a pit in her stomach. It wasn't in her nature to abandon her clientele, most notably the children who relied on her.

"Why is this his last session?" Candee asked.

"I'm moving." *So much for gently.* "Soon."

"So sudden?"

"My rent was raised to an astronomical amount. The new landlord said his parents are relocating to a retirement community, and he is taking over the property."

"Astronomical?"

"He didn't exactly use the word astronomical, but he offered a marathon explanation and got his point across."

"Can't you find somewhere else close by to live? Teddy and I have extra bedrooms on the third floor. What's more, Desiree and Kieran are hardly ever home. I'm certain they wouldn't mind if you lived with them for a while, either."

Desiree was Candee's sister, and she and her husband lived a few houses away from Candee. Kieran had opened O'Malley's, an Irish restaurant which had become tremendously well-liked. Desiree had set her profession as a lawyer on hold in order to assist Kieran.

"I refuse to inconvenience anyone," Belle replied.

"You're no inconvenience, and your horse can stable here."

"Jenkins? One never can predict how he'll behave."

"We're currently only boarding Joseph's and Megan's horses. Besides, Jenkins is a sweetie—despite his behavioral issues."

Belle chuckled. "He'll figure out a way to get out of his stall and invite the other horses to slip away with him."

"He did that once, right? When he was a racehorse?"

"He was tired of being a racehorse and has adapted to becoming a riding horse." Although Jenkins was notorious for bucking off a forceful advanced rider by stopping fast ensuring the unsuspecting rider sailed over him.

"At present, Jenkins is happy," Candee said.

"As long as everything goes his way. Though I'm thinking practically, and any arrangements in Roses would be merely temporary." Belle added a smile to her words to soften her refusal. "Thank you for your offer, though."

"Roses is home."

"For you." Belle shifted her attention back to the road. "Not for me. My home is in Wilmington, where my roots are."

Wilmington? Roots? She'd made a decision?

Apparently yes, at least in her subconscious.

"Teddy has contacts in Wilmington," Candee was saying. "Besides, I'm a Realtor … are you looking for anyplace special?

"I'd like to live near the ocean. We'll talk more when I arrive."

The women said their goodbyes and hung up.

As Belle merged into traffic, the slam of a door broke her concentration. A man strode onto a second-floor balcony and leaned over the railing. His broad shoulders were starkly outlined in a crisp white shirt. His breaths were slow and deliberate.

And then he did something completely out of character—considering the elegant house, his tailored silhouette, and the passing motorists who could witness his despair.

He placed his head in his hands.

Belle craned her neck. Was he weeping? Should she offer support?

Behind her, a car horn beeped, and she twisted back to the policewoman directing traffic. Caught in the uneasy silence of indecision, Belle followed the policewoman's signals and kept moving.

One last time, she turned. Just as the cars picked up speed, the man raised his head. For an instant, their gazes met.

He was incredibly handsome, in a Kevin Costner sort of way. His hair was dark with a hint of crimson, layered and expertly cut. His lips were firmly drawn.

And Belle couldn't help noticing that his cheeks were wet with tears. Swiftly, he mopped his eyes with a handkerchief, and the vulnerable gesture touched her heart.

AN HOUR LATER, she pulled her truck into the driveway of Candee's Victorian style home.

On the lush, expansive front yard, Joseph swung on a rope swing tied to the limb of an enormous oak tree. His thin legs kicked vigorously and the tree branch bent in an arc as Candee pushed him back and forth.

As soon as he spotted Belle, Joseph jumped off the swing and scurried to her. "Miss Belle!" He reached up and quickly hugged her. "Did you get to see the parade?"

"You are more important than a parade." Belle pressed back tears, reminding herself there were other excellent horse therapists in the area.

She slung her backpack over her shoulder and kneeled. Joseph's brown eyes sparkled with mischief, his complexion glowed healthy and tanned. After his father had died in a horrific car accident, Candee and Teddy had steered him through several difficult years. Teddy was Joseph's uncle, and he and Candee had legally adopted the little boy.

Belle scrubbed a hand over his dark wavy hair. "Let's get started, shall we?"

An irresistible giggle lit his expression. With an "okay," he tore down the driveway as Candee fell in step beside Belle.

"Teddy is in the stable and will help Joseph saddle up the horse," Candee said. "I informed him about your move."

Because of his home-flipping and construction dealings, Teddy teamed up with workers across the state. Along with Rob, his partner—who also resided in Roses with his wife, Kathleen—their supportive network of crewmen was substantial.

"What did Teddy say?" Belle prompted.

"He provided several leads, and I found a Wilmington rental available at a reasonable price. The landlords are a young couple." Candee tucked a strand of red hair behind her ear. "The apartment is located a few blocks from the beach and is situated on a modest amount of acreage. The couple is giving up farming, but keeping their house and barn and outbuildings. They'll allow you to use their stable and grounds, because they're both taking full-time jobs in Wilmington."

"What is the rental amount?" Belle asked.

"Three hundred dollars a month."

"Perfect. The situation sounds ideal."

"*Almost* ideal," Candee hedged. "The property needs work, judging from the description and photos."

"Do you have any information?" Belle asked.

"All on my phone. Let's review everything tonight when

13

you attend my barbecue. Rob and Kathleen are coming, and Rob is baking a batch of his marvelous muffins. Kieran and Desiree are bringing Irish pub food from their restaurant." Candee laughed. "A traditional, all-American buffet with a dash of Irish flavor and delectable desserts."

Belle pushed out a sigh. "I'd love to attend, but I can't. I need to start packing."

Candee pulled out her cellphone. "Then I'll text you the information."

There was a recognizable whoosh followed by a ping as photos appeared on Belle's phone. She scrolled through, scrutinizing each one.

"I like the apartment," she murmured.

Candee peered over Belle's shoulder. "It has charm and character."

"Is that your Realtor's way of describing the paint that's peeling off the ceiling?" Belle enlarged the kitchen photo. "I'll help clean."

"You won't need to, because Teddy will provide a crew and charge a nominal fee for repairs." Candee placed a hand on Belle's arm. "I know you're going to object, but please don't because we insist."

The first shred of optimism broke through Belle's concerns. Candee was a true friend, and her relocation might go easier than she anticipated. She extended a heartfelt thank you.

"Are you done talking to my Mom?" Joseph called out while Teddy led Blackjack, Joseph's sleek black horse, from the stable.

"Yes. I'm coming." Belle placed her backpack near the fence and hastened toward them. Later, she'd ask Candee for another referral, just in case this rental didn't work out. Then again, perhaps the apartment was fate.

But fate, Belle would later realize, was a funny thing.

. . .

AFTER JOSEPH'S SESSION ENDED, Megan appeared at the riding ring, the familiar pink patch covering her right eye. Her crimson-colored hair fell to her shoulders in slight curls, a startling contrast to her fair complexion and freckled features.

"Hi, Megan!" Belle enthusiastically greeted.

While Candee, Joseph and Teddy tended to Blackjack, Belle saddled Megan's pony, Honeycrisp, and led the solid Haflinger out of the stable, securing the pony to the fence with a halter rope.

A nanny normally brought Megan to her sessions, but today a man brought her.

A man with dark hair, enhanced by a hint of crimson.

An incredibly handsome man.

An incredibly familiar man.

He strode to the fence with Megan clinging tightly to his hand. As always, her riding boots were sturdy, her jeans washed and pressed.

"Hi, Miss Belle," the child said.

"Megan, you look so pretty." Belle bent to greet her. "If it's Monday morning, then it's time for your session with Honeycrisp."

Eagerly, Megan nodded.

As Belle straightened, the man eyed Belle, and then Honeycrisp. He wiped a hand along his pinstriped suit coat and stepped backward.

"I'm Andrew Bransfield," he said. "Are you the instructor?"

"Daddy." Megan giggled, her dimpled cheeks expanding in a wide grin as she handed Belle her riding bag. "Miss Belle teaches me every week."

His expression held no glimmer of recognition. He

15

merely stared at Belle while her own pulse gave a leap of acknowledgment.

"Hello, Mr. Bransfield," she managed. "It's a pleasure to meet you."

She accepted Megan's bag and dug through it until she found the riding helmet. She crouched to fasten the helmet under Megan's chin.

"Andrew."

"I'm sorry?" Belle glanced up.

"Please, call me Andrew."

"Andrew," Belle repeated. She stood, tightened her pony-tail, and extended a friendly grin. Wow, up close he was even handsomer than she'd thought. And she couldn't determine from his clear, emerald-colored eyes whether he'd actually wept on the balcony. Perhaps she'd imagined the entire scenario.

Or perhaps he'd experienced a moment of desolation he couldn't contain.

Desolation was completely acceptable, wasn't it? She'd suffered through it, especially after her divorce.

She kept her grin. "I'm glad you're here so I can speak with you, Mr. Bransfield."

"Andrew." He returned her grin with one of his own. "Is anything wrong?"

She pressed her lips together, grappling to find the right words. "Megan is making excellent progress."

Coward. Tell him you're leaving and this will be his daughter's last session with you.

"She is, isn't she?" He gazed at Megan. "And she's adorable in her pink riding helmet."

"She certainly is. And we believe in safety first."

Brilliant, Belle. As if a father wouldn't understand the importance of safety for his little girl.

Andrew regarded his daughter with unabashed pride.

"The doctor said that the patch therapy for her lazy eye made a difference. Her eyes are beginning to work together."

"That's such good news," Belle replied.

Still wearing his shiny blue helmet, Joseph ran up to them. "My parents are in the stable," he assured, as he and Megan skipped away hand in hand. Amused and impressed by their easy camaraderie, Belle smiled. While Joseph often giggled during his sessions, Megan's lips usually never spared a curve.

"I'll be along shortly," Belle called after them.

"So, I'm finally meeting the famous Belle." A lyrical Scottish accent enhanced Andrew's baritone voice. She pictured him wearing a kilt, knee socks, and a clan badge, rather than a business suit.

"I can assure that I lead a quiet, uneventful life."

"In these parts, you are remarkable."

"Hardly." Compared to his voice, hers sounded fluttery and breathy.

His presence was commanding, partly because of his six-foot tall frame, and partly because of the self-confidence he exuded. And his smile. Oh, his smile did funny things to her pulse. Gone was the bleak man from the balcony.

She studied him. In his pinstriped suit and carrying a leather briefcase, he was completely out of his element in the dusty surroundings of a riding ring. He belonged in an uptown high-rise office on Wall Street.

Yet, despite his buttoned-up appearance, a lock of that crimson-colored hair fell across his temple, giving him a slightly disheveled appeal.

In any event, he was far too fine looking for his own good. And from her limited experience with men, he was probably well aware of his charisma.

"Here in Roses, your skill is renowned," he said. "Megan's

physician recommended equine therapy. I checked numerous references before I chose you."

"Horses have the best hearts and are excellent listeners."

"I was referring to you, not the horses." He rubbed the back of his neck and eyed Honeycrisp.

"Horses are awesome."

"Sure." His jaw set. That is, until he smiled. "Your compassionate skills are highly regarded."

"Thank you." He didn't provide her the opportunity to refute his obvious dislike of horses. "I love these kids. I love my job." Belle ignored Candee's scrutiny as she and Megan emerged from the stable. Teddy, with a wave, strode to the house with Joseph.

"How about a proper hello?"

"We've been talking for several minutes."

"But a proper handshake comes first." He reached out his hand, sending an unexpected quiver through her as their fingers touched.

Oh, my. What on earth?

She kept her hand in his, although she should let go. Shouldn't she?

As she ended their handshake, she focused on the ground.

The ensuing silence between them was interrupted only by chirping birds and chattering squirrels.

"Are you captivated by dirt?" he inquired.

"Candee made certain the ground was ideal for a ring. You see ... clay-based soil is the best for riding because ..." She was babbling. She never babbled. To her chagrin, her cheeks overheated.

No, no. This was absurd. She wasn't a woman who melted because a man shook her hand.

Candee called out and Belle performed a smooth turn.

"I'm coming," she replied, then turned. "Mr. Bransfield ..."

"Andrew."

He backed up, keeping a watchful eye on Honeycrisp.

On several occasions, Megan had confided that her father didn't like horses.

Or was he afraid of them?

With a knowing grin, Belle nodded in Honeycrisp's direction, admiring the horse's flaxen blond mane and tail. "You purchased a stunning horse for your daughter."

"Right."

Belle hurried to Megan as she climbed up on the mounting block. The child put her small foot in the stirrup, grabbed the saddle horn, and swung onto the horse.

"I promise there's nothing to fear," Belle called out. "Horses are gentle."

"In your opinion," he returned. "In mine, horses are large and awkward."

"Honeycrisp is small. A pony, actually. She's only thirteen hands."

"That's a lot of hands," came his quick reply.

WHEN MEGAN'S SESSION ENDED, Belle became distinctly aware of the laughing conversation between Mr. Bransfield and Candee as they stood outside the fence.

She extended a professional smile as Candee entered the ring.

"I'll tend to the horses while you and Andrew talk." Candee snatched Honeycrisp's halter rope and, with Megan, led the pony's return to the stable.

"Miss Belle? May I have a word with you?" Mr. Bransfield unlocked the gate and cautiously stepped into the riding ring. "It is *Miss* Belle, isn't it?"

"Yes." She wondered how he'd learned she wasn't married. Most likely, Candee had told him. And, Belle didn't wear a wedding band. Angling toward him, she glimpsed his ring finger. No wedding band, either. "But may I ask *you* something first?"

He scowled.

Belle glanced over her shoulder to be certain Candee had let the horses out into the adjoining pasture to graze and drink at the creek. When she faced him again, he watched her with quiet contemplation.

"I saw you in town," Belle began. "In any event, I believe it was you."

"Because it *was* me."

He muttered in a Gaelic dialect she didn't understand. Nonetheless, she drew a breath and forged ahead. "Whatever happened that made you so upset on the balcony?"

CHAPTER 2

*A*ndrew kept his expression carefully bland. "What led you to believe that was my house?"

His challenge was an excuse to pause while he fitted his response into a plausible answer. He wouldn't admit he was prone to tears. Nor would he discuss his former wife's behavior regarding her interest in their daughter.

Or rather, her disinterest.

His divorce had induced him to frustration, anger, and heartache. Megan deserved her mother's love. Weren't mothers supposed to be devoted to their children?

"That was you on the balcony, wasn't it?" Belle asked.

"Yes, we've established that."

"We have?"

"We have now."

"You looked … distressed. I considered stopping my truck to come help you."

"Were you planning on rushing up to rescue me?"

Okay, that snappish reply was uncalled for. He softened his response with a quiet "sorry."

"I like to help." She sighed. "Were you rattled about a

business deal that went wrong?"

"Rattled?" *Another question, another deflection, another ploy to delay responding.*

"Distressed … troubled …." She glanced sideways. "I was concerned."

"No need. I can take care of myself." He sent an indifferent shrug.

Nonetheless, she was obviously worried and there was no disdain in her voice. Again, his reaction had been uncalled for. "Are you normally this inquisitive, Miss Belle?"

"No." A hint of embarrassment crept into her gentle voice, along with a pink blush on her cheeks. And those incredible eyes. At first, he'd thought her eyes were blue. At closer range, they were a gorgeous, smoky gray.

"I'm a fixer."

"I don't require fixing, but thanks." He suppressed a smile at the trace of rebelliousness and curiosity warring across her attractive features. Her slender fingers fluttered, and she bent to tug on the hem of her snug fitting jeans. They enhanced the slim curves he'd been admiring for the past hour.

"A business problem is easy to resolve," he continued. "Mine is personal and heart-wrenching."

"Men don't often use the word heart-wrenching."

"I believe heart-wrenching is two words."

She laughed. "It's a relief to meet a sensitive man who is comfortable describing his emotions."

He nodded to the stable. "I'm not all that comfortable."

"Will I have a weeping man at my feet because of a horse?"

His gaze shifted to her. "Nope, although you may have a man sprinting away from a charging horse."

"You harbor many misconceptions about horses."

"Realities," he corrected.

"Yet you allow your daughter to ride."

"Honeycrisp is a pony as you've kindly explained, and Megan's sessions are the result of our doctor's recommendation."

"Well, you enlisted the expertise of a wise doctor." Belle shuffled her feet. She was petite and trim, reminding him of a nimble gymnast. "At any rate, I'm sorry for prying."

"You're young," he said.

She blinked. "What does that have to do with—" Her chin lifted. "I'm almost thirty."

"You're not married."

"I was, for a brief spell."

"Therefore, you're divorced?"

"Yes. He …he left me."

"Why would a man leave a beautiful, empathetic woman like you?"

She shook her head. "Wow. Mr. Bransfield … Andrew … our conversation is becoming too personal."

"I'm forty."

"Thanks for the information, but I don't remember asking your age."

"I'm also divorced. Thus, I have a decade of experience on you."

She pulled blue-rimmed sunglasses from her denim pocket and wiped off the dust. "Perhaps in years."

"But not wisdom?" He waited for a reaction and was rewarded with her tinkling laugh.

"Because you're older, you assume you're more knowledgeable?"

"That's the way it usually works."

"What can you fix, Mr. Knowledgeable?"

"Personally or professionally?"

"Personally."

"Evidently, not much." His gaze rested on her face. "The

Scots have a saying, 'Ye'ill dee a thousand deaths ye'ill never see.'"

She quirked a delicate eyebrow. "Please explain the meaning?"

"Don't concern yourself with fixing others."

"Are you sharing your older, better informed advice?"

Something about her teasing voice and pure gray eyes stirred the ashes of his loneliness.

"Yes."

"Mr. Bransfield, not only is our conversation becoming too philosophical for such a lovely day, but you're beginning to sound a lot like my Aunt Lucinda."

"I hope I don't look like her."

"You don't." She chuckled. "My aunt wears a cobalt-blue beret, and her white hair hangs to her shoulders." Belle fidgeted with her sunglasses. "In any event, I've had an upsetting morning and didn't intend to take it out on you."

A breeze ruffled dark-brown wisps from her ponytail. In the shimmering sunlight, she brushed a fine strand from her cheeks. He had the urge to stroke her hair gently, as if she were a precious bird.

Because he felt something. And so did she. He'd felt it in town when they'd locked gazes. And he felt it now.

"Your apology is accepted, though you deserve clarification about my circumstances." He folded his hands together. "Rowena, my ex-wife, never returns my phone calls. As usual, I'd left several messages for her."

"She must be busy."

"She's not busy. She's selfish."

"It's not my place, but perhaps you'd feel better if you didn't judge her."

"Now *you're* becoming too philosophical. When you saw me, I had walked onto my balcony to breathe in some fresh air."

"I crave fresh air when I'm upset too," Belle said softly.

As if on cue, a delicate breeze rustled the leaves of a nearby Elm tree. More strands flew across her cheeks, and he resisted the urge to brush them away by keeping his hands at his sides.

"I had phoned my ex to inform her that Megan wouldn't be needing surgery," he said.

"Such wonderful news."

He'd conversed with Belle for fifteen minutes, but there was something about her easy-going nature that gave him comfort. She seemed genuinely interested in Megan.

"The patch will come off within a few weeks," he said. "Then she'll be fitted with eyeglasses. When she gets older, she can wear contact lenses if she prefers."

"I've prayed for her full recovery."

"Prayers are always appreciated."

Their gazes stayed connected, and Belle wiped a bead of sweat from her forehead. Scents of sunshine and leather, with an undertone of interest, held them together. Or rather, it held him, for Belle had turned toward the stable.

He wavered. Should he call out to her?

Earlier, when he'd pulled into Candee's driveway, he'd intended to drop off Megan at the riding ring, say hello to Candee and Teddy, and return to his SUV to resume a lengthy list of important business calls to secure new clients.

Besides, horses weren't his thing. They were, as he'd remarked, big. As a rule, he didn't like animals in general.

After he'd met and talked with Belle, though, he'd leaned against the fence and set down his briefcase.

He'd been impressed by her in action. Her silky hair was pulled back into a severe ponytail, and her worn jeans and denim shirt showed off her flawless curves.

She'd walked quietly beside his daughter as she completed the therapy session, talking encouragingly, and he'd hardly noticed when Candee had come to stand beside him. Often when Belle spoke, Megan had giggled. And his heart had swelled. Since his ex-wife's abrupt departure, laughter had been infrequent in the Bransfield household.

He'd been overly involved with dwelling on the hurt she'd caused him and their daughter. As a result, he'd concentrated on his work, allotting precious few occasions for fun. Or joy. Resentment was more comfortable.

"Is there anything else, Mr. Bransfield?" Belle glanced at him. "Megan likes to spend time with Honeycrisp after her therapy sessions, and I left a few treats for the horses."

He still stood in the ring, staring at Belle like a besotted fool.

"Andrew," he reminded with a sardonic smile. "And there is no hurry."

Except for that lengthy list of business calls, though he'd forgotten why they were so important.

Yes, he wanted something else from Belle. He wanted to get to know her better, although why that particular thought floated through his mind was beyond him. The petite dark-haired beauty—who couldn't be any taller than five feet, nor weigh more than a hundred pounds—was stunning. How did she manage those one thousand-pound horses with such ease?

"Miss Belle … I'm not sure how to address you."

She came around to face him. "Just call me Belle."

"What is your last name?" He studied her delicate hands as she plucked a package of what resembled baby wipes from a backpack, then wiped the dust and grime from a saddle.

"Leather wipes," she explained at his questioning gaze.

He nodded. "Your last name?" he inquired again.

She coupled her hesitation with an awkward, indrawn breath. "Boots."

Andrew lifted his eyebrows. "Your name is Belle Boots?"

A telltale flush heightened her high cheekbones, and she smiled. "I know, I know. It's a ridiculous name for a woman in the equine therapy profession. Belle Boots."

"It's my turn to apologize." He chuckled—he couldn't help it—and was grateful when she joined in. "It's just that you work with horses—"

Her smiled widened, enhancing full, heart-shaped lips. Another attractive feature. "What if my parents had named me Bronco?"

"Bronco Boots," he said easily, "has a nice ring."

"Or Bridle Boots."

"Or Bucking Boots."

She laughed. She had a wry sense of humor, coupled with the ability to joke about herself. Few people were prepared to do that.

"Please accept my compliments on the fine job you're doing with Megan. Did I tell you that already?" He motioned Belle to the railing again. He wished to continue conversing with her, although he was keeping her from her tasks.

"Not in so many words," she replied. "But thank you."

"My daughter has blossomed these past few months." He slipped behind the gate—one never knew when a horse might bound in from the pasture.

"Any credit goes to Megan and Honeycrisp. Their hard work and effort paid off." Belle made a show of shaking the dirt off her brown Western boots—first one boot, then the other. "Megan's face lights up whenever she's riding, which brings me tremendous satisfaction."

In an instant, Andrew relived his daughter's appointments and the trauma she'd undergone—the lighted magnifying glass the doctor had used, the eye drops to blur the vision of the strong eye, the pictures and letter exams when she'd been younger.

"Me too." He swallowed the lump in his throat. He always choked up when he spoke of her welfare.

Certainly, society deemed it acceptable for a man to cry, he'd often told himself.

But was it acceptable?

He'd never seen a grown man cry. None … except himself.

Surely not his overbearing father.

Rowena had seized on Andrew's perceived weakness and found endless opportunities to chide him. He'd always felt like he was on the outside looking in, anyway.

"Mr. Bransfield," Belle began.

"Andrew."

"Your nanny has referred to you as Mr. Bransfield so often that it's difficult for me to make the transition."

"I'll correct you every time."

"Considerate of you," Belle said wryly.

He smiled. "Although I'm biased because I'm her father, Megan is a delight. Her mother doted on Megan—until she drove off with the delivery man."

Belle's thoughtful expression changed to surprise. "You're joking."

His gaze restlessly shifted to the pasture, then Belle. "Such a cliché, but it's true."

Although he and Rowena had reached a divorce agreement before she'd left because fidelity had never been Rowena's strong suit. He grimaced at the understatement.

That was the thing about a woman as pampered and beautiful as Rowena. She'd demanded only the best, which included a red sports car easily reaching eighty miles an hour in mere seconds. Fast cars and a fast life that had ended with a fast departure.

He trained his gaze on Belle's small hands; she was clutching such an enormous horse's saddle.

"Andrew." Another hesitation. "I'm glad I finally met you."

"We've established this."

"Normally your daughter's nanny brings her to the sessions."

"Nancy, and I'm aware of that fact because I pay her."

"Yes, Nancy," Belle agreed. "Anyway, Megan's sessions with me are coming to an end."

"Really? Why?"

"I'm moving."

He jerked back. The stable, the focal point of his gaze while he stared past Belle, was not lost on her.

"When were you planning on sharing this little tidbit of information?" he asked.

"I didn't intend to withhold anything. I considered emailing you since I just found out this morning. In all fairness, I'm still reeling from the news myself."

"Isn't the decision to move yours?"

"Yes and no. Circumstances happened without warning and prompted me to make a hasty decision." Belle hung the saddle on the fence railing with quick, efficient movements. "I'm relocating to Wilmington. Candee found me an apartment near the beach, on a small farm with a stable. I thought she may have told you when you two were talking."

"Nope. We discussed other things."

"Her barbecue this evening?"

"Yes. Are you going?"

"I can't spare the evening." She sighed. "Unfortunately, I have a bag of potatoes that will go to waste."

"Neither can I." With a dry grin, he added, "No potatoes, though."

Those 'other things' had centered around Megan before he'd asked about Belle. The conversation had ended when the therapy session finished, which was sooner than he'd anticipated.

"Naturally, I will miss your daughter desperately," Belle was saying.

"Then why leave?"

"It's time." Conflicting reactions flickered across her lovely face. "However, my stable in Wilmington needs extensive renovation."

"As well as your apartment?"

"Yes, if the photos are any indication. Fortunately, Candee insisted that Teddy's crew will repair everything for a nominal fee."

He shook his head. "This is a lot to take in."

"Teddy is more than generous."

"I wasn't referring to Teddy's generosity. We've been acquainted for years through our business connections, and he's reliable and honest." Andrew displayed an engaging smile while he assembled a plan. "Exactly when are you leaving?"

"By the end of the month. I'll transport my horse, Jenkins, who is quite nervous. Hopefully, he won't fly into a sweaty panic when he's trailered and—"

"Miss Belle, you're moving?" Megan raced up to them. Wide-eyed, she lifted her freckled face to Belle.

"Yes, and I'm sorry, Megan," Belle said. "I'll miss you very, very much."

"Why are you moving?" The little girl's bottom lip trembled. His daughter's pink cherubic lips were a clear indicator of her distress. As Andrew gazed down at her, timeworn anxieties clustered in his mind. She was still a child, and he intended to shield her from life's disappointments.

"My landlord raised my rent to a rate higher than I can manage," Belle said. "Plus, Wilmington is my hometown, and my aunt lives there."

Megan's shoulders crumpled. "You mean I won't ever see you again?"

"We'll only live a few hours apart. I promise I'll visit Roses whenever possible."

The child balled her tiny hands into fists. She did that, Andrew noted, not in anger, but in frustration whenever she was upset. Now, with Rowena gone, Megan's frustration level had escalated. Again, Andrew was thankful for the equine therapy.

"What about Honeycrisp?" Megan asked.

"I'm certain Honeycrisp can continue to board here," Belle said. "There's no reason why not—"

"As it so happens, Belle," Andrew broke in, "I'll renovate your stable at no charge."

She was a bargain-hunter, right? Anyone who fretted about wasting a bag of potatoes wouldn't be able to resist his offer.

"Thank you, but Teddy's crewmen will provide the repairs," she replied.

"Yes, so you mentioned." He greeted her reply with all the enthusiasm of a root canal. "How's this?"

"How's what?"

"I'll renovate at *no* charge, including the work on your apartment." His competitiveness kicked in. Why not? The trait had contributed to his company's significant success. However, he was in the business of making money, not losing it. Therefore, providing a service and materials without payment was not a keen business practice.

Nonetheless, he was significantly more interested in Belle Boots than any monetary gain. Surely she couldn't resist the rock-bottom offer of a lifetime. Nothing beat free.

"Thank you." Belle looked away. "Still, I can't accept your kindness. We are hardly acquainted, and it wouldn't be right."

Her response only encouraged him.

Lightly, he placed his hand on her shoulder. "Considering all you've done for my daughter, most definitely you can consent. I'm expanding my company, Bransfield Designs, to Wilmington. Moreover, I've considered purchasing a beach house and residing near the sea with Megan in a calm, relaxing little place. Maybe I'll rent the house when we're not there."

He did? Since when? He didn't have a second to cavort on a beach or deal with renters—not with his schedule.

"We're moving to be near Miss Belle, Daddy?" Megan perked up as she tugged on his shirtsleeve.

"We're flitting to live closer to the ocean."

"Flitting?" Belle inquired.

"A Scottish term for moving. We'll use the house on holidays." He lifted Megan onto his shoulders. "You like the beach, don't you?"

She clapped her hands together. "I love the beach!"

He swung toward Belle. "What say you, Miss Belle Boots?"

"I've never been the object of a bidding war. Are you certain Teddy won't mind?"

"I'll tell him myself. No worries."

Belle smiled. "What about you, Andrew?"

"What about me?"

"Do *you* like the beach?"

"Doesn't everyone?" His lips twitched. "Oceanside living, dining on fresh caught fish, surfing …"

"You fish?"

"Nope."

"Surf?"

"Never."

They shared a chuckle.

Quiet walks on the sand with Belle accompanied by a chirpy Megan gathering seashells. He grinned inwardly at the agreeable prospect.

"Megan and I will appreciate a change of scenery and an

opportunity to escape the sweltering summers in town. A beach house where we can savor sunsets and watch the tide roll in."

"Savor sunsets?" Belle chuckled. "You are a remarkably poetic man."

"Sensitive," he corrected, planting a kiss on Megan's chubby leg. "Blame it on my Scottish ancestry. We Scots are a thoughtful people."

"Don't forget stubborn," Belle quipped.

He laughed. "You've been watching too much Braveheart."

"I've never seen the movie."

"Someday, we'll watch it together."

"The movie is about Scotland's history, right?"

"Somewhat." He combined his shrug with a grin and his shoulders relaxed. The pleasant mood was a respite from his usual tenseness "The cinematography is stunning."

He and Megan deserved peace and closure, he rationalized. A beach house was the ticket, along with the opportunity to see the lovely Belle. Yet, actually finding the perfect house would involve an experienced Realtor who acted quickly.

As he set Megan down, she turned her face to his. "Daddy, can Honeycrisp move with us to Wilmington?"

"Absolutely. Perhaps we can board Honeycrisp at Miss Belle's new stable." He smiled and met Belle's gaze. "Obviously, I'll pay the usual boarding rate."

"Do you have any idea what that is, Andrew?"

"Candee charges six hundred dollars a month. I expect you'll charge me a fair price as well."

"Rest assured, considering your free labor." Warily, she regarded him.

"So." He displayed his most charismatic smile, "I assume everything is agreed, then, right?"

CHAPTER 3

*S*omehow, this entire situation seemed mildly unethical, Belle mused, as she gazed at the two horses in her newly renovated stable in Wilmington. In record time, Andrew had enlisted a crew. They'd completely gutted the stable—replacing the tack, feed rooms, and wash stalls. After installing the latest lighting and a septic system, she'd opted for sliding stall doors and a concrete floor. The damaged fence lines had been repaired, as well as the post gate's hinge.

She might be a bargain hunter, but when it came to her horses, she never scrimped.

Straightaway, Andrew had notified Teddy that he was taking over "Belle's Project." From her conversation with Candee, Belle learned that Andrew and Megan had moved into a two-story oceanfront beach house.

In the month since, Andrew's crewmen had transported Honeycrisp to Belle's stable, and the gentle pony now had the finicky Jenkins as a neighboring stall mate.

Belle had ensured that a bag of Honeycrisp's feed was available, and hand walked the horse around the fence line in an effort to ease her into the different environment. System-atically, she familiarized Honeycrisp with the pasture. Once she was stalled, Honeycrisp and Jenkins eyed each other at a distance. After a few days, Belle turned them out together in the pasture, placing their feed over a large space with ample room around the water source. Sure, there'd been some biting and chasing—mostly by Jenkins, because he hadn't been thrilled with the situation.

Fortunately, both horses had ultimately settled into a contented routine.

In a flurry of busyness, Belle had moved her belongings into her sunlit and welcoming new apartment. Boasting a wide, fully equipped breakfast area, an adjoining living room with a pull-out couch, and a small bedroom with an attached bathroom, it was upscale and chic. She was impressed by the renovation, scarcely believing the home was now hers.

Through numerous texts, Andrew had inquired about her vision for a dream kitchen and she had described espresso cabinets, stainless steel appliances and wood-style flooring. After hand-sketching the design and emailing her for approval, he'd taken her words to heart and delivered to the letter.

Thrilled to discover her place was a mere six blocks from the ocean, she jogged on the beach every morning and again at sundown.

As always she woke at dawn, showered, dressed and went to the stable. She opened the door, and both horses stuck their heads out of their stalls to greet her. She fed them grain in a bucket, distributed the hay, and cleaned and refilled the water buckets. After brushing their coats and applying fly spray, she haltered and walked the horses to the pasture.

Chores came next, which began with sweeping the stalls.

Once finished, she hiked through an overgrown shortcut to the beach, removed her waterproof muck boots and jogged barefoot along the shore. The soothing splash of water on her toes brought her spirits up. Surely, she'd made the right decision in relocating to Wilmington.

Her eccentric Aunt Lucinda had been thrilled Belle was back in their hometown, and Belle visited her often. Her aunt had never married, spouting that a man would tie her down. Nevertheless, there had been one man in her life, she'd confessed. A man she'd loved, although she'd never divulged his name.

Men were too much of a bother, she'd stated on numerous occasions.

After her divorce from Tyler, Belle had agreed. Nevertheless, after numerous hours talking and texting with Andrew, she'd changed her mind. He displayed a kindness, courteousness, and indisputable attentiveness that proved both disarming and heartening.

With a tremulous smile, she recalled their initial meeting. Apprehension had been written across his handsome features when he'd surveyed Blackjack and Honeycrisp. Just wait until he came face-to-face with the cantankerous Jenkins. She'd need to introduce them gently.

After her jog, Belle returned to the stable. She intended to clean the hay out of the stalls, replace old tack, and carry out the million other chores awaiting her.

Tires crunching on gravel prompted her to shade her eyes and peer toward the road, as Andrew drove into the driveway in his shiny silver SUV.

He got out of the SUV and strode to her with a decidedly mischievous grin. He wore slim jeans, a white T-shirt that clung to his broad shoulders and work boots. In one hand, he carried a toolbox.

Her heart did a thump.

He looked entirely different from the fine-looking professional of a few weeks ago.

Because today, wearing jeans and a T-shirt?

Oh, my.

The morning at Candee's stable he'd been pin-striped proper, and Belle couldn't choose which look she preferred.

The jeans, she decided. Definitely the jeans.

"Hi, Andrew." She smiled as he neared.

"Greetings, Belle." He withdrew a bouquet of slightly wilted yellow flowers from his toolbox.

To discount the treacherous jump of her heart, she tried to think of something to say. "Tools and flowers," she observed. *Just brilliant, Belle.*

"Do you like flowers?" he asked.

"I love flowers, and the color reminds me of a burst of sunshine."

"I like flowers too. However, the tools aren't for you. Only the flowers. When I passed by the florist in town, I thought, 'Beautiful flowers for a beautiful woman' and I couldn't resist. What's more, they were on sale, so I knew you'd approve."

"I hope they were at least fifty percent off?"

"Try a dollar off."

"What was the original price?"

"Fifty dollars."

"What?" Raising a hand, she checked him from continuing. "You paid forty-nine dollars for a bouquet?"

He bent to nuzzle her ear and whispered, "For you, I would have paid a hundred dollars."

She couldn't contain her grin.

He liked flowers. He liked *her.* And he was a wonderful father. Contrary to his rugged exterior, he possessed a sensitive nature. She wondered if he wrote poetry.

Probably.

"Thank you." She accepted the bouquet and sniffed.

"Flowers as pretty as dahlias should have a strong, fragrant scent, but they don't."

"We think alike. I told the florist the same thing."

"They're gorgeous."

"They're a house-warming gift."

"You didn't have to do this."

"I wanted to."

Her cheeks heated beneath his steady, admiring gaze. "You've done too much already."

"You've heard the familiar adage." He finger quoted. "'It's better to give than to receive.'"

"You mean, there's no Scottish saying?"

"'Don't judge each day by the harvest you reap, but by the seeds you plant.'"

She plucked a petal from the dahlia's stem. "That's Scottish?"

"By Scotland's very own novelist, Robert Louis Stevenson."

"Which I assume means, 'It's better to give than to get?'"

"Nope." Unabashed, he chuckled. "Sadly, it's the best I can come up with."

She placed the bouquet in a shady area. "You knew my favorite flower?"

"I asked Candee, and she mentioned your former apartment was painted yellow. Thus, I selected dahlias."

"Most people think of daisies for a yellow flower."

"I studied the meanings of both. In our situation, dahlias were more appropriate."

She made a mental note to research the meanings. "Andrew Bransfield, you're an extraordinarily thoughtful man."

He nodded. "I also was compelled to see if the stable area begs for my finishing touches."

"No begging is required." She gestured to the fencing. "Thanks to you, every inch is repaired."

He eyed the pasture where the two horses sunbathed. "Are they safe?"

"Do you mean, are we safe from them?"

"Both."

"We are all safe and secure," she said.

He set down the toolbox. "Just in case, I'll keep a safe and secure distance from them."

"Why are you afraid of horses?"

"When I was young, I was attacked by a large dog and required stitches."

"I'm sorry." She paused, picked up a rake and piled dry straw into mounds. "That must have been frightening."

"It was traumatic for a ten-year-old kid who loved animals."

"Past tense?" she inquired. "*Loved* animals?"

He shrugged. "I suppose."

She let the comment pass. It wasn't the time to analyze him. "What type of dog attacked you?"

"If you're suspecting a mean, vicious dog, you're wrong. The day was scorching, the hottest on record, and I ran up to the dog to pet him. His name was Rusty, and he belonged to a neighbor. Apparently, I startled him, and he bit me." Andrew pointed to a thin white line on his forearm. "Consequently, animals aren't my number one love."

What was his number one love?

Without a doubt, it was Megan. His devotion to his daughter was undeniable.

"I guarantee you're safe from any galloping horses," Belle said.

"Whew!" He forced a larger-than-life wipe at his forehead, but his posture tensed as his gaze canvassed the pasture. "Are you certain?"

"Totally." She decided to hold off telling him that a stray tabby had found his way to her front yard and she'd immediately adopted and dubbed him Ginger. Or about the two white goats, Hester and Hilda, who were already members of the farm when she'd showed up.

Andrew would find out soon enough.

He paused and gazed at her. "You are gorgeous, Belle," he said quietly.

Donned in a pair of military-green cropped pants and a striped crewneck shirt, she highly doubted it. She opened her mouth to dispute him, but he forestalled her by leaning over the fence and gently sliding a finger across her lips.

His touch was casual and friendly and brought an unexpected tingle. Dumbstruck, she shook her head at the strong attraction.

"Sorry." He dropped his hand. "Did I invade your personal space?"

Not a bit, she wished to tell him, but refrained from speaking.

She returned to tackling the raking with outward efficiency, though her fingers trembled so significantly she could hardly hold the rake. She gave up, set the rake down and glanced at her watch. "Are you on a lunch break, Andrew?"

He gestured to his jeans. "Does it look like I am?"

"No, but it's Friday. We've texted often enough for me to be aware of your grueling schedule."

His green eyes sparkled with laughing speculation. "What might my grueling schedule entail?"

"At seven a.m. you eat breakfast with Megan. Once her nanny arrives, you report to your office by eight. You allot a half hour for lunch and leave work by six in order to spend an hour with Megan before her bedtime."

"If I'm lucky. I wish I had more time," came his frustrated reply.

"Oftentimes you take your computer home," she went on. "And I know you're up at all hours of the night, because I've received texts from you at three a.m. asking which flooring style I prefer."

"You've memorized my schedule in only a few short weeks."

"You're easy because your routine is always the same. Work, work, work." She tried a lame attempt at sternness. "Any robber could watch you for a couple days and then fleece you blind."

He grinned, but his eyes darkened, reminding her of pine trees in the subdued light of a summer sunset.

"Are you planning to rob me, Belle? Of my senses, perhaps? Because I lose track of time when I'm with you. In fact, I'm not certain of anything since we met."

Surely he joked. They were business acquaintances. Yet he sounded surprisingly off balance. Seeking to lighten the strangely intimate mood, she said, "You certainly lost your senses when you offered your services for free."

"Let's not forget my phone and text consultations."

"Is there an added fee?"

"Certainly."

"We talked about other matters," she reminded.

The way he watched her filled her with compassion and affection. Although business had dominated their exchanges, he'd spoken about his daughter and the challenges he'd encountered upon becoming a single parent. His intent was to make everything right in his daughter's world, he'd said. Or rather, it seemed, he was bent on make everything right in the *entire* world.

When silence had rung out, he'd encouraged Belle to discuss her reservations regarding her relocation and leaving behind her clients. She felt as though she had abandoned them.

Andrew had immediately corrected her when she had used the term "abandon," and she could almost see him visibly flinch. "You're a kind, caring woman," he'd declared, and her refutes were no match against his thoughtful assurances.

Belle grabbed the rake again and swirled the dry grass round and round. She concentrated on the areas near the gate that got the highest traffic. When Andrew stayed silent, she motioned to the stable. "Are your rates generally expensive, then?"

His dark eyebrows rose in a teasing challenge. "Extremely."

"Could I afford you if you charged me your regular fee?"

"Highly doubtful."

Their laughing gazes joined.

"In truth, helping you was my pleasure," Andrew said softly.

She slanted him a glance and yanked up a garden hose to water the riding ring.

Andrew held up his hands. "Do you intend to spray me, Belle?"

Hmm. No. Or maybe?

"Push the notion from your mind." He retreated a step. "We are both adults, and a prank like the one you're thinking would be extremely childish."

"How do you know what I'm thinking?"

"I just know."

"And why should I obey you?"

"Because I asked politely."

"Politeness only goes so far, Andrew." She inched closer to him and unlatched the gate. Sunlight glinted through his hair, lightening the shade to a shiny copper penny.

He refused to retreat any further. Her beating heart brought a knot of longing and indescribable attraction. Now? Yes, now. It had been years since her divorce. Although she wasn't actively searching for a relationship, she appreciated the company of a good-hearted, kind man. A man who laughed at silly pranks. A man with substance and confidence.

"The hose?" he reminded. "You're aiming at me rather than the ground."

"What's more, I'll continue aiming at you until you admit you lead a highly regimented life."

"Where did that come from?" She expected him to take flight, but he held his ground. "Is this truth or dare?"

"Possibly," she hedged.

"I'm a businessman." He shrugged with an indifference Belle suspected was partly feigned. "Need I explain more?"

"Yes." With an innocent smile, she turned the hose on him.

CHAPTER 4

*A*ndrew toppled backwards and landed on the grass while Belle's chuckle pealed through the air.

He peered at his wet shirt then up at her. "Was that necessary?"

She dropped the hose and hurried over, taking stock of him sprawled on the ground. "Was it necessary for you to display such an ambitious dramatization?"

"I was startled."

"Uh huh. You're hardly wet."

"I'm wet enough."

Her gaze narrowed. "Aren't you getting up?"

"Maybe."

She came to stand over him. "Time to get up," she repeated.

"Why?" he countered. "Are you standing by to spray me again?"

"Maybe." She repaid his question with uncharacteristic sarcasm. Belatedly registering his frown, she guardedly asked, "Are you hurt?"

"Only my pride. Fortunately, I have a thick skin in my

business." His tone sounded forced despite his assertion, bringing an ache to her throat. She considered his wet shirt, and regretted spraying him. What had seemed like a fun, playful idea a few seconds earlier now wasn't quite as humorous.

He was under obvious emotional strain, trying to keep his architectural firm prosperous while spending considerable time with his daughter. Which was the very reason why she'd injected light-heartedness into their morning. That, and the fact he'd given her the idea. Why, he'd practically goaded her.

Now, seeing him defenseless, the solemn expression on his ruggedly handsome face caused her pulse to quiver. He had a mysterious effect on her she couldn't shake, whether he was upright or on the ground.

Her memory of him when he'd strode onto his balcony flashed through her mind. She remembered thinking how pleasingly male he looked, so urbane in his sophisticated home. The fact that his ex-wife had brought such sorrow to him and his little girl prompted Belle's empathy.

His skin might be thick in business, but he was an exceptional breed—emotional and vulnerable while exuding a tough exterior.

He continued to lie in the grass. He was either milking the situation or trying to tug at her heart strings. He accomplished both quite successfully.

If, indeed, the force of the water had knocked him off his feet.

"I apologize," she began offering him the benefit of the doubt. "You're right. That was childish of me."

"I accept." He squinted up at her, shielding his eyes from the sun. "That is, unless you're planning to hose me again?"

She held out a hand to help him to his feet. "I hardly call dampening your shirt hosing you down."

With an overstated sigh, he stood and brushed the grass

sticking to his white shirt. He'd have grass stains, which were difficult to wash out, but she didn't tell him that.

"I brought no change of clothes," he said.

"With the hot July sun beating down, your shirt will dry in five minutes," she assured.

Together, they walked back to the riding ring holding hands.

There, she paused to consider the fencing. "Thank you for combining wire mesh along with the wood. As I explained, otherwise horses might catch their legs. Plus the fence is more resilient."

"Are you always this conscientious, Belle?" he asked.

"I've lived around horses and pastures since I was a teen. Fencing and barns come with the territory."

"Both are alien territories to me."

"Because you sit in an office all day."

"You're a master at describing me, but could you toss in a few descriptions other than businessman now and then? I'm an architect and work outdoors often. While we're discussing the subject, let's not forget *you're* a businesswoman."

"I'm proud of the distinction." Her dignified reproof brought a grin to his lips. "Studies prove professional women are more emotionally intelligent than men."

His steady, green-eyed gaze met hers. "Please continue."

They still held hands. He didn't seem to want to let go. Neither did she.

"Well," she adopted a formidable instructor's manner, "a woman values a person's well-being."

"And I don't?"

"You're taking my words personally. I was comparing men to women—not all men in general."

They reached the spot where she'd dropped the hose. He

released her hand, eyed the hose and grinned. Quietness billowed between them.

"Therefore, I'm not necessarily referring to you," she clarified.

"It's important to spell out the difference."

"I did." She tilted her head and granted a genuine smile. "Furthermore, women aren't as ego-driven as men."

"I agree that men like to win." Still grinning, Andrew grabbed the hose, held steady, and aimed at her.

She gaped, steering away from the sudden stream of gushing water. "You, Mr. Bransfield, are incorrigible," she shouted.

He shut the hose. "Did I win?"

"Definitely not. And because of you, my hair will stick out straight the rest of the day."

"Your hair will dry in a few minutes. Remember? The hot sun and all that ..." He gestured upward to the airy white clouds floating in a blue sky.

She ran a hand through her hair, squeezing the ends with her fingers. Helplessly, she laughed. "If you even consider turning that hose on me again ..."

In three quick strides, he reached her. "Do you give up easily?"

"Never." With a cool dose of spitfire, she included, "Unless this is a water fight."

"It may yet become one."

"Andrew ... don't you dare ..."

"Now I'm Andrew again? Which is it, Belle? Mr. Bransfield or Andrew?"

"I told you already. Because your nanny referred to you as Mr. Bransfield so often—"

"You and I have progressed to a first name basis since then."

"Are you asking a question?" She shied backward. She was

ready for the game to end, especially while he still held the hose.

"It's a statement." He looked positively boyish, a sparkling gleam in his eyes as he set down the hose. "And I promise I won't spray you again under one condition."

"Now there's a condition?"

In reply, his laughter was deep and intimate. His gaze fell to her lips.

She drew a shaky inhale. They stood within inches of each other.

"What is the condition?" she asked again.

"This." Tenderly, he brushed his knuckles across her cheek, outlined her lips with his fingertips. The rhythm in her veins accelerated, taking on a mind of its own as he bent his head and kissed her.

She melted, responding to the radiant heat of his mouth as he drew her into his arms. Her heart beat much too fast, but in that moment she was aware of only one thing.

She'd been waiting for his kiss, anticipating it. He'd been waiting too. She had seen the desire in his gaze, heard the underlying huskiness.

When had their magnetism begun? In Roses?

Or here? In Wilmington?

He framed her face and deepened the kiss.

No, no, no.

But she couldn't surface from the delicious pleasure of his lips.

She slid her hands around his neck and kissed him back, reacting to the instinctive tightening of his arms as he brought her tightly against him. So close, she felt the beating of his heart.

When he loosened his hold, she leaned against the fence until their breathing slowed. After a lingering silence, he said softly, "I've had an urge to kiss you ever since we met."

"You evidently have no objections to personal space," she half-joked.

"None at all." His voice quieted. "Not when it comes to you."

How should she respond? Start with the truth. Confess she had the same feelings.

Absolutely not, that would never do. A woman shouldn't wear her heart on her sleeve.

She swallowed. When she was with him, she was vaguely aware that she was negotiating a land mine, with no relationship experience to guide her except for a degrading ex and a marriage that never should have happened.

Andrew, on the other hand, with his charisma-plus charm and velvety Scottish lilt, left her no choice but to examine each of her words, because to say exactly what she thought and describe her emotions would expose her. She was attracted to him, very attracted, but it was too soon in their friendship for those thoughts.

This was merely a kiss between a man and a woman who had worked together the past few weeks and had become close.

Andrew appeared to take the change in their relationship with an easy-going stride. His face was calm, his features neutral.

"You're getting off the hook easily with your personal space reply, if that sums up your explanation," she said shakily.

"With you, all bets are off." He chuckled when she frowned. "Belle, you are beautiful and desirable. Be proud of that." When she continued frowning, he chuckled louder. "You know, there is simply no substitute for a smart, perceptive businesswoman."

With a self-conscious laugh, she didn't refute him. Unfortunately, her conscience deemed this as the appropriate time for an admonition.

Remember? Andrew was the father of one of her clients.

Should she have accepted his help so willingly? Or kissed him? Their association was professional, not personal.

Yet, Andrew had done more for her than anyone.

How could she repay him? Everything—materials and labor—is free of charge, he'd insisted. In the short weeks they'd been acquainted, he'd proven a wonderful friend.

Friend, she reminded herself.

He had the resources, restating that this was his opportunity to repay the kindness, patience, and understanding she'd shown his daughter.

She stood motionless. Hesitant to speak, hesitant not to speak.

Andrew broke the silence by fixing his thumbs in his pockets and stepping away. "Back to business," he remarked.

No beat was missed. He bent to inspect the fence, tugged on the gate, and began measuring the replaced wood.

He hadn't dismissed her, had he?

"Business as usual," she echoed. She wished her voice sounded as unshaken as his. "Are you resuming duty as my project foreman?"

"I never went off duty."

Sure he had, when he'd kissed her a moment earlier, but some thoughts weren't meant to be shared.

He cleared his throat. "Is everything falling into place the way you imagined?"

At the stable? Unquestionably.

In the heart department? She wasn't so certain.

He pulled a hammer and nails from the toolbox and secured a piece of wire mesh to the fencing.

"I love this area. It's my hometown," she began answering

his question. She stifled the urge to gush on and on about herself. "How about you and *your* new place?"

"Couldn't be better. I'm delighted with the house now that Megan and I are mostly unpacked."

"Where is Megan? I meant to inquire when you arrived."

"Her nanny took her to play on the beach."

"Nancy?"

"I hired Adella, a new nanny, and I'll rehire Nancy if Megan and I return to Roses."

If.

Was he thinking of settling in Wilmington indefinitely?

"I mentioned Adella to you the other day," he was saying.

He had, she admitted to him. In the torrent of activity, she'd forgotten.

"Megan will begin again soon, right?" he asked.

"I scheduled her on Monday. I'm looking forward to our weekly sessions because I've missed her."

"Excellent." His mouth tilted up whenever he spoke of his daughter. "She misses you too and mentions you constantly."

During Belle's move, Andrew had texted or phoned often. There was an easiness about conversing with him behind a safe screen which had served as a safety net. However, communicating in person was something else entirely. Suddenly feeling awkward, she drew up the rake and concentrated on a rutted area.

"Do you like your new home?" she inquired.

"Very much. Thanks to our super Realtor friend, Candee, my house is in a secluded area by the ocean. Megan and I will invite you for dinner some night. Our evenings are quiet and lonely."

Somehow, watching this undeniably compelling man, she sincerely doubted he spent his evenings alone.

"You cook?" she asked.

"My housekeeper does. She is from Scotland."

"I'm not familiar with Scottish food."

"Have you ever eaten haggis?"

"I've never heard of haggis. Is it a variety of sausage?"

"A little more." He chuckled. "My sister, Kate, who lives in Scotland, used to prepare authentic haggis."

"Used to? How long since you've last seen her?"

His features shuttered. "Many years."

"Why? Don't you ever visit Scotland?"

"Kate retained the rights to our ancestral home with my blessings." He crossed his arms over his chest. "Scotland is dead to me."

"You aren't keen on visiting?"

He stepped away, his posture rigid. "Nope."

"How many sisters do you have?"

"Only Kate. As a young boy, I was surrounded by femininity—my mother and several maids, and a wee elipel."

"Meaning?"

"Kate was a tattle-tale."

"You're holding a juvenile grudge against her because of that?"

"I'm not shallow, and this is an adult feud." He propped his elbows on the fence. "You?"

She shook her head. "I'm an only child. Do you have any brothers?"

"No other males aside from my father who was too busy womanizing to take care of his business properly. He couldn't be trusted with holding on to the family fortune."

In the wake of Andrew's unemotional attitude, Belle floundered.

"Both of my parents were domineering and opinionated," she finally said. "Fortunately, my Aunt Lucinda doesn't subscribe to artificiality. She's my mother's sister—spry and wiry and a hoot."

"She lives in Wilmington?"

"Yes. She lives alone, although she traveled the country on a Harley in her younger years. Finally she retired, boasts numerous friends and enjoys entertaining. She is free with her jokes … and her colorful phrases."

"I'd like to meet her. Her experience and wisdom must span decades."

"It does. Fair warning, though. She narrates her adventures with a larger-than-life laugh." Belle paused to study him. "I wager she'd like to meet you too."

"Thus, we have a date." Before she refuted, he grabbed a handful of nails. "I'll ensure the other side of the fence is solid."

Wait. There was more to discuss, beginning with … he had an overbearing father?

She counted on Andrew to elaborate, but he apparently didn't wish to discuss his family any further. Only hers. Only work. He had a way of doing that.

After he strode away, Belle pulled out her cellphone.

She discovered that haggis was a national Scottish dish comprised of the liver, heart, and lungs of a sheep. The recipe got better, or worse—depending on a person's appetite—because the mixture was boiled in a sheep's stomach. If haggis was ever on a menu, she'd stick with a more appetizing entrée, such as mashed potatoes and turnips.

She then texted Candee to inquire about Andrew's new house.

Five bedrooms and five bathrooms, including an in-ground pool, came Candee's immediate text. *From the photos, it's spectacular and even boasts an elevator. The address is One Carolina Way.*

Why would he rent such a large home? Belle texted.

The inventory for oceanfront is sparse, and hardly any are available. And he liked the lines.

What does that mean?

Architectural talk, LOL, and the house has an option to buy.

Belle paused. *He's considering purchasing a home in Wilmington?*

Do you realize who he is? He owns Bransfield Designs, the most profitable architectural firm in the Carolinas. Also, he's been praised in numerous magazines as being a creative genius.

No, Belle hadn't realized, although Megan's nanny had mentioned Andrew's firm on occasion.

The creative genius description fit him, though.

"I honestly don't care what people think about me," he'd once said.

And he kept odd hours, sometimes texting her in the middle of the night. When she'd asked when he slept, he'd replied that his mind was always racing.

When it came to his wealth, he paid the monthly invoices for Megan's sessions quickly, which marked the extent of Belle's knowledge regarding Andrew's finances. He owned a grand home in Roses and now rented in Wilmington and employed a nanny and housekeeper.

Thanks, she texted.

Andrew stood at the other end of the fence, scrutinizing and hammering, looking as if he would happily spend the entire afternoon repairing fences.

When she typed his name on the Internet, her jaw literally dropped. He came from a notable line of aristocrats who had resided in the Scottish Highlands. His biography detailed the family's relocation to the United States when Andrew was young because his father's investment business had gone under.

Andrew had attended public schools and there was no mention of college.

A quick scan detailed his propensity for architecture and how he'd begun Bransfield Designs with little capital. Nowadays, he didn't work for professional gain. He was compelled by something else.

A driving force within him he couldn't quell, perhaps? She admired him for making it on his own resolve.

Impressive. Very impressive. That explained his refined jaw, his straight, regal bearing, and her realization that he wasn't a millionaire. Because, in actuality, he was a billionaire.

With a quick mapping she learned he lived a short distance from her apartment, his home located on a private stretch of beach.

She looked up as he ducked into the stable, then quickly exited.

As he advanced toward her, she snapped her cellphone shut and jammed it into her pocket.

"There's a mirror in the horse stall," he said.

"Right."

"Why?"

"Years ago, I rescued Jenkins from a racetrack because he'd been mistreated. Sadly, he fretted about being closed off. Thus I brought in the acrylic mirror for companionship. He's high strung."

"Not only is Jenkins a horse, but he's a high strung horse?"

"He can't help being a horse, and he's rewarded my rescue with affection and loyalty." She gestured at the fencing. "All set?"

"The fence will hold for years. I'm pleased with the workmanship."

"Because you and your crew were responsible for the repairs."

"Something like that." He gave a short laugh. "Nonetheless, there are always improvements—even for my spectacular crewmen."

55

"Always the perfectionist."

"Does it show?" A sardonic smile tugged at his lips. "By the way, there's another reason I'm here today. I hope to take you to lunch."

And to kiss her.

"I'm flattered," she replied. "I had wondered why you stopped by unexpectedly. I assumed it wasn't solely to bring me flowers."

"A man needs no excuse to gift flowers to a stunning woman. Do you accept my offer?"

"For lunch?" She considered her appearance—jean shorts and a T-shirt, and promptly shook her head. "Unfortunately, I can't."

"Why not?"

"Look around," she averred. *Just look at me.* Her hair was still damp and plastered to her forehead. Any makeup she'd applied that morning, a light peach gloss, had surely disappeared hours ago.

"Can we reschedule?" he asked.

"Feasibly." He looked so disappointed, she supplied, "Although I can whip you up an exquisite omelette. A French omelette, not your run-of-the-mill American-style scrambled eggs."

"What's the difference?"

"Basically the way the eggs are rolled."

"You cook?"

"Not gourmet, but I get by. I'm pretty much an amateur."

"Are you inviting me to lunch?"

"I snagged a great deal on a dozen eggs. What's more, you can inspect the remodel on my apartment. All you've seen up till now are photos."

He smiled. "That being the case, I gladly accept." He gathered his hammer and nails and placed them neatly in his toolbox.

He was clearly a man who didn't object to rolling up his sleeves, working alongside his crewmen, and getting calluses on his hands. He was also equally comfortable in a board room wearing a fine woolen suit.

He directed his gaze toward the pasture. "Are the horses okay if we go inside?"

"On a nice day when the humidity isn't high and there's no rain or bad weather in the forecast, grazing in a pasture is ideal for horses." She lifted an eyebrow. "Why, are you concerned about them?"

"Just wondering."

"One might say you actually like horses."

"One might say you're wrong."

"Despite your reservations, I applaud you for placing the well-being of your daughter before your fears," Belle said. "You allow her to experience the joys of riding. Someday you'll realize that horses are like family. Speaking of Megan, how does she like Wilmington?"

"She met a girl her age who lives nearby. She loves inviting friends over for play dates. She used to be a fun-loving kid. Hopefully, she will again …" He fell silent, but Belle heard the catch in his voice.

He was a father who loved his child.

She nodded. "Are you ready to taste my delectable omelette?"

"More than ready." He bent to pick up his toolbox when Hester bleated, drawing Belle's attention. And, unfortunately, Andrew's as well.

Andrew paused. "What's that?"

Belle slanted him a wry glance. "A goat."

"You mean while I was fixing the fence, that goat was hiding?"

"He wasn't hiding. Hester and Hilda were preoccupied in the patch of woods beyond the stable."

"So while I was feeling safe and secure, I truly wasn't." Cautiously, Andrew peered around. "Hilda? There's a Hilda?"

"A male and a female. Hilda is Hester's sister. To alleviate your concerns, goats are intelligent, gentle creatures."

He scratched his head. "Goats as in plural?"

"I have a little herd of two. Or rather, the farm does. Goats don't like being alone."

Andrew retreated as Hester and Hilda rounded the stable. "What type of goats are they?"

"They're referred to as myotonic goats."

"Will they charge at us?"

"Hester never has. I doubt Hilda will." The air stilled apart from Andrew's quiet, indrawn breath as he suspiciously eyed the two white goats.

"Should I walk carefully?" he asked.

"Definitely, as running or a loud noise will startle them. They might faint."

"Seriously?"

"I couldn't be more serious."

Gingerly, he stepped to his SUV, opened the door, and placed the toolbox on the back seat.

Belle nodded her approval and placed a forefinger to her lips. "We'll walk quietly to my apartment," she whispered.

With a nod, Andrew lifted his foot to close the door. It slammed shut.

Belle jumped.

And the goats fainted.

*C*omfortably sitting on a stool in Belle's cozy kitchen ten minutes later, Andrew favorably assessed the improvements. The walls were now painted the color of butter, and despite the small size, the breakfast area was expansive. A brilliant yellow cuckoo clock, sporting a bird and leaf motif, recapped the hour with a dual chime.

A sizable granite countertop island separated the kitchen from the living room. Barn-style doors led to the hallway, bathroom, and Belle's bedroom. Wide-plank oak flooring, stainless steel appliances, and a glass tile accent wall enhanced the espresso cabinets.

Once they entered her apartment, they stepped out of their boots. She padded to the kitchen and filled a plain white vase with water, setting the dahlias in the center of the island. Quickly, she'd shown him the apartment.

He pointed to a stain on the hallway ceiling. "There's a roof leak? I presumed we fixed everything."

"Me too. The other day it rained, and I quickly grabbed a bucket. I alerted my landlords, Abby and Felix, but they're a young couple and struggle financially."

"I'll take care of it," Andrew said.

"Thanks." She pinned back her hair and washed her hands at the kitchen sink, requesting he do the same. She tied an apron embossed with lemons around her waist while Andrew texted Adella.

He was reassured that Megan was enjoying a delightful afternoon building a sandcastle in front of their home.

Are you using lots of sunscreen? he asked. He always kept Megan's fair, freckled skin in mind.

She is plastered from head to toe, came the nanny's reply. *Her playmate has joined us.*

Good. He smiled and snapped his phone shut. Yes, a move to Wilmington was definitely in his daughter's best interests.

He gazed at Belle. And his interests, too.

"Is Megan having fun at the beach?" Belle inquired.

"Her nanny said she's loving it."

"Did they go to a Wilmington beach?"

"They're closer to my home."

"Your home is near the beach?"

"It's beachfront."

When she responded with silence, he upbraided himself. He certainly hadn't intended to flaunt his wealth, but in all fairness, Belle was also within walking distance of the beach. His place happened to be oceanfront.

She spread her arms wide. "Your house must cost two thousand dollars a month in rent."

The lease was more like five thousand, but he didn't share that information.

Belle pulled a frying pan from the cabinet and added a pat of butter to the pan to sizzle on the stove while she cracked and beat a half dozen eggs into a mixing bowl.

"Is a cheese omelette okay?" She poured him a glass of her "famous" southern style iced tea from the refrigerator.

"What exactly is southern style iced tea?" he asked.

She set the pitcher on the table. "You live in the south. Don't you know?"

"I'm originally from Scotland."

"You moved to America when you were eighteen."

"Where did you hear that?"

She flushed, which prompted his grin. She'd done her due diligence—perhaps gleaning her information about him from Candee.

"Anyhow, with your Scottish brogue, how can I forget where you're originally from?" She smiled. "Southern iced tea requires heaps of sugar and freshly squeezed lemons. Also, the lemons were on sale."

He grinned and reclaimed the stool. He drained his glass and concluded that sugar was the gateway to happiness. He set down his glass and Belle quickly tipped the pitcher and refilled.

"Did the grocery store offer a deal on cheese this week too, when you went for your messages?" he asked.

"What messages?"

"The Scottish term for groceries."

"You Scots have such interesting words."

He lifted his glass as a salute. "So do you Americans."

"I assume you're American too."

"Yes, I claim dual citizenship, although I haven't been back to Scotland for many years." He surveyed the stove and its contents. "Will your French creation ooze with Camembert and fresh lavender?"

"I can't afford Camembert." Her lips curved easily as she headed for the cheese board. "Swiss cheese was only two dollars a pound this week, and I asked the woman at the deli to slice the cheese extra thin."

"Did she oblige?"

"Indeed." Belle returned to the stove and glanced at him over her shoulder. "The clerks recognize me. For your information, coupons and specials can result in substantial grocery savings."

He savored another sip of the refreshing tea, allowing the flavors of sweet and sour to linger on his tongue. "Is this a fact?"

"From first-hand experience."

He gave an overstated groan. "Are you one of those customers who hold up the entire grocery line so that the clerk can scan your fifty cent coupon?"

"That's me."

She was so serious he chuckled. His ex-wife had never clipped a coupon in her life.

For several minutes he sat silently, allowing his luncheon hostess an opportunity to prepare the omelet, correction *omelette*, without interruption.

He used the minutes to contemplate the next phase of his firm's expansion, but soon chose to reflect on his surprising good fortune.

Belle Boots stood five feet away from him at her shiny, stainless steel stove.

And he liked that—being with her, sharing lunch.

During the never-ending evenings he'd spent alone since his divorce—he'd never envisioned himself living in any other manner other than as a single man. Absorbed in his business and raising his daughter, he'd convinced himself that he was better off alone.

For starters, just look what he'd accomplished since his divorce. Why, his firm had doubled in size. Imagine if he had a demanding wife to please, as during the seven years of marriage to Rowena.

Therefore, he'd be happier if he remained unattached, apart from an occasional, impersonal date. Any free time was earmarked for his precious daughter.

After weeks of texting and phoning Belle, he was inclined

to remain on the same course. Belle had encouraged him to examine aspects of life he'd overlooked—the outdoors, nature, and humorous banter—and that made him uncomfortable. However, not so uncomfortable he'd give up his frenetic work pace.

Besides, by Sunday evening he'd be on the road again, continuing his commitment to excellent design over cheap construction, connecting with Megan through Skype, while reassured that the nanny provided excellent care.

He and his firm fought for projects to be completed without politics interfering. That was all well and good, but left little time for laughing conversations with Belle, or water fights with a hose, or heartfelt discussions concerning his daughter.

Or, he amended with a smile, any fainting goats.

Whenever he mentioned Megan, compassion and concern would immediately touch Belle's features.

As he lifted his glass, Belle flipped the omelette as adeptly as any French chef. She shook the pan constantly over the gas stove's flame.

When she slanted him a glance, he made a show of applause. She flamboyantly bowed, then turned back to the stove to flick dashes of black pepper and basil on the eggs.

His heart skipped a beat at her exuberance, her enthusiasm. He sat back, indulging himself by staring at her slim profile and exquisite features. She was a natural beauty.

What if he'd met her soon after his divorce? Would she have been able to teach him how to forgive, to assuage his jaded heart? Would she have encouraged him to seek ambitions more gratifying than wealth and influence and acknowledgment—motivations that had molded his childhood and adulthood? He was, after all, a Bransfield, and well aware of his illustrious legacy.

The improbability of ever meeting Belle when he was at

an earlier age surfaced, and he checked himself. At what cocktail party would they have connected? His life had revolved around affluence before his father had lost everything because of laziness and indifference. To be successful, a business required continuous monitoring and long business hours.

Sure, monetary and societal advantages had been a given in Scotland, and Andrew and his sister's seats among the elite were secured.

During those years, an equine therapist named Belle would never have entered his sphere of aristocratic friends.

Even if they'd met, would he have been interested? More than likely not, for she would have been overshadowed by the fashionable and ostentatious women. Belle wouldn't have been comfortable if he had escorted her to an exclusive country club dinner.

Or would she? No doubt, she was as gorgeous in a fancy ball gown as in jeans.

Distractedly, he envisioned her in an elegant green silk, her dark hair combed to the side and secured with a glittering diamond pin.

He rolled his glass between his palms, striving to be completely truthful with himself while Belle focused on her skillet creation.

When he was younger, he would have respected her intelligence and openness, her kind-heartedness, her pure, fresh nature.

But he wouldn't have asked her out.

However, that was then. This was now.

"Watch, Andrew." Belle signaled him over as she tilted the pan, added a generous sprinkling of cheese and slid it onto a plate. "This is what makes a French omelette different from an American-style. It's all in the rolling. See? The omelette is in the shape of an oval, whereas an American omelet is folded in half."

"Thus, you produced a perfect omelet," he said.

"*Omelette*." She held up the plate. "Voila!"

Laughing, he pressed a kiss on her forehead.

He couldn't help himself. She was a woman who needed to be appreciated and kissed.

"Belle Boots, you are priceless." He chucked her beneath her chin. "Thank you for helping me to laugh again."

"It's good to laugh, isn't it?"

Her assertion called for another kiss. "I haven't enjoyed myself this much in eons."

"Eons?"

"Months … years."

"I haven't laughed this much in eons, either." She reached for napkins, plates, and forks, then arranged two settings on the kitchen island.

"Did you study cooking in college?" He waited for her to sit before taking his place across from her.

She shrugged and looked away. "Most of my college courses were related to equine therapy.

"Is that a bad thing? Equine therapy?"

"Not at all."

"What courses did you study?"

"I earned an undergraduate degree in counseling. Afterward, I completed a certification program, focusing on equine interaction."

"Which is?"

"To treat patients, particularly children, with emotional or physical disabilities through a mutual affection for horses."

"You're obviously passionate about your work."

"I am. Except …" She grimaced and shifted in her seat.

"Except?"

"Except my parents expected me to become a doctor like my father. I might have satisfied them if I had pursued a veterinarian degree." Belle sighed. "I considered it ..."

"And then?"

"I love animals but also aspired to help people. My major seemed a suitable way to incorporate both."

"Did you? Please your parents?" he asked.

"No. They tried to steer my aspirations to match theirs. Obviously they didn't succeed." A sheen of tears shimmered in her velvety gray eyes, and she concentrated on a circle of copper pots hanging from the ceiling.

"Embrace your profession." He grabbed her hand. "You're improving lives and helping your students overcome emotional and physical trauma."

"Am I? Truly?"

"I speak from experience because you changed Megan's life." Reassuringly, he squeezed her fingers. "Most definitely."

She kept her focus on the pots. "Or maybe I studied equine therapy to become something my parents didn't want me to be."

Had she suppressed those contemplations, or silently contemplated them all these years? She'd spoken quickly, then seemed to regret her outburst.

"We are all rebellious once in a while," he said. "I was certainly unmanageable when I first moved to America."

"Why?"

"Because going from affluence to poverty, especially in an unfamiliar country, was disheartening." Andrew rubbed his forehead. "My mother never forgave my father for his poor business decisions."

"And you?"

"I did my own thing, made my own way."

"Your sister?"

"In Kate's opinion, my father could do no wrong." He

drew a long breath and curled his fingers around hers. "Tell me something, Belle. Are you content?"

"Undeniably."

"Then stay true to who you are and be happy with your choice. My grandfather in Scotland used to say, "'You're a long time deid.'"

"Dead? That goes without saying?"

"Once you're dead, you're dead for a long time, so enjoy life."

"Not the most heartening of Scottish sayings," she muttered.

"But true, nonetheless."

The thought flitted through his mind that he should take the saying to heart. He was committed to a continuous strive for perfection and success, pushing too fast on a narrow lane, but he couldn't help himself.

He remembered what it was like to lose everything.

Never again.

Belle eyed their plates. "Our food is getting cold."

"We can't let your creation go to waste. I'm impressed by your expertise."

"I watch numerous demonstrations on television, and you can learn a lot from YouTube."

"I'm sure, and we mustn't waste all those eggs."

She bowed her head and said grace, something Andrew had never done, although his demeanor was suitably prayerful. When she finished, he forked a mouthful of omelette and closed his eyes, savoring the delectable combination of finely cooked eggs combined with the velvety smoothness of milky sweet cheese.

"Pure dead brilliant," he said, and Belle smiled at the compliment.

He washed down the omelette with another glass of iced tea.

After lunch was over, he helped her clear and rinse the plates.

When the kitchen was tidied to her satisfaction, she brewed a pot of coffee and arranged a set of glass mugs on the island.

Over steaming coffee, he said, "Again, I'm sorry the goats fainted. My habit is to shut the door with my foot because I usually carry papers or tools—"

"No explanation is necessary, Andrew." Lightly, she touched his hand. "The goats are healthy, and actually, they didn't faint. Myotonic goats just stiffen and fall over, appearing to faint."

"I felt like I should rush over to splash cold water on their faces to revive them." He hadn't, because he didn't care to be near two stiff goats, especially one as ornery looking as Hester. "But they were up again in a few seconds and didn't seem hurt."

Belle's eyes sparkled. "No negative consequences."

A radiant sun lit the kitchen, and tiny silver hoops glinted from her ears.

Beyond the expansive window over the sink, vibrant purple zinnias blossomed beneath carefully trimmed hedging and a white oak tree. Belle had mentioned that Abby and Felix were avid gardeners.

Belle smoothed the napkin on her lap. Her movements were elegant, and he admired her aura of kindness. Despite the hard manual exertion in the stalls, her fingers were long and slender and diligently clean. Poignantly, he recalled her adjusting Megan's horse helmet, ensuring that his daughter was safe and protected.

"To put your mind at ease," she continued, "fainting doesn't hurt a goat nor cause any pain."

He gazed at her and smiled. He couldn't get enough of seeing her, being with her. She was naturally sophisticated, humorous, and captivating. She'd been forced to move from Roses quickly, and the sadness she felt at leaving her precious students was real. Despite her optimism, the move hadn't been easy.

And the attention she showed her animals was diligent and caring.

He was a decade older, and a hundred times more world-weary. Yet, every minute with her put another chink in his inflexible armor toward life.

Where Belle was concerned, things weren't all business, and her empathy softened him.

"I leave on Sunday to work in Roses for a couple days. Adella will care for Megan." He glanced at his watch. They were scheduled to return to the house so Megan could take her afternoon nap.

"If you see Candee in Roses, tell her how much I miss her and her family," Belle replied. "With the blur of moving, I haven't had time to phone, except for a quick text to refer Joseph to another therapist."

"How is he doing?"

"The therapist is excellent, although I miss Joseph."

"I'm sure he misses you too." Andrew pushed back his stool. Belle did the same. "I'll return to Wilmington by midweek. Thank you for a delicious lunch."

She walked him to the entryway. "Thank *you* for the gorgeous flowers."

"My pleasure. I'm a romantic at heart.

He was? Well, with Belle he was becoming a regular Romeo.

"You're a sensitive and kind man."

"And princely?"

"Sure."

"And you're a wonderful woman. A princess." More than wonderful. More than a princess. That prickle of awareness whenever she was near flooded his senses.

Out of the corner of his eye he spotted an orange tabby. The cat shot from the hallway and skirted around his legs before disappearing.

"Ginger," Belle supplied.

"Ginger. Right. Okay. Will Ginger bite?"

"Not that I'm aware."

"Does Ginger have a sister or brother?"

Belle elbowed him. "No."

"I'm starting to think you live in a glorified petting zoo."

She burst out laughing. "Don't tell me you're going to make a scene whenever you see one of my animals?"

"Never." He tugged her close. "But I'll show you what a scene looks like."

He didn't give her time to catch her breath nor fire a snappy rejoinder, because he kissed her, long and deep.

"That's quite a scene," she murmured between his kisses. "An extremely romantic one."

"It's from a Scottish movie."

"Which is?"

"Braveheart."

"You mean the movie with the stunning camera work?"

"The very same." He nuzzled her neck. "I'll text you while I'm gone. Will you miss me?"

She pulled back and brushed stray blades of dried grass from his shirt, giving him a tender look with those gorgeous gray eyes. "I'm a pushover for a man who shows up at my riding ring bearing flowers. Especially flowers he snagged at a great sale." She granted him one of her heart-stopping smiles.

Thus, she offered all the proof he needed. He kissed her again and would have continued. Unfortunately, his cellphone chirped, jerking him back to reality.

He snatched the phone from his pocket while muttering a

string of colorful Scottish phrases. As Belle stepped away, he scanned the text message from his foreman.

Problem with a work site in Camden, SC, boss.

Which site? Andrew texted.

The healthcare renovation at the senior living facility. Construction debris containment, and an extremely vocal town board who are concerned about infection control. They're demanding a meeting with you at eight a.m. on Monday morning or they're shutting the project down.

He pushed out a sigh.

"Troubles with Megan?" Belle asked.

"Thankfully, Megan is fine. An addition to an existing building I've designed is more complex than anticipated, and the board insists the healthcare facility remain in operation while the addition is completed."

"Is it possible to keep the facility open?"

"Not easily, but necessary because the logistics of moving senior citizens to another facility would be difficult." He shoved a hand through his hair. "Part of the problem is economics. The city paid for the renovation. The crew isn't as fastidious about debris as they should be, which leads to a cleanliness issue. The town requires a meeting with me or construction ceases."

"Is a solution possible?"

He slipped on his boots. "Anything is possible."

He insisted on a standard of excellence, not adapting lightly to changes. He thrust his cellphone into his pocket after replying to his foreman. *I'll arrive in Camden by Sunday afternoon so we can talk this over before the Monday meeting.*

This issue would push back his trip to Roses, and consequently, his return to Wilmington.

And this newest demand reminded him that what had happened in Belle's apartment would never happen again.

His work was a part of himself he wouldn't relinquish. Through his designs, his visions became realities.

In truth, being recognized by pleased customers motivated him. Consequently, he would carry out whatever orders were enforced in order to satisfy the requirements for the Camden, SC, town board.

CHAPTER 6

*S*ummer visitors flooded Wilmington, and the intense heat of a southern July eased on.

Belle began offering equine therapy sessions and hadn't seen Andrew since he'd departed for Camden. His texts to her were short and concise.

The first arrived on Sunday.

Hi Belle. I'm in Camden. Here is Adella's cellphone number. Store it in your contacts and text her directly regarding Megan's sessions.

In other words, no communication with him.

Will do. And your drive to Camden was …? Belle texted.

She grimaced. She'd never been good at texting. She was literally all thumbs.

Uneventful, came his reply. *What did you do this weekend?*

I was busy. Still unpacking. Plus, I visited my Aunt Lucinda.

Her aunt had remarked that she was pleased Belle had begun a new chapter in her life, grinning when Belle mentioned Andrew numerous times. With each recounting of the services he provided, Aunt Lucinda had stretched her hand across the porch swing to pat Belle's arm. "You found someone special. Don't throw love away, like I did."

"Didn't you once say men were a bother?"

"A woman has the prerogative to change her mind and admit her mistakes. If the right man comes along—"

"Andrew and I aren't serious," Belle had protested.

"You will be."

Belle had a swift, unbidden thought that Aunt Lucinda might be correct.

With a sigh, she batted away the contemplation. Sure, she felt special when she was with him, and they chatted about everything because he was easy to talk to. But she'd given her heart to someone only to have her dreams broken.

How is your aunt? Andrew texted.

Eccentric, as usual. She insisted on wearing green gloves and an Indiana Jones hat when we shopped at the Farmer's Market.

Did anyone remark on her appearance?

After all these years, they're accustomed to her.

Does she use coupons too? he asked.

LOL, no. What about you?

No coupons.

I mean, how was your weekend?

More unpacking, same as you. Spent hours with Megan before I drove to Camden. Look, I gotta go. My foreman is pounding on my hotel door.

Good luck with the meeting.

Thanks. Hope your week goes well.

You too.

Impersonal, affable, informal. Hurried. No mention of their lunch together. No mention of French omelettes or tabby cats. This wasn't the teasing, good-natured man who had kissed her by the fence, or in the entryway of her apartment.

This was a different Andrew. The entrepreneur. The billionaire. The man firmly out of reach.

When her cellphone pinged the following week, her heart stopped when his name crossed her screen.

Crazy busy here, Andrew texted. *How are you?*

Fine. You?

Overloaded in work.

The project is taking longer than anticipated?

Much longer.

She waited for him to continue. When he didn't, she asked, *Are you there?*

Sorry, Belle. I'm preoccupied. A local crew was hired, and it's up to me to maintain a high benchmark. Safety is our first priority.

Lots of details?

Yes. I've divided off part of the construction with barriers and stay on site to ensure the crew is complying with town regulations.

Numerous problems waiting for only you to solve?

Okay, that was edgy, but it was too late to take it back. Another long hesitation, and she watched her phone screen for the telltale bubbles indicating that he was texting.

Architects like solving problems, Belle. BTW, Megan is loving her sessions with you.

She's a pleasure. Belle's fingers hovered over her phone's keyboard. Should she inquire when he planned on returning to Wilmington? She typed the question, quickly deleting it. Too needy.

Take care of yourself, she typed in its place. *Don't work too hard.* Ugh. Such a cliché. She pulled at the collar of her sleeveless denim shirt.

That's my job, Belle.

That's your life, she wanted to fire back. Instead, she said nothing.

. . .

SEVERAL DAYS AFTERWARD, she claimed a stool at her kitchen island and examined the bouquet of dahlias—the petals brown and curling, the stalks drooping.

Nonetheless, a slight yellow tint remained. A sign of hope.

She re-cut the stems, changed the old water to fresh and returned them to the vase.

What is the meaning of yellow flowers? she typed into her cellphone.

Daisies mean cheerfulness and innocence. Dahlias represent a forever commitment between two persons.

She sucked in a breath. She couldn't focus on any words with tears flooding her eyes.

"*I looked up the meanings of the flowers,*" Andrew had told her. "*Dahlias seemed more appropriate.*"

Slowly, her annoyance at him for being preoccupied in Camden gave way to regret that he wasn't with her in Wilmington. Unfortunately, her practical brain reminded, that same romantic man had forgotten all about her only in a matter of days.

ON A LEISURELY WALK A WEEK LATER, Belle came upon a street sign that read Carolina Way. Andrew was in Camden, she rationalized, and she was more than a little curious to see his house. Besides, she enjoyed viewing real estate, assuming that someday she'd have a home of her own.

As she strolled the shore, she relished the slap of ocean water against the rocks, the Atlantic-blue churning surf. All familiar. All soothing. She loved living in Wilmington again.

She neared a secluded mansion and verified the location using the map on her cellphone. One Carolina Way. Andrew's house.

Her lips parted. She stood silent in mute confusion.

His "little" place? Painted a vivid turquoise blue, the spectacular home sat directly on the ocean and claimed a broad, sandy beach.

This was his rental—with the outsized swimming pool flanked by elegant Roman columns, complemented by faultlessly groomed shrubs? Really?

Yes, really, because, clutching a cellphone, he waved to her from the second-floor balcony.

Her legs froze in place. Wasn't he supposed to be in Camden? He'd caught her spying on him.

At any rate, he'd returned and had obviously neglected to phone her.

And what was it with this man and balconies?

Despite her compulsion to flee, she gathered her courage and feigned a smile. "Hi." She enhanced her smile with a high-spirited wave. "I took a walk and—" *Happened to be strolling along Carolina Way? Why were her thoughts so muddled?* "This is private property, correct?"

He clicked off his cellphone. "It's *my* private property, Belle, and you're always welcome. Adella just left, and Megan is in bed."

Belle's hands curled. "I assumed you were out of town." Okay, she was incriminating herself further. Not to mention that she was shouting and had no right to question his whereabouts.

"The problems in Camden are resolved, and I arrived home an hour ago. I showered and read Megan a story before her bedtime. I planned to phone you when I finished this last business call and here you are. C'mon over." He waved her forward.

"I can't." She peered at her cut-off shorts. Her hair must look a sight, and sand had taken up permanent residence in her sandals. "Thanks for the invite, but I'll take a raincheck." She hastened her steps and backed away from the house.

"Belle, please. I'll meet you on the deck." That Scottish lilt, affirming an unpretentious warmth, both enchanting and entrancing. He slid his cellphone into the pocket of his gray polo shirt. "We can watch the sunset together."

Ever the romantic.

She swallowed her protest, slowly starting up the lush expanse of emerald lawn. He was sensitive and seemed sincere, she conceded, and the combination was irresistible.

As she approached, she took in the inviting scene. Candles were lit on a teak credenza, and a Mozart piano sonata played from an invisible speaker. The dancing flames from a rectangular fire pit beckoned, and potted red zinnias brought radiant color to the deck.

He finished arranging two white Adirondack chairs on either side of a wooden table, set a child monitor nearby, then surveyed Belle from head to toe. Striding forward, he grasped her hands in his. "Miss Belle Boots, you are adorable."

"Adorable?"

"You always remind me of a poster woman for … I don't know … small-town goodness."

"Is that a Scottish compliment?"

"American." He laughed. "In any event, you're gorgeous and a perfect package."

Promptly recognizing that after two weeks on the road, any woman would undoubtedly be a perfect package, she took a guarded step backward.

"How are you?" A Scottish burr laced his words, trilling the 'r.'

"I'm fine. You?" She gazed up at his impossibly attractive face. Would he welcome her into his arms?

He didn't, murmuring he was also fine and gesturing for her to sit. "Can I offer you anything to drink?" he asked. "You name it, I have it."

"Iced tea."

"Ah, sweet iced tea. My beverage of choice is non-alcoholic Scottish ginger beer this evening. Adella picked up a six-pack at a local specialty store. Are you up to trying it?"

"Sure. Was the beer on sale?"

"We're just glad the store carries it." He grabbed two bottles from a free-standing mini fridge tucked in the corner of the deck. "Adella would have paid any price, especially because it's on my tab." He grinned and Belle reciprocated.

He gazed at her as he poured beer into her glass. "You are lovely."

"A minute ago, your choice phrases were adorable and small-town goodness."

"Pure dead brilliant also comes to mind and beautiful and I—" His words rushed together. "Sorry. Scots don't give praise well."

She studied the glass as he continued pouring. "You're spilling the beer," she noted.

He muttered a lively Gaelic phrase, reached for a linen napkin to mop the overflow, then handed her an overflowing glass.

She sniffed, then tasted, rewarded with a sampling of spicy ginger and citrus.

He set the bottle upright and waited for her to sit, then claimed the chair beside hers. "Good?"

She lifted her glass. "Delicious."

Judging from his reddish beard stubble, he hadn't shaved in several days. His hair was still damp from the shower and his shirt, open at the throat, was tucked into olive-colored shorts. Involuntarily, she memorized the way he looked, the rigid planes of his chest, the strong profile—every inch the charismatic male. She also noted the fixed lines of fatigue around his eyes and mouth, which she hadn't noticed when she'd last seen him.

He smiled and leaned back. "Do I meet with your approval?"

"Sorry. I was staring, wasn't I?"

"Don't be sorry. You meet with my approval too." There was no mistaking his quiet assertion. Despite his laid-back teasing, her pulse doubled.

She shifted. Swallowed. Even if she had the courage to ask him why he'd texted her only twice, she couldn't be certain whether her question wouldn't come with an answer she wasn't prepared to hear.

"Thanks for repairing my leaky roof," she said. "Abby and Felix gratefully appreciated your generosity."

"My pleasure." Andrew stretched out his long legs, picked up his glass and watched the fire's cheery blaze leaping and flickering. "I, too, fix things, except my specialty is buildings."

She sat straighter. "You remember I'm a fixer?"

"There's nothing about you I ever forget." A warmhearted gleam shone from his eyes. "Did Candee mention I visited her when I was in Roses?"

Belle placed her glass aside. "Briefly, yes."

"Did she say who we discussed?"

Recalling their phone conversation, Belle replied in a cool voice, "She was evasive." And that had made Belle uncomfortable. "I assume you two discussed Joseph's new horse therapist, or Megan, or Bransfield Designs." Noting the rigidity in his jaw, Belle ended with a short laugh. "Correct?"

ANDREW SET down his glass and reached for Belle, although she drew away and planted her hands on her lap. Despite her off-the-cuff response, he had the uneasy impression he'd unintentionally upset her. Determining their conversation required a clearer explanation, he began, "Candee and I discussed you."

"Me?" Belle tilted her head. "Why?"

"I was eager to learn more about you. After considerable prodding, Candee was kind enough to share the details of your marriage with me."

"You mean my divorce?"

"From what I understand, you were married to a guy named Tyler who didn't appreciate you."

Slender eyebrows snapped together. "Why were you two discussing my personal life?"

He caught the resentment lacing her tone. "I explained why. I'm interested in you, Belle. Surely you realize that."

Well, that wasn't the entire truth. He was *more* than interested.

In Camden, he hadn't been able to think clearly, which had put him in a state he wasn't accustomed to, causing the job to take twice as long. He'd been certain when he'd left Wilmington that a relationship with Belle was too emotionally harrowing to contemplate. However, sitting next to her now played havoc with his sentiments.

She kept her gaze on the ocean. Her fingers toyed with the silky hair at her temple.

"Look at me." He touched his lips to her restless fingers. "Talk to me."

"About my failed marriage? About Tyler?"

"If you wish."

"Hasn't Candee regaled you with all the tragic, pathetic details?"

"They're not pathetic," he said. "And I'd like to hear them from you."

Her gaze darted to his. "We're friends, aren't we?"

"Without question."

"Alright then." She plucked up her glass. "To begin with, Tyler was in my life for several years. I believed I loved him."

Despite the irrationality of it, a surge of jealousy went through Andrew.

The air became unnaturally quiet.

"When I first met him, he asked if I could keep a secret. He'd been hurt by several unpleasant relationships and had lost faith in women. I felt bad for him and privileged that he confided in me. He was such a stoic man. He was a professional accountant, you know."

Andrew gave a bitter laugh. "I heard."

"A string of unfortunate luck, Tyler told me." Belle's heel incessantly tapped on the wooden deck. "His sad stories inspired me to prove to him that he shouldn't lose faith in women and love."

"Did you succeed?"

Belle choked on her beer. "A month after we were married he verbally degraded me after a horse competition, mocking that I smelled like a barn."

The sadness, the humiliation brimming from her gray eyes, drew a dawning of compassion within him. That frozen ocean of deep uncertainty—to care for a woman again—to care for anyone save his precious daughter; began to crack.

He laid a palm on Belle's cheek. He longed to embrace her, to hold on to the intense emotions gripping him, the first real emotions he'd felt in years. He wanted to share more than a moment with her. He anticipated sharing a lifetime.

The knowledge surprised him, but only for an instant. He embraced it for what it was. The truth.

A tear ran down her face and he kissed her there, sampling the saltiness. He rifled through his intentions to continue the conversation, half-heartedly rejecting the subject of her beauty, her mesmerizing smile, her declaration that they were friends.

They were more than friends. Much more.

"Go on," he said tenderly.

She fixed her glass on the table. "Six months into our marriage, Tyler screamed at me for not keeping myself up to his excessive standards. He scolded me for always wearing informal clothes." She bit down on her bottom lip as it quivered. "I tried to reason with him. Jeans were, after all, what a therapist wore when around horses all day. But he merely yelled louder. His profession required a well-dressed woman he could escort to corporate dinners." She gazed up at Andrew with tear-filled eyes. "I didn't provide a proper fit for him."

Andrew kept his features neutral, although his insides churned with fury. "Your beauty rivals any of the prettiest starlets."

"I'm adorable, if I remember your words correctly."

"And lovely," he emphasized.

She waved an airy hand, dismissing his compliments. "The next day Tyler apologized for his outburst. Nonetheless, a few days afterward he filed for divorce. He told me I couldn't compare to his glamorous ex-girlfriends if I tried."

"He told you he'd dated glamorous women?"

Her chin lowered. "Often."

Andrew recalled Belle's hands gently fastening Megan's helmet, her soothing, encouraging voice, their shared giggles when his daughter rode Honeycrisp.

He marveled at her kindness, suppressing a frown because now she was assiduously avoiding his stare. For all her dauntless independence, wit, and spirit, she became hesitant and withdrawn when talking about Tyler.

"The papers from his lawyer decreed irreconcilable differences," Belle was saying.

"You should have been glad to get rid of him." Andrew evened out his voice, seeking to reassure her while tamping down the impulse to physically strangle her ex.

"My aunt said the same. So did Candee. I should've known by the way Jenkins reacted the first time Tyler entered his stall."

"Your horse, you mean?"

"Yes, I believe animals have a sixth sense." Briefly, Belle closed her eyes. "I keenly remember Jenkins' soft brown eyes going hard, and his ears pinned back. That marked the last time Tyler ever entered his stall."

"Tyler never tried again?"

"Once, but Jenkins threatened to kick him."

"So Tyler got the memo?"

"Loud and clear." She grinned, but her expression swiftly turned sober. "But you know what?" She picked up her glass. Her hand shook. "When the divorce documents arrived, I accepted and signed while my heart broke."

"Why? You clearly were abused."

"In my mind I was a failure—trying to fix Tyler, trying to fix my marriage, and ultimately not gratifying my parents' wishes."

"You chose to follow your own professional path, and for that I commend you." Andrew raised his glass for a toast.

She clinked her glass against his. "True."

They exchanged congratulatory glances.

Her thick hair gleamed in the firelight, spilling forward across her face. Her lashes, dark and lush, cast the hint of a shadow across her unblemished cheeks.

"I'm wondering if you ever really loved Tyler." Andrew voiced his thoughts aloud. Although perhaps he shouldn't have because her eyebrows pulled together and she frowned.

"Maybe. Maybe not." She stood, and he admired her pure loveliness, the subtle finesse in the way she wore her clothes, no matter how casual.

She peered at the sun setting on the horizon, the sky a brilliant brush of vivid rose and intense orange, the waves shimmering like diamonds as an unflinching moon cast silvery beams on the water.

He came behind her and enfolded her in his arms, tracing the curve of her ear with his mouth. She trembled. He hoped she would turn to gaze at him so he could see her face.

When she didn't turn, he brushed his knuckles against her cheek and delicately kissed her shoulders, her nape, her hair.

"Andrew, I—"

"Don't, Belle."

"Don't what?"

He drew in a slow, leaden breath. "Don't ever change."

Because he was falling in love with her.

She brought him a quiet sense of joy. In quick-thinking texts, emotional moments, and dazzling smiles, she'd stolen his heart.

His words wrung a hesitant chuckle from her. "Don't ever change what? My profession?"

"Anything about you."

"Are you saying that you're beginning to like horses?"

"Fortunately, you're not a horse."

"I'm around them all week."

He smirked. "I'll manage."

"You haven't met Jenkins face to face yet." She threw a rueful smile over her shoulder, and he set his sights on her alluring lips.

He laughed, deep and throaty, steadying himself, marveling at her bewitching effect on him. Impulsively, he tightened his arms around her. He couldn't get enough of her, and this was a unique experience. Yes, women had been a social duty all his adult life, but certainly not his entire world. He'd never been preoccupied with a woman before.

"Andrew?"

He closed his eyes. "Hmm?"

"Are you interested in hearing the rest of my story?"

Even with his eyes closed, he felt her gaze on him as she turned and rested her soft cheek against his chest.

The simple affection of her movements plunged his spirits. Effectively, it reminded him that if he stopped seeing her, there would be no further tender moments.

He should let her go. He was committed to his work, to his daughter. There was no room in his life for another relationship. Another failure.

Not in business. Not personally. He'd learned that hard lesson from experience.

But he *couldn't* let Belle go.

"Yes. Tell me everything." He opened his eyes. "Under one condition."

"What's that?"

Huskily, he murmured, "I can keep my arms around you."

For a beat she was silent, followed by a quiet sigh.

"I'd love that," she whispered.

He tipped up her head, prompting her with an over bright smile. "I'm listening."

"Right ...well ... " She inhaled. "When I rationalized my situation, I attributed my divorce to a marriage gone wrong at an early age and a manipulative husband. I shouldn't have tried to fix his problems."

"Fixers place other people's needs before their own," Andrew said.

"I have an overwhelming urge to support folks, and try to come up with a solution to make things better. Sometimes, I can't help myself."

"Sometimes?"

"Oftentimes," she conceded.

Her eyes reminded him of the color of dove feathers, soft and gentle, which perfectly described his selfless, caring Belle.

The last beams of sunlight streamed down, enhancing her shiny hair with golden highlights.

She interrupted his delightful contemplation by rhapsodizing, "Isn't the sky picturesque? The sun sets over the ocean in so many colors. It resembles a portrait."

"Or a painting on canvas." He cradled her close to his chest. "Sometimes I forget to appreciate the precious things in life."

Like love.

He'd never known what love felt like. Now he did.

The exhilaration, the joy. The feeling that every last breath had been taken from his lungs.

Love wasn't planned. It never was.

And love was the only thing in life that truly mattered.

CHAPTER 7

*T*he night Belle had watched the sunset with Andrew, she'd agreed to text him the minute she returned to her apartment. Touched and flattered when he'd insisted, she'd happily obliged.

Twenty-four hours later, he suggested dinner with him and Megan when he came back to Wilmington the following weekend.

She accepted.

He canceled soon afterward. Problems in Camden.

The days merged into another week before he arrived back in Wilmington.

When can I see you again? he texted. *My foreman told me there are wild horses on a beach in the Outer Banks.*

You mean in Corolla? she asked.

Yes.

Megan will love this, Belle replied.

I missed you while I was away.

Audibly, she swallowed, processing Andrew's comment.

And you? he pressed. *You love horses.*

A given. But he'd been gone. Now he assumed she was at his beck and call.

Wild horses will be a grand adventure, she hedged.

I agree. BTW, Megan's eye patch was removed this week.

I know. I saw her when she came for her session. How wonderful.

I wasn't around. I relied on Adella to bring Megan for her eyeglass fitting, because work necessitated that I stay in Camden. Still, I should have been there.

I would have enthusiastically joined them, Belle responded.

Really?

Without question. I love Megan.

Thank you. A hesitation filled the space between them. *That means a lot.*

Wait ...The horses at the Outer Banks wander freely, Belle texted. *What if a horse gallops near you?*

I'd jump into the ocean.

She laughed out loud. *Sounds like a plan.*

Not a particularly good plan, but a plan, nonetheless.

Are you aware Corolla is four hours away from Wilmington by car? she added.

It is?

Aren't you aware of the distance?

I've been so preoccupied lately.

Perhaps a beach trip somewhere a bit closer?

I missed you, he texted a second time. *Will you come to the beach with us?*

She squeezed her cellphone, briefly closing her eyes while her heartbeat soared.

"You missed me," she whispered to the phone screen, visualizing his handsome face.

She'd missed him too, but she wouldn't tell him that.

You work too much, she typed instead.

No, no, too bossy.

She deleted it. He'd just arrived after several nonstop workdays.

I'm trying to change, he texted, as if he had read her mind. *I tuned in to a bunch of self-help audiobooks during the long drive. How to balance work with everyday life.*

Were the books helpful?

Interesting. Thought-provoking.

Perhaps he should practice what he listened to.

Still, a much-needed beach respite would allow Andrew a renewed and refreshed outlook.

Don't mention anything else on this subject, she warned herself before her fingers touched the keypad. She had no right trying to fix him.

Shall I pack a lunch? she inquired.

No. You have enough to do. There's a certain colonel who makes a delicious fried chicken.

I thought you loved fresh seafood?

Who said that? Me?

Uh, huh. Fresh caught fish for dinner…

Hmm. We'll order seafood when we get closer to the beach. Pan-fried scallops and fried pickles are my favorite. Megan likes chicken strips.

Scallops sound good. Undecided on the pickles. Which beach?

The beach in front of my house.

You just went from a four-hour car ride to a one minute car ride. Have you considered Carolina Beach?

Is it far?

About twenty minutes away.

She loved the sun-drenched feel of the modest town and hadn't had the opportunity to visit since landing in Wilmington.

Excellent. I'll pick you up at ten on Saturday morning.

. . .

Two days later, Andrew and Megan arrived at Belle's apartment exactly as her cuckoo clock chimed ten a.m. Punctuality was a trait Belle admired about him.

What did it cost him to juggle a multi-million-dollar business while single parenting? Sure, he had the means and domestic help, but it still required resourcefulness and a perseverance she seldom witnessed in men. Certainly not Tyler. Certainly not any she'd dated since her divorce.

Of course, she and Andrew weren't dating. They were friends who shared a common interest in his daughter's happiness and security.

And horses.

Well, not horses, exactly. Goats. Nope. Tabby cats. Umm, no.

Nonetheless, they got along splendidly.

As was his custom, Andrew got out of his SUV as soon as Belle emerged from her apartment.

He opened the passenger door for her. "You are stunning," he said.

"Thank you, but hardly." She glanced down at the khaki shorts and red ribbed tank top she'd worn over her swimsuit. "I appreciate your earlier home-town goodness compliment, though."

"Small-town goodness," he corrected. "Here's another compliment. 'A pretty face suits the dish-cloth.'"

"Now I look like a dish-cloth?" She hung her hands on her hips. "Is that a step up or down from small-town goodness?"

"It's Scottish flattery. You are stunning in anything you wear." He chucked her under the chin. "So it's a step up."

"Well, perhaps if you said it in Scottish …"

"English will do." He grabbed her raffia bag and feigned a groan as he fixed it in the trunk. "What's in this? Lead?"

"All the necessary supplies. Sunscreen, towels, water bottles and my script." Belle displayed a tablet from her tote bag, settled into the SUV's plush leather upholstery and greeted Megan with a jovial smile.

The child sat securely buckled in her car seat. Her emerald-colored eyes, enhanced by raspberry eyeglass frames, twinkled with excitement.

"Hi, Miss Belle." Megan lifted her terry cloth cover-up with exaggerated flair. "Do you like my bathing suit?"

"I love pink unicorns," Belle replied. "And you are utterly adorable."

"Daddy helped dress me, but I picked out my own clothes."

"Kudos to you and daddy." Belle grinned as Andrew winked at her.

"A script, Belle?" He slipped into the driver's seat. "As in a movie script?"

"Not quite Hollywood, I'm afraid, but yes."

"You act as well as offer equine therapy? I'm impressed."

"Thanks. The Little Theater in Wilmington put out a casting call for The Lion, The Witch, and The Wardrobe." She glanced at her tablet before embarking on details.

"C.S. Lewis?"

"Very good."

"Daddy, you read that story to me," Megan said. "I like the part when the four kids go into the wardrobe and all the animals talk."

"Their world is magical." Belle grinned at Megan over her shoulder, then gazed ahead. "The story's message focuses on faith and courage."

"Don't forget love," Andrew said. For a split-second he

watched her, the heat in his tone igniting his words. "Because in the end, it's all about love."

His deep voice, that Scottish brogue, his green, fathomless eyes, had an alarming effect on Belle's heart rate. The remark was so typical of his romantic nature that she smiled.

"Is it?" she asked.

"What the world needs now ... All you need is ... you've heard the lyrics to these popular songs, correct?"

"Of course."

"I wasn't certain, because you're younger than me."

"By only a few years." She rolled her eyes in amused exasperation. "You're certainly brimming with all sorts of sayings this morning."

He wore a pair of swim trunks in a dashing pattern of tropical leaves, and a royal-blue T-shirt that read *Bransfield Designs*. He was drop-dead handsome, and his debonair attitude mesmerized her. Another Andrew she was beginning to know better—this one playful and humorous.

When he rolled down the windows, a breeze grabbed her hair. Deeply, she breathed in, delighting in the scents of fish and salt, the promise of the ocean.

He switched on the radio to a station with kid-safe lyrics and transferred it to the back speakers. Immediately, Megan and Belle hummed along to a familiar tune.

"Belle, are you auditioning for the role of Mrs. Beaver?" Andrew asked.

"Mr. Beaver's wife?" Belle stopped humming, glancing at him as he concentrated on the road. "The obsessive, overly careful woman?"

"If I remember correctly, Mrs. Beaver is kind-hearted."

"I'll need to audition first before I'm cast in one of the bigger roles. Fortunately, there's always a place in the supporting cast for a forest squirrel or chipmunk."

"That's the part where the animals turn to stone," Megan chimed in.

"Little ears hear everything," he whispered.

With a chuckle, Belle twisted, brushing her hand reassuringly up and down Megan's bare, freckled leg. Lovably innocent, she presented an endearing picture in an oversized nautical bucket hat, and Belle found herself wanting to protect her, similar to Andrew's instincts.

"In Narnia," Belle assured Megan, "everything works out for the best."

Leaning back in her seat, Belle recalled that in the play, the children were separated from their mother. Some animals died, as well.

"Megan and I will attend your performance, providing it's a mild version," Andrew was saying.

"It might not be," Belle replied.

He frowned. Belle could see his brilliant mind turning, reviewing the tale.

"In any event," he continued, "I'll be the one clapping the loudest when you take your final bow."

She grinned. "Good to know."

"I enjoy live plays." He brightened. "I especially liked *My Fair Lady.*"

"*My Fair Lady* is a musical, not a play."

"Same difference."

"Hardly." Her lips quirked. "But you haven't seen me act yet. You may snatch up your program and dash from the theater at intermission."

"I'll support you no matter what. Good, bad …" He squeezed her hand. "Exactly as you supported my daughter through her rough times."

THEY REACHED Carolina Beach a half hour later.

"It's illegal to intentionally come within fifty feet of the horses at Corolla," Belle informed Andrew as he opened her door. "We wouldn't have been permitted to feed or pet the horses, anyway."

He gave a thumbs-up. "Best news I've heard all day."

"Daddy!" Megan admonished as he unbuckled her seat belt. "Horses are nice."

"These horses are different, Megan," Belle explained. "Think of them as Honeycrisp's wild cousins."

"They don't faint, do they?" Andrew muttered.

Belle smiled, then drew a wobbly breath. She and Andrew already shared a history of memories and fun, private jokes.

Years earlier, when she'd first acted in minor roles, she'd waited for the director to give her cues. Now, with Andrew, she felt as if she were exactly where she was supposed to be. With him and his daughter. No direction was needed. She just *knew*.

When it came to finding a man she could genuinely love, she hadn't been looking.

But here he was.

A single father. A man of principle. A man who felt real emotions and wasn't ashamed to show them. And she was falling in love with him with a ferocity she could hardly explain.

She brushed her hand against his. "Wild horses don't faint. Only goats. Or women who haven't eaten lunch."

She grinned at his perplexed intake of breath.

"We are grabbing fried scallops later," he said. "Shall we find a place to eat first?"

"Lunch is this afternoon," Belle reminded.

"But we can snack anytime, right, Daddy?" Megan asked. "Didn't you pack corn curls?"

At Belle's lifted eyebrows, he explained, "I'm better with packaged food requiring no preparation."

"Sliced carrots and hummus are nutritious and easy to pack."

"Special days merit special treats."

At his affectionate gaze, her cheeks heated.

Fifteen minutes later, Megan was thoroughly drenched in sunscreen and their beach chairs, towels, and a portable cooler were arranged beside them. Belle and Andrew dug a moat around a castle Megan erected, tamping down wet sand with oversized shovels.

The sky, a brilliant Carolina-blue, mirrored the sunlight and a briny wind whipped across Belle's cheeks. Oftentimes, she'd visualized living near the beach again. Walking barefoot while the waves lapped at her ankles, the golden sand warm and comforting.

And here she was.

"Daddy, can we dive in the water?" Megan, apparently tiring of filling buckets, yanked on Andrew's arm. He held out his hand to Belle although she declined, preferring to lounge on a reclining chair.

She adjusted her sunglasses and easily spotted father and daughter as they splashed in the surf. Andrew's tall, trim body dripped with water, and his drenched swim trunks slicked against his powerful thighs. He had an indisputable magnetism, and she tracked him with her gaze.

Her cellphone pinged, and a text message from her Aunt Lucinda slid across Belle's screen.

How's it going? her aunt inquired.

Alarm prompted Belle to waver. *Are you okay?*

Perfectly fine. I'm sixty, not six hundred.

We're enjoying a day at the beach.

We're?

Andrew and I and Megan.

His daughter? You mention her frequently.

She's precious, Belle responded.

You always wanted children.

Belle touched her throat. Aunt Lucinda invariably stated whatever was on her mind. She had no filter.

Yes, but— Belle began.

I predict you and Andrew will have a big family.

Belle pulled the phone close to her chest. *We've hardly—*

In the meantime, I'm still waiting to meet him.

Dear aunt, I'll arrange something soon. I love you.

I love you. I also love the idea of finding your true partner. Someone to share your joy and sorrow. Do you agree?

Belle nodded, recalling Andrew's song lyric comments. On a promising day like this, love definitely made the world a brighter place.

She snapped her phone shut and shook the sand from her sandals, intending to join Andrew and Megan along the water's edge.

He met her before she'd taken ten steps. She paused, the water fizzing and bubbling at her feet.

"Take a swim," he said. "We'll watch from the shore."

"I'll go in later." With a smile, Belle followed them back to their chairs.

Megan rubbed her eyes, her rosy-red mouth set in a cherubic smile. "Am I a good swimmer?"

Belle gave her a high-five. "The finest on the entire Wilmington shore."

"Sun and water wear her out, although she fights nap time," Andrew mouthed. He wrapped his daughter in a beach towel and tucked her into a chair with an umbrella overhead. Within minutes, the child was asleep.

He slung a towel over his shoulders. Grabbing two water bottles from the cooler, he offered one to Belle. He took a swig of the other and landed on a lounge chair beside her. Their bare feet were so close they almost touched.

"Beach living is the best," he announced.

"You said something similar before. You mentioned surfing—"

He slipped his hand through hers and chuckled. "Do you remember everything I say?"

"Absolutely not." She hid her lie behind an amicable smile and quickly bent her head, concentrating on the water bottle.

"A pity, because I remember everything about you," he murmured.

She reminded herself that Andrew was part of an imaginary life, similar to this brilliant beach day—bold, dazzling and memorable, yet transitory.

He gazed at the ocean. He still held her hand as if he craved her near, craved her touch. She liked that, liked that about him.

"Did I ever tell you about my ex?" he asked.

His serious tone conveyed the importance of the subject.

"A little," she ventured. "You cited the delivery man." She waited for him to offer a Scottish proverb or witty jibe. When he didn't reply, she said softly, "It helps to talk about our concerns."

He nodded. "After Rowena's abrupt departure, Megan was devastated."

"It's only natural. It must have been difficult."

His laugh was brief and grim.

"Rowena didn't give any notice?" Belle asked.

"None. She taped a note to the front door and drove off. We haven't seen her since." Andrew tossed down his water and rested his gaze on Megan.

"How long has Rowena been gone?"

He shifted positions. For several minutes, he focused on the vast expanse of sparkling water reaching the horizon, the sunlight reflecting an intensity of colors.

"Then what happened?" she finally inquired.

Andrew glanced at Belle as if he'd forgotten she sat next

to him. "These past two years she's missed Megan's birthdays and Christmases. I'm the primary custodial parent, and Rowena hasn't contested the lawyer's papers."

"Although I'm sorry for everything, be grateful Megan is in your life." Belle tried to sound untroubled by Rowena's startling lack of interest. "Your daughter adores you and she's happy."

Belle studied the bleak expression on Andrew's face, sensed the somber mood that had descended. Despite his mumble of agreement, he wasn't at peace.

"Don't be sorry for me," he said. "It sounds like this happened all of a sudden, but breakups don't occur in a vacuum. Rowena and I were headed for divorce court several years beforehand." His tone took on a sharp edge. "I can't forgive her."

Belle touched his hand. "Surely, Rowena has attempted to see Megan."

"No," he said shortly. "And selfish is too kind a word to describe her."

Sea gulls cried in the distance, the ocean waves foamy and white. Near them, a group of giggling children made angels in the sand. Carolina Beach was a favorite of Belle's. As a child she'd spent hours wading in the sea spray, and loved the unique, family flavor of the beach and adjacent boardwalk.

She searched her mind for a pleasanter topic rather than dwelling on Andrew's divorce details.

"Ask me anything about Wilmington, and I can answer," she declared with a bright smile.

He wrinkled an eyebrow. "Anything?"

"For instance, the rare Venus flytrap grows here in the wild."

Although his lips were pressed together, a grin slipped through. "I'll keep a look out for it."

"And the flytrap flourishes in a sixty-mile radius around

Wilmington." Belle bobbed her head, delighted and thankful her subject change had worked so swiftly.

"At the risk of dispelling any Venus flytrap myths, if a fly just sits in the trap and doesn't resist, the plant will open, and the fly can leave in the morning," he replied.

"Did you pick up that specific scientific fact from your audiobooks? You are an architect and study ... building structures."

"I am. I do. I learned about the Venus flytrap from science *class* in secondary school."

Belle grinned.

She intended to ask more questions—about the bitterness he harbored toward his sister and ex-wife, because she believed she could help him heal.

However, sensitive to the quiet mood, the way it had changed for the better, she held onto the comfortable silence.

The tautness in his jaw relaxed, and she almost missed the genuine affection in his eyes when he smiled at her, because she'd gazed down at their hands, still entwined.

a couple days afterward, Belle stood in her riding ring and announced to Megan, "If it's Monday, it's time for …"

"Equine therapy!" the little girl chortled as she raced from Andrew's SUV.

"Hurray!" Belle dragged the mounting block to the center of the ring, then bent to secure Megan's pink helmet.

"What about me?" Andrew baited indignantly as he reached the fence.

"Are you wanting a horseback ride?" Belle met his grin with a teasing one beneath her lashes. "Jenkins is in the stable along with Honeycrisp and Felix, my landlord."

"Can I see the horses?" Megan asked.

"Sure," Belle replied, "they're expecting you."

Andrew considered the surroundings. "Where are the goats today?"

"Around."

"Around is a little too vague. I'll stay here." He reached for Belle's arm and shifted her to face him. "First, I'm here to confess that I missed you."

"You confess that a lot."

"Because I think it a lot."

"If you recall, we spent last evening together. Adella watched Megan at your house while we strolled the boardwalk." Belle well remembered the sticky blue blobs of cotton candy she and Andrew had fed each other, the windswept sand dunes, the noisy arcade games lining the two-mile boardwalk. Inside a quaint shop, Andrew had purchased Megan a handmade shell bracelet.

'I like Wilmington,' he'd said to Belle. *'I appreciate the feeling of normality. I tend to forget how valuable leisure time is to a person's health.'*

Belle had agreed in a matter-of-fact voice.

They proceeded, beaming at couples who passed them with affable nods.

"Happily, I finally met your Aunt Lucinda," Andrew was saying.

"Finally." Belle smiled at him. "She prefers living near the boardwalk, so it was an easy walk for us."

"Does she like living close to all these stomach-churning rides?"

"No rides," Belle replied. "Although every Sunday, the Farmer's Market is her chosen spot for homegrown kale. She also shops the adjacent booth for chocolate-covered bacon."

"I suppose healthy cancels out unhealthy when you're sixty years old."

"She buys me bacon too," Belle said. "And I'm not sixty."

He laughed. "So, you like chocolate-covered bacon too?"

"No, but I won't hurt her feelings."

"Let me guess—the bacon is on sale."

"It depends," Belle replied. "I figured out that the man who owns the bacon booth is attracted to her. He becomes all animated when he sees her."

"Vice versa?"

"If I know Aunt Lucinda, it will take more than a pound of chocolate-covered bacon to court her." Belle muffled a laugh. "In any event, you two got along famously when we arrived at her bungalow unannounced."

"She is everything you described and more."

"How much more?"

"Shall I begin with her outfit?" Andrew stifled a grin. "I admit I'm not up-to-date on women's fashion—"

"You object to her Indiana Jones hat?"

"I was prepared for the hat. For her remarks, not so much."

Belle paused. "Aunt Lucinda doesn't mince words."

"I noticed."

"She likes you."

"I like her too. I especially like what she suggested."

"Who's Aunt Lucinda?" Megan bounded up to them. "What did she say, daddy?"

Belle's cheeks burned as Andrew extended a helpless smile. Aunt Lucinda had given Andrew the once-over and candidly declared he was exactly the man Belle was destined to marry.

Andrew had agreed, pulling Belle into his arms and kissing her. Belle had returned his kiss with all the love brimming in her heart.

Because Andrew had agreed.

"Aunt Lucinda is Miss Belle's aunt. Soon, you'll meet her." He kissed Megan on the cheek and looped an arm around Belle's waist.

A HALF HOUR LATER, Megan finished her therapy session, and Felix offered to bring Megan to the stable to unsaddle Honeycrisp, then turn the horses out to pasture.

"I'm in town all week," Andrew said, when Belle met him

at the fence. "Will dinner and a movie at my place suffice for a date?"

"More than suffice."

"I can stream Braveheart."

"So you're in a sentimental mood and reminiscing about Scotland." Belle opened the gate and stepped over to him. "Are you serving haggis?"

"Are you brave enough to sample a plate?"

"You mentioned your sister makes the best haggis. Next, you'll probably charter a private jet to Scotland to see her."

He rubbed his hands over his face. "Nope."

"Potatoes and turnips will do, then. Both are favorite Scottish dishes."

"You've done your Scottish homework." His mouth tilted at the corners. "I assume it's because you were eager to learn more about me?"

Thinking of an excuse to refute his claim, she ended up simply nodding. There was no sense hiding her feelings. He knew she was interested.

He just didn't know how much, because she was unquestionably, unequivocally falling in love with him.

"I'll ask Adella to prepare a Scottish meal for us." He rubbed his palm against Belle's cheek and grinned. "When we watch Braveheart, be prepared to see some of the most gorgeous scenery you'll ever witness."

The ache of longing in his voice for his homeland tugged at her. She squeezed her eyes shut as his fingers wandered to stroke her hair.

He missed Scotland. He should resolve the issues with his sister. There was no purpose in holding onto a grudge. What was the Scottish phrase?

"You're a long time deid," she murmured.

The grin vanished from his features. "What did you say?" He dropped his hand and stared at her.

"Nothing."

"You're parroting one of my Scottish sayings?"

"They're not *your* sayings, they're your country's sayings, and you should embrace them. Life is short. Forgive your ex. Forgive your sister."

"Why?"

"It's obvious. Forgiveness will set you free."

He glanced toward the stable before fixing his gaze on Belle. "Sometimes there are too many wrongs to right."

"Forgiving the people who may have wronged you will provide peace of mind."

"I am at peace."

"Are you?"

"You're an equine therapist, Belle, not a human therapist." His brief smile didn't reach his eyes. "If I need advice, I'll check a self-help book out of the library."

She recoiled, but pushed on. "Begin the process of healing. Do it for yourself."

Instead of agreeing, he stared past her.

"Furthermore, Andrew," she touched his arm, "you work too much."

"Thanks for the advice. Unfortunately, this isn't a good time for a psychological discussion."

"When? When is a good time?"

He brought up a hand, interrupting her with utter finality. "Let's put this conversation behind us."

Belle held her tongue, quelling her reflexive reaction to offer more suggestions.

His cellphone buzzed. He read the text and frowned.

"What is it?" she asked.

"There is trouble in Camden. A resident was hurt, and they're blaming the accident on the worksite not being properly secured and safe." He blew out a breath as Megan emerged from the stable. "Let's take a raincheck, okay?"

Belle didn't respond, and he hardly noticed as he signaled to Megan that they were leaving. He brushed a kiss on Belle's forehead as he passed, murmuring an assurance that he would text her as soon as he arrived in Camden.

She waited. Surely he would turn back to her, so she could suggest that he stay.

Maybe he would ponder his quick decision. Maybe he would declare that his foreman could easily handle any problems.

But he didn't, and neither did she, swallowing her protests because they were futile.

Knowing he would refuse, anyway.

CHAPTER 9

*B*elle braced a hand on the window frame over her kitchen sink, and admired the purple zinnias flowering in the garden, the whitish-gray bark of an oak tree, the sun setting on another September day.

Summer was over, and so was her romance with Andrew.

That is, if it had ever begun.

Andrew. First in her thoughts, first in her heart.

They'd been friends before their relationship had deepened to romance. Good friends, confidantes, really. She could tell him anything.

But love was elusive. Yes, there were moments made just for them—the boardwalk, the sunsets, the shared laughter.

Followed by longer moments, like today, when she felt utterly alone.

The beautiful dahlias he'd gifted had died, and she'd replaced the flowers with a ceramic bowl of fake oranges.

Andrew. With him, she believed she'd found a genuine love. A deep connection, both large and small. In his arms, she was beloved and cherished.

She shook her head. She'd been so wrong.

She suppressed her heart's disloyal leap whenever she envisioned Andrew's striking features, his enthralling smile, his endearing Scottish brogue.

Forcibly reminding herself that he was gone, she brewed peppermint tea in a glass mug and claimed a kitchen chair.

Andrew was content expanding his architecture firm and raising his daughter. What more did he need?

When he Skyped Belle from Camden a few minutes later, Belle told him as much.

"That's your version of a hello?" His features sharpened beneath the brash overhead light of his hotel room.

"You left the riding ring quickly the other day," she answered.

"Belle, there is a lot going on here. I can't deal with any more guilt—if that's where this conversation is headed." Although his words were firm, there was no harshness. His tone with her and his daughter was always kind, gentle and respectful.

By now, however, Belle understood the rules, his rules. He'd made them clear. Don't discuss his life, his choices, his priorities.

"In any case, will you heed my advice?" she pressed.

"Which is?"

"Appreciate your life. You employ a large staff and shouldn't do everything yourself." She took a deep breath. "Not to mention you carry a heavy burden you should confront."

Immediately, she regretted her outburst when his features became firm and unbending.

"Are you trying to fix me?" he asked.

"No. Well, yes, maybe. I can't understand your unreasonable work ethic. You love your daughter, yet you leave her alone constantly."

"I've provided a magnificent home, enrolled Megan in an exclusive private school, and bought her a horse. Aside from that, Adella is an excellent caretaker."

"Still, you should—"

"I need … I should…" He shot her a wearied look. "I am who I am."

She stared at the phone screen as he looked away. When she caught his gaze again, his eyes glistened. With frustration? Unshed tears? Now she wasn't certain he'd handled their discussion as dismissively as she'd assumed.

I love you, which is why I'm trying to help you, she wanted to tell him, but his manner became patronizing when he inserted, "I'm older than you, remember? Be a good equine therapist and don't worry about fixing a jaded architect like me."

"You're right, then. I won't." Her chin came up. "And it's time I resume my quiet life with my animals."

"What are you saying?"

"I'm ending our discussion, Andrew. The horses need to come in from the pasture."

Her wounded pride wouldn't permit her to say anymore.

"Right now?" he asked irritably. "All day I looked forward to talking to you. It was what got me through a very wearying meeting with the Camden town council."

"Sorry, but you'll need to conduct both ends of our conversation because I'm clicking off."

"I'll phone you tomorrow night."

"Rehearsals are beginning for The Lion, The Witch, and the Wardrobe."

"So you got a role? Are you Mrs. Beaver?"

"I'm a forest animal."

"Which one?"

"A squirrel."

"That's nuts. Get it?"

She couldn't suppress her grin, though her heart was breaking. She'd miss his wit and Scottish phrases, but she'd made up her mind. A long-distance relationship that relied on his unpredictable work schedule would never be successful.

"I'll be back in Wilmington on Saturday," he said. "Dinner at my place?"

His simple request almost brought her to tears. She tugged her gaze from the cellphone screen, grappling with the desolate mood settling over her. It took all her limited acting skills to summon a spirited attitude as she uttered a final goodbye.

When he clicked off, her breath pushed out in a rush. She'd never see his home again, never watch a sunset with him, never experience his tender kisses.

She struggled to control the agonizing tug in her heart.

But she failed, put her head in her hands, and wept.

IN TYPICAL ANDREW FASHION, he texted daily, updating her on his work progress before declaring the problem in Camden was solved and he would return to Wilmington by the weekend.

He didn't, and one week became two, then three. Days merged into weeks, and the end of September loomed. The weather remained sticky-hot as the final days of torrid temperatures descended on the Southern beachfront town.

Although Belle continued seeing Megan, and Adella briefed her on Andrew's whereabouts, the sessions weren't the same.

With a wobbly smile, Belle responded to Adella's updates with a cheerful acknowledgement.

To Andrew's credit, he communicated with her often, although she continuously cut him off. Instead of wasting the hours alone, she immersed herself in caring for the horses, her clients' therapy sessions, and nightly play rehearsals.

Aunt Lucinda had little doubt behind the reasons for Belle's ceaseless round of activity, but as their afternoon at the Sunday Farmer's Market faded into twilight, her worried glances whenever Belle became teary-eyed when Andrew's name was mentioned came less often. And even her aunt wasn't bold enough to continue asking why Belle no longer would discuss the man she loved.

There were mornings when Belle didn't contemplate how her life would have been with Andrew, evenings when she didn't revisit his texts, and dawns when she didn't lie awake staring listlessly out the window, recalling his Scottish brogue as he whispered loving words to her.

Nevertheless, those days were few.

"How is Andrew?" Candee inquired when she phoned Belle one evening.

Belle settled on the living room couch with the cat stretched out beside her. "He's still in Camden, I think."

"You *think* he's in Camden? Where else would he be? Don't you trust him?"

"Of course. It's just—"

"There isn't a man who works harder, except for my husband Teddy, or Rob, or Kieran."

Belle murmured a concession at Candee's fierce protectiveness of Andrew, as well as all the other men in her life. Teddy worked alongside his crewmen on job sites, plus flipped homes. Rob assisted his wife, Kathleen, at her teahouse. Beforehand, he'd owned several bakeries, Rob's Marvelous Muffins, in Florida. Kieran, who had married Candee's sister, Desiree, ran an Irish pub in Roses. In all three cases, the wives were supportive of their husbands' endeavors.

Why couldn't Belle do the same?

To begin with, she and Andrew weren't married, much less engaged. He'd never declared his love for her, not in so many words.

"Andrew is consumed with his business and when he isn't, he deserves to spend any precious free hours with his daughter," Belle responded. "Which is, of course, as it should be."

"Should it be? Why?"

Belle sighed. "I don't know if he loves me enough to spend time with me, anyway."

"You're being absurd. From what I understand, he spends every spare moment with you when he's in Wilmington. Has he texted you?"

"Constantly."

"And?"

"I hardly respond. What's the use? I can't depend on him, because, well, he's never here."

Candee cleared her throat. "First, I can assure you that he's in love with you. The look on his face when he visited me in Roses a few weeks ago … well … he's completely enamored with you, Belle."

"Candee, you're a true friend, but you're wrong."

"Andrew keeps to himself. Did you know his family moved to America with literally nothing?"

Belle didn't respond.

"Give him a chance. Accept his phone calls and texts. He's a complex man."

And brilliant, Belle thought. And sensitive, honest, and attentive.

Still …

"I can't." A quiet dignity firmed Belle's assertion. "I don't understand his intense drive to succeed. What is he proving? He's accumulated a fortune already."

"It's not about the money, Belle. His father lost his business, his wealth, and that left an impression on Andrew. Teddy and I have discussed him at length."

"Someone should tell Andrew to stop working so much."

"A Type A personality rarely listens to good advice, or any advice, for that matter."

With a ragged laugh, Belle agreed. "Even if he heeded our suggestions, I won't take him away from his daughter."

"He has enough love for both you and Megan, just as I love Teddy and Joseph."

Belle tried not to listen to Candee's words. She'd continue to push Andrew Bransfield out of her heart, out of her life, by ignoring him.

And by doing so, she had never felt as forlorn.

"By the way," Candee was saying, "Andrew purchased the Wilmington house he was renting."

Disregarding the lump in her throat at the realization he would live only a few blocks away, Belle sat up. "He did? When?"

"A week ago. Sorry. He may have intended to spill the news as a surprise."

Through a sheen of tears, Belle pulled her knees to her chest.

Firmly, she repeated to herself that she had no reason to be angry just because Andrew Bransfield was moving forward with his life, while her life had stalled.

So, she continued to ride her finicky horse, nurture the animals, and treat her therapy clients with fastidious care. She'd put herself in neutral; an emotional balance she maintained, ensuring she'd shed no more tears over him. It was better this way, ending the relationship slowly, with no confrontation.

.   .   .

When Andrew returned to Wilmington the following Friday evening, he texted Belle and invited her to his home for takeout dinner and a movie.

She declined.

He suggested a Saturday boardwalk date, but she declined, citing the excuse of busyness.

"Right. Okay." She visualized his frown as he accepted her refusal. "Shall we try for Sunday? There's a Mexican restaurant serving the best—"

Before he finished, she made up an explanation about studying her script, although they both knew her part in The Lion, The Witch, and The Wardrobe had no words.

It hardly mattered, because he texted her on Monday. He was leaving for another job site in the Carolinas.

A pattern formed as the days drifted through the month of October. He'd text her, and she'd respond with quick one-sentences.

How are you? he'd ask.

Good. You?

The same. Equine therapy still on for Monday? I will finally be in town for a while. Can we have dinner together? There's a new Italian place in town.

Sorry. Too busy, she texted. *Opening night is next Friday.*

Finally. These play rehearsals have gone on forever. Did you nail your infamous role as a squirrel?

Soundly. Complete with a white vinyl tail and furry gray mitts. Can't wait to see you.

Perform? Visit her? He knew where she lived. She didn't touch that one, instead replying with, *Can't. Rehearsals are till ten PM.*

Through the weeks of correspondence, he'd finish his

texts with smiling emojis, flashing red or pink hearts. Tonight he concluded with a questioning face.

CHAPTER 10

*W*hat was more exciting, more intoxicating, more nerve-wracking, than opening night at a theater? It hardly mattered if the production was professional or amateur, the thrill, the rush, was the same.

Belle adjusted the tail on her squirrel costume and peeked at the audience as the curtain raised. The Lion, The Witch, and The Wardrobe had sold out for both weekend nights, and the crowded community theater shifted with anticipation. Posters hung in various businesses, in addition to the announcements on local radio stations, and the advertisements had proved beneficial. The director insisted on staying true to the book, incessantly occupied with the imaginative sets and choreography.

Belle searched the rows for Aunt Lucinda, who had arranged to meet her backstage afterwards, but didn't spot her. In many instances, her aunt had made a late grand entrance, so not seeing her wasn't cause for alarm.

Aunt Lucinda had mentioned bringing a surprise. Perhaps the right man for her had come along after all … perhaps the man from the Farmer's Market?

Belle ducked into the hallway, the canned music began, and the narrator intoned:

"Once there were ..."

THE TWO-AND-A-HALF HOURS of the play passed in an exhilarating blur. Afterwards, Belle hugged and congratulated the actors and actresses, then reported to her makeshift dressing room. Settled on a stool in front of a mirror, she yanked off her mitts and scrubbed away her face make-up while she waited for her aunt.

Muted voices made her pause. Aunt Lucinda's voice, followed by her larger-than-life laugh, announced she was near.

But it was the other voice, a rich Scottish brogue, that forced Belle slowly to her feet. This man was not the bacon shopkeeper, nor the suave, sophisticated Andrew of her dreams. This Andrew was an irresistible force. As he rounded the corner, his rugged features were torn between distress and tenderness.

He was real. He was here.

ANDREW DIDN'T HEAR Aunt Lucinda, nor the performers they passed in the hallway. He was already striding into a cramped dressing room, packed with discarded water bottles, headphones and a clothes rack jammed with costumes.

Belle stood by a mirror, holding a cloth in one hand, a pair of furry gray mitts in the other.

Entranced, he remained by the doorway, observing her radiant smile as her aunt scurried forward, holding her arms wide for a congratulatory hug.

He advanced, standing five feet away from Belle. He kept

his hands at his sides, clutching the flowers he'd brought. He was uncertain what to say, how to move.

He stared at her freshly scrubbed face, devoid of make-up, her dove-gray eyes filled with tears. The eyes that had gripped his nightly dreams and consumed his daytime thoughts.

He hadn't the slightest notion if she still cared for him. Or worse, had she forgotten all about him? He hadn't known what kind of reception he would receive from her when he'd phoned her aunt, requesting a ticket to the production.

Or, if he could now prove to Belle that he was worthy of sharing her life.

Her aunt gave them both a look of profound satisfaction. "Say what you came here for, Andrew, before Belle starts to cry."

His gaze trained on Belle's delicate face as he set down the flowers and wiped his eyes. "I'll cry with her."

"Men don't cry." Aunt Lucinda clucked her tongue. "Especially strong Scottish men."

"Dear aunt, you've been watching too much Braveheart," Belle said, as she rushed into his arms.

He cradled her, shielding her from her aunt's observant stare.

"I missed you," he whispered, knowing Aunt Lucinda heard every word, and not caring.

"You always say that," Belle replied.

"I couldn't figure out any other way to see you. Adella agreed to watch Megan, although Megan wanted to come. I wasn't sure about this production, though."

"It's okay. Next time. Andrew, I love your little girl."

He smiled. Belle carried enough love for everyone.

"If I asked you out again," he continued, "I assumed you would make up another excuse to avoid me."

She gazed up at him. "What's better than tonight, coupled

with my triumph as a squirrel?" She grinned, but then her shoulders shook with sobs as she glided her hands around his neck, and snuggled her tear-stained face close to his chest.

Her aunt's sing-song voice made them both jump. "I'm grabbing a bite to eat and headed home. Well done, Belle. Your performance did me proud."

"All thirty seconds of my debut."

"You were the prettiest squirrel on stage," came Aunt Lucinda's reply.

Belle brought her head up and offered her aunt a dry smile. "I was also the *only* squirrel on stage."

Andrew grinned. "Thank you, Aunt Lucinda." He hesitated. "May I call you my aunt?"

"You're welcome. And now that you've finally come to your senses, then yes."

He kept Belle firmly in his arms. Desperate to be alone with her, he speculated how to politely ask her aunt to leave without being blunt.

Aunt Lucinda caught his uneasy gaze. "It's a jubilant day when two people find true partners to share their lives." At the far end of the room, she switched the lights to dim, and was gone.

Belle stepped back and regarded him. "I still can't believe you're here. An hour earlier, I felt so desolate and—"

"Hollow?" he provided. "Unfulfilled?"

"And yet, you came to my performance."

"Because musicals are my favorite."

"The Lion, The Witch, and the Wardrobe is a play."

"Right." He picked up the flowers. "I bought these dahlias for you. They're a bit wilted."

She accepted, sniffed, and clutched the bouquet to her chest. "They're beautiful. Thank you."

"Why are you crying again?"

"Because I know … I know what they mean."

"A commitment shared forever by two persons." He took her slender hand in his. "Belle Boots, I love you."

She answered with her lips, parting them as he stroked her luxurious hair. She responded with the same ardor as when they'd kissed at his home, the night of the sunset.

Then she pulled away. "Can we talk?" she asked, her gaze honest and direct.

"Now?"

"Now is the best time."

"I forgot you're as blunt as your aunt."

"Andrew, I love you, but you're always working."

"Not anymore." Somehow, he managed to control his tone, recalling the weight that had been lifted from him when he'd come to his decision. "I offered my main foreman more responsibility, and he accepted. We've worked together for years, and I trust him."

"That's so encouraging. But there's more, Andrew. For your sake, can you find it in your heart to forgive your sister?"

"I can't."

"You can, with me standing beside you."

"What is it about you that brings out the best in me?"

Her hand tightened on his arm. "So you might reach out to Kate?"

"These things take time, but I will try."

"Thank you." Her infectious laugh that had lightened his days conveyed a trace of innocence. "And there's one more thing."

"More?"

"What about horses?"

"What about them?" Distracted, he kissed her, relishing the delicious combination of joy and love she brought to his heart.

"Will you venture into the riding ring with me, when the horses are there?"

"Under one condition."

"Which is?"

"Will you marry me?"

"You're bartering horses with an offer of marriage?"

"Exactly."

"Then yes." She nodded, replying with the response he'd waited for.

"I can't guarantee I'll stay in the ring for more than a minute," he warned. "But I expect our marriage will last a lifetime."

"I know it will." She lifted her delicate eyebrows in a challenge. "I also know that you and Jenkins will get along. He's an excellent judge of character."

"Does that mean he'll like me?"

"If you're a beginning rider, then yes."

"How did we go from entering a ring, to actually riding a horse?"

She stood on her toes and kissed him. "We'll take it slow."

He reached into his pocket and handed her a program. "I wrote a poem." On the back of the program, he'd written in large letters, "You're the woman I want, you're the woman I need."

She scanned the words. "You write poems," she said quietly. "Why am I not surprised?"

"Not very good ones because they don't rhyme, but yes." He held her close, reciting the last two lines of his poem with her:

"Because in the end, it's all about love."

And he sealed his words in Scottish Gaelic.

"Tha-mi-gad-ghradh."

I love you.

THE END

A NOTE FROM JOSIE

Dear Friend,

Thank you for reading *1-800-SUMMER.* I hope you enjoyed it. This the fourth book in my contemporary sweet romance series: *Flipping for You.*

Fate tells her it's time to saddle up and ride on. But home beckons in one man's eyes...

This sweet romance begins in the charming town of Roses, North Carolina, and then moves to the beautiful city of Wilmington, NC, for a summery beach setting.

In 1-800-SUMMER, I introduce two new characters to our beloved mix of familiar heroes and heroines. I also researched the heroine's fascinating profession of equine therapy.

If you loved this story as much as I loved writing it, please help other people find *1-800-SUMMER* by posting your amazing review.

1-800-SUMMER is available in ebook, paperback, Large Print paperback, Audiobook, and Hardcover.

I'd love to meet you in person someday, but in the meantime, all I can offer is a sincere and grateful thank you. Without your support, my books would not be possible.

As I write my next sweet or inspirational romance, remember this: Have you ever tried something you were afraid to try because it mattered so much to you? I did, when I started writing. Take the chance, and just do something you love.

With sincere appreciation,

Josie Riviera

My Spotify Play List for 1-800-SUMMER is here.

Love the 1-800- books? Be sure to grab The 1-800-SERIES. 3 Books in one boxed set.

KATE'S OLD FAMILY HAGGIS RECIPE

Ingredients:

1 lb. lean mutton - ground

1 pound chopped suet

1 lb. organ meat (lungs, liver, heart) (chicken livers work well)

6 onions peeled & chopped finely

1 tsp. salt

1 pint liquid

¼ tsp thyme, ¼ tsp coriander, ¼ tsp savory, ¼ tsp. marjoram, ¼ tsp nutmeg, ¼ tsp basil, 1 tsp garlic powder (or fresh garlic, chopped), ½-1 tsp freshly ground black pepper, ½ tsp cayenne pepper, 1 bay leaf

2 cups finely ground oatmeal, toasted (make sure you toast it. This step makes a big difference.)

Stomach bag of sheep or muslin bag. (You can use an oven bag - like those you use to roast a turkey.) If you don't use the sheep stomach, dissolve 2 crushed rennet tablets in water and add to the meat mixture.

Preparation:

Wash the stomach bag in cold saltwater. Boil organ meats for 1 ½ hours, leaving windpipe attached to lungs & hanging out of the pot. Impurities will drip out, so put a pan underneath. Cool. Cutaway windpipe skin, & gristle. Put aside some of the liquid in which the organ meats were boiled. Mince organ meats & add to other meat & suet. Toast oatmeal in the oven and add to meat mixture with chopped onion and spices. Add enough liquid from boiled organ meats to make a soft consistency.

If you use a sheep stomach or muslin bag, fill a little more than half full. Close tightly, prick, and put into a pan of boiling water with a plate at the bottom. Boil 3-4 hours. Prick occasionally to stop bag from bursting.

If you use an oven bag, put in an aluminum pan on top of a baking sheet. Kind of pat the bag flat. Turn and mix periodically until it looks done. Timing depends on how much you make and when it looks done.

And the most important part, the oven temperature!

Serves 8-10   Oven temp 325-350 (if you bake it)
Enjoy!

ACKNOWLEDGMENTS

An appreciative thank you to my patient husband, Dave, and our three wonderful children.

JOSIE RIVIERA

a Chocolate-Box Summer Breeze

PRAISE AND AWARDS

USA TODAY bestselling author

CHAPTER 1

*A*t seven o'clock on a Thursday evening, Emily Varon sat alone in a corner booth in Olive's Diner. She swallowed some black coffee, pushed the cup aside and checked her watch.

Joe Vertucci was ten minutes late. Odd, because he was always punctual when he phoned her.

Emily bit her bottom lip, drew back the diner's thick tan-colored curtains, and peered out the window at a sultry California evening. The parking lot was empty except for the few cars that belonged to the customers who were dining inside.

She grabbed her cellphone from her leather handbag and read the last words Joe had texted.

After all these months, I'm looking forward to seeing you in person again, Emily.

Her stomach fluttered as she imagined their reunion. She was looking forward to seeing him too and told him as much. He'd responded with a thumbs-up, which had prompted her to smile. She'd attempted to explain different emojis to him, he didn't always have to use a thumbs-up.

However, he couldn't seem to get the hang of new technology.

Of course, emoji stickers weren't new, and he'd beamed on their video chat when she'd assured that she'd teach him how to use them.

Their only disagreement had taken place when Joe had insisted on paying for their meal. Eventually, she'd conceded and offered to leave the tip.

He'd concluded their conversation with a quip. "That's why I'm crazy about you, Emily. You don't take advantage of me."

Frequently, he'd referred to himself as a blue-color, working-class guy, and she'd heard a trace of disparagement in his voice, as if he was putting himself down. Although people took pride in referring to themselves in that way, she repeatedly wondered if he genuinely believed in himself.

He should. He was a thoughtful, good-natured man.

Again, her gazed flitted to the window. He could have been delayed by rough weather, or unexpected traffic delays. Hazards on the road occurred in seconds, and driver fatigue often caused serious accidents.

Or, perhaps … Joe wasn't interested in her after all.

She rubbed her cheek with the back of her hand, attempting to pry herself free from the anxious speculations. She hadn't dated in years, and her nerves wavered as if she were a schoolgirl.

This isn't a date, she reminded herself, nor a naïve teenage crush.

She opened the menu and scanned the dinner selections. The special featured grilled chicken, and a baked potato, which suited her nicely. However, the diner's delicious coconut cake would surely ruin her diet.

It was her proper upbringing, she supposed, that kept her focused on the latest fashion trends. Often, though, she pondered if there was a reason to watch her weight anymore. The only people she encountered besides the diners were her son and his family, the weekly grocer, her hair stylist, and Sunday morning churchgoers.

A Moonglow Chocolatiers truck pulled into the lot, and Emily's heart leaped. A man with silver-white hair emerged from the driver's side. Several patrons whispered Emily's name, like the murmurings of a breeze rushing through a forest. Somehow, they knew Joe was here to see Emily.

"I haven't seen Joe in a long time." Oliver, the owner of the diner, stepped over to her booth. He held a steaming pot of coffee.

Emily jumped. She was so focused on Joe's arrival that she hadn't realized Oliver had approached.

"You're eating dinner later than usual." Oliver grinned and gestured toward the window. "Are you waiting for Joe?"

"Yes." Hastily, she jammed her cellphone into her purse. "He's overnighting near here for a couple days."

Oliver refilled her cup. "How did you know Joe was in the area?"

"Why are you asking?" She sat straighter and adjusted her flawlessly creased white slacks. Through all her months at the diner, she'd kept her personal life private. "Sometimes, people need to eat dinner with someone else, rather than all alone."

At the swift, questioning look he shot her, she grimaced. Her response had a breathless, edgy quality. "Sorry."

"No worries, Emily, and you're one hundred percent right. I shouldn't pry." Oliver patted her hand. "I can't help being an old-fashioned Cupid, and I detect a romance is brewing."

"Hardly." She dismissed any further inquiries Oliver poised on his lips with a wave. "Joe and I regularly talk on the phone."

"Ever since you met him here in my diner?"

"Yes," she acknowledged. For an instant, she closed her eyes and relived that stormy February night.

After panicking because she'd never been in a situation like that before—stranded in a diner—her nerves had settled, and she'd enjoyed several hours conversing with Joe. The narratives about his over-the-road travels had made her laugh. It felt good to laugh, especially after she had visited with her son the previous weekend. He, his wife, and her grandchild had been cordial, but their life was hectic and Emily had felt useless and in the way.

She knew they loved her, but they didn't need her.

"May I call you?" Joe had politely inquired that evening, after the road had been cleared and the customers could safely leave the diner.

His request had wrung a reluctant chuckle from Emily, but the sight of his incredible smile had done odd quivery things to her pulse.

She'd agreed and wrote her number on a napkin before handing it to him.

Following an exchange of "safe travels", she'd driven back to her large, empty home in town, and hadn't felt quite so lonely.

"I remember you two got along well." Oliver grabbed a cup and paper placemat from an adjacent table and set them across from Emily. "You never mentioned that your relationship with Joe had blossomed. You eat dinner here nightly."

"Your food is delicious."

"Thanks. I might use your testimonial as advertising." He paused. "However, you're not answering."

"Is this a question or a statement?"

"Both, considering I'm an old-fashioned Cupid," he reminded.

"Joe and I are too timeworn for a romantic relationship."

She tasted the coffee, which was always perfect, then dabbed her lips with a napkin. "Even though I gave him my phone number, I didn't expect him to call me."

"Why not? You're an attractive, classy lady."

She shook her head. She wasn't. She'd continually considered herself plump and the opposite of model-thin, but she wasn't about to introduce a lengthy psychological discussion. Plus, she'd been obsessed with tanning salons, believing a tan made her look younger. However, she'd finally recognized that tanning aged her, and had given that up after she'd met Joe.

One didn't need any more wrinkles at her age.

"Thus," Oliver said, "you've been talking to Joe for—"

"Nearly four months. Joe and I believe in phone calls and occasional video chats," she said.

"There's something about hearing a person's voice. It's more personal."

"Yes, definitely. These days, everyone relies on texting." Emily took another sip of coffee. "Young people stare at their cellphones waiting for bubbles to appear when a phone call accomplishes twice as much in half the time. In addition, there's constantly a risk you'll be misunderstood."

In accord, she and Oliver nodded.

"I'm glad he's here now," Oliver said. "Beneath the flannel shirt and jeans façade, Joe is a romantic guy."

Romantic. The idea brought a funny catch to her chest.

Once, romance had made life worth living.

Now?

She lowered her gaze to concentrate on her cup.

She'd lost all sense of romance after Krandall—her tall, striking husband—had unexpectedly died three years earlier. At the image of his well-heeled demeanor, his poise in the board room, his focus and goal-setting ... "I've set my eyes on you, Emily," he'd declared, and the remembrance brought a thickness to her throat. Her moneyed parents had extended not-so-subtle nudges for her to accept his advances so that she could "marry well."

Emily fingered the black-gold and sapphire bracelet, the last piece of jewelry Krandall had bought her before he'd gotten sick.

In fact, he'd purchased many gifts for her, mostly to apologize for his outbursts. He'd been super-critical and continuously chastised her. Sometimes, she believed she was little more than a fixture on his arm that he could show off at high-class fund-raisers.

Glancing up, she realized that Oliver was studying her.

"You're categorizing Joe as a romantic?" she asked him.

"Absolutely. We chatted at length the night he was stranded here, and our conversation was poignant and enlightening."

"Poignant?"

"Guys use fancy words too." He grinned. "From what I gathered, he yearns for a connection with a woman. He was widowed several years ago."

"Companionship ... most people are seeking mutual support."

"Joe confided that he longs to feel loved again." Oliver scanned the diner, then set the coffeepot on the table and perched across from her. "Is this a first date? Or a second?"

"Oliver, you're not listening. A widow and widower who are seventy years old don't date."

Although this meeting with Joe was, in every sense of the word, a date. Wasn't it?

No, she repeated to herself.

She fished in her handbag for pink lipstick and a mirrored compact. Ordinarily, she wouldn't fuss as much with her appearance, but the anticipation she'd soon see Joe face to face ...

Where is he? the question intruded. It shouldn't take that long to park a truck.

"He's been rummaging for a while." Oliver echoed her thoughts.

Carefully, Emily arranged her silver-blond hair and applied a dab of lipstick. "He keeps track of his hours in a logbook and is doubtlessly making certain the load matches the manifest sheet."

"Manifest sheet?"

"The list of deliveries and shipments." She cast Oliver a sideways smile as he went to the counter to pour two glasses of water.

She'd learned a lot about trucking from her conversations with Joe. What's more, she'd gained an understanding of the man himself. He was frugal, efficient, and fit. He was also sincere, sensible, and because of his job, mechanical.

With an inner sigh, her gaze wandered back to the parking lot.

Tonight was so different compared to the night they'd met. That eventful evening, a severe storm had flattened a tree in front of the diner. Now, four months later, the California rains were nonexistent. Summer bloomed, intense and motionless, the sky a mellow golden hue.

A painter embraced the tints of the sunset, bold tones of orange and crimson. For her, the spectacular evening marked the beginning of another lengthy, desolate season.

Summertime, the potential for light-heartedness and unexpected delight. Days to flaunt straw hats and sundresses, pretty floral blouses, and sandals.

Don't be ridiculous, she scolded herself. The season didn't matter. Not for a grown woman of a particular age.

"What is taking Joe so long?" she blurted, as Oliver returned with two glasses.

"Most likely, he's planning something extraordinary for you."

"From the back of his truck?"

Her thoughts drifted to their conversation the previous evening. As was his custom, he'd phoned at six o'clock, and suggested video-chatting.

"I chuckle whenever I consider Oliver and his diner," Joe had said. "The former owners had named the diner Olive, and Oliver kept the name, declaring it had a nice ring to it."

"Even though we've all told him there's a considerable difference between Olive and Oliver."

Joe laughed. "So let's have dinner together at the diner while I'm in town ... the place where it all began."

"Where *what* began?" she'd responded.

"Our ... our friendship."

Friendship was a safe word. Although, she'd read in a leading scientific journal that men and women weren't capable of being "just friends" because romance bubbled just around the corner.

Her cellphone buzzed. She pulled the phone from her handbag and checked the screen.

"Who is it?" Oliver stood and plucked up the coffee pot.

Her pulse quickened. "Joe is here. He sent me a thumbs-up."

"I know. We saw him get out of his truck, but now I'm staring at him." Oliver pointed to the doorway as Joe entered. "He looks great. Did he lose weight?"

Indeed he had—twenty pounds and counting. She knew he'd been trying because he'd outlined his nutritious diet, reiterating the calorie and fat content.

And indeed he did. Look great, that is.

Joe's handsome, rugged face was clean-shaven. He adjusted his eyeglasses, then shoved a hand in his jeans, his gaze searching the diner. Searching for *her,* Emily realized with a wide grin.

His manner was comfortable, almost boyish. But it was his genuine, inviting smile, a smile that reached all the way to his blue eyes when he spotted Emily, that encouraged her to grin in return.

She stood, flattened her fine, white linen blouse and hailed him. "His route takes him across the state and back," she informed Oliver.

"Sounds like you're proud of him."

Briefly, she savored the moment as she regarded Joe.

"I am," she said truthfully. "We talk for at least an hour until Jeopardy comes on." Her face sobered. She was showing too much excitement. "Oliver, are you taking note of my social life?"

Oliver chuckled and shook his head. "I can hardly manage my own."

"I imagine that Sally Elliot keeps you on your toes?"

Sally was the woman who owned Bloomingfield Candy Shop. She'd been stranded at the diner that same February night along with Emily, Joe, and several others.

"You're imagining correctly." Oliver wiped a hand on his clean white apron. "I see Sally and her daughter, Clarissa, every weekend. Nevertheless, our busy work schedules produce challenges, because I'm here in Evanville and she's in Bloomingfield."

"Challenges you both are apparently overcoming?" Emily teased.

"For love," Oliver replied, "anything is possible."

CHAPTER 2

*E*mily caught a quick breath as Joe hastened to her table. He carried a package wrapped in blue paper, and she silently groaned, hoping it wasn't another baked good. Thus far, the cupcakes and brownies he'd sent to her had been dry and tasteless.

Joe's bright eyes fixated on her. "My lovely Emily." He laid a hand over his heart, confirming he was as elated about their meeting as she. His voice cracked as he placed the package on the table, then took her hands in his—completely disregarding Oliver except for a brief nod. "Thanks for waiting. I'm sorry I'm late."

"Joe, you're only fifteen minutes late. I'm glad you drive slow and conscientious." She glanced at her watch. Okay, he was twenty minutes late, but that was because he'd spent a few minutes in the back of his truck.

"By the time I finished my deliveries, then sorted the chocolate—"

"Anything on the road can slow your progress," Oliver broke in. "Did you deliver to Bloomingfield?"

"I did, indeed." Joe winked. "Sally said hello. She and her

daughter will see you later this evening when she gets off work. And tomorrow you're both playing hooky in order to take Clarissa to the aquarium at the new mall in Santa Rosa."

"Exactly the plan." A satisfied grin spread across Oliver's features as he wended around the tables, filling cups of coffee for his customers and stopping to chat.

"How are you?" Joe waited for Emily to sit before settling across from her. She appreciated his gentlemanly traits. He was chivalrous in a traditional manner some people labeled as out-of-date.

Emily didn't. Gallant and respectful behaviors never went out of style.

"I'm fine," she replied. "You?"

He beamed, never taking his gaze from hers. "I couldn't be better."

"You're staring at me as though I have food on my chin."

"I was thinking about how gorgeous you are in person. A phone screen doesn't do you justice. And your hair, it's blonder?"

Self-consciously, she touched her hair. Earlier that morning, she'd asked her stylist to color over the platinum silver. After a half hour of consultation and assurances, Emily had decided the two hours in the salon had been worth it.

"What do you think?" she asked. "It's my natural color, minus the years in between."

He chuckled. "I love it."

"I wanted a change."

"It's a marvelous one … I mean … I liked your previous hair color too."

"It's not that much different."

He studied her. "No, it's just … blonder."

Emily tried not to chuckle at how ridiculous their conversation might sound to anyone who happened to listen.

Judging from the patrons eating and conversing, no one had heard them.

Joe nudged the gift toward her. "I brought something for you."

"Chocolates from Sally's shop?" *With any luck*, she thought. Joe was so intent on creating low-fat goodies he'd forgotten that in the end, taste mattered the most.

"Nope," he said. "I baked these German chocolate mini-muffins in my own kitchen."

She kept her grimace at bay. "Are they healthy?"

"Naturally. I substituted unsweetened applesauce for the vegetable oil. The muffins got jostled during the trip, but I re-wrapped them."

Two weeks earlier, he'd mailed her a batch of chocolate chip muffins, followed by brownies. Each time, he used a thin cord of gold ribbon to create a delicate bow. Although stunning to look at, the baked goods inside didn't prove as delicious as the packaging. The last batch had been too sweet, and Emily had tactfully suggested he use real sugar instead of artificial, which frequently left an aftertaste.

He'd agreed, but the following week, his chocolate-coffee muffins had arrived on her doorstep. Those muffins had tasted odd, and she'd (respectfully, of course), urged him to check the expiration dates on the ingredients.

Sure enough, flour had been the culprit.

She glanced up. Expectantly, he watched her as she examined the package.

"Thank you, Joe. You're becoming a baking expert." She smiled.

A little white lie never hurt anyone.

She nudged aside the fake potted lilac plant Oliver always placed on every table, unwrapped the package, and peeped inside. Immediately, she inhaled the aroma of rich, dark chocolate.

"I bought a new bag of flour," Joe said.

She extended a brilliant smile. "Thus you baked two perfect muffins."

Hopefully.

"Maybe not perfect, but I figured that after dinner we'll try them for dessert."

"Joe, you always persevere."

"All I can do is try."

He was sincere and put his whole being into everything.

The knowledge caused her to smile. "Oliver's special dessert tonight is coconut cake," she said.

"My muffins have fewer calories than cake." Absently, Joe perused the menu, then grasped her hands. "Is there anything in the world more captivating than you?" he asked softly.

She moved back. "What brought on that compliment?"

"You. Just seeing your lovely face and new hair style."

"New hair *color,*" she corrected. "My style is the same." With a laughing sigh, she leaned her head against the green vinyl seat. "There are countless subjects more captivating than me."

"You're not a subject. You're my Emily."

She concentrated on his words. Nonetheless, she drew her hands away and clasped them properly on her lap. They were friends, she repeated to herself, and she wasn't about to get cozy in a public diner. She'd grown accustomed to living life alone, although, through Joe's direct and indirect hints, she intuitively knew he craved more from their relationship.

Joe frowned at her response. There was that directness about him she admired, the way he wore his sentiments on his sleeve. Her late, by-the-book husband had controlled his emotions.

Krandall had been a generous provider, fixating on his net worth and savvy with his fortune, believing the money from his investment business liberated them.

Joe remained silent, evidently waiting for her to say more. When she didn't, he said, "We've established dessert. What is your choice for dinner?"

"I've decided on the grilled chicken special and a bowl of Oliver's homemade vegetable soup."

"Low calorie and hearty, but please choose the most expensive meal on the menu." He held out his palms in a generous gesture. "Remember, dinner is my treat."

"The grilled chicken is the most expensive entrée tonight."

He laughed. "Then I'll have the same, because this is a celebratory evening."

After they'd placed their order with an efficient teenage waitress, Emily leaned in. "Do you eat all your meals in diners, Joe?"

"Usually." Yet again, he grasped her hands. "What about you?"

"I never eat out anywhere but here, and only for dinner. I prepare my other meals at home."

"We should dine together more often. When I'm driving, all I can think about is phoning you from my hotel room. You're the highlight of my hours and I love hearing your voice."

The heartfelt attentiveness in his gaze and the enthusiasm in his tone made Emily feel warm and cherished.

"I feel the same," she said. In fact, his calls had become a lifeline, and she looked forward to telling someone about her day. "Although I wish you'd cut back your working hours—for your sake."

"I can't, Emily. I'm paying off my daughter's college tuition loan because she recently lost her job. As a single mother, Lydia is struggling. She applied at the bank for a debt consolidation and seeks employment every day."

You're struggling financially too, Emily thought, but she didn't share her contemplation with him.

The fact that he was compelled to work an exhausting job in order to pay his daughter's bills brought a sadness, an infuriation, to Emily's chest. By now, Joe should be ready to retire.

Managing his route and the truck's contents while staying on schedule was arduous for a younger man, and ever more so for someone Joe's age. Yet, he managed it all while maintaining a courteous demeanor with his suppliers and customers. Even when describing his workdays he never complained, and she innately knew he wouldn't welcome her observations or sympathy.

Emily blew out a breath. "Your actions are admirable. However, your daughter is a grown woman."

"Wouldn't you do the same for your son? From what you've mentioned, he's doing well financially, but if he wasn't—"

"Naturally," she agreed. "But I wish you would relax more."

"Relaxing isn't a word in my vocabulary." Joe downed his water, then fidgeted. "So Emily, where do we go from here?"

"We? Why? Where are we going?"

For the first time, she questioned if there was another purpose for their arranged meeting that Joe was easing into. Since this was a special and upbeat reunion, she followed his lead. Perhaps she'd shift their discussion to small talk, rather than student loans and debts. At cocktail parties in the past, she'd been a pro at engaging people in light conversations.

"It's a figure of speech." Joe cleared his throat and scratched his chin. "I have the next few days off."

"Good. You deserve it."

"How about you?"

"I don't work."

He scanned her face. "I mean, what do you have planned for the weekend?"

"Nothing."

Oliver wandered to the juke-box, and the jingle of coins dropping in the slot followed as he selected a song, throwing a grin at Emily over his shoulder.

Several seconds later, Frank Sinatra's voice crooned the first few measures of "You Make Me Feel So Young," an upbeat romantic ballade.

She grinned at Oliver and awarded a wave. There was something about being in a familiar place—with an attractive man who was obviously interested in her sitting across the table—that brought an excitement she hadn't envisioned. Add the music, and the night was magical.

"Are you a Frank Sinatra enthusiast?" Joe inquired.

"I love his music, particularly 'Come Fly With Me.'"

"I'm a Beatles fan."

"Rock?" She scoffed. "All the music sounds the same —rebellious."

"Not the Beatles. Their music is fresh and innovative. How about country songs?"

"No, but I adore musicals," Emily replied. "Especially *Cats,* by Andrew Lloyd Webber."

"I've never seen a live musical, nor listened to any."

"You've never visited New York city, or strolled on Broadway?"

"Nope." He sat on the edge of his seat. "What's the musical about? A cat?"

"Several cats, and my favorite song is 'Memory'." With a soft murmur, she called up the lyrics ... "being alone in the moonlight with remembrances of the past."

"Is there a storyline?"

"Of course. The old cat, Grizabella, is mourning her

youth." Emily tipped her head to the side. "Sometimes the older you get, the more it seems like you've disappeared."

Sometimes, oftentimes, she'd felt that way with her son and his family.

"What's your favorite song?" she asked. "Besides anything by The Beatles."

"Give me any tunes by Journey."

"You're going on a journey?"

"Journey is the band's name, Emily."

She offered an abashed smile. "I'm joking."

"I know." He shifted but didn't grin. "Are you spending the Fourth of July with friends?"

She automatically tensed at the question. Any social life since she became a widow was nonexistent. Her core of socialite friends had avoided calling, and Emily learned that several wives considered her a threat because she was single.

To keep active, she'd tried a sip and paint class before concluding she wasn't good at sipping wine or painting. Hence, she'd given up on a night life, or a day life, or any social life, for that matter.

"No plans," she replied.

Joe kept his features reserved, although the affection in his deep-blue eyes betrayed him. "Will you see your son?"

"He and his wife and my grandson are taking a hiking trip to the mountains."

"They didn't invite you?"

"Not in so many words, but I suppose the invitation was there." She kept her voice a monotone. "I'll call him. That is, if he has cell phone service where they are camping. Oftentimes he doesn't pick up. However, I always leave a message."

Joe extended a half-smile. "I do the same."

"Our adult children and their families lead hectic lives."

"Yes."

Emily focused on the ceiling. "Anyway, I've never slept in

a tent before and informed my son that I'm certainly not starting at my age."

"So you prefer creature comforts?"

"Totally. You?"

"Delicious food, a pleasant home, and a delightful woman by my side is my vision of paradise," Joe said. "I could probably climb into a sleeping bag … however, climbing out is a different matter entirely."

"Because of the zipper?"

"Because I'm seventy." He smirked. "It's not easy for me to get up."

His upbeat banter was so infectious that she grabbed his hand before she could stop herself. "Not exactly a simple task for me, either."

"Unless we're both planning to become Olympic athletes in our seventies, sleeping in bags on the ground probably isn't a satisfactory plan. You're physically fit, though, Emily. I presume you work out."

There was no mistaking the admiration on his features.

Her face flushed. The two-mile walk on the treadmill every morning was tiring, but obviously worth it.

She drew back but didn't release her gaze.

"My daughter and her little girl won't be around either." Joe picked up his coffee cup and smiled at her over the rim. "What I'm trying to ask is … are you interested in riding to Cambria with me? I'm scheduled to pick up another chocolate delivery near there, but not until Monday. Therefore, my days in between are clear, plus I'm paid for the vacation."

"And you choose to spend those days with me?"

"Absolutely."

"You mean … ride with you to Cambria … in your delivery truck?"

"Sure, and we can enjoy the long weekend together. Cambria is a little seaside town. I've visited a number of times because there's a major chocolate distribution center close by. Tourist attractions in Cambria include a castle and a boardwalk, and we can watch the sunsets on Moonstone Beach."

Emily attempted to tamp down her excitement, although her senses reeled. "Where is Cambria?" she hedged.

"About five hours away."

"I'm not sure—"

"No pressure." Joe set down his cup and grasped her hands again. "No expectations. Just two friends taking pleasure in one another's company."

She eyed the Moonglow Chocolatiers truck in the parking lot. "Is there enough room for me?"

"I'm driving a box truck, Emily. There's plenty of space."

"I'm not accustomed to packing lightly."

"Bring whatever is best for a beach trip, especially if it fits into a duffel bag."

She frowned. She couldn't recall if she even owned a duffel bag, but she owned a set of white designer suitcases.

"Fair warning," Joe said. "If I keep any clothes and items in the back, they tend to smell like chocolate."

"Tend?"

"They do. They will."

With a quiet giggle, she assured, "Chocolate is my favorite."

"Me too, or I wouldn't have lasted two decades transporting it across the state."

She pressed her lips together, still debating. "Is there a downside of riding in a truck?"

"Well, dust always lands in the passenger seat."

"Can anything go wrong on the road?"

"Plenty." He caressed her fingers with his thumb. "A punctured tire, a cracked windshield—"

Halfheartedly, she stifled a grin. "Joe, are you trying to talk me into going? If so, you're hardly succeeding."

"Because I saved the best for last." He sat straighter. "My truck has something no other can boast. Besides having you along for the ride, of course."

"Which is?"

"A year ago, I installed an eight-track cassette tape player in the dashboard."

"The proprietor agreed?"

"I leased the truck for five years, and now I own it."

"I commend your entrepreneurial spirit, but where did you find cassettes?"

"Several big-box stores, vintage record shops, and online. It's a niche industry, but many people prefer tapes."

"Therefore, there is no CD player in your truck?"

He quirked a white eyebrow. "What are those?"

"CD's are—" She caught his smirk and joined in. "At any rate, eight-track cassettes are antiques. Like us."

"We're not antiques, Emily. We have an exciting life ahead of us and an entire world to experience."

She shrugged. "Maybe." She wondered exactly where that world was located … sometimes. At other times, she was content in her quiet, daily routine.

Wasn't she?

Of course.

Moreover, repetition was excellent for aiding memory, and her routine was invariably the same. She drove the short distance to the diner for dinner, conversed with the other customers and Oliver, and returned to her comfortable brick house in the center of the small adjacent city.

Rinse and repeat, her conscience chided, noting that her days had become repetitive and dreary. Was Joe's invitation an opportunity for adventure?

"What are the accommodations in Cambria?" she asked. "Are there hotels?"

"There are numerous motels and hotels and quaint bed-and-breakfast spots. At last count, Cambria's population was around six thousand."

"You described a seaside town." Emily envisioned starfish, tumbling waves, and a smart pier harboring million-dollar yachts.

"Cambria is near the Pacific Ocean," Joe continued. "The community boasts an abundance of sea life, including otters and seals. We can book a boat excursion if you'd like. I did once when I was there … by myself." He paused. "We can swim, although parts of the coast are rocky."

Emily's head came up at the swimming reference. "Decades ago, I was a member of my college's swim team."

"What was your best stroke?"

"The backstroke." She met his gaze. "Were you on the swim team in college?"

"I didn't attend college, but I know how to swim. To support my family, I took the first job offered as soon as I graduated from high school. My father had died when I was young, and my mother cleaned houses for a living. We constantly struggled to make ends meet."

When she didn't respond, Joe granted a broad, disarming grin. "May I confess something?"

"Why not?"

"I rented a tiny, quaint cottage by the sea. It's not as fancy as the deluxe resorts where you vacationed when Krandall was alive." He hesitated. "I know you summered in Europe and wintered in the Bahamas."

She shook her head. "Contrary to what you might presume about me—"

"You prefer the finer things in life."

"Admittedly, but Cambria sounds enchanting."

Joe blinked. His eyes rounded. "My tiny cottage will suffice?"

"Nicely." She bit back a smile at his enthusiastic tone. "However, if you've already rented the cottage, then you assumed I'd agree to your invitation?"

"I wasn't certain." He squeezed her hands. "Nonetheless, I was hopeful."

She turned to the window. Night had descended, the golden colors of afternoon had dimmed to twilight, then blackness.

And there was one more subject to resolve.

"Joe, without sounding prudish …" She subjected him to a delicate raise of her eyebrows. "We both were married, but my mother instilled Victorian values in me that I still ascribe to."

"Excellent." He grinned. "Your mother must have known my mother."

When he continued to grin, Emily reiterated with utmost honesty. "Consequently, I won't share a bedroom with you."

"I respect you too much to ask otherwise. The cottage I rented has two bedrooms, and I'll sleep in the smaller of the two."

CHAPTER 3

*W*as this beach trip a wise idea?

The following morning, Emily pondered the question while she finished packing. She'd selected casual, comfortable clothes. After all, it was a spur-of-the-moment invitation. For the drive, she opted for a black and white jersey knit sundress, black leather sandals, a thin silver bracelet, and a cardigan sweater to drape over her shoulders.

When had she last gone on a vacation, or anywhere at all since Krandall had died, except to visit her son and his family?

Pausing to rest on the tufted sofa in her cozy sitting room, Emily set the duffel bag on a table and drew a knitted blanket over her lap. Because of the air conditioning, she was often cold.

She leaned her head back. Too excited to sleep the previous evening, she'd risen when stars still flickered in the sky. She hardly ever slept well anymore, waking frequently.

After their dinner at the diner, Joe had phoned when she'd returned to her house, describing in enthusiastic detail the places in Cambria she might be interested in—the charming boutiques lining the boardwalk and an artifacts gallery displaying art painted by local California artists. She envisioned a Nantucket-style cottage, a coastal retreat with lattice greenery growing over the roof. A sunny, gleaming oasis decorated with cane chairs and needlepoint pillows.

A thumbs-up text from Joe brought her to her feet. She stifled the kick in her pulse as his truck rounded the street corner.

A minute later, she was partway across the living room when the doorbell rang. Although she was overjoyed to see him, she was determined to stay poised and attempted to tamp down her enthusiasm as she opened the door.

He stood on her front steps with his hands dug in the pockets of his khaki shorts, wearing a smile that revealed white teeth. His strong pride showed in his rough-hewn features, and the firm mouth that had tenderly kissed her goodnight.

He wore sunglasses, quickly pointing out they were prescription when she complimented him on his appearance.

He held her hands in his, then slanted his head. "How much stuff are you bringing?"

"Stuff?

"Clothes … stuff."

"This and that. Somehow, I managed to fit most of my toiletries into a duffel bag."

"Somehow? Almost?" He peered around. "I don't see a duffel bag, but I do see two large white suitcases."

"My duffel bag is in the sitting room."

"Sitting room?" He shoved up his glasses. "What's that?"

"A place where you … sit. I needed something slightly bigger and couldn't fit all my clothes into one little bag."

"A duffel bag expands."

"Not enough," she countered. Because she'd added another one-piece swimsuit, a cover-up, two more sundresses, nightclothes, a bold pearl necklace, white cotton slacks, and a couple flowery-print blouses. In addition, her makeup and night clothes took up more space than she'd anticipated, which had necessitated the second suitcase.

Joe rubbed his temples. "I'll store your suitcases in the back. Be ready to smell like chocolate when you open them in the morning."

"You warned me already, and I'm prepared." She hung her hands on her hips, opting for a more logical approach. "What woman can fit all her weekend outfits into a duffel bag, anyway?"

"Certainly not anyone as fashionable as you." He placed his arm lightly on her shoulders. "I phoned my daughter. Did you speak with your son?"

"He seemed pleased I had plans for the holiday." *Immensely, overly pleased.*

With a twinge of heartache, Emily had detected her son's relief. Definitely, she was joyful because he had a devoted wife and an adorable son, but oftentimes she felt abandoned.

"Excellent." Joe brought a hand to his forehead and peered toward the hallway. "Are you ready?"

"Whenever you are." She retrieved her duffel bag, secured the windows and snatched her purse, and house keys.

Joe lifted her suitcases and feigned an amplified groan. "Imagine if we traveled for a week. What would you pack then?"

"Enough for at least four suitcases." At his incredulous stare, she quickly inserted, "Just kidding."

As they walked to his truck, he paused to regard her. "I still can't believe I persuaded a fine, wonderful woman like you to come along with me."

"It was the eight-track cassette player," she reminded with a laugh.

He opened the passenger door, then waited as she

climbed in and buckled her seat belt. "Thank you for agreeing to ride with me, Emily. This trip means more than you can imagine."

"Me too," she said quietly.

He was a thoughtful man with a tender heart, and she hardly was able to contain her happiness that she'd met him.

He started the ignition and eased onto the street, then the interstate, while Emily fiddled with the radio stations. When the disc jockey's voice introduced the next song as country/western, a man in an SUV pulled up next to them at the stoplight. His SUV blasted the same station.

"My cassettes are in the glove compartment." Joe had evidently noticed Emily's pained expression as Willie Nelson blared from their twin speakers. A woman, apparently, was always on Willie Nelson's mind.

Emily sifted through the row of cassettes—ranging from The Eagles to an assortment of Beatles collections—and her hand stilled. "Frank Sinatra's Greatest Hits? The soundtrack from *My Fair Lady*?"

"I couldn't find the musical you mentioned … the one about dogs."

"Cats," she corrected. "And I thought you didn't care for—"

"This morning, I patronized an oldies store in town."

"You were searching for music for me?"

"Only for you," he said affectionately.

She was special to him, and the knowledge filled her with delight.

The miles passed rapidly, and Joe remarked on the numerous tourist attractions. Traffic moved at a crawl when they hit construction sites, and he braked slowly and gently. Whenever they picked up speed, acceleration was seldom quick.

"We're in Bloomingfield," Joe announced when they drove

along the main street of a charming town. He angled his steering wheel toward the curb. "This is where Sally Elliot owns her candy shop."

"Don't stop," Emily said. "Sally isn't working today because she and Oliver and her daughter are visiting an aquarium."

"Oh, right." Joe stared out the front window and carefully merged into traffic. "Her sister, Julie, owns The Pasta Junction, a fine Italian restaurant here in town, and she makes her own pasta. Her eatery doesn't open until dinnertime, though. Have you frequented either place?"

"I don't travel much farther than the diner," Emily answered with a broken laugh. She shook off her defeatism and said graciously, "But Oliver's food is tasty."

"His meals are the best in the state," Joe agreed. "We'll stop in Bloomingfield some other time, alright?"

"Alright."

He glanced at her. "Is that a promise?"

"Indeed." Emily nodded and stretched out her legs. Her limbs felt weightless, and her expectations were positive.

Some other time. A promise of a next time.

"I've never ridden in a truck before," she confessed. "I'm up so high."

"There's a first for everything, and the view is better."

"Is driving difficult? The ride is a bit rough, and I noticed you swing wide on your turns."

"Yep, and I take ramps and curves unhurriedly."

For the next half hour, they covered an expansive stretch of highway while serenaded by Frank Sinatra's soothing voice singing, "That's Life." Up ahead, a billboard advertised a fast-food restaurant at an upcoming exit.

"Are we stopping for lunch?" Emily asked. "I'm content eating at a drive-through."

"I packed sandwiches," Joe replied. "Or rather, the deli prepared them. There are several roadside picnic areas."

"I haven't picnicked since … forever."

"The spot where I'm headed is on a riverfront."

"Krandall preferred to dine at the country club," Emily mused.

"Nothing against a country club, although I've never even entered one. I prefer to eat outdoors. Food tastes better, particularly a classic turkey sub with roasted red peppers, which I requested especially for you."

She clutched her fingers together. "How did you know some of my favorite foods?"

"Easy." He chuckled at her reaction. "I phoned Oliver. I ordered the same sub for myself, except I requested mine garnished with green peppers instead of red."

When they broke for lunch, she heartily agreed that food tasted better alfresco, further declaring she was becoming a nature lover. To her surprised pleasure, she wasn't immune to the ambiance of an unassuming meal and devoured an amazingly marvelous lunch. As she reached for a cold bottle of water from the sack of drinks and sandwiches, she marveled at the backdrop of their location—the grove of redwood trees, the rushing river, and the scenic, towering mountains.

They disputed whether green or red peppers were tastier, and she did fun things—simple things—such as sitting by the river and skipping rocks.

"Find the smoothest, flattest rock," Joe instructed, demonstrating that a simple flick of the wrist produced the best bounce. "Also, face the water."

"Where else would I face?" She laughed out loud, relishing the friendly competition as she thrust rapidly and the rock flew airborne.

"Next time, I'll teach you how to spin rocks," he said. "You're certainly a pro."

"My newfound skill," she jested, "is skipping rocks."

"You beat me on every throw."

She shoved the hair off her forehead, her lips twitching with laughter as she embraced the finest, most relaxing day she'd ever experienced.

But of course she was with Joe, and as she'd previously determined during their numerous conversations, he had the ability to change ordinary events in life into memorable ones. No fancy meals for him. Just plain old-fashioned fun that didn't rely on a high-priced atmosphere or over-the-top chef creations.

Afterwards, Emily lounged against the truck while Joe filled the tank with gas. She relished the soothing breeze against her face and the brilliant glow of the afternoon sun, grateful for the straw hat she'd worn to protect her complexion.

In a few short hours, they exited the highway. The day had flown by, and soon they arrived at the cottage. Emily rushed across the stone walkway, taking in the appeal of the classic Cape Cod style—the weathered cedar shingles and white wooden shutters.

And then she stopped.

The cottage looked neglected, as if it hadn't been updated in decades.

"The website stated that the cottage had a run of owners, but the reviews were pretty good," Joe said. "Plus, the rental rate was reasonable."

Pretty good. Reasonable. Emily made a quiet groan in her throat. Half of the dilapidated wrap-around deck faced the shimmering Pacific ocean, and two rusty pink bicycles sat propped against an abandoned rose trellis.

"I haven't ridden a bike since I was a teenager," she

murmured, sidestepping the fact that the bicycles screamed for a major repair, as did the rest of the property.

"Neither have I." Joe gestured to a younger woman who stood on the sandy beach and stared at them. With his arm draped around Emily, he steered her toward the doorway and tipped her chin up. "I bet our neighbor thinks I should kiss you before we enter our weekend escape."

Emily tucked her hands at her sides. "I bet she's not thinking any such thing. She doesn't even know us."

He lowered his head. "Let's show her what two happy people look like … two people on top of the world."

Emily bit back a helpless smile as their lips touched. "Make it quick," she murmured.

"I can't kiss you quick when you're laughing."

"I'm laughing because you are."

As their breaths merged, he extended a friendly wave to their neighbor.

THE MUSTY, dry odor of the cottage's interior hit Emily first.

"This place was advertised as sparkling clean and boasting divine beds," Joe muttered.

"Nothing that an airing can't solve," Emily chirped. "We'll open the doors and windows."

They stepped on creaky, white-washed wooden floors and came upon the larger of the two bedrooms. A red and white buffalo checked quilt covered the single bed. An ancient air-conditioning unit blocked most of the cracked window, and slivers of light shone through. Outside, rolling sand dunes, and tall grass swayed in a wind gust.

"If I owned a cottage in a splendid location like this," Emily said, "I would remodel the bedroom, install central air-conditioning, and let the sunlight in. The view of the ocean is spectacular." She ran her fingers over the dusty oak veneer chest and studied a watercolor depicting a fisher-man's boat set against a backdrop of jagged cliffs. Embla-zoned in blue letters on the boat's stern was *Summer Breeze.*

"Sometimes, owners name their boat after a pleasant memory," Joe remarked.

"*Summer Breeze* brings to mind hope and joy. It's easy to forget any concerns with the promise of summer to cheer you." Emily balanced on her toes to examine the initials etched in the right-hand corner. "K. S. Who do you suppose that is?"

"There was a Keaton Smith art gallery in town a few months ago when I was here," Joe replied. "Let's include the gallery on our itinerary."

"I like itineraries." Emily offered a smile, then reluctantly returned her attention to the bedroom, particularly the cobwebs. Her smile faded as she pondered how long it had been since the walls had absorbed a fresh coat of paint, or the four rooms had been filled with the aroma of a Sunday pot roast.

"When you stare at the floor," Joe said, "you make me think the cottage is inadequate."

Quickly, she shook her head. "No, no, not at all. It's lovely ...really. Only, I'd anticipated something more modern." Belatedly registering his wounded expression, she focused on a point over his shoulder, regretful for allowing her expectations to prompt her to blurt her reservations aloud.

Several seconds of unpromising silence followed.

She stiffened, expecting a verbal set-down. When Joe didn't respond, she encouraged, "Please talk to me. I'm sorry."

"What would you like me to say?"

"To begin with, you can chastise me about my comment."

"I'd never chastise you."

"Okay, but you can tell me that I was rude and ungracious."

"I won't do that, either." He sighed. "This is a cottage built in the 1920s, Emily. You can't expect modern. I told you it was quaint."

"I realize you tried to find the best place on a budget." She drew a long breath. "Are you upset by my remark?"

"I'm not sure."

"I don't understand."

"When it comes to you, my thoughts haven't been clear since we met. In addition, my insecurity grows heavier every second we're together." He kept his stare downcast, which prompted Emily to smile.

She rattled him because he was attracted to her.

"I'm thrilled to hear that," she declared.

Joe didn't appear nearly as thrilled. He rubbed the back of his neck, sat on the edge of the bed, and invited her to sit beside him. "We should come to a clearer understanding of what is happening between us, and, more importantly, how we should continue."

"Joe, we just arrived. This conversation is too serious."

He steepled his hands. "Shall I speak first, or you?"

She flinched. He'd ignored her statement.

"Go ahead," she relented.

"Fifty percent of the time I shake myself, a reminder that I'm really here with you and this isn't all a dream," he said. "You're too attractive and elegant to devote your days to a guy like me."

"Don't put yourself down. I respect you a great deal."

"We're not having this conversation because I'm fishing for compliments, Emily."

She fingered the silver bracelet on her wrist. "And the other fifty percent?" she prodded.

"Despite how well you may perceive me and my lifestyle,

I'm a galaxy away from being inexperienced. The perfectionism I strove for in my youth, the same perfectionism I believe you still want, disappeared for me many years ago. We're both seventy and should acknowledge our differences. I'm the opposite of a wealthy millionaire. I earn an hourly wage and will never receive a six-figure, end-of-year bonus." The grin had long since vanished from his features. "This isn't a senior prom, and I'm not speculating about whether I'll kiss you, because I already have, and—with your permission—will do so again."

Her cheeks heated. He was frank about expressing his feelings. She liked that.

Politely, she folded her hands. "Are you finished?"

"Should I be?"

"Can't you understand that I'm proud of you and what you've accomplished?"

"I own a delivery truck, Emily, and my house is a quarter of the size of yours."

Their earlier excitement was rapidly disintegrating, and an imperceptible strain slowly descended on the tiny bedroom.

"Those things aren't important to me," she replied.

He tapped his fingers on his knee and didn't look convinced.

She inhaled and smiled. "Well then, everything is settled."

"What's settled?"

"You have my permission."

"For what?"

She peered at the doorway. "It's been nearly a half hour since you kissed me and …"

Realization dawned on his face.

Smiling, he cupped her chin and silenced her next words with his lips. As further proof she was sincere, she flung her arms around his neck and returned his kiss.

Several minutes later, they walked hand in hand through the narrow hallway to inspect the galley kitchen, which was painted a dark cobalt blue and boasted glass cupboard doors.

She scanned the chipped Formica countertop. "Where's the coffee machine and pods?"

"There is a coffee pot on the stove." He indicated a stainless steel percolator, then stepped to the white refrigerator and peeked inside. "I also arranged a grocery delivery for necessities."

Sure enough, a quart of milk, a dozen eggs, a loaf of bread, butter, bottled water, and ground coffee perched on the top two shelves.

"You planned everything." She darted a glance at the shabby surroundings, forcibly reminding herself that this was a beach cottage, not a five-star resort. "Where is the bathroom?"

"It must be through here." As he freed a jammed door, his voice went quiet. Water leaked from the sink's faucet, and the mirror reflected tarnish. Although only one person at a time could fit in the cramped space, the tiles gleamed and fresh white towels hung on the towel bars.

She peered inside. "There's no shower stall."

Joe strode to the living room and grabbed a brochure off the coffee table. "I read about an outdoor shower, but I assumed it was to rinse off the sand after a day at the beach." He swung wide a saloon-style door in the kitchen which led outside.

"Hmm."

"Hmm?" she asked.

"I guess the shower is truly outdoors." He hesitated before facing her. "I assume that's okay … because … because you're a nature-lover, right?"

CHAPTER 4

*N*ature, Emily soon realized the following morning when she stepped into the outdoor shower, presented a challenge. And clearly she wasn't a nature-lover after all.

Spiders and creepy-crawlies naturally gravitated to a damp area. In addition to the leaves and sand piled in the corner, clouds rolled in while she was soaking wet and the wind picked up, leaving her shivering and taking the fastest shower of her life.

And then there was the bigger problem.

In addition to the compactness of the space, she was *exposed.*

Not to mention that she had to hang her rosy-red sundress and clean undergarments on the door and hoped they didn't fall into the dirt while she quickly scrubbed herself. Thankfully, the warm water, plus the fragrant eucalyptus spearmint soap she'd brought from home lifted her spirits.

She didn't bother with make-up except for a pastel pink lipstick, foundation, and mascara. She had secured her neatly coiffed hair with a shower cap beforehand so it didn't get wet, and later swept back the ends with a thin, glossy-red headband.

Despite the obstacles, she was determined to impress Joe.

Why did she care about impressing him? she challenged herself. They were two friends sharing a weekend. Romance wasn't part of the equation. Furthermore, there was no attraction between them.

Hah, her conscience chided, and she thrust it aside. Oftentimes, her conscience was an annoyance.

A half hour later, fully dressed and made-up, she slipped on easy, closed-toe shoes and entered the kitchen.

The front door and windows were wide open, and the weather promised a silvery-blue sky and comfortable temperatures. Emily caught a whiff of a salty sea breeze and the echoes of percussive waves hitting rhythmically against the shore.

Joe stood near the stove, brewing coffee and popping bread into the toaster, and his efficient movements made her smile. The attractiveness of his robust physique, his purple polo shirt tucked into navy shorts, hastened her breathing. Feeling suddenly shy, she shoved her hands into her pockets and wished him a cheerful good morning.

"Good morning, beautiful." He met her smile, and her heartbeat doubled at the affection in his gaze. "Red becomes you."

She braced her fingers on the counter and took a slow breath. *Friends, friends, friends*, she reminded herself.

"How was your shower?" he asked.

"Quite an adventure." *Talk about an understatement.* "A stunning sanctuary isn't the first description that comes to mind."

"The second?"

"Um, no. Perhaps airy?"

"Therefore, the experience was …"

"Harrowing. And my clothes smell like a chocolate factory."

"I warned you." He grinned. "I encountered a large spider."

"That's all?" She laughed, then feigned disappointment. "You were lucky."

"Why? What did you see?"

"The better question is … what *didn't* I see?"

He barked with laughter. "I rose before dawn and showered early."

"I didn't hear you."

"You were fast asleep. Did you rest well?"

"Surprisingly, yes. I opened my window and the sound of the ocean waves lulled me to sleep. Usually it takes me a long time to fall asleep."

"Me too, but not last night. It must be those divine beds." She giggled her assent as he reached into the cupboard for mugs and poured two cups of coffee. She inhaled the deep, rich aroma.

"You take your coffee black, right?" he inquired.

She nodded and relished the first sip. Of course he'd remembered her preference.

Standing, she spread butter on their toast, and they worked companionably, bantering while they set their dishes in the sink after a light breakfast.

"No dishwasher," he murmured. "Sorry."

"I can certainly wash and dry a few dishes. There's nothing to apologize for." She glanced his way and her pulse quickened. Her feelings for him multiplied the more hours they spent together.

"Let's venture into town and stock up on more food supplies," Joe suggested. "I want to try a new recipe while we're here."

"Another brownie that promotes weight loss?" Emily teased.

He draped a dishcloth over his shoulder and perched his hip at the edge of the table. "Lydia emailed me a recipe for peanut butter bars. She insists they're delicious." He pulled out his cellphone and scrolled.

Emily eyed the tiny stove, and oven, then peeked over his shoulder. "All my favorite ingredients. Butter, peanut butter, and chocolate."

He frowned. "Hardly low-calorie."

"Excellent news." Emily placed the last of the clean plates in the cupboard. "A modest amount of fat isn't necessarily bad, as long as you balance the foods with a nourishing meal plan."

He didn't appear convinced but tucked his cellphone into his pocket. "This afternoon we can visit William Randolph Hearst's castle. I reserved two tickets for a tour of the grand rooms."

CHAPTER 5

a few hours later, as the tour guide detailed the history of the magnificent Hearst Castle, Joe scanned the gardens, then concentrated on Emily. With her hair pulled back by a red headband and a hint of pink lipstick on her full lips, she presented a stunning vision. Her complexion was clear, and her heavenly blue eyes were framed by black lashes and elegant eyebrows.

"Can you believe the castle took all those years to finish?" Her demeanor was upbeat, and her gaze shone with excitement as she pointed out the architecture surrounding the opulent pool.

Joe nodded. "Right."

"From 1919 to 1947! And building on the mountaintop in order to capture the breathtaking views was brilliant. I am in awe of Mr. Hearst's vision."

Again, Joe nodded.

She squinted and slipped on her sunglasses. "Hence, you agree?"

"Yep."

"Uh, huh. Did you hear what I said?"

"Of course."

She hung her hands on her hips. "Tell me, then, word for word."

"You began with … we're on a mountaintop." He continually lost his train of thought as he gazed at the curves of her figure, her stunning smile, and the sun shining on her face.

"Therefore, you weren't listening. First, I remarked on the views because they are awe-inspiring." She drew in a breath. "I wonder what the rooms that were not included on our tour look like."

"You do?"

"Yes." She paused, and he sensed an uncertainty in her voice. With any luck, she was exploring a dignified way to suggest another road trip with him.

"You'd like to see more of the castle?" he encouraged. "With me?"

"Am I that transparent?" Studiously, she observed the rose bushes and avoided his gaze. "You must realize you're the ideal—"

"Companion?" He drew her nearer and chuckled, the scent of her spearmint fragrance uplifting. Steadying himself, he pondered why she had such an insane effect on him. "You're my ideal companion too."

She hesitated and pulled at the neckline of her dress. "Joe?"

Whenever she uttered his name, her delicate, pure voice had a dreamlike quality that stirred his senses.

"Hmm?"

"I'm glad we met."

"Me too." He held her close. "I believe fate has a hand in these things—how people meet, when they meet. Sometimes events take place that are beyond our control."

Slightly, her lips parted. "Fate is from the Latin word, fatum, which means 'that which has been spoken.'"

"Did you study Latin in college?"

She rested her head on his shoulder and grinned. "I read a lot, but I learned that from Webster's Dictionary."

THE REMAINDER of the day was a blur of shared hugs and a peaceful walk on the beach. Later, a stroll through town revealed that the Keaton Smith Art Gallery had shuttered a few months earlier. However, they appreciated the sense of originality in the flourishing community that especially beckoned to Emily. She stopped often and browsed—particularly at the stalls where local jewelers created white polished necklaces, rings, and matching bracelets, and crafters wove bright-colored quilts.

She purchased a nautical souvenir for her son's home, plus a bag of caramels for her grandchild, and Joe did the same.

When an antique dealer invited them inside his shop, Emily murmured that his pieces seemed ideally suited to the cottage's ambiance.

"You mean because they're old?" Joe jested.

"Nothing can be as old as that cottage," she solemnly returned.

Simultaneously, they both laughed.

He hugged her then, right in the middle of the shop. He couldn't get enough of her, which was a unique experience for him. Since his wife had died a decade before, he'd found little claim in socializing because no woman appealed to him. Sure, his friends arranged double-dates, but Joe had made up his mind. He wasn't interested in anyone or anything except his daughter, his grandchild, and his work. Any dreams before his beloved wife's death had been lost.

That is until now.

Emily fit effortlessly in the curve of his arm. She was

appealing, curious, and captivated him with stories about her experiences traveling around the world—Europe and Asia and Africa—places he'd never envisioned outside of magazines and television. In her enthusiastic style she'd encouraged him to imagine new possibilities again.

He'd also been impressed by her understanding of technology when she'd adeptly showed him where to find the emojis on his phone. That had resulted in a half hour of experimentation as he'd texted her pink hearts, red hearts, dazzling hearts, and an array of golden stars that had prompted her to giggle until tears streamed down her cheeks.

Sometimes she was stubborn, other times she charmed him with her smile. She was refined and elegant, never showy, topped with so much love bottled up that she mesmerized him.

"All my life I've lived for my son," she said.

"Live for yourself, not others," Joe replied. "Although it's entirely understandable when it comes to our children. They are an important part of who we are."

Emily's eyes had glistened with tears. "There are instances when my son is too preoccupied to spend time with me and I miss the noise and clatter of a crowded household. I remember when I believed the outside world was fraught with peril, and my mission was to protect him."

"You describe memories I also hold close to my heart," Joe admitted. "I miss those years too."

He was living proof of that emptiness. It was the main reason why he preferred to be on the road—to avoid going home to a desolate, lonely house.

Although he and Emily were the same age, he was a million times more world-weary, because he had grown up in a poor neighborhood, whereas her life had been one of affluence. Nonetheless, something about her relaxed him, and that was novel.

However, she avoided any discussions about their future, explaining she didn't wish to ruin their hours together with talks about anything other than the present. Besides, they were too old for any of "that foolishness."

The foolishness of love?

Or was she ashamed of him, his modest background and line of work, and too considerate to vocalize her feelings? He was suitable for a fun, light-hearted weekend, but beyond that … nothing.

He'd always been a plain, unassuming guy, accustomed to simplicity. At eighteen, he had taken the first job that had come along and was grateful. He'd noticed Emily's barely disguised disapproval when he'd mentioned assisting his daughter financially and couldn't understand why it seemed to upset her. At his stage, he was pleased to help his family while they were down on their luck. In addition, he'd managed to tuck away a fair amount of savings.

ON SUNDAY, Joe spent the afternoon assembling ingredients for the recipe his daughter had sent. Emily came and stood beside him in the kitchen and assisted. As a team, they creamed butter, spooned in the peanut butter, and measured the oatmeal.

After the peanut butter bars finished baking, they assembled a tray and two mugs of herbal green tea and headed into the living room. The only TV displayed a makeshift antenna, and they caught tidbits of black and white Andy Griffith Show reruns, which suited them nicely. The everyday activity of passing time—relaxing and watching TV with a special woman—was something he hadn't enjoyed in years.

As Emily placed the half-eaten tray of cookies on the

coffee table, he spoke with a grin. "I decided I prefer regular butter over the low-fat stuff."

"Hurray and don't forget extra chocolate." She stood to brew more tea. As he observed her walking gracefully to the kitchen, he admired her effortless, natural style and the understated sophistication in which she carried herself.

At his insistence, she'd dressed up for their Sunday together. She'd strung a large pearl necklace around her elegant throat, and her deep-blue sundress matched the color of her vivid eyes. With her shiny hair pushed back, her face radiated a sun-kissed glow. After getting ready, they'd found a white-steepled church in town and attended services.

After the service, he'd caressed her cheek and kissed her.

"Tomorrow is our last day," she said, and he detected the conclusiveness in her tone. Or perhaps he imagined it.

"Unfortunately, yes," he replied, his voice shaky. "But we have several hours together while we pick up the delivery, and the ride back home."

He envisioned her attending various social functions when she was married to Krandall—charity balls and Broadway musicals in New York City, and couldn't imagine how he'd forgotten that he'd never be a part of those scenes. He wouldn't escort her to extravagant events because he couldn't afford them. Furthermore, his awkwardness would embarrass her.

In that instant, he understood that not having her in his life was going to be hard, but there was no other choice. Emily deserved better than anything he could offer.

Vacantly, he focused on the paneled wall in the living room as a hollowness filled his chest.

"What are you thinking?" she asked, returning with two steaming mugs.

"Nothing." He shifted. *Nothing he would share with her.*

He offered his best imitation of a smile. "Shall I bake the

next cookie batch using spray butter and artificial sugar?" He suspected that she didn't care for his low-calorie baked goods. She'd never told him, not in so many words, but oftentimes a person conveyed more by what they didn't say, rather than by what they did say.

"No! Please!" Emily sputtered, almost dropping the mugs before setting them on the table.

"I can save several hundred calories—"

"At the expense of taste."

"I've lost weight since I lowered my calorie intake," he loftily responded. "However, this is our vacation, so I'll just sit on the couch and eat more cookies." He gave her a side-long smirk, snatched a cookie from the tray, and took a bite. "Although the middle is undercooked."

Emily nestled closer, and he shared his cookie with her. "Blame it on the tiniest oven in the universe, not your daughter's recipe."

"Are you saying … never blame the cook?"

She laughed and lifted her lips to his. She tasted of chocolate and sweetness and all that he'd missed for so many years. "Never, ever blame the cook."

"Emily, you're the best thing that has happened to me in a long time," he whispered. "Always remember that."

If she wondered why he'd uttered that last part, she gave no indication. Instead, the bonus for his admission was a dainty brush of her fingers against his chin, and a kiss that stole his breath away.

SEVERAL HOURS LATER, they rode in his truck to Moonglow beach and strolled the planked wooden walkway of the boardwalk. Along the way, they searched for moonstones. Yes, there were really moonstones, he assured Emily, and many people made jewelry with them—such as the necklaces and rings and bracelets they'd admired in town. As they found shiny black pebbles and polished sea glass, they often rested on the benches lining the pathway. Joggers ran past, riders on bicycles flew by at a brisk clip, and a couple stopped to converse—describing the playful seals they'd spotted earlier in the day.

As Joe and Emily continued, an easy summer breeze ruffled Emily's hair, and the tang of the ocean filled his nostrils. Fingers entwined, they admired the rock-strewn cliffs and jaw-dropping coastline.

"We didn't have time to take the boat excursion," he said. "Or to swim."

"Maybe next time."

He turned to gaze at the ocean, his heart heavy, knowing there would be no next time.

One last night together.

He wanted all that they were sharing—tomorrow, the day after that, and the day after that. He longed to paint the town red... would she know that old expression? He suspected she would.

He yearned to embrace life and celebrate every hour with her, because time went by too quickly.

She snuggled against him and he squeezed his eyes shut for a moment. Nearby, people threw red, white, and blue confetti in the air, waved American flags, and cheered.

He soaked in the ambiance of the enchanting pint-size community, its gentler pace, and the way the sun scattered bits of golden sequins on the Pacific Ocean. Fireworks marked the July Fourth celebration, and patriotic music blasted from a loudspeaker in the distance.

A flood of affection, of contentment, radiated through him.

He loved their little cottage. Unquestionably it showed

maturity, but the weather-beaten shingles proved it had lived successfully through another season, despite its age.

Much like him. Much like Emily.

He loved this ageless place that hinted at a kinder lifestyle from a date long forgotten.

And then he realized what he'd known in his heart all along.

He was in love with Emily Varon.

CHAPTER 6

*S*unrise came quicker than expected, and Emily snuggled under the buffalo-checked red and white quilt longer than she'd planned. A sea wind whistled through the cracks of the window as she reluctantly opened her eyes.

They were leaving.

Quickly she showered and then packed, appreciative of the coffee and toast Joe had placed on the oak chest in her bedroom. When she tried to swallow, the coffee tasted bitter in her constricted throat, and the toast was dry and flavorless. A disturbing awareness hit her, setting in motion sadness and confusion. She didn't want to return to her private and solitary existence.

Making a concerted effort to maintain her composure, she pondered why this trip with Joe had come to mean so much.

However, she couldn't let him know, choosing not to appear needy. Especially when she suspected that her son and his family considered her clingy and desperate.

She finished arranging the last of her toiletries in the duffel bag and stepped to the doorway. The Moonglow

Chocolatiers truck idled, exhaust coiling densely from the tailpipe into the sultry morning air.

"Good morning, lovely." Joe adjusted the emerald-green silk scarf she'd tied carelessly around her throat. "Are you ready? I brewed an extra thermos of coffee for the ride, and I included leftover peanut butter bars to nibble on before we stop for lunch."

Emily bobbed her head, but her legs refused to move.

"There's rain in the forecast. I'll need to drive slower and keep my lights on." He peered at the gray clouds on the horizon, then hoisted her suitcases.

"Okay. I'm in no hurry." Emily went into the kitchen and slowly picked up the coffee pot, disposing of the coffee grounds and washing the mugs and plates they had used. She held Joe's mug against her heart, tracing the rim with her finger before she placed it back in the cupboard.

With a muffled sigh, she glanced around. Much as the cottage was in disrepair, she would truly miss the place.

After they collected the cases of chocolate at the delivery center outside of town, the rains started. Joe kept the radio volume low and made no mention of playing any cassette tapes. He increased his following distance and checked the truck at a deliberate, safe speed.

After an hour, he pulled into a rest area, and Emily grabbed the thermos and poured them coffee. They stood under a tree, and a car sped past, splashing water against the truck.

Hazardous weather. Rain. Construction. Joe was under a considerable amount of strain, regularly driving under challenging conditions, and this had been his occupation for countless years.

They stopped several more times for gas and food, and the mood remained solemn.

They made it through Bloomingfield an hour later than it

had taken to cover the same distance in sunny weather. Soon, they would be back in her hometown.

As they covered the last stretch, Emily sat straighter and gathered her courage. She'd never declared her feelings openly, certainly not to a man she'd known for mere months.

Nonetheless, the time had come.

She couldn't envision a life without Joe, couldn't accept the agonizing awareness of resorting to repeated phone and Skype calls with him again.

Despite her jittery stomach, she dismissed her reservations and single-mindedly focused on one objective. She didn't care anymore about sounding needy. In truth, she *was* needy when it came to continuing their relationship. And she would tell him, employing her 'small talk' finesse.

"Joe?" she began.

"Hmm?" He kept his gaze forward, the wipers beating a recurring back-and-forth flap against the windshield.

"I'd like a more permanent courtship."

So much for finesse.

He blinked. For a split-second, he took his gaze off the road and regarded her.

"How? I constantly work, Emily."

"Perhaps you can drive less." She took a quick breath. "Or, preferably, not at all."

"I need to continue working, Emily."

She pushed on, crossing and uncrossing her legs. "Move to my town, so we can be together more often."

"You're talking marriage?"

"Well—"

"In summary, I'd have no income and would rely on your money to support me?"

"I didn't say that."

"I noticed you didn't ask to move in with me. I assume you're ashamed of my house, although you've never seen it."

His shoulders curved forward as he concentrated on the road. "Let's face it, Emily, you're ashamed of *me* because I'm a common truck driver."

"You're misconstruing all my words."

"Am I? What would my daughter reckon, and my fellow drivers, if they learned I was with you? They'd suspect I was after your wealth."

"You assume this is about money, and you're worried about your self-esteem?" Letting out a shocked gasp, Emily sat back. "It's about a full-time relationship rather than a part-time one. I deserve better than that."

"You deserve better than *me*," Joe countered. "Someone who fits into your world."

She flinched, and her stomach hardened. As they passed Olive's Diner, she stayed silent. When they arrived at her house, Joe parked the truck and came around to open the door for her.

"Thanks for coming with me," he said briefly, and leaned forward.

In case he wanted to kiss her, she held up her palm to ward him off.

He grimaced, grabbed her suitcases and duffel bag, and carried them into the living room.

"Thanks, Joe. Goodbye. Safe travels." Her chest hitched. She couldn't say more.

His grimace remained. "Goodbye, Emily." He stumbled back a few steps, then spun. Without another word, he got into his truck and drove away.

CHAPTER 7

*S*even days went by. Then fourteen.

Despite her efforts to occupy herself, Emily pined for Joe, missing him desperately. He'd sent a brief text saying he was driving to another part of the state and would be gone for a while.

And then, nothing.

Naturally, she was too proud to phone him, and awaited a call that never came. Obsessively, she checked her phone and waited.

The weekend they'd shared had begun like a fairy-tale. Oftentimes, she imagined another scenario, a happier ending. If only their relationship had turned out differently.

Yes, she loved him, and believed he cared for her.

But now it was over.

On a typical Thursday evening a week later, she sat at a corner booth in Olive's Diner, staring out the front window at the sunset. Fresh pink and tangerine orange colors ignited the sky. The month of July was coming to a close, and the days had been reduced to a smudge of summer. She'd gone into town more often, holding on to the breeze as she chatted with people she passed. It felt wonderful not to disconnect from strangers anymore.

She'd even enrolled in a painting class again, surprising herself when she discovered that she did better when she put forth more effort. Her earlier lack of talent had grown from mental obstacles, and she'd been hesitant to try anything new since Krandall's death for fear of failure.

Failure was a matter of one's experience, she supposed. The fear of risking her heart and subsequently losing it, had almost broken her. That is, until she'd relaxed her tight muscles, taken a fortifying breath, and stepped into the art studio again. Her first attempt had produced a watercolor of a fishing boat, which she'd proudly hung on her sitting room wall. On the stern, she'd penned, 'Summer Breeze' in scripted calligraphy. In addition, she'd filled her home with vases of pink and yellow seaside daisies, a display of cheerfulness she seldom felt.

Oliver stepped to her table, bringing her musings to the present.

"The air-conditioning broke," he said.

"I noticed it's warm in here tonight, but I don't care for air-conditioning, anyway."

"Have you seen Joe lately?"

She swallowed hard. "No." They'd been over this every day since she and Joe had parted.

"Are you ordering tonight's special?" He grabbed a pencil from behind his ear and tugged an order pad from his apron. "I'm serving lasagna."

"Excellent. I expect the pasta is loaded with extra ricotta cheese and heaps of calories."

"Guaranteed." He tapped his pencil on the edge of the table and peered at his watch. "Look, Emily. I wanted to surprise you and probably should have told you earlier, but—"

"Lasagna isn't a surprise, Oliver." She gazed at him with frustration. "You serve lasagna on alternate Thursdays." She glanced out the window and her head jerked back as a familiar Moonglow Chocolatiers truck pulled into the parking lot.

"It's about time," Oliver muttered, perching across from her. "He's running late."

She grabbed Oliver's arm. "It can't be ... Joe is in town?"

"We've had nightly conversations, and I knew he was coming this evening to see you."

Her heartbeat accelerated as a short, handsome man—carrying a package wrapped in blue paper and a thin gold bow—strode into the diner.

His usually neat flannel shirt puckered at the waist, his white hair was disheveled.

"When did you arrange this?" She squinted at him. "How?"

Oliver set the order pad on the table, a doodling of two hearts in the corner. "I'm an old-fashioned Cupid, and recommended he take action."

"Hi, Emily." Joe strode to her booth. Tears were in his eyes as he hesitantly set the box on the table. "I brought you a gift."

She stared up at him. "Joe, if it's brownies ..."

"I think I'm done playing Cupid." Oliver shoved to his feet and moved to the counter. "Shall I prepare two servings of lasagna?"

Emily regarded Joe.

"Absolutely," he agreed.

Still reeling, she said stiffly, "You could have mailed the package, Joe."

"I'm not here to deliver brownies." He settled across from her, gazing at her with boyish eagerness. "I'm here to offer you what's in this box."

"Did you bake another low-calorie recipe?"

He shook his head. "Not low calorie. No calorie."

"What?" She couldn't help herself. She was staring at him.

"Please open it."

She did, and then she gasped. A polished moonstone ring, exquisite in its simple luminous beauty, was set in a magnificent gold setting.

"I wasn't sure of your ring size. However, the jewelry maker in Cambria assured me that the size can be altered."

"You bought this in Cambria?"

"I ordered it ahead, left my house before dawn and picked it up this morning. The way we parted … it's not over. *We're* not over. I traveled halfway across the state to be with you."

"Five hours each way. That's a long drive."

"Not for the woman I love."

He loved her and was uttering the words out loud. The knowledge made her breath catch.

His voice was deep and gripping. She'd longed to hear from him, to see him.

"All this effort … for me." She fixed her hand on top of his. He was warm, animated, dynamic.

"Our life together," he said. "There's a wonderful, exciting world waiting for us to explore."

She opened her mouth, and then closed it, celebrating the upcoming years in her mind.

He pressed his fingers to her lips. "I want to marry you, Emily, and I won't take no for an answer."

"You said you didn't want to be with me. You were

concerned about what your daughter and co-workers might assume."

"I'm ashamed of myself, because it was my own self-esteem and fears that caused the problem. I couldn't allow people to speculate that I was with you for your money. I would never use you."

"Joe, I don't care about other people's opinions."

"But I do, and I will protect you from any disparaging remarks because I love you, Emily."

"And I love you."

"Good. Good." He beamed. "I've spent many hours pondering our situation, and I figured out a workable solution."

She nodded, waiting for him to continue.

"I'll drive part time, and when I go on a trip, you'll come with me."

"But, Joe, where will we live?"

"Anywhere." He paused, then grinned. "I have nowhere to go, though, because I sold my house. However, I managed to purchase a quaint cottage in Cambria with part of my savings. It boasts an outdoor shower and is situated near the sea."

She pressed her fingers to her throat. "You bought our cottage?"

"Yep. It needs a painting, though."

"I can paint."

The infectious grin that had filled her days in Cambria settled on his features, along with a charismatic trace of conscience. "I approached the owner who was more than willing to sell for a fair price. He even threw in the two bicycles at no extra charge."

"Generous." She shared his grin at that. "What about my house?"

"Keep it, sell it. We can discuss the logistics later."

"After living there for thirty years, I'll sell." She gazed up at him with a helpless smile. "I expected to never see you again."

"Yet, here I am." He pushed up his glasses. "Will you marry me, Emily Varon?"

"Yes. Yes. Yes." For the first time, she noticed the stubble of his white beard, the strokes of weariness at the corners of his bright-blue eyes.

He secured the ring on her left hand finger, then leaned over and kissed her, gently and lovingly and expressively. She curved her hand around his nape, and he buried his kisses in her hair. From the corner of her eye, she spotted Oliver placing a cassette tape player on the counter.

"Now?" he asked Joe when they pulled back from their kiss.

Joe turned to Oliver. "Perfect."

The poignant music from Andrew Lloyd Webber's musical, *Cats,* floated through the diner. The handful of patrons looked up from their meals and smiled. Apparently, the entire diner was in on her surprise.

Emily's heart tightened. "That's my favorite song. 'Memory'."

"I found the cassette online, and I've listened to the music ever since."

"You discovered musicals," she said.

"Especially the lyrics to this song. You're not alone, Emily. Not in the moonlight, not in the daylight. We're here, together, living for today and tomorrow. We'll create our own memories."

She glimpsed Oliver opening several windows to let in a flurry of air, and then her gaze settled on Joe.

The man she loved. Their journey in unison.

"We'll create our own life events," Joe was saying.

And the beckoning of a summer breeze, lighting the landscape of their lives.

The End

A NOTE FROM JOSIE

Dear Friends,

Thank you for reading *A Chocolate-Box Summer Breeze.*

I wanted to write another story centering around the characters in the "Chocolate" series, and chose an older couple—Emily and Joe—to share a summer romance with you.

If you loved this sweet romance as much as I loved writing it, please help other people find *A Chocolate-Box Summer Breeze* by posting your review.

A Chocolate-Box Summer Breeze is available in ebook, Paperback, Large Print Paperback, Hardcover, and Audiobook.

My Spotify Play List for A Chocolate-Box Summer Breeze is here.

With sincere appreciation,

Josie Riviera

Love the "Chocolate Box" sweet romances?
Be sure to check out the other books:

Click here.

RECIPE FOR LYDIA'S PEANUT
BUTTER BARS

#1 CRUST:

1 cup margarine
1 cup brown sugar
½ cup white sugar
4 cups oatmeal
Mix together, PRESS in an 12 x 18 ungreased pan.
Bake 375 degrees for 12 minutes. COOL.

#2 Spread over crust.

1 cup creamy Peanut Butter
(Place in the garage or outside to harden.)

#3

12 – 18 ounces of chocolate chips

1 ½ - 2 Tablespoon butter

Melt together. Dot evenly over peanut butter and spread out.

#4

COOL. Cut into squares. Place into a cookie tin or a plastic container.

Refrigerate. Keeps well for up to a month.

Enjoy!

JOSIE
RIVIERA

a Summer *to* Cherish

PRAISE AND AWARDS

USA TODAY bestselling author

#43 Amazon Contemporary Christian Romance Books

#75 Amazon Contemporary Christian Romance

5 Star Crowned Heart InD'Tale Magazine Review:
A Summer To Cherish

"When the main ingredient in David Fodero's artistic career threatened to shut everything that defines him, he withdraws from the rest of his world to a secret place where he hopes no one, from the life he is choosing to exit, can ever locate him. Ashley Madden who solely relies on David's art supplies, though indirectly, to keep her business alive, has to do something when the man holding the keys to her business disappears. Not knowing where to find him, she makes a trip to one of her close friends, Sarah, hoping to get a lead. True to her instincts, her friend gives her the much-needed help to locate the famous artist who has decided to shut the door to the business world. She barely knows the man. How will she even start questioning his disappearance?

What begins as a casual attempt to keep one's livelihood afloat takes a huge spin when the curtain of the artist's cool cabin split open. When the witty character of Ashley and the stoic no-nonsense stature of David mix, a rainbow of humor, hope, joy, and a great romance is born.
What an artistic piece of literary art!

The reader is totally carried away by the sequential waves of storyline that keeps the boat rocking, making it a perfect read for any day, any time. The theme of how to deal with people's disabilities through compassion shines throughout Ashley's role, making "A Summer to Cherish" a perfect mirror for the contemporary society.

Undoubtedly, lots of work, thoughts, and amazing talent went into what became this wonderful read. " - JM Lareen

"A delightful romance from Josie Riviera, reminding readers to value moments spent with those who fill our hearts with joy."
--SHANNA HATFIELD, USA Today bestselling author

CHAPTER 1

Every child is an artist. The problem is how to remain an artist
once he grows up.
- Picasso

A famous artist didn't just disappear.

Ashley Madden steered her beat-up Chevy convertible around the final treacherous curve connecting her hometown of Greenwood, South Carolina, to Cherish, South Carolina. Earlier, a storm had kicked up, leaving a debris of tree branches and leaves. Fortunately, the trip was under eighty miles and took less than two hours to drive by car.

The route led her through the center of the town, which boasted peaceful, immaculate streets, brick-paved sidewalks, and a decided lack of skyscrapers.

She lowered her car window, drew in a breath of a rain-soaked breeze, and snagged the last peanut butter cup from her stash. She took a bite and exhaled a contented sigh.

Unhealthy food was definitely the tastiest.

Her gaze fixed on the road ahead, and she eased up on the gas pedal as she neared her destination. She kept her chin high, her eyes alert. This artist needed to be found, and she intended to find him. She was determined to preserve her free art program for handicapped children and their families low on funds.

Art made people think, made people feel. Art inspired her students to dance and jump up and down with joy.

And art lasted a long time—certainly longer than her relationship with her ex, who'd dumped her with a quick text:

Sorry it didn't work out between us.

And just like that, the relationship was over.

She eased her convertible into the first available parking space near Thumbs Up, a plant retail store and greenhouse. Squinting in the rearview mirror, she patted down her cowlick. Why couldn't it grow in the same direction as the rest of her hair?

It never occurred to her to fuss with her appearance. She didn't consider herself pretty—she was slight, though her feet were too big. People often remarked on her ready smile, though.

Today, she'd dressed in her typical uniform of a plain white T-shirt and chambray shorts. She couldn't imagine styling her honey-blond, shoulder-length hair other than tying it in a haphazard ponytail. Her makeup ritual consisted of sunscreen and a rosy lip gloss.

She shut off the ignition, unbuckled her seatbelt, then walked across the damp grass to the entrance of the greenhouse. Thick summer air hung heavy, the sun appearing through a gauze of humidity.

She shaded her eyes and peered at the sky. God's golden assurance, sunlight, was forever faithful. Regardless of the rain, He repeatedly guaranteed something better was around the corner.

Ashley entered the greenhouse, instantly recognizing the dark-haired woman engrossed in watering a pot of mauve African violets.

"Sarah?" Ashley came up behind her and tapped her on the shoulder.

Sarah whirled. "Ashley! Twinkle!"

Ashley smiled. Her nickname from a precious student. The name had stuck.

Sarah set the watering can to the side and tugged the apron from her slim waist. "How was the drive?"

"The roads are a mess from the windstorm." Ashley spoke slowly to help Sarah read her lips. Sarah had been diagnosed recently with a hearing loss and wore hearing aids.

"Were the roads littered with trees?"

"It could've been worse." Ashley embraced her friend in a hug. "However, I'm here and I'm fine."

"I'm due for my lunch break. Will you help me haul these bags to the storeroom first?" Sarah pointed to several bags of soil and sheepishly smiled.

Ashley returned the smile. "Of course."

Afterward, they headed toward the rear patio. Sarah grabbed a couple of bottles of water, a turkey sandwich on rye bread, chips, and a chocolate bar.

"Want to share?" She handed Ashley a bottle of water.

"Sure." Ashley slid onto a picnic table beneath a pink-flowered crepe myrtle tree. "I'll take the candy."

Sarah sat across from Ashley and whispered a prayer of grace before unwrapping the sandwich.

Ashley opened her candy bar. Chocolate, her favorite. "Any luck locating David Fodero?" she asked.

Sarah unwrapped her sandwich. "You mean, your reclusive painter?"

"He's not *my* painter. He's Nancy Trainor's painter," Ashley corrected between bites.

Sarah frowned. "Why would an artist like David have his work carried in a small gallery in a tiny southern town?"

"He and Nancy studied together in New York City. She decided her talent lay more in finding and promoting artists than in being an artist." Thoughtfully, Ashley chewed. "David is happy to help out her gallery by having her represent him."

Sarah raised an eyebrow. "Doesn't his artwork sell for tens of thousands of dollars?"

"He allows his works to be sold for lower prices in her gallery. The smaller pieces, not his large canvases." Ashley took another bite of her candy bar. "Without his paintings to sell, her gallery may close. The income his works provide allows her showroom to remain open. Luckily, he's prolific."

"Which implies your art studio will also be shuttered if he disappeared for a long haul," Sarah said.

"No one will rent me space as inexpensively as Nancy does. Plus, her showroom is a source of inspiration for my kids."

"So David Fodero isn't *your* painter, but the kids in your program are yours?"

Ashley grinned. "Every child is unique, and I love them all for their special talents and gifts."

She'd worked hard to make ends meet to provide for her students—whether it was brushes, soap, or an artist's table—and it was all worth it. Truly, she was blessed. She adored teaching kids and had shaped a satisfying career for herself.

"Maybe you can persuade David to donate funds for your art supplies." Sarah grabbed a chip. "He's certainly wealthy enough."

"If I can ever find him, I just might."

"Poor unsuspecting fellow." Sarah threw Ashley a smirk.

"He doesn't realize what he's in for. You don't put the brakes on until you achieve your goals."

"Poor unsuspecting, *mysterious* fellow," Ashley amended.

"It's odd no one has been able to reach him." Again, Sarah offered Ashley half her sandwich. At Ashley's refusal, Sarah happily finished it. "I wonder what happened."

"These genius artists are impossible. Nancy said he's very serious and oftentimes difficult. She walks on eggshells when she deals with him."

"I researched him on the internet." Sarah stood, indicating her break was over. "He is celebrated for his avant-garde portrayal of everyday subjects. Have you seen his *Woman by the River?*"

"That painting has been analyzed and torn apart by critics, though it's a fan favorite. When Nancy displayed it in her showroom, a student of mine, a nine-year-old girl with Down syndrome, continuously stared at it and smiled." Ashley's eyes welled. Her emotions, her affection for each precious child, brimmed inside her. "The girl didn't need any language to convey how she felt."

Sarah gave Ashley's hand a squeeze. "You care too much for people. You're eternally optimistic."

"I can't help it."

"That's why you're special. Don't ever change." Sarah retrieved the discarded wrappers and tossed them in the trash, along with their water bottles. Arm in arm, the women revisited the outside garden center before doubling back inside.

"For the record." Sarah's forehead furrowed. "I never figured out where the river actually was in David's painting."

"Neither did I."

"Who is the woman with the chestnut-brown hair in the corner?"

"Art enthusiasts have speculated about that for years. He's

been photographed with every leading actress on the planet. Perhaps the woman is one of them."

Ashley well remembered the day David Fodero had stridden into Nancy's showroom, the one and only time she ever saw him. He'd worn scruffy jeans and a casual navy-blue T-shirt. Yet he looked as handsome as when he'd been photographed wearing a black tuxedo at a glitzy fundraiser. His picture had been splashed on several society pages the following morning.

Nancy had confided he was growing tired of the endless social functions that demanded his attention, and he sought clean air and a calmer lifestyle in Cherish, a small Southern town not far from Greenwood.

Sarah gazed at the ceiling, as if David might miraculously appear. "He's drop-dead gorgeous, and every female on Earth wants to date him."

"Except you."

"I'm happily married to Max. But you're single."

"Yes." Ashley sighed. "Now and forever."

"Never say never." Sarah examined the African violet. Satisfied, she smiled. "Don't lose heart because of one failed relationship."

Don't lose heart.

What woman wouldn't lose heart after being dropped by a guy she'd dated on and off since college? Well-meaning acquaintances speculated she'd set the bar too high. Perhaps her ex couldn't live up to her expectations.

Which were what, exactly?

To show up when he promised her a date at the movies? To phone when he was out of town for long weekends?

Was there a man anywhere who was true to his word, a man who would sincerely care about her, and loved God as much as she did?

She shook off her reflections.

"I'm here on business to help Nancy." Ashley admired a particularly lush plant with cherry-red blossoms and considered buying it. However, she wasn't certain the plant would survive. Unlike her friend, her thumb was the opposite of green. "Nothing more."

"Unfortunate." Sarah sighed dramatically.

"Why?"

"You and David both like art. You couldn't ask for more."

"We're from two different orbits. He lives in New York City with a population of eight and a half million, while Greenwood has, what, five thousand residents?"

"Greenwood and Cherish are similar in size."

"A similarity we don't share with New York City." Ashley couldn't help a giggle. "It'll take more than art appreciation to ignite a spark between David and me. A distinguished painter and a woman who can't draw a stick figure to save her life isn't an ideal match."

"Perhaps." Sarah waggled her eyebrows.

Sarah, the incurable romantic. The women had shared a relaxed candor ever since they'd attended a friend's wedding five years earlier.

Bending, Sarah checked the water level of a particularly dry-looking violet. "David is better looking than your ex."

"Looks aren't everything."

"Looks are something."

"My ex is currently dating a knockout." Uttering the words aloud hurt, and Ashley pressed her lips together. "I saw them together at an upscale restaurant. Luckily, they didn't see me."

"You're a knockout too."

"Thank you." Ashley gnawed her bottom lip. Her ex had stripped away her self-confidence. In fact, he'd been cheating on her the entire time they'd dated. "However, I don't trust men anymore."

"All men?"

"Men in general."

"You enjoy reading romance novels."

"Those men are fictional."

"Never give up. Love will arrive when you least expect it." Sarah's tone was low and steady. "By the way, I discovered why David came to Cherish. Marge Addyson, the pastor of Memorial Street Church, commissioned him to paint a church portrait for their one-hundredth-anniversary celebration."

"And?"

"Last week, he was spotted on the church steps taking photos. Tall man with longish black hair, a trimmed beard, and crystal blue eyes, correct?"

"Yes. Or you could just say *brilliant and gorgeous*."

"Uh, huh. So I've heard."

Ashley belatedly pondered the wisdom of her description, although it was her first thought whenever she pictured him.

Sarah slid her a wise glance. "You know him better than any of the Cherish residents."

"I don't, because we never formally met. I only laid eyes on him for an instant when he appeared in Nancy's showroom to drop off a sketch. I was sitting on the floor of my adjacent studio, stenciling with an eleven-year-old boy. David glanced my way before he chatted with Nancy and gave me his legendary, wry smile."

"What did you do?"

"I smiled back, and we exchanged a friendly wave. His entire conversation with Nancy lasted all of five minutes before he dashed out the door."

She'd estimated he was several inches taller than her, which placed him at over six feet. Muscular and tanned, his physique contrasted sharply with her image of an artist—a thin, whiskered chap sporting a beret and wielding a paintbrush. David's broad shoulders and masculine features were a stark reminder he was light-years beyond her—a teacher who spent her days amidst classes of giggling children, hanging art pieces on austere gray walls while complimenting drawings of princess castles.

Ashley shifted from foot to foot. "Nancy just sold his last oil painting and is adamant about connecting with him."

Much as she wanted to help her friend, Ashley's search for David Fodero was self-serving. Her studio and a café owned by a friend were both connected to Nancy's bustling gallery—a setup that benefitted all three businesses. If any failed, all would be left on rocky financial ground.

Ashley and Sarah reentered the store part of the nursery and were hit with a blast of cold air. The whir of an air conditioner ensured customer comfort from the relentless seasonal heat.

"People say he stays to himself and lives out on the edge of town." Sarah grabbed a metal watering can and filled it with water from a hose. "When my husband went bird-watching at Juniper Mountain yesterday, he saw David standing by his easel near a grove of trees."

"Where is Juniper Mountain?"

Sarah reached in her pocket and pulled out a discarded receipt. Flipping it over, she drew a makeshift map. "The mountain is in the state park. Max hikes the Walnut Forest route."

"Is it difficult?"

"Aren't you an exercise fanatic?"

"Sure. On a treadmill."

"Walnut Forest isn't challenging. David told Max he welcomes the solitude of nature and seemed absorbed in whatever he was painting."

"He is a true artist." Goosebumps rose on Ashley's arms whenever she envisioned his paintings. She speculated about what inspired him to create his pieces—and why he chose certain textures and shades of colors, the scope of the canvases. "I wonder if he finished it."

His landscapes commanded thousands of dollars. It didn't matter what he painted. If patrons discovered his name signed on a canvas, they were willing to pay exorbitant sums.

"Trees, birds, and a pond were in the vicinity. I imagine those were in there somewhere." Sarah set down the watering can and began pruning a flamboyant-fuchsia flowering petunia. "Folks in town say he's polite, but his responses crackle the air like a broad band of heat lightning if someone dares to ask a personal question."

"He's known to be reclusive. Anything else?"

"I imagine Max led a painstaking description of all the birds in the park because he's the resident bird watcher." Sarah grinned. "But we all know how fiercely David guards his privacy, so few will infringe on that—not even talkative Max."

"Which may be why he hasn't answered any of Nancy's phone calls or texts for the past three months."

"He donated an oil landscape to Canine Helpers for their annual fundraiser—the cutest depiction of a dachshund who accompanies him everywhere." Sarah pulled dead leaves off the petunia. "At least, I think it's a dachshund in the painting. The dog's body is sketched in blue, and the ears are purple and red."

"Classic rebellious David." Ashley grinned. "Your information is appreciated."

"One more thing."

Ashley glanced at her watch. Sarah had been due to clock in ten minutes earlier. "I won't keep you any longer."

"No worries. I usually work overtime." Sarah brushed a piece of soil off her dark-green pants. "Max spoke with a park ranger who told him David purchased a dilapidated cabin a few miles outside the state grounds. He's been reno-vating it these past few months."

"That's where he's living? He bought a—Ashley made quote marks in the air—'dilapidated cabin'? He's not renting?"

"No. The cabin is on ten acres, bordered by state land on all three sides."

"What's the name of the road?"

"Pine Knoll Lane, and it's the only habitable property near the park." A wide smile crossed Sarah's face. "If you touch base with the ranger, he'll provide the general location. Although I warn you, solitude seems paramount to David."

"He's becoming a hermit."

"Right. So don't think you can just appear on his doorstep."

"I'm not here to marry him."

Sarah chuckled. "You're staying for the weekend, correct?"

"Yes. A substitute is teaching my Sunday school class." Ashley raked her hair from her forehead. "What time are the church services in town?"

"Memorial Street Church offers two services at 9:30 and 11:30. The pastors are outstanding, and the worship music is uplifting. I'll introduce you around if you attend."

"Count me in. I rented a room at the Cherish Hills Inn."

"Julian Wilson is the owner, and the church is a short walk from there. David drops by there for takeout meals, so maybe you'll meet him there."

"What are the odds? He may not stop in for another month." Ashley hesitated, then perked up. "Although a happy coincidence may occur."

Sarah frowned. "I've seen that look before. Are you up to something?"

"Have you ever heard the saying, if the mountain will not

come to Muhammad, then Muhammad will go to the mountain?"

"Sure. It means, if things don't go your way, then you change events so that they do."

Ashley tapped her fingers on a shelf stacked with clay pots. "Precisely."

"Are you Muhammad or the mountain?" Sarah tipped her head. "How can you run into someone who is rarely seen in public and doesn't answer his phone or email?"

"I'm whoever I need to be in order to locate him."

A foolproof plan had formulated. Well, perhaps the plan wasn't foolproof, but it was a start.

Her instincts shouted *no*. The plan was filled with the likelihood of failure, although she couldn't think of anything better.

She dismissed her reservations because her brain shouted yes.

Ashley was Muhammed. And Muhammed was going to the mountain.

CHAPTER 2

Art is a lie that makes us realize truth.
- Picasso

*D*avid had spent the entire day painting. Or, more accurately, attempting to paint.

He stood at his easel surrounded by oak trees, a jewel-like river bubbling in the distance. Shadows cast by the branches shielded him and his dog from the sun. He'd brought water for them both, in a thermos and doggie dish respectively, as well as an energy drink for himself.

New Yorkers who were accustomed to snow and temperatures below freezing weren't supposed to be fond of penetrating summer heat. Yet he relished everything about Cherish, including the weather. This quintessential Southern town was proving private and off-the-grid, boasting natural beauty and a sunny climate. In just a few months, he'd met more sincere, down-to-earth folks here than in his entire two decades in a large, impersonal city.

As the afternoon gave way to early evening, the sun glowed with a burning hue.

The golden hour. The hour most flattering. The light was diffused, the silhouettes intense.

"Red and soft and magical. Right Pickle?"

His dog looked up at him with shiny oval eyes and angled his head.

David grinned at his devoted dachshund, consistently in tune with him and his moods. Pickle's long, low body always seemed balanced, his black-and-copper coat smooth, his demeanor curious. Never farther than a few trots from his master, Pickle proved that adopting a dog from a pet rescue center was one of David's finest decisions.

He stood back from the easel to assess his work.

One tree.

Two endless weeks of sweat, countless energy drinks, and one tree.

What was he doing? Anyone could paint a tree. A child could paint a tree.

Just because he'd framed the tree in a garish-orange stained glass window didn't make it any better. Any more unique. There was a fine line between avant-garde and absolute nonsense.

He tossed down the last of his energy drink and regarded the river, the sun's rays glittering along the water's surface. Some days, the anger and sadness at his loss subsided, as he appreciated the splendor of his surroundings.

Not today.

His designs from earlier years had been described as radical and unorthodox, and he'd been acclaimed as a prodigy. Newer pieces were applauded because of his experimental approach to design and color.

When he'd first become recognized, he'd scoured every email and text he received, checked the tweets that mentioned him, holding out hope his older brothers would recognize his contribution to the art world. If they did, they hadn't bothered to inform him. And his father? Hardly a word of praise, even when David used to phone him on weekends. Their relationship had always been strained.

Once, he'd fantasized about moving back to the mid-sized city where he was born and purchasing the original homestead, just to prove he could. He'd amassed enough money with his art sales to buy the entire city. His livelihood was effectively guaranteed and predicted to become even more impressive.

But currently?

Though too soon to determine, he was certain he'd despise his latest piece when it was finished. Inspiring paintings didn't come easily anymore. In retrospect, they never had.

Neither did innovation. All artistry required direction, analysis, and exceptional ideas to execute, with a healthy dose of diligence and confidence.

He wanted to create pieces the artistic community had never seen before. He wanted to rescue his career. The sad truth was he hadn't liked anything he'd painted the past few months. Not since he'd woken up one morning, barely able to see out of his right eye.

He was an artist. This wasn't supposed to happen to an artist.

So what?

He had nothing left to prove. He'd accomplished every artistic milestone at a relatively young age.

The knowledge he could no longer paint anything worthwhile left him humbled and dispirited. He'd considered other art forms—perhaps picking up his oboe again or writing poetry—for fulfillment. Or purchasing another estate, or docking a yacht on an exclusive island, or escorting a starlet to a dazzling social gathering.

He couldn't bring himself to engage in any of those activities anymore. A part of him—ethics, morality, the boy who had once believed in God—was dejected by a shallow, affluent lifestyle.

So much for doctors. So much for irony. So much for God … taking away an artist's eyesight. What sense did that make?

"C'mon, Pickle." David grabbed his easel and paints, and then picked up his ten-pound dog, being sure to retrieve the dog's favorite toy—a plush, striped elephant.

David buckled Pickle into the dog car harness in the back seat of his crew-cab pickup truck. Then he buckled himself in the front seat and drove the short distance to his cabin. He had no trouble driving. Just as his ophthalmologist had predicted, David's brain had adjusted to compensate for the loss of depth perception.

"You'll be fine," the doctor had assured him.

Right. What, exactly, described *fine*?

Claude Monet, the French Impressionist painter, suffered from cataracts, and his eyesight had been impaired as he aged. He'd complained of foggy vision and undergone surgery. His paintings had changed as a result of the deterioration.

David certainly shouldn't compare himself to Monet, but he recognized his work was shifting—and not for the better.

He pulled his truck into the gravel driveway of his home and regarded the remote area and vast acreage. His cabin was concealed from the road by thick woods.

Rustic, yet remarkably well-appointed following David's renovations, the cabin offered an ideal retreat. The timbered ceiling was braced by beams of weathered cedar, and a spiral staircase led to a bedroom loft, which offered a panoramic view of forest and mountains. On a vibrant, sunny day, the scene was magnificent.

He kicked off his shoes as soon as he entered. The hours ahead promised peaceful solitude and reflection. In winter, a crackling fire in the massive stone fireplace would be a requirement. For a June evening in the Carolinas, he'd opt for a riveting adventure thriller audiobook, while he and his dog settled in his favorite chair, a redwood armchair. He prized the exposed rustic tree knots and polished design.

In former years, devotions to God would have highlighted his reflections, as well as Bible study. He especially enjoyed reading from the Old Testament. When despondent, he had absorbed the poetic, inspiring psalms that described God's love and mercy. The words had entered him like an inspirational melody.

Those were days long past.

God had taken too much away. As a result, he maintained a distant relationship with God. His plea for help had never been answered.

David's foundation was gone, his faith unfocused.

The feeble protest of his conscience to utter a prayer, any prayer, fell by the wayside.

With a harsh sigh, he gazed out the living room's front bay window. Flecks of dust danced in the pitch of afternoon sunlight. The windowpanes needed dusting.

Aware of the fleeting minutes, David regarded the plot of land he considered ideal for a garden. He'd never tended soil. Perhaps now he would. A garden offered order to the forest, direction for his thoughts.

He scratched his temple. What vegetables and flowers grew under a fierce summer sun? Was June too late in the season for planting?

His deliberations drifted to work and obligations.

Tomorrow, he'd begin sketching the commissioned

painting of Memorial Street Church he'd agreed to finish by summer's end. He'd taken various photographs of the church's white painted exterior, ornate wooden doors and high-arched windows, from different angles.

He threw an ironic glance at his reflection. How could he complete a project he hadn't begun? Procrastination wasn't his style, though with a few words, the ophthalmologist's diagnosis had altered everything.

David's optic nerve to his right eye wasn't getting enough blood. He was slowly going blind.

AN HOUR LATER, after a quick shower and dressed in his usual T-shirt and jeans, he situated himself on a bench facing the tree painting. He couldn't help himself, couldn't stay away from painting. Pickle sat on a woven wool rug, his striped elephant beside him.

A tap on the door brought David and Pickle to their feet.

No one visited. No one, thankfully, knew exactly where he lived.

With an irritated shake of his head and the dog at his heels, he padded to the entry.

A slight, dainty woman stood on the porch steps, dark glasses covered her eyes, her blond hair swinging from a side part and spilling to her shoulders. Wayward, shiny strands drifted across her cheek. Dappled sunlight shone through towering pine trees, and shadows formed on the ground. Somewhere, the fluttering of unseen wings broke the silence.

Her figure was slender. The thought came to mind that a strong windstorm could blow her off her feet.

"Hi." Her voice was bright and breezy, resembling her appearance.

"May I help you?" He opened the door wider. "If you're selling cookies, I'm not buying."

"Who said I was selling cookies?"

"You don't look any older than a university student."

"Do university students sell cookies?"

"For fundraisers, I suppose."

She paused. "Do you have any?"

"University students?" He glanced over his shoulder. "Nope."

"Funny. Not."

"Oh, you're referring to cookies." He surveyed her from the top of her smooth forehead down to her manicured toes, peeking out from strappy sandals. She wore slim-fitting jeans and a green floral blouse. Her complexion was healthy, a sun-kissed tan along her cheeks and the bridge of her freckled nose.

He grinned. "I stored a couple boxes of cookies in my freezer."

"What kind?"

"Chocolate with a creamy-white filling."

Her generous lips pulled into a smile. "My favorite. I have it on reliable authority most cookies thaw quickly, though I've often eaten them frozen."

He patted his stomach. "I've inhaled half a box in one sitting."

"Frozen?"

"Microwaved."

Inwardly, he shook his head. They were actually discussing cookies. If this was considered lighthearted conversation, it felt foreign. He had forgotten the pleasure of conversing with a lovely, quick-witted woman.

She slid the dark glasses down her nose. Huge, hazel-green eyes flicked him a glance.

A shadow of a smile crossed her lips. He wasn't sure why.

With an about-face, she gestured toward a blue Chevy

convertible parked in front of his cabin. "Unfortunately, I'm stranded."

"I'm sorry. Trouble with your car, ma'am?"

"Miss." She plucked off her glasses and perched them on her head.

They locked gazes.

Time stood still.

He wasn't an overly emotional guy, yet feelings that hardly made sense bombarded him. Attraction, an instant connection, a familiarity he couldn't explain.

"My convertible stalled, and my cell phone battery is dead." Her statement sounded far away, and he dragged his mind to attention.

"I'd offer assistance." He scanned the road. "Regrettably, my skills as a mechanic are sorely lacking." *They were, in fact, nonexistent.*

"May I use your phone to call a friend? I don't intend to drive these deserted roads at night. The curves are difficult to navigate."

He peered outside. The sky was etched in pinks and grays. Dusk set slowly in the Carolinas, and darkness wouldn't occur for another hour. "You're on Pine Knoll Lane. I'm surprised you made it this far without realizing there's no outlet. Loop around, and you'll connect with the state park entrance in a few miles."

"Once my car is running again." Her tone was easygoing, her smile angelic. "My sense of direction is faultless, though I obviously lost my way."

"Obviously." He shifted. Why was he thinking this woman was special? He didn't even know her. "If you're looking for a tree-lined residential street, head to Cherish. There's nothing of interest on this road."

"There are lots of things of interest." She caught his stare, then turned to peer at the deserted road. "I planned to hike Grandfather Mountain today."

"Isn't Grandfather Mountain in North Carolina?"

"Oh."

Oh? She was in the wrong state?

"I'm a mountain climber."

She certainly didn't look like a mountain climber, and she didn't know her mountains very well, either. Where was her backpack, and why wasn't she wearing sturdy shoes caked with mud? Her sandals were white and clean.

No business of his. Perhaps her gear was packed in her car.

Still, why hike at dusk?

He watched her in silence. Soon she'd be on her way. The sensations that raced through him, that instant flare of attraction, would soon disappear.

"May I use your phone?" she repeated.

"Certainly. C'mon inside. I left my phone in the kitchen."

"Thanks." She offered a helpless laugh. "I hope I'm not putting you out."

He glanced at his canvas by the window and reminded himself that people were more important than work. He strove to achieve balance, although it wasn't easy.

"You're not putting me out at all." He led her into the living room. The worn hardwood floors creaked beneath their feet, and he motioned to the L-shaped sofa. He suspected the sofa hailed from the 1960s, judging from the plaid pattern and velvet armrests, but it was clean and homey and comfortable. He hadn't replaced all the furniture yet. Likewise, he hadn't gotten around to a kitchen remodel.

Pickle trotted beside them and sniffed the woman's sandals. Quickly surmising she was a friend, he brought his striped elephant close to her and flopped on his back for a belly rub. She accommodated him while cooing that he was the cutest dog in the county. Judging from the dog's rapturous pose, her compliment delighted him.

"Adorable." She nodded at the elephant.

"His favorite toy."

"I've never owned a dog."

David looked at her as if she'd uttered a statement entirely foreign to him.

"I can't," she explained. "I've fantasized forever about adopting one, but my apartment is tiny, and I spend most of my days and evenings at my studio teaching." She smiled. "I love animals, though."

"Visit your local rescue center, adopt a miniature chihuahua, and bring the dog with you to your studio."

"Helpful advice." Her smile faltered. "Perhaps someday."

"Someday." David glanced from her to Pickle.

"You can't beat a pet to combat loneliness." She went on rubbing Pickle's stomach. "Animals help humans reconnect with nature. Some say dogs are God's messengers because they grant us grace."

"Pickle is a significant part of my life. He's my comrade."

She looked up at him, her gaze sparkling. "Pets are extraordinary."

He nodded in agreement and headed for the kitchen. "Extraordinary, indeed."

He reached in the freezer for a box of cookies and decided on bottled water instead.

Retracing his steps into the living room, he asked, "You're not from around here?"

"No."

He had assumed she'd be sitting on the sofa, rubbing Pickle's belly.

She wasn't.

Pickle was snuggled in his doggie bed by the fireplace. She stood facing David's unfinished tree painting.

She refused his offer of hospitality by shaking her head at the water and gestured to the painting. There hadn't been graffiti on the tree, although he'd added it, enhancing the graffiti in bold purple letters. The blue sky, devoid of clouds, conveyed a curious juxtaposition against the solemn moss-green grass. Carrot stained-glass windows stood out sharply in the background.

She surveyed the canvas. "Is this a happy or sad painting?"

He set the water bottles on the coffee table, noting she hadn't answered his earlier question about where she was from.

"Paintings don't have feelings."

"People do."

He clasped his hands. "I haven't decided."

"About people's feelings or the painting?"

He didn't reply. Instead, he handed her the phone and provided her with the local mechanic's number.

"Thanks." She focused on the canvas. "All your paintings bring up complicated emotions."

"All? How do you—?" She must be an art enthusiast who recognized his work. He was obliged for the support, though lately he couldn't muster any sentiments—gratefulness, productiveness, motivation. Everything he'd taken for granted had evaporated when he'd received his eyesight diagnosis.

She wandered away with his phone to her ear, muttered a few sentences, then disconnected. "I called my friend who can repair anything that goes wrong with a car."

Already feeling useless as an artist as well as a mechanic, David murmured, "Good." If he were one of his brothers, he would've dashed to her car, yanked the appropriate tools from his pickup, and fixed the problem for her.

He wasn't that kind of man, though. He'd never been mechanical.

Left brain, right brain, he theorized. He was the opposite of a methodical thinker. His right-brain dominance made him creative, prone to day-dreaming, intuition, and visualization.

"No tools here beyond a couple screwdrivers and a hammer." He shrugged. "My truck is loaded with canvases, watercolors, and an easel."

"No worries. Everyone can't be a pro at everything."

"Your worldview theory?"

"I look at life through God's perspective."

Noncommittally, he shook his head. "Whatever works for you."

She peered at him. "You sound like you're hard on yourself. Are you?"

"Not enough to be psychoanalyzed in my own living room."

"Right." She chewed her lower lip. "So, my friend will be here soon."

The longer he gazed at her, the more familiarity niggled, though he couldn't place her. Her blond hair was a hundred shades of gold. Those startling hazel eyes seemed to change from green to brown at will. Doe-eyed. Perceptive and luminous.

He cleared his throat. These intense feelings roused recollections of his teenage years over two decades earlier.

He bent to go after a paintbrush lodged under the sofa. "How long?"

"Hmm?" She stepped closer to his canvas.

"How long?" he repeated.

"How long what?"

He stood. "How long before your friend arrives?"

"Not long." She laser-focused on the painting. "This tree really is magnificent."

"You figured out it was a tree?"

"Yes. Is that good news or bad news?"

"For an avant-garde artist, I'd consider it bad news."

She folded her hands behind her back, peering at the landscape. A clear invasion of his privacy. Then she fixated on the rusted coffee can on the fireplace mantel.

"Quite an unusual decoration," she noted.

"Thanks." He searched for an explanation and decided on none.

"And the redwood chair in the corner is … rustic."

"I moved it here from my Manhattan apartment." He set the paintbrush in a bucket. "I helped create the design."

"Is it comfortable to sit on with all that wood jutting out all over the place?"

He smiled. "Chair pads soften the experience."

"The sitting experience."

He chuckled. "Correct." He couldn't stop drinking in the sight of her slim figure. Her jeans hugged her curves to perfection.

What? He gave himself a mental shake. He was seeking a laid-back lifestyle without complications. Perhaps then he'd be inspired to paint something worthwhile.

She concentrated on the coffee can. "Is there an artistic significance in that?"

"Maybe." He crossed his arms, narrowed his gaze.

"Is the living room your studio?"

"This room gets the most favorable light in the house since it faces north."

Canvases slanted against the walls, wrong side out. She gestured to them. "Do you ever show your work?"

"No." True enough since he'd moved to Cherish.

"Why not? You should paint often and sell everything."

To dissuade her from asking any more questions, he flashed her a frown. "Look miss, I don't even know your name."

Not losing a beat, she held out her hand. "Ashley Madden."

He tilted his head to the side. In some way, the name was recognizable too.

He took her hand and shook. Her fingers were fragile and delicate, sending a warm tingle through him.

Indeed? For a woman's hand? He really needed to get out more.

"David Fodero," he replied.

Admiration shone in her gaze. "Hello, David."

"Likewise, Ashley."

She arched her graceful blond eyebrows. *"Likewise?* Quite the introduction."

"I'm not known for flowery words. What I meant was ..." His formal upbringing kicked into gear. "My pleasure."

He assumed he'd let go of her hand, but peering down, he realized he hadn't.

"My friend should be here within a half hour." Ashley continued their earlier conversation as if no lapse had occurred, then dropped her hand. "I assume that's okay?"

Did he have a choice? "Of course."

"Why not?"

He took a sip of water. "I'm not following." Clearly, this woman shifted topics with the speed of a tornado.

"Why not show your pieces? Your art is thought provoking."

Respect threaded her tone. He recognized it, appreciated it, but couldn't respond except for a nonchalant, "My work isn't good enough."

"You're joking, right? Surely you don't believe such a thing."

"It's my opinion, which is the only opinion that matters."

He indicated they should sit, and they chose either ends of the sofa. She was silent. He was well aware she had set aside her curiosity and inquiries about his paintings because of his blunt reply.

"I have iced tea in the fridge." His statement broke through the silence. "Care for a glass?"

"No, thank you." She shot him a measured smile across the breadth of the sofa. "I prefer sugary soda."

"I'm an energy-drink guy."

"I noticed." She darted a glance at the empty cans in the wastebasket near his bench.

His brain faltered for something else to say. He wasn't chatty—unless discussing art or photography—and lately even those subjects made him uncomfortable.

He gazed around the room for a way to restore their earlier banter because he regretted the loss. Playfully and without thinking, he tossed a fringed throw pillow at her.

She let out a startled shriek. The dog leaped up, barked, and circled the table. The friendly mood returned as Ashley laughed and threw the pillow back at him.

"Don't you dare!" She held up a hand to fend off another throw.

"Give up?" He stood and swung the pillow back and forth. "What's a little pillow fight to a seasoned mountain climber?"

"You're right. You win." She switched an innocent smile on him before grabbing another pillow from the sofa.

A knock brought their hands to their sides. Ashley tidied the pillows they'd disarranged. With her pink cheeks and a sparkle in her eyes, she created a fetching picture.

"Now who might that be?" He rubbed his chin. "Someone else selling cookies?"

She grinned, peeked out the window, and waved. "I'll get it."

"Be my guest," he mumbled with wry courtesy.

Her laughter rang out as she opened the door. An auburn-haired woman stepped inside.

"David Fodero, meet Sarah Archer," Ashley said. "She's my handy repair person."

A woman.

Sarah offered a hello and took a step back. Reserved and a bit shy, he mused.

"All set, Twinkle," she said to Ashley.

Twinkle? David opened his mouth to inquire about the name, but Ashley ignored him.

Sarah mumbled something about a mysterious engine part, and Ashley responded by using sign language.

Wait. Ashley's friend was deaf?

Sarah offered him an abashed smile. "I'm losing my hearing. I denied it for ages, until my husband, Max, prodded me to confront my fears and visit an audiologist. I believe you met him at the state park."

"The birdwatcher who always wears a bow tie?"

"Yes." Sarah smiled. "Now that I've adjusted, my hearing aid is a blessing, along with signing."

He turned to Ashley. "You know sign language?"

"I run an art studio that's attached to a couple other businesses, one being a café." Ashley reached for her water bottle. "A waitress who works there is deaf."

"You own a business?"

"Yes, for handicapped students. I cared for my dad when I was young and missed a lot of school. I fell behind and the teachers labeled me as a slow learner. After a while, I quit trying. Then I met a wonderful mentor, and he was an inspiration. From then on, I vowed to help others." She waved a dismissive hand. "More information about me than you would ever possibly want."

"No, not at all." He was still reeling from this personal insight about her. "Is your studio in Cherish?"

"No."

More questions came to mind.

Before he could inquire, Ashley gestured to Sarah. "My friend has the greenest thumb on the planet."

He considered congratulating Ashley for another rapid subject change. Instead, he remarked to Sarah, "I've contemplated planting a garden."

"I work at Thumbs Up, the nursery in town." She pulled a business card from the back pocket of her jeans and handed it to him. "Give me a call."

"Thanks." He pocketed the card and glimpsed the two women, a little unnerved at the smile that passed between them.

Sarah eyed his dog, who had permanently attached himself to Ashley. Crouching, she rubbed his stomach. It was amazing what dogs did for a belly rub.

Sarah glanced up at him. "What type of plants are you interested in?"

"Whatever will grow in this hot sun."

"I recommend zucchini and squash and carrots."

"Sugar-coated carrots are delicious," Ashley chimed in.

"All my favorites," he joked, then sobered. "I'm sorry. I'm not sure how to converse with you, Sarah. I never studied sign language."

She stood. "I read lips and understand you perfectly."

"Are you a musician?" He perched his hip on the edge of the redwood chair.

Both women frowned in confusion, and he immediately regretted his words. But Sarah's disability had made him think of his own—although it was constantly on his mind anyway—and he'd wondered if she was an artist too.

"My husband plays harmonica and is in a band with my uncle," Sarah answered. "Why?"

Were they really discussing musicians? Yes, and he had initiated it.

He peeked at Ashley. This woman knew hardly anything about him, yet he sensed her interest in his answer.

His muscles tightened. He was up for the challenge.

"Beethoven suffered from deafness." He picked up his water bottle and rolled it between his hands. "Any theories why that would've happened to him?"

Ashley regarded him with a sideways glance. "I'm not certain."

"I assume you'll lay it on God. That He works in mysterious ways."

"Often, He does." She stood straighter. "Faith is fragile. Faith takes time. Hold on to faith when there's too much of life and too little of you."

"Is that what Beethoven did?"

"I don't know."

He sighed heavily. "Therefore, according to you, I should take a step toward believing in God."

"God is always working on a solution."

How had this become a theological discussion?

"Then tell me this," he challenged. "Is a musician losing his hearing comparable to a painter losing his eyesight?"

He saw the shock in Ashley's eyes, knew when the impact of his words struck her.

She pressed a hand to her lips. "David, is there anything—?"

In the soundless aftershocks, he kept his features bland and didn't answer. He'd revealed too much already and hoped she wouldn't read into his response.

"David Fodero is going blind?" Ashley whispered to Sarah as soon as they left David's cabin. The women stepped along a stone path and hastened to their cars. Rather than broaching the subject further, Ashley had opted to remain silent. Sarah had wordlessly agreed. Besides, he'd quickly banished any questions by his cool response. Or rather, lack of response.

"He wasn't necessarily referring to himself," Sarah said.

"Of course he was." Ashley tried not to appear as troubled as she felt. The pride stamped on his face, the jut of his chin, declared that David Fodero wasn't the type of man who resigned himself to his fate. Yet there was a profound sadness in his eyes. "Who else might he be referring to? Van Gogh?"

"I thought Van Gogh was supposed to be color blind."

"Judging from David's voice, he was referring to his own disability. I want to help him find a solution."

"Your infinite optimism is surfacing again." Sarah inclined her head toward the cabin, then at Ashley. "You constantly try to solve other people's problems. Rest and leave it to God."

The air was eerily stagnant, the sun beginning its descent as Ashley and Sarah hugged each other goodbye. As soon as she reached her car, Ashley leaned her head against the door to collect herself. Her chest knotted at the awareness of David's blindness. Despite his attempts to sound casual, his expression and deep voice had revealed raw emotion.

Now she knew the reason why he hadn't responded to Nancy's emails, phone calls or texts. Ashley's heart missed a beat at the image of his troubled, handsome face. The consequences of his disability plagued her long after she'd retired to Cherish Hills Inn for the evening.

She sat on the cozy white comforter on her bed, drew up her legs, and wrapped her arms around her knees.

He wasn't blind *now*. He'd looked at Ashley as if he saw her with no trouble. He didn't seem to encounter any difficulty moving from room to room. And he obviously still painted.

His depiction of the tree was wonderful. Different from

his earlier works, this canvas was darker, more melancholy. According to well-informed art critics, David's talent was phenomenal, an unstoppable force that had shaken up the art world.

She couldn't make that sort of judgment. She simply respected his talent and skill, his distinctive portrayals of nature and everyday life expressed his recognizable style.

In Greenwood, she was on a mission to make a difference, providing an art platform for handicapped children.

In David's case, surely his condition could be treated by a skilled physician.

And prayer.

CHAPTER 3

Art washes away from the soul the dust of everyday life.
- Picasso

*S*unday, Ashley rose early and breakfasted in the inn's solarium. The room had been recently added onto the original building, a hostess explained. Benefitting from the natural light, the lavender paint on the window trim and the pops of greenery, along with white wicker tables and chairs, completed the cheery environment.

The breakfast offerings included fluffy French toast drenched in pure maple syrup and black coffee that Ashley doused with sugar and cream. All served by Samantha, a pleasant young waitress with ice-blue eyes and dark hair. She worked during her summer break from college, she explained to Ashley. Her father was the owner.

"No work-out room?" Ashley asked, scanning a colorful pamphlet with descriptions of the inn's services.

"Sure, we do." Samantha gestured toward the hallway. "Complete with a weight machine and treadmills."

Ashley made a mental note to exercise the following day.

As she watched the comings and goings of other diners, she focused on how next to approach David.

The prior evening had gone as planned. She'd found him at his cabin.

Her breath had caught at how good-looking he was—wearing jeans and a white T-shirt that clung to his wide shoulders. His hair was rumpled, his strong jawline appealingly stubbled. He'd padded barefoot through the living room, his strides long and purposeful, and he'd been welcoming, inviting her to make herself comfortable.

She'd felt a strong attraction to him, a pull she couldn't deny.

With a nervous lungful of air, she'd seized the chance to study his one visible painting when he went into the kitchen for his phone. Of course, she hadn't needed to phone Sarah, and a tinge of remorse for her deception tightened her stomach.

Soon, she'd reveal to David the real reason she'd come to Cherish. She'd also acknowledge she was mechanically inclined and could've fixed her own car if something had actually gone wrong.

She attributed her self-reliance to her father. He'd raised her as a single parent and made certain she could take care of herself. He had also been a devoutly religious man, frequently reminding her that God knew her life from beginning to end—and to release any burdens she carried to God.

She'd vowed to pass her father's teachings along and did what she could to minister to other people.

A peaceful determination swept through her, banishing any reservations and leaving her mind sharper. She was here for a reason.

Yes, to help Nancy. But something more.

God's hand was imperceptible, but He was never idle.

That flutter of excitement? The butterflies in her stomach when she and David had locked gazes? She dismissed it as a passing attraction.

Nevertheless, her reaction confused her. She couldn't get him out of her mind.

She drained her coffee and left the restaurant with a fast-paced stride, phoning her two part-time employees and asking them to cover her for the upcoming week.

She stopped at the lobby and extended her stay, then walked the few blocks to Memorial Street Church. Sunday mornings were meant for more than a leisurely breakfast and steaming coffee. Sunday mornings were meant for reverence and allowing God to provide a path. Specific details? They weren't needed. All that was needed was trust.

AFTER BEING SEATED for dinner at the inn's restaurant later that evening, Ashley spotted a painting on the wall. The landscape—wildflowers, trees and water—seemed to be in David Fodero's familiar signature style. The colorful wild-flowers were upside down, the bubbling river noticeable only if an observer looked closely. David's brushwork was detailed, his design abstract.

She was so lost in thoughts of him, it took a few seconds for her to realize the owner had approached her table.

"Complex, isn't it?" Julian Wilson, a tall man with gray eyes, held a silver water pitcher. He eyed David's painting as he filled her glass.

"Thanks." Mesmerized, she perched her chin on her hands to continue to stare at the painting, then turned to him.

She'd spoken with Julian on several occasions when she'd

made her reservation. He was always pleasant and helpful and seemed able to accomplish numerous tasks with ease.

"Distinctly David Fodero," they remarked at the same time.

"David doesn't title his artworks." Julian pointed to the top of the canvas.

"He used to, probably for cataloguing and sales purposes." She dismissed Julian's observation with a shrug. "Not anymore, though. His art is so unique people recognize his work immediately."

"Notice the dog." Julian set the pitcher on her table and edged his finger along the strong lines of a tiny dachshund in the upper right-hand corner.

"David inserts minute details a casual observer might miss." Ashley folded the cloth napkin on her lap. "However, the bold yellow and orange tints of the wildflowers stand out."

"He pushes boundaries. When I first saw his work, he was painting everyday objects and enhancing them."

"Such as?"

"The sides of a barn painted lime green. Daffodils were growing out of the roof."

"He still paints the everyday objects, only now his paintings are more intricate."

Julian hesitated. "You're an artist?"

"No." Ashley smiled at his question. "I own an art studio for handicapped children in Greenwood. My studio is connected to a café and an art gallery run by a friend. She has sold quite a few of David's works, including his lithographs."

"He moved to Cherish a few months ago, but I haven't seen much of him. When we talk, I brag about the advantages of living in a close-knit town where faith emboldens the residents."

Ashley grinned. "What's his response?"

"He replies with a noncommittal shrug." Julian brushed an invisible speck off her linen tablecloth. "All we can provide is prayer and trust God to show David the right direction."

"I've perfected worrying, and I worry about David."

"Why?"

"He's remarkably talented. Maybe too talented." She paused, frowning at her reply, conscious it made no sense. She chose not to divulge David's vision loss in case Julian was unaware.

He studied the painting further. "Everyone in the community is thrilled he decided to live here."

"An acclaimed artist who fled the center of the art universe when he reached the pinnacle of his career."

"New York City's loss. Cherish's gain."

Her server set down her appetizer, which had been recommended—sweet and sour meatballs.

Ashley bowed her head to say grace, then helped herself to a meatball. "Delicious." She dabbed a smear of sweet sauce from her chin.

"All the credit goes to Melissa, our magnificent cook. Her secret ingredient is orange marmalade." Julian threw a satisfied glance toward the kitchen. "I understand David hasn't completely cut his ties to New York. He still owns a penthouse on Central Park."

Ashley nodded. "I remember seeing photos. Glass-wrapped and two full floors, with a whopping eight thousand square feet of space."

Julian glanced at the New York guidebook Ashley had set on the table. "Have you ever visited Manhattan?"

"Never, though it's on my list of places to see."

"If David felt the need for a change of scenery, I guess it makes sense that he decided to buy a cabin here. I hear he did extensive renovations. Rumor is the place is a stunner."

She nodded. Her lips quirked in a smile. What she'd seen of David's place was stunning, with a distinctly masculine vibe.

"Once in a while," Julian added, "he breezes in for a takeout meal."

"He never dines in the restaurant?"

"No." Julian turned to an unoccupied table, fine-tuning the glassware. "He seems a good guy the few times we've spoken. He's generous to the shopkeepers and an excellent tipper. He donated his artwork to various businesses including a silent auction for Canine Helpers, a volunteer organization that supports veterans, and his piece raised thousands of dollars. When word of his contributions spread, tourism will surely increase."

"Which would be great for Cherish. It's such a quaint and charming town."

"I agree. I first came here a few years ago to supervise the opening of a new restaurant. I expected to stay only a few months, but I ended up meeting the woman of my dreams. Now, we're married and I'm helping raise Samantha, my precocious stepdaughter. She recently turned twenty."

"I met her at breakfast. She is lovely."

"She is musically talented, as well." Julian beamed, then fired a glance at a waitress displaying an assortment of desserts to an older couple who hadn't yet finished their meal.

"What's the name of the new restaurant?" Ashley bit into another meatball, savoring the tasty blend.

"Fresh 'n' Good, and it isn't new anymore. You may have seen the building." Julian's gaze swung to another waitress who attempted to balance too many entrees on a single tray. He stepped over to assist.

"I haven't had time to explore the town," Ashley said when he returned, "although I'm familiar with the chain."

"The restaurant is near the train station and was a former shoe store. I like to think we're friendly competition. Keeps both of our restaurants on our toes." He grinned. "Get it? Toes? Shoes?"

"Clever." Ashley laughed and turned toward the enormous picture window overlooking the street. The night sky glowed with the lights from the town. Traffic was easy—a brown Jeep and an old-fashioned Volkswagen drove by. At the intersection was a gas station attached to a bustling diner. When she had checked in the day before, Julian had told her that men sat there for hours solving the world's troubles, and coffee was poured nonstop.

"The town is growing, yet Cherish remains a faithful community honoring God," Julian said. He gave her an inquisitive glance. "What brings you here, besides the wonderful accommodations, religion, and delicious food?"

She grinned. "Wonderful accommodations?"

He actually puffed out his chest. "Tried, tested, and true."

She smirked. "Sarah Archer and I met at a mutual friend's wedding a few years ago."

"I know her and her husband well."

"We stay in touch through phone calls and emails and wanted to catch up in person."

There was more, a lot more, but Ashley couldn't divulge anything else to this gracious innkeeper.

"Samantha and I play a game." Julian shifted their conversation. "Whenever we see a David Fodero original, we try to describe it in two words."

"You narrow his complicated pieces down to two words?" Ashley considered the idea, staring down at her water glass. "It's not possible."

"Sure it is. My turn first. Radical and imaginative."

"Not fair. You've had loads of practice." She lifted her glass to salute him. "Scenic and surreal."

"Excellent." He reached for the water pitcher and waved down a waitress balancing another dessert tray. "David painted that landscape when he first moved to town and brought it here one afternoon. He insisted I hang it wherever I wished."

"And you wished to hang it on a prominent wall in your restaurant."

"Why not? I'm a businessman and publicity is publicity." Julian grinned, held up a hand to the waitress and mouthed, "I'm coming."

Ashley nodded at the painting. "Where is the place David painted?"

"Close. So close, in fact, you can walk there. When you reach Memorial Street Church, go a little farther and you'll see an abandoned rail line bordered by a river."

"I'll check it out."

"Are you an art lover?"

She contemplated her answer, choosing to be 100 percent honest. "Actually, I'm the planet's most enthusiastic fan."

Especially of David Fodero, she amended to herself.

CHAPTER 4

Inspiration does exist, but it must find you working.
- Picasso

When the sun rose the following morning, Ashley considered checking out the work-out room, but then decided to wait another day. Instead, she showered and washed her hair with lemon-scented shampoo, then chose a pair of cotton tie-dyed shorts and a chambray button-up top. After a quick breakfast to spoon a container of yogurt and drink a cup of sugary coffee, she exited the inn. She couldn't resist pausing on the front porch to rock back and forth on one of the inn's wide-slatted rocking chairs before heading to the town square.

She picked up a basket of ripe peaches from the farmer's market, inhaling whiffs of buttered popcorn and spun sugar, and treated herself to an herbal lavender tea served in a miniature paper cup.

She decided to bring the peaches to David's cabin as a

gesture of gratitude for his hospitality. Sure, it was an excuse to speak with him further, though she couldn't explain away the urge to see him again so soon.

David. She smiled just thinking about him.

Polite but distant, he'd offered to help with her car. She well remembered the quirk of his dark eyebrows when he'd remarked on Grandfather Mountain being located in North Carolina. His chuckle had been deep, holding good-natured amusement.

She must come clean with him, and soon. Still, she hesitated. She suspected David didn't appreciate dishonesty.

Slow. Think it through. Use finesse. And pray.

She tramped back to the inn, then drove to the town's outskirts. Following the exit that led to the state park, she soon sighted Pine Knoll Lane. She parked in front of David's cabin and followed the stepping-stone path to the door.

With a rapid knock, she called out, "Anyone home?"

She peered around. No dog bark from Pickle, and David's green pickup truck wasn't in the driveway. She peeked through the expansive bay window. The living room looked the same—neat and orderly, with assorted canvases, paints, brushes, and a metal tray stacked and sorted.

She tried the handle, surprised when the door opened. Fearful the fruit wouldn't tolerate the heat well, she set the basket on the foyer floor. A glimpse of the distinctive redwood chair prompted her to peek further inside.

The entryway led to the living room. Beyond, a full bathroom and a study. A wooden desk was cluttered with art books, and a laptop computer sat closed. A layer of dust begged for a housekeeper, and she had the sense he must employ someone once in a while. As she doubled back to the living room, a sleek black metal spiral staircase beckoned.

No. Too personal.

Should she? She twisted her hands, then craned her neck

upward. No, she shouldn't, but she couldn't resist. Quickly, she mounted the steps. An upstairs bedroom boasted a double bed with a wood paneled headboard and brown tweed comforter set. The air smelled of him—sandalwood and pine.

The room was neat and clean, the exception being a pair of jeans and a T-shirt draped over the bed. An elaborate sound system took up one corner, and a stack of audiobooks stood on a nearby shelf.

Odd that a man who painted such abstract art chose traditional décor for his personal space. It didn't fit his narrative, although nothing about David surprised her.

She retraced her steps downstairs, and the kitchen proved a shocker. Despite the meticulous renovations throughout the cabin, this room appeared untouched, as if taken straight from her grandmother's era.

She returned to the front door and grabbed a scrap of paper and a pen from her purse.

Sorry I missed you! I stopped by to thank you for the use of your phone. I hope to catch up with you soon.

Ashley Madden

She skimmed the note. Ugh. Had she mentioned her last name when she'd introduced herself at his cabin? She couldn't remember.

Was the wording too forward? And what about the exclamation mark? She *was* sorry she missed him, but she didn't want him to suspect how much.

Well, she couldn't wipe out her message and begin again, as with an email. The note would have to suffice. She placed it with the peaches, closed the front door, and walked along the gravel driveway back to her car.

In the town center a while later, she wandered through the appealing boutiques, thrilled to discover David Fodero originals—quirky, fun and bold—in nearly every shop.

The owners all recounted the same tale when she inquired about the small canvases. David requested they not sell them but were free to display them. The paintings were gifts because he was pleased to be part of a caring community.

In Musically Yours, a music store in town, Ashley introduced herself to Dorothy Edwards, the owner. She was a spunky woman with emerald-green eyes and a slim figure. Dorothy was a pianist and her husband, Ryan, an opera singer.

"Please attend our outdoor concerts in the village park this summer." Dorothy gestured to a bulletin board tacked with the town's events.

"I'm only in Cherish for the week. I'm visiting."

"What brings you here?"

"A friend. You may know Sarah Archer?"

"Certainly. This is a tiny community. Her husband sings and plays harmonica in our church." Dorothy bobbed toward a mountain of sheet music on the counter. "The latest hymn arrangements just came in."

"I teach art to children, and also teach Sunday school."

"Art and music are closely related." The continuously busy Dorothy moved on to arrange a display of Percy Grainger statues, explaining that the store was celebrating the composer's birthday all month.

"I've never heard of him," Ashley confessed.

"Many people haven't, which is why we're spotlighting him. He was born in Australia and became an American citizen. Listen to his arrangements, especially 'Seventeen Come Sunday,' an English folk song. Or, his piano rendition of 'Country Gardens.' You'll recognize the tune."

Ashley's gaze returned to David's canvas behind the counter. "Outstanding. I can identify his paintings immediately."

"He presented the painting to me as a gift when he first moved here," Dorothy said as she filed a pile of Percy Grainger posters. "I got the impression he was subtly giving a message—he valued friendship but didn't want his privacy breached."

"Fair enough." Ashley's gaze skirted again to David's painting.

Nancy's art gallery displayed his larger canvases and sold them for several thousand dollars. Upon closer inspection, Ashley preferred his 8 x 10 inch, more intimate pieces— always with a hidden, or not-so-hidden dog in the upper right-hand corner.

She might even be able to afford one of his smaller works, and mentally redecorated her apartment, finding blank wall space where she could hang his paintings. However, they weren't for sale anymore, not in Greenwood, not in Cherish. Not anywhere.

She detoured to where David had painted the landscape he'd donated to the inn. She parked at Memorial Street Church and walked a short distance to an abandoned railway. The pavement glittered with the hotness of the midday sun.

After she worked her way through a narrow trail and reached a clearing, she didn't expect to encounter him. But there he was. In the same grove, surrounded by a kaleidoscopic array of wildflowers, with oak trees and a river beyond.

The air was scented with moss and earth, and the hint of summer blossoms.

She stared at him, open-mouthed, thrilled with her good fortune.

His heather gray T-shirt touting a well-known New York tourist attraction and slim-fitting Bermuda shorts enhanced his muscular physique. Again, he didn't fit her image of a reclusive painter.

But then, he wasn't painting. Rather, he was taking photographs, the camera slung around his neck by a strap, a tripod beside him.

She approached him from behind, on his right side, and he didn't seem conscious of her until she stepped in front of him. Or perhaps because his dog raced over with welcoming barks and sturdy tail wagging.

David looked wildly around and raked the dark hair from his forehead. The skin bunched at the corner of his eyes. "Ashley Madden. I didn't see you at first."

"Hello, David." Her heart shouldn't tingle because he'd uttered her name. And why wasn't there a sense of strangeness? They'd only just met.

"Sorry," she went on. "I didn't mean to come up on you so quietly." She stepped back while inwardly reprimanding herself. She'd been inconsiderate for advancing on him without warning.

He ran a thumb across his camera. "When I'm involved in my work, I'm focused and block out everything else."

She couldn't ignore the pride on his handsome face when he'd recovered from being startled by her approach. Surely a man like him never succumbed to weakness or defeat. Clearly, he hadn't seen her, though he'd object to anyone feeling sorry for him. Still, he needed support and morale boosting from someone.

And who might that someone be?

Nope. Not going there.

Sure, he was talented, an animal lover, and definitely generous.

And she'd begun to daydream about him, although she stifled any romantic notions. Nevertheless, she was drawn to him.

"How did you come upon these broken-down railroad tracks?" He grinned. "The running train is located on the opposite side of town."

"I'm not going anywhere." She smiled from ear to ear. "Today, I'm discovering Cherish."

He set the camera on a stool beside him. "You're still looking for Grandfather Mountain?"

"Grandfather Mountain? Why would I—"

"Remember? You're a mountain climber."

A glimpse of his boyish grin, more relaxed now, and she forgot her reasons for anything besides him.

"Grandfather Mountain is a distinctive mountain in the Blue Ridge Range," she informed him. As soon as she'd gone back to her room, the first day she met him, she'd done her research on the internet.

"How tall is it?"

"What is this? *Jeopardy?*"

"Just asking."

"Five thousand, nine hundred, and forty-six feet."

"Excellent." He laced the word with teasing amusement. "What other mountains do you climb?"

She bunched her hands into her pockets. "I stick to the basics."

"Basic mountains?"

"I'm referring to my gear."

"I assume you bring a rope, climbing pack, helmet and a harness."

She fumbled for the right words. "Yes, and a ... a headlamp." Once, she'd watched a television documentary about a mountain climber and he'd used a headlamp.

David feigned absorption in the rushing river behind her. Yet when he met her gaze, she caught a glimpse of unaffected warmth in his blue eyes.

"A climbing headlamp is useful after sundown," he suggested helpfully.

"A super bright lamp is crucial." She stalled, searching her mind for helpful details, counting on someone, anyone, who might appear and come to her rescue. In the end, it was David.

He moved closer. "You don't know all that much about mountain climbing, do you?"

"An understatement to say the least." She scooped up Pickle, who rewarded her with a dozen licks to her chin. "How did you guess my secret?"

"Call me a regular Sherlock Holmes. Or maybe it was the headlamp reference." Lightly, he brushed his knuckles over her cheek, disarming her. "I'm just messing with you. I don't know anything about mountain climbing, either."

"I'm ignorant when it comes to mountain ranges too."

"Well, you could've fooled me." He seemed to try his best not to look surprised. "By the way, someone broke into my house today."

"Huh."

"Huh? Meaning?"

"It was me." She held up a hand. "Although to clarify, I didn't break in because the door was unlocked. Plus, I had an excellent reason."

"I can only imagine." He waited, shifted. "Go on."

"I was worried about … about the peaches."

"I wasn't aware peaches had feelings."

"The heat is excessive, and the peaches were already ripe when I bought them at the farmer's market. I feared they might spoil. Your doorstep gets a lot of sun."

"You're blaming your break-in on my sunny doorstep?"

"It wasn't a break-in," she clarified, straightening her shoulders. "But yes, it's all your fault."

"Well, that explains everything." His laughter rang out,

and the last bit of tension vanished from his face. "Thanks for the treat. They're delicious. I already ate two."

"You're welcome."

"What made you decide on peaches?" He shifted to face her. "They're my favorite fruit."

"Peaches were a wild guess, though they're in season and I assumed everyone likes them." She set Pickle down. He lapped up the water in his dish and found a shady spot in the grass beneath an oak tree. "Thanks again."

"Glad to oblige." David's smile was candid. "Next time we'll devour a box of cookies and drink sugary soda."

Next time? She muffled a self-conscious laugh while her heart skipped a beat.

She stepped over to the tree and crouched to give Pickle a belly rub. The dog rolled onto his back, feet splayed to provide better access to his stomach.

"Did you peek through my house while you were inside today?" he asked.

"Snoop?"

"Peek, snoop …"

"Neither is flattering. I was in and out quickly. *Fairly quickly,* she amended, sending a prayer to God. In retrospect, it had been an intrusion on David's personal space.

God is within me. God is rooting for me. Focus on His word and God, please forgive me.

Now was a suitable time to explain to David why she was really in Cherish. But he was smiling, and the mood was congenial. She didn't want to spoil it.

"You mentioned you're not from around here," he said.

"I live in a town fifty miles away."

"Not far."

"Not far. It's similar in size and population to Cherish, though Cherish has more of a quintessential…"

"Charm?"

"The optimal description."

He waited, apparently, for her to continue.

"I own an art studio for handicapped children. I allow my students the freedom to create art in any form they choose. There's no right or wrong."

"Admirable." He yanked open a portable cooler at his feet and offered her a bottle of root beer and an almond biscuit from a bakery in town, which she gratefully accepted. He grabbed an energy drink for himself.

"The soda isn't sugar free." All the while, his gaze stayed on her. "Neither is the biscuit."

"Best news of the day."

He laughed. "I assume your teaching is challenging?"

"My students are a pleasure, and my studio is a work in progress. I love sharing the beauty and wonder of art."

He transferred his weight from one foot to the other. "Why are you here in Cherish?"

She blinked, caught by his question, scarcely able to breathe because of his closeness. "I'm searching for distinctive art supplies to stock my studio."

Actually, she was in Cherish because of the tall, handsome man eyeing her with undisguised interest.

He reached for another biscuit. "Aaron's Art is an excellent shop in town."

"I'll stop by while I'm here."

"I can show you sometime."

She answered with a surprised smile. "I'll take you up on your offer."

She tried to ignore the leap of her pulse at the sight of David's dazzling grin. He gave a thumbs-up.

"Do you pay for your studio items out of your own pocket?" he asked.

"Of course, although I charge minimal tuition." An abrupt memory of the many months when she'd scarcely been able to pay the heat and electric bills flashed through her mind. "Sometimes, I receive donations from my church, which is a huge help."

"If you ever need anything, I own a warehouse in New York filled with supplies."

"Thank you. I'm always running out of metal buckets and paint brushes and canvases. It's all worth it, though. Art is healing."

"Exactly." He treated her with a mixture of courtesy and sincerity. There was a guarded attentiveness from this urbane, handsome man. She couldn't shake the feeling he sensed their growing attraction, too.

He uncapped his energy drink. "What else do you provide for your students?"

"Unconditional love and support."

"There's nothing better." His gaze, shining with respect, met hers. "You're staying at the Cherish Hills Inn?"

"Yes. I booked a room for the next few days. The owner is accommodating, and the food is fabulous." She paused, the biscuit in her hand temporarily forgotten.

Nerves kicked in. Why was he asking? Was he interested in her? In a sense, he'd asked her out by offering to show her the art shop. And he'd mentioned sharing cookies.

"Julian is a hands-on owner, and his cook, Melissa, produces marvelous dishes."

Thinking of her exquisite meal the night before, she nodded. "The restaurant offers top-notch service. I enjoyed dinner there, and the sweet and sour meatballs are scrumptious."

"You ate alone?" David asked. He finished his second biscuit and drank half his energy drink.

"I'm single and usually eat by myself."

Something stirred in the immeasurable depths of his eyes.

Something warm. "I prefer to dine with a beautiful companion."

Judging from photos she'd seen of him through the years, there was often a glamorous starlet hanging from his arm. Ashley swallowed, torn between awkwardness and self-consciousness. She was neither stunning nor a starlet.

The warmth in his eyes was replaced by an emotion she couldn't pinpoint. And then he became unreadable.

"In all honesty," he said, shoving his hands into his pockets. "I'm surprised."

"Why?"

"A breathtaking woman like you should've been snatched up long ago."

"I'm a seasoned solo diner with no romantic commitments. I'm also a foodie."

"I eat by myself more often than not."

Her eyes widened. She couldn't imagine him dining alone. "Do you prefer it?"

"Not a bit."

She smiled. "When dining in a restaurant, the secret is to take along props."

"A fork and a spoon?"

She choked on a laugh. "A travel book is good. I recommend *The Lonely Planet*."

"Where do you travel?"

"Nowhere, though I've always wanted to tour Italy, particularly the Campania region and Naples."

"I've visited. The word *scenic* doesn't capture Italy's breathtaking coastlines. Traveling is my passion, and that country is a favorite."

"I've read that every meal in Italy is a memorable experience."

"Tuscany resembles something straight out of a picture book."

Now they had Italy in common, besides art and a love of animals.

"When dining alone …" She paused for a dramatic effect. "I pull up the e-reader on my phone."

"How about taking a companion with you to dinner?"

Her eyebrows raised, along with her spirit. She couldn't be certain if he was flirting, but elected to participate. "Do you have anyone in mind?"

"Me, because I haven't eaten there yet."

"I heard you frequently order takeout." She prayed she wasn't initiating a topic too prying, but took the dive, anyway. "Julian Wilson mentioned it last night."

A sparkle lit his eyes as he placed a hand on her shoulder. "I'm the center of a conversation?"

Her mouth went dry. She swallowed. Truth? These days, he was the center of all her conversations. All her thoughts.

She dismissed his teasing query with a chuckle. "You were worth a quick mention."

"Thanks for letting me down gently." He granted her a rueful smile. His hand leisurely massaged her shoulder. "Hence, will you?"

"Hence? Will I …Wait. Are you asking me out to dinner, or am I asking you?"

A softness shone from his blue eyes. His eyes, she decided, were designed to mesmerize. She couldn't look away.

"To clarify, I'm asking you. I hope you'll accept." His hand remained on her shoulder, and the chemistry between them heated. He realized it, too. She heard the evidence from the tenderness in his tone.

"You're splashed on the front page of gossip newspapers with models and actresses—" Ashley stopped herself. Whoa. This chat was becoming overly personal.

"Gossip newspapers don't reveal a factual story. Many of

those women simply craved publicity. I was the man of the hour, though insincerity isn't my thing." The edginess vanished from his voice, replaced with a hint of gratefulness. "The woman of my dreams has a sense of humor and is a delight to be around."

"I've never dated anyone famous."

He rubbed his forehead. "Why bring up that particular word at this precise minute?"

"Because I'm the opposite of your usual choice in women."

His gaze narrowed. "You're an authority on me in the short time we've known each other?"

"You mentioned insincerity wasn't your thing," she continued. "I'd welcome the same consideration."

"You don't believe I'm sincere?"

"I don't know you well enough to determine either way."

"So I'm guilty."

"I didn't say that."

She had, though.

Too late, she noticed his troubled expression, and regretted allowing her emotions to steer her toward such a blunt outburst. She braced herself for a verbal lambasting, but after a blink of silence, he replied, "I value your honesty. You're a refreshing change in my jaded world."

She drew in a breath and didn't meet his gaze.

Her conscience tapped her on the shoulder. Insincerity? She was the one being dishonest. What about the bigger explanation of her sudden appearance in Cherish?

"Ashley?" David's tone was just enough of a caress that she ignored her conscience. Though if he was extending a genuine invitation, she wasn't sure how to respond. She only knew she was pleased and thrilled and welcomed the excitement seeping through her body.

"Yes?"

"I'm sincere." His gaze dropped to her mouth.

In a state of expectation, she waited for him to kiss her. When it proved apparent after awkward seconds passed that he hadn't planned any such thing, she disguised her disappointment beneath a luminous smile.

"I'll accept your dinner invitation under one condition," she replied.

"Which is?"

"Cookies are on the dessert menu."

"Any particular kind? Frozen, I assume?"

She chuckled. "I have an affinity for chocolate. Frozen is incomparable. Thawed is acceptable."

"I'm certain the innkeeper can arrange chocolate cookies to your liking." David burst out laughing, then pressed a fleeting kiss to her forehead.

She tipped up her chin. "What's that for?"

"The laugh or the kiss?"

"The kiss."

His admiring gaze roved over her from head to toe. "My kiss is expressing gratitude for keeping me on track. For granting me the unexpected freedom to laugh out loud. For looking incredibly enchanting in a simple outfit of shorts and a chambray blouse."

That described her to a T. Simple. Not striking. Not glamorous.

Simple.

His compliment was nothing more than lighthearted flattery. She gazed past him at the spectacular scene of mountains and sky far beyond the crystal-clear river.

He chucked her under the chin and the romantic moment, if that was indeed what it had been, eased.

He nodded toward the stool and gestured for her to sit.

She threw him a questioning glance. "But there's only one stool."

"And it's for you." An amused sparkle lit his eyes as he leaned against a tree. "Unless you'd like to share it."

Rather than disagree, she sat as he requested, and set the soda beside her, leaving no space for him. She was certain her cheeks had heated to a flushed pink that had little to do with the warmth of the day, and more to do with the good-looking man standing a few feet away.

"You asked a lot about me," she said, "but why are you in town, David?"

"I'm here on Marge Addyson's invitation. I was commissioned to paint a portrait for the centennial celebration of Memorial Street Church." He grabbed a third biscuit, thoughtfully chewed, then drained his energy drink. "Marge is the associate pastor, my benefactor, and a kind, thoughtful woman. Based on her request, the artwork will be personalized with a then and now quality."

"Two paintings?

"I haven't decided. Perhaps two-sided art, or two renderings of the church, the older version drawn in charcoal."

"On the same canvas?"

"Maybe."

"I'm certain anything you paint will be marvelous."

"Let's settle on acceptable."

Her heart skipped a beat at the uncertainty in his expression. If she hadn't glanced up, she would've missed it, so fleeting had it crossed his face.

She groped for an upbeat topic. "Do you intend to live in Cherish permanently?"

"I signed a contract."

"For the commission or the cabin?"

"The commission, which is to be delivered the final week of August. I purchased the cabin outright."

Mentally, she gauged the price. With David's extensive

renovations, she estimated a cost of at least a half million dollars.

"I'm single with no ties," he went on. "I wanted a discreet out-of-the-way house. When I first visited, this town fit the bill. The right place, the right season in my life."

She hung onto the beginning of his sentence. "Why?"

"Why I'm not married? I'm only thirty-five. There's still time." He rubbed his eyes. "I suppose the first reason is because no woman seemed interested in dating a starving artist."

"You're hardly starving anymore."

"I was dirt-poor for many years." His eyes shuttered, a sharpness carried his tone. "You've heard of overnight successes?"

"Hasn't everyone?"

"Whatever you're inclined to believe, there is no such thing. Almost 100 percent of anyone who has achieved any semblance of success worked hard to get there."

"You mentioned a first reason." Ashley rounded on him. "Is there a second?"

"Second what?"

"Second reason you're not married."

"I never allow a relationship to last over the three-month line." He rubbed his temples. "I found it's easier that way. No one gets hurt."

She fixed her stare on the tranquil scene of wildflowers and water and a sleeping dog. He'd certainly given her something to mull over.

David picked up his camera, slung the strap around his neck, then began taking photos. He used his left eye to focus.

"I'm left-eye dominant too." She stood and stepped to an oak tree near the river. "Most people are right-eye dominant."

No answer, only more camera clicks.

"Gorgeous and natural," he murmured.

She surveyed the base of the tree. "Do you fish?"

"Nope."

"There's certainly access to fishing in this town."

"Yup."

Pickle woke, stretched, then dozed again.

"Will you use these photos as a reference to reproduce on canvas?" She anchored her foot on the lowest branch of the tree.

A fair question, though again, David didn't respond. Instead, he stepped back and muttered something about tight and wide shots.

She squinted up at the sun. "What's the ideal light for outdoor photography?"

"It depends on what I'm shooting."

She curled her fingers around the next tree branch, testing to be certain it would hold her weight, then scrambled to the sturdy upper limb.

He swiveled toward her, open-mouthed. "What are you doing?"

"I'm climbing a tree."

"I'm quite aware." His lips quirked. "May I ask why?"

"So I can sit."

"There are stools for the same purpose."

"I see better up here."

"Isn't that a bit childish?"

"I'm an adult, but it doesn't mean I should give up everything I loved to do when I was young. The view is different up here. Better. I can see beyond the river to the grassy knoll bordering the mountains." At his curious look, she added, "Haven't you ever climbed a tree?"

"When I was ten."

"What was it like?"

He blinked and averted his gaze. "I climbed an old maple tree higher and higher. Then I looked down."

"And?"

"I closed my eyes and gasped for oxygen. When I opened them, I was sweating profusely."

"What happened next?"

"I lost my balance and fell out of the tree."

"Oh, no." She clung tighter to a skinny branch. "I hope you weren't hurt."

"Only my pride." He gazed up at her. "My brothers thought it was the funniest thing they'd seen in a decade. They laughed for days."

"Did you ever try again?"

"Nope. Do I look like a fool?"

"Chicken."

Her prim correction brought a chuckle. Then a sigh. Then another series of clicks as he lifted his camera.

"How many shots do you usually take?" she called down to him.

"Thirty or forty." His manner was preoccupied. "I file my photographs in an image library."

"All part of the creative process." She shifted to a different branch. "I've learned that subject is most important in art and photography."

Again, he placed the camera close to his eye and took aim at the river. "And in life."

His statement, his philosophy, she wasn't sure.

She looped strands of hair slipping loose from her ponytail behind her ear. She repeated to herself that she was in Cherish for a purpose, to discuss if he planned to sell his artwork anymore. Equally important, he should consult an eye doctor.

Perhaps he already had. He certainly had the financial resources.

Should she ask? Wouldn't that be prying into his personal affairs?

And why couldn't she keep her gaze off him for longer than half a second?

By now she had surmised he was losing, or perhaps had lost, total vision in his right eye. He was discernibly uncomfortable discussing the subject, though he'd alluded to the eyesight loss in his cabin. Just as easily, he had shut the discourse down before she'd uttered a word. He had a knack for dictating a conversation.

Another stretch of silence. She climbed down from the tree, reached for her soda and took a sip. The drink was warm, and flat.

When she brought up how summer colds were sometimes worse than winter colds, citing various reasons, David teased her about being a regular Dr. Google.

Then, she focused on the wildflowers.

"They're exquisite, aren't they?" she rhapsodized. "I especially love red and pink. The shades are vibrant."

"Yup," came his reply.

Not much of a response. Artists realized the power of color, and she'd taught her students that color brought out emotions. She recommended vibrant, cool, warm, and complementary paint in every piece her students created.

When she had exhausted any further attempts about uncontroversial subjects—the weather, various dog breeds, favorite television shows—hers was the *Andy Griffith Show*, David packed his camera and tripod in a brown leather messenger bag. He expelled a breath, hoisted the bag over his shoulder, and leashed Pickle.

"Are you headed to the inn, Ashley?" He glanced at his watch and frowned. "I'm giving up for today."

"Giving up what?"

"Work, photographs, art. Nothing is cooperating, including the weather."

"Why? Is it supposed to rain?" She caught his frown, then raised her gaze to the heavens. As if the mention of rain had conjured up the finale of a picture-perfect sky, clouds had begun to form.

"Nothing in the forecast, and the weather is warm but pleasant." He cut off any further questions by stating, "It's getting late."

Four o'clock in the afternoon was hardly late for two grown adults. Tree branches swayed in the breeze, and squirrels scampered from tree to tree.

She scowled at her flat soda. Suddenly, David had become aware of her again.

"As a matter of fact, I am headed to the inn," she said.

"I can walk you there."

Was he sincere or offering out of courtesy?

Around him, her thoughts became increasingly tangled. She felt like she was on a roller coaster—thrilling, adrenaline-filled, and exhilarating when he was near. At other times, the hours slowed, and she could hardly catch a breath.

Both instances had the same common denominator.

Him.

An hour ago, they seemed in perfect accord. Presently, she was trying her best to ignore the blow to her pride by his sudden memory loss. Had he forgotten he'd suggested they have dinner together?

"I'm fully aware of the inn's location," she said. "I don't require an escort to walk a few short blocks." She sought to sound indifferent and knew she didn't when the words trapped in her throat.

Nonetheless, she didn't appreciate the way he'd dismissed her.

Typical difficult artist.

"Besides," she added, "my car is parked a short distance from here." She offered a grim smile. "Thanks anyway. Good day, David."

Later, she'd wonder how she pulled off ending the conversation with such supreme self-confidence. She kept her posture straight, whirled on her heel, and marched away.

CHAPTER 5

Every act of creation is first of all an act of destruction.
– Picasso

*H*ours later, David shook his head. *Wow, had he bungled that badly.*

When he and Ashley had stood near the oak tree, he'd watched her delicate eyebrows knit together in a frown before she'd stomped away. Contrary to his expectation she'd accept his offer to walk her to the inn, she'd done the opposite.

It was his fault.

She'd given such a jaunty declaration that she knew where the inn was, that he'd wanted to take her in his arms and kiss her soft, full lips.

Standing by the window in his cabin, he gazed out at the night sky. The slender leaves of willow oaks flickered under the silver light cast by a quarter moon. He stared blindly at his reflection and raked a hand through his messy shag, begging for a haircut.

He braced an arm on the frame and surveyed the last of the clouds. Despite the forecast, it had rained earlier. He opened the window to allow the breeze to wash a freshness through the room.

He hardly knew how to cope with the range of emotions he was experiencing.

An attractive, charming woman had expressed interest in his paintings, perhaps in him, and he'd been less than enthusiastic. He reprimanded himself over the unfairness of taking his frustration over his lost eyesight out on her, but he hadn't been able to see into the camera as easily as he'd anticipated. He'd been in the zone initially, snapping photos intuitively and envisioning them. Exhilaration and enthusiasm had pressed him to continue. Soon, he'd questioned himself as he realized he couldn't identify subjects as clearly as he liked.

In addition, he'd felt disheartened when Ashley had remarked on his fame.

If anything, he felt like a failure. Sure, he'd spent his entire adulthood beneath the celebrity umbrella, but the mention always made him uncomfortable.

Was that all she saw in him?

He wasn't an award for a woman to parade on her arm. He was a living, breathing man, not a slicked-up magazine cover. Similar to newsworthy men in the public eye—movie stars and prominent sport figures—his tranquility had been invaded by women fascinated not by him nor his art, but by the prospect of enlisting him as their escort for popular media events.

Not the man. Not him.

Rather, how the reclusive, mysterious artist might bolster their career.

The afternoon with Ashley was the first time he believed

a woman was drawn to him solely for himself. He'd learned a little about her and had been captivated by her kind-heartedness and ideals. She was a breath of pure air, and refreshingly uninterested in money and power.

Thus, he was surprised he'd been wrong about her.

But no, no, he wasn't wrong. He'd recognized the interest in her gorgeous hazel eyes whenever she gazed up at him.

Something was happening between them. Something special. Something magnetic.

While he'd taken photos of the landscape and river, he'd caught her staring at him from the corner of his good eye. Involuntarily, he'd begun to memorize her face—all pink-cheeked and beautiful and captivating.

His feelings were utterly illogical. He'd just met her. Nevertheless, the upsetting emotional and physical unbalances he'd faced because of his eyesight, coupled with the hours in her charming company, had merged together.

The result was excitement, a kind of euphoria he'd never experienced before.

The result was chaos. His reaction and judgement weren't functioning clearly.

Part of the time, he had the wildest sensation that she couldn't possibly be as genuine as she seemed. Vivacious and enchanting and embracing life, she brought to mind an eighteen-year-old girl on the verge of becoming a woman.

On the other hand, she made him feel like he was eighteen again, for she remained constantly in his thoughts.

He'd been sincere in his suggestion to walk her to the inn, hoping to prolong their afternoon together. It wasn't a big shock she refused. Why would she want to converse with someone like him, so sulky and self-absorbed?

"Ashley, Ashley." He whispered her name aloud.

Ideal on a marquee, definitely traditional, and beyond compare.

And her other name: *Twinkle.*

Why had her friend called her that?

Ashley had ignored his inquisitive stare at the time, though he intended to ask her the meaning of the nickname. She was an enigma he wanted to get to know better, and so he'd absorbed every word she'd uttered when they were together.

The first day they met, they'd shaken hands. Hers was dainty, like the woman herself, her fingers slim and firm. When she'd slipped off her sunglasses, she'd afforded him a glimpse of her startling eyes. Fascinating. Hazel eyes were set apart from brown or blue eyes because of their combination of green, gold, and brown.

She embodied the ideal subject—great cheekbones, finely arched eyebrows, and rounded, subtle features.

When Sarah and Ashley had readied to leave his cabin, he hadn't anticipated spouting about deaf musicians and blind painters. He'd just blurted it out. Shock and disbelief had flashed across Ashley's face.

She was considerate and compassionate. Her face lit up when she chatted about her students.

He closed the window, nodding quiet approval for her tender spirit.

When they'd stood by the river, her breath had quickened. He had wanted to kiss her, though he'd been uncertain if the timing was right. They were in the earliest stages of a relationship, slowly learning about each other. His heart had skipped a beat at her disappointed expression when he hadn't kissed her.

Taken aback by his next thought, he sighed. Why was he unsure about kissing her when every instinct told him it was right?

Why? Because he wasn't clear about anything anymore.

He glanced at Pickle, sleeping on a rug by the fireplace.

"Can you understand this relationship any better than I can?" he asked.

The living room lamps were on. The dog didn't respond, just continued sleeping with his legs extended. Pickle could sleep just about anywhere.

David closed his eyes and went over their afternoon again.

In addition to all the reasons he was intrigued by Ashley, she also liked his paintings and championed him. Her open praise was a welcome switch from his inner harsh criticism. Perhaps he should lighten up on himself.

THE NEXT DAY, David assessed the photographs he'd taken. Surprised, he sorted numerous shots with Ashley in them. He hadn't realized he'd included her. He hadn't been able to see her clearly whenever she stepped to his right and hadn't noticed her in his viewfinder.

Or had his subconscious known she was there all along?

Maybe...

He printed the best photos, assessed them, and chose one with her sitting in the tree, a suggestion of a fairy. She had shifted toward the water, and her profile—small, turned-up nose and lifted chin—created a fetching picture. The sun gilded her blond hair to a honey gold, her shapely legs were long and tanned, her creamy complexion sprinkled with freckles.

She'd glanced at him. He'd caught her expressive gaze, her lips poised in a smile. Rosy-red, her lower lip was fuller than her upper lip. Her chin was smooth, her cheeks velvety and dimpled. Yet he couldn't ignore the strength in her features.

Deprived of rational thinking, he'd captured her in a reflective, relaxed pose. Against the natural backdrop, Ashley Madden proved the ideal focus for a painting. Flawless.

Could he paint her from the photos without her permission?

Meeting her, capturing her exquisiteness…

Circumstances or all a coincidence?

He brought the photos into the kitchen. Well aware the kitchen was the main room to tackle when renovating an old house, he'd spent an afternoon listening to a builder explain traffic patterns, heating, plumbing lines, the latest "must-have's," and had opted to wait. He didn't need glass-fronted cabinets, stainless-steel appliances, or a marble-topped island. He preferred the rustic charm of blue painted cabinets and a stone floor.

He sat at the vintage wooden baking unit he used as a table and laid out the photos.

Surprisingly, Julian's voice rang in his ears. Whenever David stopped at the inn for takeout, Julian extolled the advantages of living in Cherish, sometimes peppering David with questions about his faith. For Julian, it was of utmost importance that the residents remained steadfast in their unwavering belief in God.

Had these last few months been guided by God's divine hand? Or could he attribute it to fate—the unexplainable law of the universe—that had brought him and Ashley together?

He poured himself an energy drink, took a gulp, then slumped back on the antique chair. Ah, the adrenaline of caffeine. Just the ticket to spur his brain's neural activity and quicken his thought process.

The dog trotted over and rested at his feet.

He scooped Pickle onto his lap and stroked the silky fur.

Perhaps Cherish was where he'd find his greatest freedom. Perhaps he should allow former priorities the opportunity to escape. Be inspired by a fresh perspective. Let go.

Let go of what exactly? His painting? His beloved art?

He wasn't certain. He just knew the faint murmur in his

heart whispered the observation that what he needed might be directly in front of him.

Nope, nope, nope. His hand stilled. He gazed at the beamed wooden ceiling. Dating? Women? Faith? Too much struggle. Too much conflict. Too much difficulty.

He well remembered his strict religious upbringing—the drone of Sunday sermons by an aged pastor when his parents had dragged him to church as a boy. His mother's insistence he dress properly in beige pants and a blue polo shirt. Their gasps of horror when he declared the sermons boring. He was an adolescent when doubts about God and Christianity had taken hold.

He gave a sad, small laugh. At himself, at the universe.

Maybe the time had come to accept whatever God had in store for him.

You're joking, right?

He shook off his musings, set the dog down, and shoved to his feet, turning to the refrigerator. He pulled a box of cookies from the freezer.

When he bit into one, still frozen, the way Ashley liked them, reality intruded.

God had been absent for decades. God wasn't interested in a man like David—with faults more numerous than the number of paintings he'd painted through the years. Besides, he was too much of a skeptic to change his religious views.

With a decisive nod, he vowed to be more attentive to his art and less attentive to his thoughts about Ashley. Surely thinking about her shouldn't consume him.

Ashley.

Any artist would clamor to paint an enchanting woman with such expressive eyes. A woman with a lean, breathtaking figure and a face that conveyed tenderness and compassion.

She was fascinating, and he wished to see her again. With

his mind made up, he placed the cookies back in the freezer. It would be better if he and Ashley ate them together. Along with bottles of soda loaded with sugar.

TIME HAD SMOOTHED over Ashley's upset of the previous day over David's not-so-polite dismissal of her. A morning workout crossed her mind, but she quickly dismissed the idea. Instead, she chose to explore the town more. In order to rationalize her morning jaunt, she popped into Aaron's Art, the shop David had mentioned. She invariably needed supplies for her studio.

Aaron, the owner, a hunched-over fellow with a white curly beard that reminded her of sheep's wool, sang David's praises. David had come into his store, learned Aaron struggled to meet his monthly rent payments because business was slow, and paid for the store's new heating and air conditioning unit. He'd made all the arrangements and sent Aaron a check to cover six months' rent as well.

"He's beyond generous. It's a shame he's hidden himself away." Aaron crossed over to her. "He'll appear for a couple hours and is gone by the time anyone realizes he was around."

"He's certainly made his mark in the artistic community." She instantly regretted saying anything, because she could almost see Aaron's ears perk up.

He stepped over to a display of pencil pocket sets. "Haven't you heard? He keeps himself scarce because he's losing his eyesight." Aaron scribbled a sign: *Superb For Traveling.*

"Rumors spread like wildfire, don't they?" Ashley said.

Aaron fixed her with a level look. "Sometimes."

Not everyone knew about David's eyesight loss, she

wanted to tell Aaron. Only those who spent a lengthy amount of time with David would have figured it out.

Like her, for instance. She was fortunate to have shared hours with him. He was complex and charming and … impossible. She hadn't broached the eyesight subject with him because she didn't want to hinder his creativity. And it seemed as if he was always creating. Also, she didn't want to interrupt their time together with upsetting conversation.

She remembered the way his gaze had dropped to her lips, the warmth of his skin. She longed to run her fingers through his messy, disheveled hair. Did he realize his hair curled at the nape?

They'd stared at each other as if they were both waiting for something.

What, exactly?

He wasn't falling in love with her, nor was he about to declare an everlasting declaration of any kind.

Neither was she.

She had resolved to preserve her heart behind a sheltered and safe wall. Love wasn't a part of her future, and any fleeting thoughts of her and David had to be quickly squelched. With him, she'd keep things businesslike. Besides, she wasn't stunning and sophisticated or similar in any way to the women he apparently preferred.

Allow me my privacy was his philosophy, and the reason why he'd attempted to conceal his whereabouts in this idyllic community.

She picked up a framed watercolor of Venice, Italy, and then gazed out the shop's front window. Townsfolk cheerfully greeted each other as they strolled along the sidewalk. Children skipped, the seniors walked slower, arm in arm.

Cherish had a glow all its own.

The simple acts of fellowship should have made her

spirits soar. Instead, they plummeted because all that good cheer effectively took her back to David's suffering.

Hiding his loss under an unbreachable demeanor might be his way. Not hers. God had placed outward limits on David's body, but His inner blessings were greater. She promised to pray and believe and lean on God. She wanted to inspire David to do likewise.

She purchased pocket sets, pens, and pencils for her students and thanked Aaron, suppressing her dismay that she wasn't able to afford more expensive items. She could've used an assortment of mason jars, but would have to wait.

She passed a sign on the corner advertising a Renaissance Faire in a neighboring town. She'd always wanted to attend one, but never had the opportunity.

Perhaps this time?

Her imagination conjured the aroma of pork on a stick, or a steak and mushroom meat pie, and her stomach rumbled. The idea of escaping to a medieval world, outside of modern everyday life, held a sense of adventure and decent, old-fashioned fun.

But no, not this trip. David Fodero absorbed all of her attention.

AN HOUR LATER, Ashley had showered and changed into a yellow sundress that hugged her slim figure, a bold necklace featuring a golden sunflower and beige leather sandals. Before she forgot Dorothy's recommendation from the music store, she listened to Percy Grainger's performance of 'Country Gardens.' She read about the pianist's fascinating life, spending more time on it than she'd foreseen, as he was praised for his talent.

Another typically difficult artist, she smiled to herself.

By seven o'clock, she was perched on a stool in the inn's

lounge, sipping a tall glass of sweet iced tea, mulling over different ways to help David.

Julian greeted her with a smile as he wended between bistro tables. He held a tumbler overflowing with fresh-squeezed limeade. He'd expounded earlier that limeade was an inn specialty beverage because of the addition of fresh mint leaves.

"I heard you were here." He leaned against the stool opposite her. "I'm the messenger this evening. Someone in the parlor wants to see you."

"Is Sarah here?" She sat forward. "I thought we were having lunch together in a few days. I hope I didn't get the times mixed up."

"I assure you it's not Sarah." Julian chuckled. "I haven't seen her tonight."

Ashley half stood. "Who, then?"

Julian toasted her glass with his. His eyes sparkled with merriment. "I'm fairly certainly you'll recognize him immediately."

CHAPTER 6

Good artists copy, great artists steal.
– Picasso

Seated on an overstuffed sofa in the parlor of the Cherish Hills Inn, David set a bouquet of wild-flowers on the coffee table, and then rifled through a pile of periodicals. Particularly catching his interest was a gardening magazine, reminding him that he planned to start his vegetable garden. He needed to contact Ashley's friend, Sarah.

"Anything I can help you with, sir?" A pleasant woman whom he guessed to be in her sixties, with curly gray hair and red-rouged cheeks, all beams and buoyancy, wheeled a trolley cart stacked with beverages and snacks toward him.

"No thanks. I'm set." He held up the magazine as proof.

Optimism all around seemed to be a prerequisite for living in Cherish, along with its close cousins—positivity and religion.

He smiled at her, then feigned absorption in an article touting the optimum season to plant pumpkins seeds. He assumed it was the fall. He was wrong. In the Carolinas, early July was deemed best. He'd better get on it so he could harvest something he'd be able to swallow. Sarah had mentioned squash and carrots and... What was the last vegetable? Something green he'd certainly not eaten before, and which was probably tasteless.

When he finished the article, he looked around, cheered by the surroundings—a stacked rock fireplace, cornflower-blue tapestry rug, and gleaming oak wood floors. A shaft of late-day sunlight slanted through the front window. Outside, the sky blazed a magnificent tangerine-orange. In the distance, a dog barked.

He'd considered bringing Pickle with him, but was uncertain if dogs were allowed. From comments on the internet, he'd learned the inn's previous owner had banned dogs. He wasn't certain of Julian's stance.

Before he had left his cabin, he'd given Pickle a gnawing toy and his favorite striped elephant. He'd tuned his radio to a country station that would provide, the DJ assured him, easy listening for Pickle. As he'd left, a male singer was crooning about how much better life would be if he only had a boat.

David smiled. Country music was fun and all about emotions. He was fairly certain there were no cleverer lyrics on earth.

The tensions of the day had drained as he stepped outside his cabin and into the sultry June evening. The air was thick and heavy, and a five-minute rain shower hadn't cooled things off.

Shifting to the present, he sat back on the sofa and pulled out his cell phone. He'd invested in a doggie camera he'd stationed in his living room, and streamed to his phone.

Currently, Pickle was participating in his favorite activity: sleeping.

"David?"

Ashley entered the parlor, a surprised smile on her face. He pocketed his phone, picked up the bouquet, and sprang to his feet. Her yellow dress complemented her blond hair, which spilled over her shoulders in delicate waves. She dressed with a casual finesse, perfectly suiting her symmetrical features.

"Hi, Ashley." His admiring gaze glided from the top of her head to the tips of her manicured toes.

"Hello." She set a glass of iced tea on a side table, her movements elegant, yet tentative. She reminded him of a pretty summer posy, feminine and romantic.

"I assume your tea is weighted down with sugar." He groped for the ideal words, stronger words, funnier words, and hoped his humor was contagious.

"I take three teaspoons. What's your preference?"

He matched her cheerful response. "I survive on energy drinks. I work better at night, and they help me stay awake."

"Not very healthy."

"Said the pot calling the kettle black."

"You realize caffeine is addictive?"

His retort was a bark of laughter. "Moderate consumption is okay."

"Now who is Dr. Google?"

He half smiled. Somehow, she'd flipped the conversation, causing him to consider the amount of caffeine he drank each day. Caffeine elevated his mood and kept him more alert. However, there was a major shortcoming. He'd come to rely on the drinks.

She raised her glass. "I assume you're a health nut."

"Me?" He wasn't smiling anymore. He was laughing.

"But you are into vegetables." She gestured to the magazine he'd been reading. "Aren't you planting a garden featuring everyone's favorite vegetable, zucchini?"

Right. The vegetable he couldn't remember.

Animated buzzing of conversation filled the inn's hallway, and the chiming of the pendulum clock had recently sounded the hour.

"I'd prefer to plant coffee beans bursting with caffeine," he replied.

"And I'd plant chocolate candy bars."

He started toward her, stopping within inches.

She stared up at him. "I didn't expect to see you tonight."

"Yet here I am." Captivated, he focused on her amazing smile. "Apparently, I can't stay away from you."

Ashley regarded him and stayed silent.

"The flowers are for you. Sorry, they're wilted. I'll blame it on the humidity." He offered her the bouquet, wrapped in paper towels. He'd stopped by the river and gathered the spray of fiery pinks, cardinal reds, and stems of gray-purple violets.

"Thank you. They're exquisite." Ashley set down her glass, then sniffed the delicate fragrance, a woodsy scent mingling with a hint of fresh strawberries. "David, you remembered."

A declaration, not a question.

He grinned down at her. "I listened to every word you said yesterday."

"I didn't think you heard me. You were preoccupied."

"My work requires me to stay focused. Fortunately, men can do two things at once."

She lifted a skeptical eyebrow. "Can they?"

"Yes. I can listen and work at the same time."

"Really?" She planted a hand on her hip. "What else did I say yesterday?"

"Before or after you climbed the tree?"

"After."

"Well, you enlightened me on every dog breed on the globe and provided next month's weather forecast." He flicked a glance toward the window to emphasize his point. The dark-green leaves of a majestic oak tree bent in the steamy evening breeze. "And your favorite television show is the old *Andy Griffith Show*."

"Because it's the funniest sitcom ever produced," she informed him. "I laugh each time I watch an episode, even though I memorized the lines and know the outcome by heart."

"I prefer to watch documentaries on my computer."

She slanted him a cheeky glance. "Anything special?"

"*Gladiator*."

"That movie is not a documentary or entirely accurate, though it's certainly wonderful. I'd categorize it as a love story."

Slightly mollified because she hadn't disputed his taste in documentaries, he replied, "The movie is inspired by factual events in ancient Rome."

"Uh-huh. Whatever you say. You never told me your favorite show."

"I don't own a television set."

"No way." She peered at a nearby wall, where a wide-screen TV was mounted. "I've never known anyone who doesn't own a TV."

"Now you do."

She met his gaze with disbelief. "Are you some type of minimalist?"

"On the contrary, I love TV." He offered a guilty shrug. "I discovered, though, that it's too distracting and robbed me of my most valuable asset."

"Which is?"

"My time when I could be painting."

"You're here." Her sigh was edgy, as if she was blaming

herself for his presence at the inn. "You could be painting now."

He felt it—a curious tug on his heart, the odd ache whenever he reflected on how she always considered others before herself.

"Time is valuable. People are valuable." He brushed his fingers across her cheek. "Spending time with valuable people is most valuable."

She swallowed. "A lot of valuables in your sentences."

"A lot of meaning too." He smiled into her gorgeous eyes. "May I tell you the truth about something?"

"Always."

"I fantasized about kissing you. Your skin is soft, and your mouth… I'm saying words out loud I've never told another woman."

He stepped closer. Their breaths mingled.

No. He was saying too much. He thought about pulling back. He didn't.

She gazed up at him, her chin tipping ever slightly. "I'm flattered." Her voice vibrated with the same emotion.

He understood.

He kissed her, a gentle brush of his lips on hers. Sparks of adrenaline in his veins didn't match the tenderness of their kiss, he thought.

And then he stopped thinking at all.

That is, until she stepped back and firmly shook her head.

She set the flowers down, her hands flitting like a wild bird. She didn't seem to know where to put them. "You're quite thoughtful for a guy who accomplishes two tasks at once." Her tone was easy, but her mannerisms indicated otherwise. She was shaken, as he was, by their attraction.

He dragged in a long breath. "I owe you an apology."

"For what?"

"Yesterday I wasn't as attentive as I should've been."

"No apology is necessary. You're more observant than I imagined." She picked up her tea and sipped. Her hand was trembling. She glanced at him, apparently wondering if he noticed. He did.

"You're an exceptional artist, David, and need your space." She set down the glass. "I respect you for those traits. Praise God for giving you a unique talent to share with the world."

It wasn't her affirming statements that brought a swift beat to his heart. It was the manner in which she regarded him—with appreciation in her magnificent eyes and subdued marvel in her tone. It was refreshing to be viewed as a man with merit, as if he were heroic and exceptional. A gift more precious than any he'd ever received.

He debated about reaching for her again, more insistently, by circling his arms around her and keeping her close. He wanted to create a magical evening for them—to cancel out his rudeness from the prior day. He wanted to begin the night with kiss after kiss.

Upon gauging her guarded reaction, however, he instructed himself to slow down.

"Are you ready for even more truth?" he asked.

His question elicited a puzzled gaze from her, and she shuffled her feet. "Truth is always welcome, David."

"There is another important reason why I'm here tonight."

She tilted her head, searched his face. "I'm listening."

"I wanted to see you again." He fought down more words, the knowledge of spending enchanting hours with her. Truth was, he *had* to see her again.

A rosy blush crept up her cheeks. "Oh."

Not exactly the response he'd hoped for, but considering their growing relationship, he'd accept it. He assessed her rigid bearing, and his stomach plummeted. He could almost hear her refusal.

He hesitated. "Will you join me for dinner?"

Her mouth lifted at the corners. "I'd love to. Otherwise, I planned on dining alone."

He blew out a relieved breath. "Did you bring any props?"

"You're referring to *The Lonely Planet* guidebook?" She laughed. "Not tonight."

"Excellent. No distractions." *Except him.* "Let's create a celebratory occasion."

Years before, he'd read an entire book about celebrations. A modern-day spirituality book, advising the reader to rejoice in every activity. He'd never done that, embracing precious happiness as it came, and he intended to begin with Ashley.

"By ordering champagne with dinner?" She nodded over her shoulder toward the hallway.

"I don't drink alcohol. You?"

"Me neither. I prefer any beverage with sugar."

"Wow," he noted with a straight face. "You could've fooled me."

Her infectious smile was his reward for following through with his plan. He hadn't been certain she'd be willing to dine with him. He'd taken a gamble, entering the lobby with a bedraggled bouquet and a whisper in his gut that honest joy might be waiting for him around the corner.

And here it was. And here she was.

His mind flashed back to several signs he'd seen on his drive into town.

There'd been one advertising the farmer's market, another for a church bake sale, and a third for a Renaissance Faire in a nearby town.

The farmer's market was a possibility.

The Renaissance Faire? He'd never attended one, although the brochures he'd seen had always seemed to suggest a gigantic costume party. He wouldn't be caught dead in one of those getups people spent months creating.

As for the church bake sale, he hadn't seen the inside of a church in years. He tried to be a good person but harbored too much pain and resentment to pray.

Realizing his presence at the inn might produce a stir of local gossip, he'd parked his pickup truck a half block away and walked to the inn. Not that it made a difference, though perhaps he might slide inside discreetly, wildflower bouquet in hand.

No such luck.

The setting sun cast long shadows on the ground as he approached. Julian greeted him with a hearty hello and a boisterous chuckle.

"I messed up when I was with Ashley yesterday," David began.

"Welcome to the human race." Julian clapped David on the back and ushered him through the hallway. "We all have our faults."

"Some more numerous than others. I'm here to ask her to dinner."

"No objections on my end, and there's nothing like an apology to set things right. I assumed you weren't hankering to dine with me tonight." With a good-natured grin, Julian continued. "Ashley is a unique, giving person. I gathered from a recent chat she highly rates your art."

David scanned the dining room, his gaze landing on his painting. "I debated calling her, but I didn't have her phone number."

"Ask her for it."

"I plan to."

"Go with your gut." Julian attended to a tray of drinks on the sideboard. "Do what's appropriate, for the finest of reasons, and you'll receive your reward."

David looked from the painting to Julian. "Is this some form of religious teaching found in the Bible?"

Julian's smirk was reassuring. "Common sense straight from yours truly."

"Then what is my reward?"

"The hazel-eyed blond sitting alone in the lounge. I'll get her for you." Julian lifted a hand in salute. "You'll learn I have a penchant for meddling in people's lives, especially when they've taken the first step and brought flowers."

With that, Julian had steered David into the parlor.

David watched Ashley now, knowing he couldn't explain, even to himself, how he felt about her. He didn't intend to examine the countless emotions compelling him to spend every minute around her. A spot-on Christian might proclaim it was God.

Maybe God. Maybe.

"David, are you coming?" Ashley had gathered the wild-flowers and started for the hallway. She darted a glance over her shoulder. "I'll ask the hostess for a vase and we can leave the flowers here."

He caught up with her in two strides. "Why don't you bring the flowers into the dining room? Julian will wave his hand and a vase will magically appear."

She offered a plucky grin. "You're probably right."

"You've met Julian. I'm not *probably* right. I'm *definitely* right."

His assertion was rewarded by her bubbling laugh. Without taking his gaze from hers, he asked, "Do we need reservations for dinner?"

"Nope. I know the owner."

As they entered the hallway, he took her hand in his. "Me too."

He was heartened by the fact she didn't pull away. If anything, she nodded her acceptance.

CHAPTER 7

Action is the foundational key to all success.
- Picasso

The Cherish Hills Inn dining room lived up to the accolades David had heard about since his arrival. The walls were salmon-colored, the decorations lush gray, and tiny tea light candles on each table created an inviting ambiance to the elegant, understated atmosphere. Here, subtlety was the key. The artist in David noted these details as well as the table settings—gleaming silverware, sparkling glasses, tapered candles, and gold-rimmed china plateware. He also noted that heads swiveled, and the noise level dropped as he and Ashley walked in.

Ashley handed the flowers to the maître d', who then pulled out a chair and seated her. He assured her the flowers would be sent to her room, a complementary crystal vase provided.

"Perhaps a table closer to the window?" David asked, gesturing toward a particular table.

"Sorry, sir. The town sheriff and his wife sit there." The maître d' wore an apologetic smile as earnestly as he wore his black tuxedo.

Ashley and David scanned the menus, both opting for the signature dish of smoked ham, scalloped potatoes, and green beans topped with almonds.

After they placed their orders, including a carafe of fresh-squeezed limeade and Cobb salads for starters, David gazed at her across the table.

He couldn't get enough of her delightful, heart-shaped face. "Thank you for allowing me to be your dinner companion this evening."

"I never would have refused you." The soft warmth in her eyes and the catch in her lilting tone gave him pause. Absorbed by the feelings expanding inside him, he slid his hand across the table and rested it on hers. In the background, the piped-in harmony of a solo saxophone and bass violin added to the emotional mood.

When their salads were served, she bent her head and whispered a blessing for their food. Although he hadn't prayed in years, David reverently bowed his head. He didn't participate, though he remembered the simple prayer of grace.

When she finished her prayer, she sampled a portion of hard-boiled egg and avocado doused in vinaigrette.

"I've never tasted savory greens." She pinched two fingers together and touched her lips. "In fact, I don't usually like greens."

He agreed the salad was incredible and attributed the delectable taste to the olive-oil-based dressing and bits of bacon. He wasn't a leafy vegetable person, but figured he'd better start getting used to it, given a garden was a part of his future.

His gaze skimmed the room, and fragments of conversation swirled around him. "I'm glad I changed out of my paint-spattered clothes and decided on dress pants and a cotton button-down shirt."

"And sport coat," she reminded.

He'd draped his navy-blue sport coat over the back of his chair.

"This is a fancy place. And well-trained staff."

Their server, wearing the inn's trademark red apron, magically appeared when they were ready to order, brought their food and kept their glasses filled. Otherwise, he was satisfyingly absent.

After they savored a superb dinner and their table was cleared, David became keenly aware they were being watched by the staff.

While their server crumbed the tablecloth and replaced the silverware and water glasses, another waiter brought a fresh carafe of limeade and refilled their glasses. As before, Ashley added more sugar to hers. A cheese plate assortment with bread, crackers, and candied nuts also appeared.

Julian joined them and asked if the meal was prepared to their liking. They assured him the food was exquisite.

"Will you be having coffee or dessert?" Julian inquired. "Our featured special is blackberry sorbet." He snagged a silver water pitcher from a side table and refilled their glasses. "Our desserts are made in-house. The sorbet is refreshing, and the blackberries are local."

"We hoped you served cookies." David smiled at Ashley, noting the laughter in her eyes. "Particularly chocolate cookies."

"I'm certain our pastry chef can create something

extraordinary." Julian snatched a menu from an empty table and flipped to the dessert listings.

"Particularly frozen chocolate cookies." David smeared spicy mustard on a cracker and popped it into his mouth.

If Julian was caught off guard, he didn't show it, except for a widening of his eyes. In the meantime, Ashley's cheeks colored a hot pink.

"Excellent choice." Julian glanced toward the doorway. "I apologize for intruding on your evening, Mr. Fodero, but my wife, Nora, and our daughter, Samantha, are hoping to meet you. Samantha is attending college and keen on her course work."

"What is she studying?"

"Baroque composers—Bach, Handel and Scarlatti."

"The arts, along with novel ideas and challenges, will help her discover where her passion truly lies." David paused. "By the way, Julian, you've called me David ever since we met."

"Of course." Julian said, as though the opposite was true. "In a more formal setting, though, everything is more … formal."

"Please ask them to come over." He had no intention of leaving Ashley out of the conversation and gestured to her. "I'm assuming they haven't met Ashley yet, either."

"I met your daughter already." Ashley scooped a handful of candied nuts.

"And I told both my wife and daughter a little more about Ashley." Julian regarded them with a warm smile.

A short while later, a dark-haired woman and a young lady, who looked to be in her early twenties, hurried to their table.

Julian quickly made the introductions while Ashley and Samantha said hello to each other.

"It's great to meet you, Mr. Fodero," Samantha said. She looped a strand of inky-black hair behind her ear, and David couldn't help but grin at her ear piercings—three in each ear, chunky gold hoops interspersed with miniature crescent moons and stars. The young woman definitely expressed her unique style.

"David," he corrected. He kept his expression pleasant, but her exuberance discomfited him. He didn't deserve it. "Ashley merits the genuine praise. She owns an art studio and gives back to the community by providing classes to handicapped children and adults. Me? I just paint."

"I adore my profession." Ashley looked at the others, then met his approving stare. "Though you are the true artist."

"In the artist-fan relationship, both the artist and admirer are important," Julian put in. "Also, a painter works at his or her own pace. The admirer is a supporter, encourager, and exhibits patience."

Ashley murmured an agreement.

"See why my dad is so smart?" Samantha grinned and turned to Ashley. "I never used to volunteer, but after my parents coaxed me into giving it a try, I discovered that volunteering is fulfilling."

"I'm liking your parents more and more for the values they're instilling in you." David lifted his glass. "What are you studying?"

"Music is my first love." Samantha continued gawking at David whenever she looked his way. "But as much as I loved the Baroque period, I'm also studying avant-garde art, which is much more modern."

"Hurray for avant-garde." He followed her gaze and realized she was staring at his painting. "I commend you. Follow your dream."

"Her major instrument is guitar," Nora said, automatically straightening the cutlery on the table next to theirs.

"What type of music is your favorite?" David asked Samantha. Considering her age, he assumed her interests were countless. "I like all kinds of music, and especially country."

"Worship music is my choice," Julian, Nora, and Samantha announced in unison.

His gaze encompassed all three of them. Yup. He was definitely surrounded by a community that valued God and family. He studied Ashley, this gorgeous woman sitting across from him. He had tasted her mouth and sensed her pleasure in their embrace. More and more, he felt an attraction he couldn't rationalize with a flippant dismissal.

"Worship music is elevating." Ashley surveyed the cheese plate and selected a firm cheese and a slice of bread. "Whenever I listen, I feel calm. The lyrics are soothing and inspirational."

Soothing and inspirational. Like her.

David struggled to arrange his thoughts in order and discovered he already had. With her, he was at peace because she had become his inspiration.

In truth, God had once been his inspiration—to create, to bring out his level best. To enlighten him.

Sure, on occasion, particularly when the going got rough, David considered revisiting prayer. However, he always talked himself out of it, which was easy. He hadn't realized all were excuses until he'd examined his motives.

Which were?

Making justifications for things he didn't want to do. For anything that made him uncomfortable.

Like God?

He presumed God didn't wish to hear from him only during the rough patches. But perhaps there was a chance to reconnect with God. Perhaps Ashley could help him.

Ashley.

He couldn't ignore the gentle tug on his heart whenever

he gazed at her. Change was happening, however subtle. With God. With Ashley.

"When are you going to start painting again, Mr. Fodero?" Samantha asked.

"Hmm?" Absorbed in reflection, he'd drifted away from the exchange.

Ashley shot him a rueful look. "He's a typical artist. Sometimes I've lost him in the middle of a discussion too."

He reached out and squeezed her hand. "In the days since we've met, Ashley is beginning to know me well."

"Uh-huh, Mr. Planter of Gardens." She plunked another sugar cube into her limeade and stirred. She did that a lot. Whenever she was uncomfortable, she craved sugar.

"Samantha," Nora said, "what a rude question." She rested a firm hand on her daughter's shoulder. "The decision is up to Mr. Fodero to decide when to paint, not you. Dad just mentioned how a fan should be patient and respect the artist."

"But the public is waiting." Undeterred, Samantha looked again at David's painting, then back at him. "More important, the entire world is waiting."

"To everything there is a season." Julian quoted the familiar Bible passage and smiled. "C'mon ladies, there's work to be done here."

"Dad, I can't help at the inn tonight." Samantha splayed her hands on her slim hips. "I have to get home and take the dog out."

"Our house is two blocks away, and the dog can wait another half hour," Nora replied, and they all chuckled at Samantha's audible groan.

"You own a dog?" David inquired.

"A golden retriever." Samantha's smile was unrestrained. It was amazing how quickly a young person's mood shifted.

"Canine Helpers is where Dad and I volunteer and it's awesome."

David nodded. "I agree. The place is awesome."

"Do you like dogs, Mr. Fodero?"

"I love dogs. In fact, I own a dachshund named Pickle." He pulled out his phone to show her a photo, then decided to go a step further. "I invested in a doggie camera so I can see Pickle when I'm not home. The camera streams to my phone."

"Pickle is adorable." Ashley favored another scoop of nuts. "Although I can't speak from experience because I don't own a pet, unless my goldfish, Frederick, counts. Fortunately, one of my friends is feeding him while I'm away. My apartment is tiny and—"

"No excuses," David countered.

The mood of pleasantness faltered, and he searched for a way to restore it.

"I'm sorry," he said. "I shouldn't judge."

Ashley frowned. "No, you shouldn't."

"Alrighty then," Julian said. "Now that we've discussed dogs and college and the arts, let's allow David and Ashley the opportunity to get better acquainted, shall we?" He smiled at them. "Your server will bring you cookies and coffee." With an apologetic grin, Julian piloted his wife and daughter from the dining room.

"Is that what we're doing?" Ashley peered at David over her glass. "Getting to know each other better? Do tell."

"First, I'm abandoning the subject of dog ownership, so you'll stop scowling at me."

She coiled a strand of silky hair around her finger and displayed a sunny smile.

"Much better." David leaned back as their waiter returned. With a flourish, the waiter poured piping-hot coffee into their cups, then positioned a crystal creamer, sugar bowl, and a glass-topped plate of fancy-looking chocolate cookies in the center of the table.

Ashley went for the sugar.

David quirked an eyebrow. "Well, my beautiful companion, shall we begin?"

CHAPTER 8

Everything you can imagine is real.
–Picasso

"You first." Ashley used a silver tong to pick up three sugar cubes and plunked them into her coffee. "How about a story from your childhood, David?"

"Anything in particular?"

"How many siblings do you have?"

He eyed her coffee, frothing with sugar. "Two older brothers and a younger sister. I'm a middle child. There was lots of boisterous shouting over the din of flag football tournaments on our front lawn or when fixing cars in our garage."

"You're mechanical?"

"Not even a little. My brothers are excellent mechanics, though."

"Are you athletic?" She gave him the once-over, her gaze lingering on his shoulders.

"I jog and I've got a workout room in my condo in New York. Plus, I played football in high school." He blew out a breath. "Mostly to please my father, who was intent on raising his sons to be jocks. He was a competitive sportsman and almost made it to the pros."

"Were you a jock?"

"Football earned me dates with girls who would never have looked at me otherwise." David laughed. "I concentrated on painting and artwork. Perusing art galleries and sketching were my favorite Saturday afternoon pastimes."

"Tell me more."

His jaw tensed, and he forced himself to relax.

He expected the interest—the "getting to know each other" conversation Julian had endorsed. He just wasn't used to opening up to people. "My father wanted his sons to live up to his legacy as a star athlete."

Ashley provided an unabashed smile. "You're a star painter."

"Believe me, it's not the same." He pushed back his coffee cup.

"Instead, you lived up to the art world's expectations and well beyond."

His nod was quick, though he fell silent. The waiter came by, refilled their coffee cups and pointedly looked at the untouched cookie plate.

"I promise we'll eat all the cookies." Ashley smiled at the waiter, who quickly disappeared, then shifted her gaze to David. "You accomplished your numerous successes in your own style."

Evidently sensitive to his moods and body language, she had realized the significance of their conversation and how much his father's opinion mattered to him. Even now, after all these years. Even now, after all the rotten things his father had done.

He lifted the glass top off the plate and offered her a cookie. "Delicious, fancy chocolate."

She chuckled. "Excellent subject change."

"I try."

"I prefer plain store-bought cookies with a creamy center."

"Are you easy to please?"

"Sometimes."

"You're hedging."

"So are you." She laughed, then bit into the cookie. "These aren't frozen and taste more like fudge."

"They're posher and more expensive."

Thoughtfully, she chewed. "As long as I'm scarfing down chocolate, I'm happy. Any food from the inn's kitchen is awesome."

His mood relaxed, and their banter once again became upbeat.

The flickering candlelight cast a gleam on her thick blond hair, transforming it to silver. Her creamy complexion glowed.

She glided her fingers around the rim of her limeade glass. Her hands were slim and graceful, her fingernails cut short and tapered. She was a natural beauty.

The cozy, romantic atmosphere, along with the melodic background violins, enhanced her loveliness and brought a sparkle to the entire evening.

He wanted her to describe her art students. He enjoyed how her face lit up whenever she mentioned them. When he was about to shift the conversation toward her, she asked, "Do you see your father often?"

"No. He passed away."

"Oh. I'm sorry."

"Thanks."

"Well." She cleared her throat. "Did you used to see your father often?"

"No."

"That was an abrupt answer."

"He was a difficult guy. Like father, like son, I've been told." David sighed. "When I attended elementary school, I learned he was unfaithful to my mother."

"How did you find out?"

"He and a woman I didn't know brought me to a circus. I was confused because the woman wasn't my mother. He made me promise never to tell anyone."

"Did you?"

"I was seven." The memory of his father's stern lectures still resounded in David's brain. "You want the short answer? No. He died over a decade ago and his secret died with him."

"Did you ever wish to snatch back your promise and tell your mother?"

"Oh, I considered it many times. My heart broke for her since she had a good-hearted and trusting nature. But I was a little kid and taught to obey. Invariably, I struggled to please him."

He'd never succeeded.

Ashley snatched another cookie, pulling it apart before dipping it into her coffee. "And your mother?"

"She was my biggest cheerleader."

"So, she never learned of your father's unfaithfulness?"

"If she did, she never let on. I guess she trusted him." Unlike David. He'd learned not to trust his father. He hardly trusted anybody.

Ashley folded her hands and stayed silent.

"My mother's beauty was ageless," David went on. "No plastic surgery for her, though she insisted on dyeing her hair to cover the gray."

"Was her hair brown in her youth?"

"I believe so. Her parents immigrated to the United States from Scotland, although none of her children inherited her coloring. We all favored our Italian father's Mediterranean looks."

"Thus your attractive combination of dark hair and blue eyes."

He grinned. "I'm attractive?"

Ashley swallowed. Her cheeks flushed to her ears. "A little."

"You're attractive too. The difference is, you're attractive a lot."

"Wait, a minute." She fixed him with a stare that wouldn't let go. "Is the mysterious woman in your painting *Woman by the River*, your mother?"

"Very observant." He tugged at the collar of his shirt. "Though the woman isn't mysterious when you analyze my motives."

"Which are?"

"I add whoever is special to me and my life to my paintings."

"Like your dog. Like your mother. Anyone else?"

"Nope. Often, my mother whispered words of praise in my ear. About my art," he clarified. "Every night after prayers, she'd encourage me to continue sketching and painting."

"I like to hear that."

"Hear what?"

"I like to hear about prayers and encouragement."

He shifted. "Right."

Her head crooked to the side. "You have a problem with encouragement?"

"Nope."

"Prayer?"

Despite her reproachful tone, her eyes held kind gentleness.

"Prayer …" He paused and pondered. "Sometimes." He replied cautiously, not wishing to tread on a religious landmine, especially with a devout believer like Ashley. This was territory he hadn't navigated since his teens. "If I'm candid, I have a problem with prayer. Or rather, unanswered prayers."

"Try again. You'll find solace by talking to God."

"To each his own." He grabbed her hand. "Prayer isn't for me. If it's for you, I'm pleased you've found comfort."

"Comfort is only the beginning." She withdrew her hand. "Your mother heartily approved of your art?"

"She motivated me often whenever I wanted to quit."

He was telling Ashley more than he'd ever told anyone about his childhood, but he refused to scrutinize the emotions welling up inside him that urged him to keep speaking.

She was easy to talk to, her gaze focused solely on him.

"Please go on," she urged.

"When I was awarded a generous art scholarship to NYU, my father finally sat up and took notice, though afterward I hardly heard from him. Which is why I settled in New York City instead of moving back home."

"Where is home?"

David wrapped his hands around his cup. "A seacoast town in Georgia."

"I'm sure the area is lovely." Ashley touched his hand, her fingers lingering. Her hand seemed to gravitate back to him of its own accord. "And now?"

He didn't have an answer. Remembrances flashed of his father's final days and how David had stayed by his bedside, although his father hadn't recognized him.

Ashley opened her mouth, closed it, opened it again. "What about your brothers?"

"We don't speak. I've tried to connect, and they seldom reply. They're simply not interested. In this day and age, it's hard to believe guys think anything to do with art is a dreamer's profession reserved for sissies. I suspect they're embarrassed of me."

"You're kidding."

"I wish." He regarded the somber twist of her lips. "Happy finish, though. After undergraduate and graduate studies, New York City started to feel like home."

"Now you've landed in Cherish."

"These days, I'm living the dream."

"Which is?"

"The freedom of answering to no one."

"A confirmed bachelor?"

"Maybe."

For the time being, he added to himself.

Her mannerisms quieted. Was she interested in him, and not thrilled by his "confirmed bachelor" declaration?

No. Not possible. She was an engaging, enterprising woman who devoted her life to helping others. He was a painter who couldn't sketch a tree branch.

She picked up her fork and pressed down the cookie crumbs left on her plate. Her silence spurred him to continue.

"Both of my brothers were varsity athletes. Quinn, my sister, played soccer all through high school and college. In fact, Quinn reminds me of your friend Sarah."

"Sarah is an extremely capable woman. She hasn't allowed deafness to hamper her story. Once she recognized her disability and acknowledged she needed treatment, she embraced it. Beforehand, she waded through stages."

He leaned forward. "Such as?"

"What you might expect. Shame, refusal to accept her body's faults."

He gave himself fair warning. He was inquiring about Sarah and how she coped, though he was also interested in his own disability. "What's the result?"

Ashley bit down on her lower lip. "Sarah exhibits more self-confidence now. She's focused, and she recently declared life's too short not to value every hour. She's pleasant, practical, and I'm proud to call her a wonderful friend."

David pushed out a sigh he didn't realize he was holding.

Perhaps he should come to terms with his own disability instead of ignoring it and expecting it to go away. Perhaps hope beckoned. The prospect brought optimism to his heavy heart.

"My sister is an accomplished woman and well-educated," he said. "Though I don't see her much anymore."

"Why not?" Ashley offered him another cookie, which he refused.

"I only like them frozen." He shook his head. "Your tastes in food are wearing off on me."

"Try another cookie, anyway." With that, she plunked a cookie on his plate and asked again, "Why not?"

"Why not what?"

"Why aren't you in touch with your sister anymore?"

He waved an airy hand. "The artistic community is incredibly active in Manhattan, and obviously, I need a presence there because of my profession."

"Obviously."

He decided to follow Ashley's lead and dropped a sugar lump into his coffee. After stirring, he sipped and grimaced. Way …too sweet. He set his spoon beside his napkin. "Quinn lives in Texas and is mostly married."

"Mostly?"

"She recently filed for a divorce from her current husband and tends to relocate often. She doesn't have children."

"Current husband?"

"Her third."

"Oh."

"Soon my sister will be footloose and fancy free. I love her, yet we fell out of step."

There was no better explanation. Quinn had never understood his art—had never understood *him*. She embraced traditional art, seeing no point in upside-down dogs and neon-green trees painted on the side of a building. Whenever the occasion arose, she told him as much.

"I'm sorry," Ashley whispered.

"I suppose it's my fault." He shrugged. "I tend to be cynical regarding relationships."

"Logical, considering your father's infidelity. Don't be hard on yourself and never forget how successful you are."

"Success is the part everyone remembers. However, failure defined my in-between years." He picked up the creamer. Perhaps his coffee needed cream to offset the sugary taste. "Enough about me. What about you?"

"My upbringing was the opposite of yours. Nothing rowdy. Mine was quiet because my household consisted of me and a parent."

He filled his cup to the brim with cream and tried it. Grimacing again, he decided black coffee was much better than the other options. "Your mother raised you?"

"My father. From when I was a toddler, he taught me all God's creatures are my friend."

"Where is he now?"

"Sadly, he died five years ago, and I never knew my mother. She abandoned us when I was a newborn. Years later, I learned she'd died in a car accident a few states away. She'd been speeding late at night and drinking heavily."

David kept his attention fixed on her. "She was an alcoholic?"

Ashley bobbed a yes.

"Why did you open an art studio for children with disabilities?"

"I had trouble reading when I was young. I assumed all the letters were supposed to be backward." Ashley ran a hand through her hair. "Turns out, they weren't."

"Did you attend college?"

"I attended a state school where I was a dual art education and disability studies major. I was a shy kid, and daydreaming became a favorite pastime. I always wanted to teach art to children with special needs, and thus my two passions merged."

David nodded. "And you're single."

"I'm thirty and definitely single."

"Then I shouldn't be looking over my shoulder for an irate boyfriend?"

"Hardly. I dated a guy for a couple years."

"What happened?"

"He dumped me."

Their gazes met. David refused to let go. "The guy is a fool."

Her cheeks colored. She looked away, focusing on the tiny pinpricks of candlelight flickering from each table.

They lingered over coffee, neither one willing to break the spell of attraction that drew them closer. David didn't want the night to end. He sensed she felt the same.

An hour later, in the nearly deserted dining room, their laughter still rang out. The waitstaff unobtrusively glanced at them and smiled as they cleared the other tables.

David peered at his watch. Nearly ten o'clock, and the restaurant was scheduled to close.

"Thank you, Ashley." He sought to remove himself from the magnetic spell they'd created by capping their evening with politeness. "Again, I apologize."

"You apologized already for not listening to me yesterday."

"Indeed, we established I *was* listening."

She propped her chin on her palms. "You thanked me for the peaches."

"Then thank you for the past few hours. Too few." His voice was hoarse, and he scarcely recognized it as his own. "After you left…"

Her eyebrows shot to her hairline. "You're referring to when I stormed off?"

"Yes." He laughed out loud. It felt freeing to laugh. "I like your honesty." He liked a lot more than that about her. He liked everything.

He fished in the pocket of his sport jacket. "May I show you a photograph I took?"

"The one of the tree?"

"And you."

She sat back. "Me?"

"You happened to be in several photos."

"*Happened*? How?"

"I didn't realize it." Or maybe he did. In any case, he'd blamed the mistake on his failing eyesight.

He slid the photo across the table. The tree and flowers were clear. However, Ashley, clad in shorts and a chambray top and sitting in the tree, took center focus. "I'd welcome your permission to paint you."

"Why?"

His gaze was steady. "Because you're beautiful."

"David, I'm definitely not—"

He pressed a finger to her lips, stopping her from protesting. "You really don't realize it? Your humbleness is disarming."

"Reality, you mean." Appreciation edged her self-conscious laughter. "But thank you."

He felt as if a warm hand had settled on his heart. This woman unearthed sentiments he'd buried long ago, bringing him a newfound excitement and pleasure. She was unpretentious, yet joyful. Kind and truthful.

Inwardly, his conscience chided him. A permanent relationship between them wasn't practical. Besides the fact she lived miles away, she was a people person.

Him? He preferred to sit back and observe the world.

Nonetheless, he captured her fingers. "Is that a yes? I can paint you?"

"You have my permission, but only if I can see the painting."

"After it's done, and not before."

That's it. Establish a practical boundary. Finish the evening with a kiss on her cheek and a "'Have a good life. I'll call you.'"

He did the opposite.

He came around the table to pull out her chair, then inched closer.

He scanned the dining room. Empty. Julian and the wait staff had disappeared. When had that happened? He had been so engrossed in everything about Ashley, he hadn't paid attention to his surroundings. Even the violins had been shut off.

He tipped up her chin. "How long will you be in Cherish?"

"A while. I intend to travel back to my studio soon, because I miss my students. Thankfully, a couple volunteer instructors are filling in for me." Her gaze drifted to his. "Initially, I arranged to be here only for the weekend."

"You're extending your stay because…?"

"I like it here."

"I like it here too." He dipped his head and brushed his lips against hers in a tender kiss. "Especially because you're in town."

"Church service on Sunday was wonderful."

"An invitation?"

"Definitely."

"Church." He sighed. "I'll paint the outside. No reason for me to venture inside. Let's leave it at that."

Her fingers teased the soft hairs at his nape. "Perhaps—"

His arms wrapped around her, and he captured the rest of her words in a long kiss.

"Dining room is officially closed, folks." Julian's deep voice came from the doorway. "You can continue smooching in the hall." He flipped the light switch, and the room sank into darkness. "Our generous Lord will give each of us another day."

A minute later, Ashley and David reached the lobby, hand in hand.

"I'll settle up for tonight's meals," David said to a waiting Julian.

Julian winked. "I'm certain you'll be back and will keep a tab running."

"I'll walk you to the door." Ashley linked arms with David and led the way to the front entrance.

"Thanks." He grinned. "What are your plans for tomorrow?"

"I want to revisit Aaron's art shop."

"Aaron is a nice guy."

"Yes." Her tone was soft, her smile warm.

David pieced together her missing words. She hadn't extended her reservation in Cherish to purchase art supplies. She was staying in town because of him. He knew this as surely as his heart took a beat.

The upcoming days held infinite appeal, though his mind shouted a reminder. What could come of a serious relationship? Three months had always been his dating limit.

Luckily, it hadn't been three months yet.

And afterward? Was a long-distance relationship with Ashley possible?

He rubbed a hand over his chin.

In fairness to Ashley, he needed to attend to his vision problem first. There was no quick fix, and although his brain had adjusted, the disability was affecting his painting. He couldn't even paint a tree.

His art, his vision, his problem.

All well and good, although he clung to a decision he couldn't believe, considering there was no future with Ashley. Still, the idea took shape without warning.

"How about a tour of the town's main attraction tomorrow?" he asked.

"What is the main attraction?"

"A surprise."

Her hazel eyes widened. "You're still a newcomer here."

"Compared to your mere days, I'm a lifelong resident." He hesitated. "May I have your cellphone number?"

"Phone the reception desk and they'll transfer your call to my room."

"I'd prefer to text you directly."

One eyebrow cocked. "We hardly know each other."

"In case you haven't figured it out, I'm trying to change that."

She drew her cell phone from her purse and handed it to him. He texted himself and checked his phone. Then he texted her back. *Will you accompany me tomorrow?*

He handed the phone to her.

With a grin reaching her eyes, she replied, *Where?*

He pulled her into his arms, more than delighted she rewarded his kiss with gratifying acceptance. "A surprise, remember? I'll text you in the morning. I have somewhere special in mind."

For tomorrow. And the next day. And the day after that.

CHAPTER 9

It takes a long time to become young.
– Picasso

At daybreak, Ashley woke in her luxurious room at the inn. She drew back the snowy-white lace curtains framing the window and peered outside. The morning streets were quiet, and the whiff of buttery, yeasty biscuits from the kitchen wafted through the air. The sky was bathed in the rosy radiance of sunrise.

She debated about working out and rationalized that walking and hiking with David sufficed.

Excuses, excuses.

The bouquet of wildflowers the maître d' had sent to her room, vibrant and cheerful, held center stage in a gleaming crystal vase on a side table. She envisioned David revisiting the river, bending to choose the exact flowers she'd favored. He was a man capable of thoughtfulness and tenderness, and no one could fault her for being helplessly drawn to him.

She resolved to keep her wits about her. Attraction was fleeting. Promises of a commitment called for something else entirely. Honesty, integrity, and a long-lasting love.

As the morning hours passed and she waited for David's text, she felt increasingly guilty.

She'd sought him out over false pretenses, and it was wrong. She was a Christian woman. How could she explain to him that her car breaking down in front of his cabin hadn't been a coincidence?

She opened the pocket Bible she'd brought with her. Her father had taught her to study the verses and pray often. Today she began with Romans 8:31 and reflected on the message.

If God was for her, who could be against her? God's presence in her life didn't mean she'd never face sorrow. Instead, the words held the promise she'd never experience sorrow alone, for He was always with her.

"Dear Lord," she whispered. "Allow faith to remain my focus. I must do better. I can count on God. Can He count on me?"

Assuredly, she made excuses and there were things she should have done differently, but she vowed to learn from her missteps and apply them to her upcoming decisions. Today she had wisdom. Today she would tell David the truth of why she was in Cherish before courage abandoned her. A relationship depended on her coming clean with him.

He had trust issues and valued honesty. Had he truly believed she'd gotten lost on a one-way street in the middle of nowhere?

Don't shift the blame onto his shoulders, she scolded herself. This was all her doing. He had no reason not to accept her explanation when she'd landed on his doorstep, which only made matters worse.

In times of conflict, she prayed. She did so now in a

hushed whisper, without reservation. "Lord, in the midst of my uncertainty, I praise your glory and honor. I value your consistent presence in my life. Please do not give up on me. I appreciate that you are ever faithful."

David's text appeared on her phone screen just as a pleasant young waitress arrived with a continental breakfast tray. After Ashley positioned the tray on a table by the window, she clicked on the text.

Good morning, gorgeous, David began.

Top of the morning to you too.

Did you sleep well?

His question unsettled her, because all her dreams had been of him. She grasped the china coffeepot and poured steaming coffee into her cup.

Ashley?

I'm here. Yes, I slept well. You?

I painted until midnight. I was inspired. Pickle stayed up and kept me company.

Against her better judgment, she asked, *What did you paint?*

He didn't reply, but somehow, she already knew. He'd been painting her. As the image took hold, she hoped he hadn't sketched her with unruly blond hair and her cowlick sticking straight up. And what about her pointed chin?

Worse, had he attached her nose to her face? One never could be certain with avant-garde artists.

I kept wondering if you enjoyed yourself last night.

She reread his text. Now why would he wonder about that? His question sounded insecure, yet David was strong and confident. She could see it in his artwork, his paintings bold and emotional.

She nodded at the phone, then felt foolish because he couldn't see her. *I enjoyed myself very much. It was fun.*

It was magical, she thought.

I still feel your hand in mine.

Her heart quickened at his message. Had he really typed something that romantic?

I'll pick you up at eleven.

She paused in the act of stirring three sugar lumps into her coffee and typed, *Where are we going?*

We might go on a hike.

Might?

I'll pack everything we need.

Food?

Are cookies okay? Just kidding. He inserted a smiley emoji. *Wear comfortable shoes.*

TWO HOURS LATER, she waited in the inn's sunny, plant-filled lobby. She'd decided on lightweight jeans, a long-sleeved blouse, cotton socks, and serviceable hiking boots. She didn't intend to get bit up by mosquitoes. Also, she carried a tan leather tote bag.

A foray into her suitcase had yielded the boots she'd brought on a whim, and she was thankful. Surely God had a hand in this.

The inn provided miniature bottles of lemon and sage soap and shampoo, and the scent was heavenly. The discovery had delighted her. She was one of those women who dashed to the hotel bathroom first to check out the toiletries.

After her shower, she'd wrapped herself in a luxurious, blue-striped terry robe and applied a touch of blush and a rosy lip gloss.

She'd secured her freshly washed hair into a ponytail, then loaded her tote bag with essentials—sunscreen, a water bottle, and a thin cotton sweater in case the weather got cool.

Unlikely, though. Sunshine poured in the front window,

the blue sky speckled with clouds, and the weatherman predicted ninety-degree temperatures and the prerequisite humidity.

Julian strode over, displaying a smirk she could only describe as amused. "Greetings, Ashley. Are you sticking around for anyone in particular?"

"David suggested we see a little of Cherish today."

Julian wiped minuscule dust particles off the bannister with his fingers. "What a thoughtful guy. I give a fellow credit when he seizes a golden opportunity and runs with it."

She raised her chin. "He's showing me around because he's been in Cherish longer."

"A whole few months longer. Though it's a superb excuse for a date."

"This isn't a date."

"If you say so." He chuckled. "Where are you two exploring?"

"He mentioned a hike."

"Probably Juniper Mountain, the town's favorite."

"Sarah spoke about the Walnut Forest route. She claims the climb is easy." Ashley shoved her hair from her forehead. "I'll point that fact out to David."

"Don't forget bug spray."

"He's packing everything."

Julian laughed. "I applaud a guy who thinks ahead."

Before Ashley responded, David entered the lobby, clad in jean shorts and a gray T-shirt, and cradling Pickle under one arm. She considered that his tanned, strong-featured face belonged on the big screen of a Hollywood movie. Yet he preferred to live as a hermit and paint.

"I trust you don't mind I brought Pickle," David announced to Julian. "As you can see, I'm holding him."

"I do." Julian nodded. "As a reminder, Frank's Pizza allows dogs."

"Thanks for the tip."

Julian extended his hand to David and exchanged a friendly shake. "And I recognize Pickle from your painting that hangs in our dining room."

"You're very discerning."

"I try."

"Good morning, Ashley." David's admiring gaze fixed on her, moving gradually down her face, hair, and legs. He bent his head and their lips touched. "You are exquisite, as always."

His words caused her stomach to flutter with anticipation, and his fleeting kiss ignited a spark she hadn't felt in years. "You're not too shabby yourself."

A smile crept across his face. "And your hair smells like—"

"Lemons," she and Julian chorused.

Julian brightened. "The inn sourced our toiletries to a local woman who makes her own garden-inspired soaps and shampoos. She's experimenting with a variety of different perfumes."

"Tell her to stick with lemons," David replied.

Ashley patted the bag hoisted on her shoulders. "I'm ready for our surprise."

"Some surprise." He dropped his gaze to her hiking boots, muttering an effective analysis for their mutual foolishness to hike on such a hot day.

She burst out laughing. "We live in the South. Get used to scorching summer weather."

He joined in with a chuckle. Reaching for her hand, he led her to the front door.

"Bye, you two," Julian called out. "I'm clearly invisible because you only have eyes for, well, you two. Oh, and by the way, Tom, the previous owner of the inn, didn't allow dogs inside."

Ashley peeked over her shoulder. "We appreciate your flexibility, Julian."

He beamed. "Who am I to enforce the rules? I'm just the owner."

DAVID PROVED A PROPER GENTLEMAN, exhibiting old-world manners. He insisted on opening the passenger door of his truck for her before dashing to the driver's side and buckling Pickle into a dog harness in the seat behind her. The truck's interior smelled of oil and canvas and paint. She recognized the scents from her art studio and recalled the same smells when she'd entered David's cabin.

After they buckled their seat belts, he switched on the radio, and while Tim McGraw sang, she stole a glance at David. He sat on the ripped leather seat beside her and stared straight ahead. She sensed his need to focus and surmised it was because of his failing eyesight.

He glanced sideways at her. "Before our hike, there are a couple places I'd like to show you."

"You're the tour guide and the driver. Will we stop at Aaron's Art Shop?"

"Let's save the art excursion for another day."

Another day. Her heart squeezed. Another day to spend with this compelling man.

Despite any misgivings, happiness drifted through her. They were two friends savoring a scenic day together. Indeed, she envisioned herself looking back someday and reliving her hours with David as summer memories to cherish.

As they passed the sign advertising the Renaissance Faire, she sighed. "If I had more time, I'd choose to spend a day at the Faire."

"You do now."

"Do what?"

He sent her a smile. "You're staying for the week instead of a few days."

"True." She relaxed in her seat. "Have you ever gone to a Faire?"

"Never. In fact, wild horses couldn't drag me there." He paused. "Unless it meant a lot to you."

She was not only speechless, but she was also unexpectedly touched. He was considering her happiness before his own. That particular trait had been noticeably absent in her past relationships.

"First stop is Canine Helpers." He slowed his truck. "The volunteers train dogs to assist veterans."

"Samantha mentioned that she and Julian volunteer here."

"Yes. Scarlett Slater will show us around."

"Who is she?"

"A woman with a heart of gold."

Ashley sighted the sign and turnoff ahead. "You donated a painting to benefit the Canine Helpers auction."

David darted her a glance. "Close-knit communities. Nothing stays hush-hush for long, and everyone knows everybody."

At the intersection, he flicked on his turn signal.

She flashed a glance behind her. Pickle was contentedly snoring in the back seat. "Is your generosity a secret?"

"I'm delighted to help." He parked and rounded the truck to open the door for her. Then he woke Pickle up, unbuckling and then unleashing him. He steered them to the entrance, where a woman with flaming red hair and a generous smile greeted them.

"David Fodero. Such an honor to see you again." The woman showed them inside, and David placed a hand beneath Ashley's elbow.

"Scarlett Slater, please meet Ashley Madden, my special friend."

Ashley smiled at the introduction. She and David were friends. Special friends. Whether she was being naive or idealistic, her pulse quickened with the observation.

She glanced at him, surprised to find him intently watching her.

Scarlett beamed at Ashley. "Any friend of David's is a friend of mine. His painting commanded ten thousand dollars at our silent auction, and the money will go toward supplies for the vets. We are a Christian facility and welcome donations of any amount."

Ashley digested the mind-boggling sum a patron had paid for one of David's paintings while David explained, "Owning a dog is like having a child."

"Dogs give us absolute allegiance." Scarlett crouched to rub Pickle's head, then stood. "C'mon into the common room. We've done various improvements since you were last here, David, beginning with a new sink."

As they toured the facility, Ashley asked what type of services Canine Helpers offered.

"We specially train service dogs and match them with veterans who require emotional or physical support." Scarlett gestured to a row of leashes hanging on a wall. "Many of the men and women in our armed forces return home with PTSD or physical restrictions."

David's blue eyes lit with compassion. "Canine Helpers furnishes the animals and the assistance at no charge to the veterans."

"Our aim is to ensure our veterans lead healthy, positive lives again." Scarlett spoke with such earnestness; Ashley was taken aback by the woman's commitment. "Luckily, grants and generous donors like David's contribution to our auction help the organization remain viable."

"I wish there was a way I could help too." Ashley's gaze encompassed the clean dog dishes neatly lined up.

"Some elderly folks are donating dogs they expect will be of wonderful service." Scarlett stacked retrieval toys—discs and balls and rope tugs. "Are you available to foster a dog?"

Ashley shook her head. "My apartment is tiny."

Scarlett bent to tidy a group of empty water bowls, then stood to face Ashley. "You aren't required to train the dog, if that's the reason for your reluctance."

"I don't live in Cherish. I'm visiting. At home, I work twelve-hour days." She replied as if the reasons were clear. "It's unfair for a dog to be alone all day."

"If you're ever interested at a later time when you're not as busy, here's my cell phone number." Scarlett handed Ashley a business card.

Ashley dragged her gaze from the card to David's face. His features were undecipherable, though he hadn't lectured her about dog ownership. In fact, he hadn't uttered a word.

He gave her hand a reaffirming squeeze. "You'll recognize when the time is right."

"Eventually." Ashley placed the card in her pocket. "A dog is somewhere in my future."

"Hopefully sooner rather than later." David paid for a bone baked on the premises and gave it to Pickle. The dog whined, carried the bone in his mouth, then quickly consumed it. "Sooner is better. A dog offers devoted companionship and you're missing out."

"I've elected Frederick, my goldfish, as my only pet for the time being," she replied.

A few minutes later, Ashley, Pickle and David emerged from Canine Helpers. Scarlett had recommended they visit the music store, Musically Yours, located a few blocks away.

"My darling husband, Joseph, teaches guitar lessons there." Scarlett's green eyes had radiated with affection. "Currently, he's on a two-week tour of the eastern United States. Often, I accompany him. This time, I opted to stay in town to facilitate the training for some new dogs. However, Dorothy Edwards, the owner, will show you the music store."

"I've met her." Ashley tightened her ponytail. "I stopped in, and she told me all about Percy Grainger."

"Who is Percy Grainger?" David asked.

"He was born in Australia but is considered an American composer. Dorothy mentioned he had several peculiar obsessions."

David looked intrigued. "Spill the details."

"He gave up meat and ate mostly fruit pies."

"Better than copious amounts of sugar," he joked.

"David donated a painting to Dorothy's music shop," Scarlett said, steering the discussion back to Musically Yours. "I'm certain she'd love to see you both. I'll text her."

Agreeing, David and Ashley linked arms and exited. When all three were settled in his truck, he started the engine. There was minimal traffic on the short drive and they soon reached the corner of Myrtle and Magnolia, where the store was located.

"Scarlett's husband is a well-known contemporary worship musician." Ashley signaled to David to move closer to the curb as he parked. "I didn't put that together until you introduced her. Have you heard of Joseph Slater?"

"I don't listen to church music. Country is better."

"I disagree. Country music lyrics are all about cowboys and muddy trucks and—"

"Are you kidding? Every song tells a story. Though I recall 'worship music is your choice.'" He finger quoted with one hand, echoing the statement she, Julian, Nora, and Samantha had affirmed at dinner.

Ashley nudged his elbow. "God's grace is the best choice of all."

"Your words, not mine."

"What did you like most about church while you were growing up?"

"You don't want to hear my answer."

His confusing reply brought additional questions to mind. She sat up straighter. "Of course I do."

"To begin with, the pastor was kind."

"And the sermons?"

"I was a kid."

"Meaning you fell asleep?"

"Meaning I carried a small pad and pencil with me and sketched the pastor."

"Flattering renditions, I hope?"

"You can hope. However, on the bright side, I recall the message from one particular sermon that always stayed with me. 'The blessing ahead of you is bigger than any battle you left behind.'"

"Hallelujah, David. You had a wise pastor."

"Sometimes."

She ignored the amusement in his tone. "Go on."

"What I liked most were the refreshments served afterwards in the basement." He studied her in a beat of silence. "My mother used to bake a spicy cinnamon coffee cake with a streusel crumb topping."

"Nothing surpasses the food prepared in a church kitchen."

"Agreed. I'd sneak a cup of coffee, which was probably the beginning of my addiction to caffeine."

"You're blaming your caffeine addiction on church and your mother's coffee cake?"

Somehow, he managed to look innocent. "I told you that you wouldn't like my answer."

"Why did you stop attending?" She prayed David hadn't gotten involved in drugs or alcohol or the wrong crowd.

"Life got busy." His tone grew soft. "Life was good. I didn't need God."

The tension in the truck became smothering. She fixed him with a level stare that might have coerced a longer explanation from him had he glanced at her. However, he lowered his window and scanned the street.

A hot breeze blew inside the truck, along with the guarantee of heavy air awaiting their afternoon.

"Do you need God now?" she asked.

He met her stare, his features completely bland. "God and I don't have a running dialogue. At least, not anymore."

"One of the most profound blessings God offers is peace." She spurred herself to press onward. David harbored fears, as did everyone, but surely God would reveal Himself, allowing David to release his burdens. "He hears you," she added.

David tapped his fingers on the steering wheel. "If only He listened."

To inspire his observations, she presented a radiant smile. "You're not confident He listens, or you don't reach out to Him?"

"Both. Neither."

Silence followed his reply.

"I waited for God to communicate with me." He expelled a heavy sigh. "Nothing. Naught. Zilch. Now that I could use His guidance, He never answers."

"Why do you need His help?" She prayed David might confide to her about his vision. She wanted to comfort him, though she didn't wish to overstep her bounds.

"Because I'm human, although I like to believe I'm superhuman."

"Don't we all."

David didn't miss a beat. "I suppose you're going to lecture me on how I should pray regularly."

"I won't, then." Too tense to say more, she gazed out the passenger side at the scenic beauty of brick sidewalks, tidy shops, and window boxes overflowing with speckled petunias and dusty miller. Then she turned back to him. "Follow your heart."

"My heart is silent more often than not these days." His expression was laced with uncertainty. "Do you remember when I asked Sarah if her husband was a musician?"

"Are you changing the subject?"

"Religion is too deep a subject for such a fine summer day."

To him, maybe. Certainly not her.

Nonetheless, she'd spent enough time with David to detect his subtle nuances. Currently, his tone brought an end to their religious discourse.

"Besides," he went on. "I have something else in mind." He drew her close for a heady, unexpected kiss.

She pulled back a cautious distance. "We should go inside the store. Dorothy is expecting us."

"I'm looking forward to meeting her. Julian told me that Dorothy is a pianist, and her husband is an opera singer."

Ashley wondered if the conversation would proceed down the same path as when David compared his blindness to Beethoven's deafness.

Instead, he said, "I respect all musicians. I'm one myself."

"You are multi-talented?"

"I played the oboe in high school." He retrieved Pickle from his dog harness. "You?"

"I've never been able to sing on pitch. I took piano lessons for a couple years when I entered middle school, though I don't remember how to read a single note."

"My sister is taking piano lessons." David set Pickle on the ground and leashed the dog. "I hope Dorothy allows dogs."

"This entire community is dog-friendly."

"Another positive aspect of living in Cherish."

They lingered a half hour in the music store, chatting with Dorothy, favoring the harp earrings, and perusing stacks of sheet music.

After they left with an assortment of classical piano books for David's sister, he declared, "Now it's time for our hike."

"I don't expect you to devote your entire day to me," Ashley said as they walked hand in hand to his truck. "I'm assuming you should get back to your commissioned painting."

"I'm taking the day off."

"Are you making progress on the painting?"

A sardonic smile formed on his lips. "It's too soon to tell."

"Have you started it yet?"

"I'm waiting for inspiration to strike."

He picked up speed as they traveled on the two-lane road toward Juniper Mountain. She slanted glances at him when he wasn't looking. He had a magnificent profile, resembling a classical statue with his Roman nose and chiseled features.

During their drive, she determined he didn't have any peripheral vision to the right and could only see her if he turned his head or she sat forward. She did so, careful to make conversing as effortless as possible for him.

When they reached Juniper Mountain's parking area, he eased his truck into a space beside a vintage turquoise convertible with a "Just Married" banner draped over the rear bumper.

"How romantic." She glanced at David and was pleased he nodded in agreement. "The newlyweds must be camping to celebrate their marriage."

"Would you ever go camping on your honeymoon?"

"I'm more of a city girl." She hid her sentimentality behind a shrug. "You?"

"Whatever my future wife wanted, I'd comply without question. Her happiness would be my first priority."

"You don't seem the compliant type."

"Depends on the woman I marry. She may wind me around her little finger." He shut the ignition and covered her teasing lips with his.

Time dissolved.

The pad of his thumb smoothed her cheek. "Ashley Madden, you unbalance me," he murmured.

Her heart flipped over in her chest. His quiet utterance had a magical effect. She closed her eyes and savored his kisses. His male scent—woodsy and sandalwood—enveloped her, and she ran her fingers along his muscled forearms.

Sensing his gaze on her, she opened her eyes. She wondered what he'd say next and was surprised when he pulled back.

He blew out a breath. "Let's plan our hike for some other time."

"Why? We came all this way."

"In Cherish, everything is close. The middle of the afternoon isn't ideal for a sweltering trek up a mountain."

"What can we do instead?" Cautiously, she considered bringing up the idea of the Renaissance Faire but decided David's reaction wouldn't be positive.

His gaze rested on her lips, within inches of his. "I'll switch on the air conditioning, and we can continue kissing."

"Try another option."

He sighed. "Let's order a pizza, then enjoy a late lunch in my vintage kitchen."

"Your cabin is tastefully appointed, except for the absurd redwood chair."

"What's wrong with my chair?"

"No one in their right mind would ever sit in it."

"Why not?"

"It doesn't look at all comfortable."

"You haven't seen my kitchen yet." Absently, he fingered her renegade cowlick. "You're in for a treat."

She *had* seen his kitchen, but decided it was best not to share that knowledge with him.

CHAPTER 10

I paint objects as I think them, not as I see them.
– Picasso

A half hour later, David, Ashley and Pickle stood in Frank's Pizza, waiting for a pepperoni pizza. From what Ashley had learned from the residents, Frank's Pizza was not just the local pizzeria, it was the *only* pizzeria in town. The restaurant was empty except for a teen boy tossing pizza dough behind the counter, and David remarked that the air-conditioning was a welcome respite from the afternoon heat.

She stepped to the vending machine near the exit. "Do you want a candy bar to tide you over until we get back to your cabin? I need a sugar fix."

"I can wait another few minutes."

"I can't." With that declaration, she plunked three quarters into the machine. She waited for her choice to drop to the shelf at the bottom, but the candy bar kept dangling from the release mechanism. Muttering, she banged on the side. Nothing.

She began shaking the machine. "David?"

"Careful. It might topple, and the glass will break." He strode over, the pizza box balanced in one hand and Pickle's leash in the other.

"My candy bar is stuck, and I lost three quarters."

He sighed, set the box on an empty table, and secured Pickle's leash to a chair leg. "This can only happen to you."

"Help."

"Wait a couple seconds. Be patient. The machine might sense your candy bar hasn't dropped."

She tapped her foot. "Nothing is happening."

"Here." He dug into his pocket and handed her more quarters. "Try again and select the same candy bar. Maybe it will jerk yours loose."

She did as he suggested. Nothing changed.

She crouched to peer up into the machine. "The flap is stuck. Now you've lost your quarters too."

He cocked his head, considering the machine, then reached in his pocket. "This is the last of my quarters. Choose another candy bar from the row above."

"Grand idea." She inserted the quarters, made her selection, then exhaled. "Sadly, it isn't working."

"Right. Okay. Let's shake the machine. You take one side; I'll take the other."

No amount of jostling dislodged the candy bar.

"I wish I had those frozen chocolate cookies from the other day," he said, once they were back in his truck and following the road to his cabin. "They might alleviate your chocolate craving."

"Where are the cookies?"

He grinned. "I ate most of them. You're right, they're much better frozen. I refroze the rest."

"Frozen, thawed, and refrozen? David!" She sputtered in righteous exasperation.

After they parked in his driveway, he pressed a kiss on her forehead. "There are cookies left."

"You're trying to placate me."

"Maybe."

Before he opened her door, she jumped from his truck, the dog at her heels, and grabbed a Frisbee off the ground.

"Fetch, Pickle!" She threw the Frisbee across the lawn, and Pickle gleefully dashed after it. The sky was a dazzling blue, the sun blinding overhead. She enjoyed the radiant heat and had grown accustomed to it, though she would've welcomed a breeze. The air was motionless.

"Let's feast on pizza, then plan a walk after dinner," David said.

"Do you know what I have to say about that?" Amidst a cluster of buttery-yellow dandelions, she plucked a fluffy sphere and poised it before her lips.

"What?" He stepped closer and squinted at her, shading his eyes from the sun's glare.

She took a hearty lungful of air and puffed, sending delicate cottony seeds through the air.

He laughed and ducked. "What's that for?"

She blew again.

Another shout of his laughter almost drowned out her reply. "For making fun of me in the pizza parlor when I lost my quarters."

"You nearly broke the vending machine with your muscling."

"Muscling? Muscling?" Delighted she could make him laugh, she softened her voice and cooed, "The machine eats quarters and stole our money."

"We're the ones who put the money in to begin with." He set the pizza box on the ground and regarded Pickle, who had discovered a cool spot under the massive oak tree in the side yard. The dog's newfound Frisbee lay beside him. "Blame it on a machine malfunction."

"Sure, stick up for the vending machine instead of me."

David moved so swiftly she didn't have time to react, save for a surprised screech as he plucked a handful of fluffy dandelions.

"Now David, I assume you're not childish enough to retaliate."

"Do you recognize the foolishness of needling someone who is bigger and smarter than you?" he asked.

"Hah! You wish!" She hurled her hands to her hips. "Absolutely not."

He chased her to the oak tree, and she picked dandelions while she ran and flung them at him. Her shrieks of laughter sounded across his secluded acreage.

When he caught her, his boyish smile sent her pulse reeling. A bead of sweat trickled down his forehead, and she wiped it with her forefinger.

"You're a treasure, Ashley Madden." He brought her into his arms, and their laughter faded, replaced by a deep kiss.

She gazed past him, eyeing the oak tree. Somewhere overhead, a robin chirped. "David?"

"Hmm?"

"That tree is ideal for climbing. The branches are low-hanging and sturdy."

"Don't even think about it."

Once inside the cabin, Ashley yanked off her boots and set her tote bag on the redwood chair. She filled Pickle's water bowl at the sink while David grabbed cold drinks, plates, and silverware from the kitchen cabinets. He excused himself to freshen up and reappeared minutes later, wearing denim shorts and pulling on a white T-shirt. Her breathing stopped as she stared at his bare chest and broad-shouldered physique. The magazine photos of him had pictured him unfairly. In person, he displayed a reserved strength and a strong allure that film couldn't capture.

He gave her one of his devastatingly lazy smiles, and she scolded herself for allowing her mind to wander where it had no business wandering.

I'm falling in love with him.

Panic bumped. What? No. Never.

David Fodero is infinitely appealing.

Yes, but…

David Fodero basked in a wealthy Manhattan lifestyle she could hardly fathom. He was unreachable, unattainable, and altogether out of her league.

"Quite the kitchen, David," she joked, clamping down her emotions. "Vintage is a suitable adjective." She adjusted the faucet and splashed cold water on her cheeks. She dried her face with a clean towel, then spun to arrange the place settings on the wooden table. A window overlooked the unaffected rural surroundings. A grassy meadow beyond evoked a scene from a different era.

"Everything here is marvelous," she added. Beyond marvelous. His park-like location brought to mind temperate summer days spent resting in a hammock and reading the Bible.

He stepped to her, pulling her close to his chest. "I can see the stars at night."

"It must be beautiful." She smiled, trying to contain her growing tenderness for him.

"So you like the kitchen?" A faint catch in his voice disarmed her. He was always so self-assured, yet he valued her opinion.

"Stone floors and blue cabinets." She twisted and discovered he was studying her. "What's not to like?"

"Nothing." He offered a self-indulgent grin. "My kitchen has periodic appeal."

"Perhaps an acquired taste, and it may lack a little… modernization. Let's begin with the yellow stove and blue oven."

"Yellow and blue don't match?" He reached for two green speckled ceramic cups from the cabinet, then opened the refrigerator for an energy drink and a sugary soda.

"Stainless steel appliances are in style." She teasingly smacked him with the towel. Then, sobering, she focused on a paint splatter on the floor. "David, I have a confession."

His hand stilled for a split second before he closed the refrigerator door. "Go on."

She lifted her gaze to meet his. "I've already seen your kitchen."

"When?"

"The day I dropped off the peaches. I couldn't resist a peek." She folded the towel on the counter. Silence reigned for too many seconds.

"I'm sorry."

He poured their beverages into the cups. "Please explain."

"I was curious."

"No." His jaw was tight. "Explain why you didn't tell me sooner."

She dug her nails into her palms. "I should have. I let you down. I let myself down. Please accept my apology."

"I'm not quick to point a finger. We've all made mistakes and I'm grateful for your honesty. It means a great deal to me."

She drew back slightly. "All is forgiven?"

"All is forgiven."

Because of the lump in her throat, she couldn't form any

words. She picked up Pickle's water dish and stepped into the living room.

"The stove is a cast iron antique," David said from the kitchen. "I'll grant the oven might require replacing, although it heats up to temperature."

"What temperature?"

"Two hundred degrees Fahrenheit."

"That's not hot." She set Pickle's dish down. "Do you bake?"

"Never. There's a tasty bakery in town, though."

She rolled her eyes in humorous exasperation. "Spoken like a true guy."

"I'm practical," he called out. "Why replace a working appliance?"

"I see. You're aiming for retro, whether the oven heats or not."

"I heard that. Two hundred degrees—"

"Isn't hot enough to bake a cupcake," she muttered.

She paused, noting the rusted coffee can by the fireplace. She cast a quick glance toward the kitchen, then grasped the can and peeked inside. Two dollar bills lay crumpled at the bottom.

David strode into the living room, sipping from his speckled cup. "Ashley, do you prefer your soft drink in here?"

"I'm fine for now. Thanks."

He stopped. Swallowed. Propped a shoulder against the doorjamb. "What are you doing?"

She held up the coffee can, regretting the timing of his entrance. "I'm sorry. I didn't mean to snoop—"

"You did, though." His face became expressionless, his voice sharp in contrast.

She set the can back down. Tears stung her eyes. "I said I was sorry."

"C'mere." He set his cup on the table and beckoned her to sit on the sofa.

"What about the pizza?"

"I prefer cold pizza. I hope you do too." He raked a hand through his hair. "I didn't intend to charge you with a crime for picking up a rusty old can."

She planned to answer when she was good and ready. She planned to sit when she was good and ready. But there was no contest when it came to David's quiet apology.

She perched on the edge of the sofa. "Sometimes, you are thoroughly impossible."

"Others have said the same. I'm working on becoming a better person. I make excuses, though I try to take full responsibility for my words and actions."

She had leftover anger to challenge him. Nevertheless, she wasn't *that* upset. Besides, she was a Christian and granted forgiveness graciously. Nor could she ignore the mindlessness of upsetting their precious minutes with a needless misunderstanding.

He settled on the sofa and requested she sit closer. Once she scooted near, he slung an arm around her shoulders. "We've spent hours together, yet we're virtual strangers in many respects."

After all their banter, an upscale dinner, and endless delightful kisses, they were still strangers?

Still, she bestowed her best smile. "More sharing? You go first."

"Why am I always first?"

"Because you owe me a candy bar, and the suggestion is yours."

He kept his gaze on the fireplace. "Are you ready for more accounts of my artistic struggle?"

Stunned and flattered because he'd relented so quickly, she nodded. He was a private man, yet he chose to share his personal stories with her. And she sensed that this story held special significance for him.

"Did you ever hold on to something that meant the world to you, even though it carried little monetary value?" He smiled, and the curious tug on her heart occurred again, that tender odd ache.

"A rusty coffee can?" she teased.

"The can is a symbol."

"For what?"

"Do you recall when I told you the road to success is built on hard work?" His tone was strangely hoarse.

"And you mentioned it takes years and years."

He stared at the can. Abundant silence. With David, she was learning patience.

"When I attended NYU…"

"You were awarded a full scholarship." She patted his forearm, a congratulatory pat he probably considered sophomoric. Still, their relationship was tentative, though for her, it was on the verge of becoming more serious with each of his tales. "Your family must've been proud and thrilled." She switched to an encouraging note.

His features remained somber, and she doubted his father had sent any gratifying "*Atta boys*" his way.

Every minute she spent with David, she understood him more. He was complex. He was smart and talented. And he'd been hurt. His recollections brought a broader comprehension of his nature. He was kind, yet vulnerable.

"A scholarship doesn't compensate for everything." His voice deepened. "Tuition and books, sure, though not the infinite art supplies."

She nodded in commiseration. "I can't operate without the countless paintbrushes and watercolors I resupply for my studio each month."

"Nor did my scholarship pay for meals and living costs."

She looked up at him. "Your parents didn't help you financially?"

"My father didn't want his son to become an artist, remember?" David reached for his cup and sipped. "He was pleased about the scholarship. Nonetheless, I was on my own."

She sat engrossed, listening to every sentence, every tenuous shade of David's voice. She had learned already that whenever he mentioned his father, aloofness laced his expression. In this case, she suspected his father's reaction had hurt David the most. She considered remarking that his father's disinterest was cruel, for it had deeply wounded his talented, impressionable son. However, she reserved judgment. "How did you earn money in college?"

"I staked out busy street corners and sketched people. I carried a stool, drawing paper, charcoal pencils, and a kneaded eraser."

"An artist's favorite friend," she agreed. "The eraser doesn't leave any heavy marks behind."

"Hurray. A woman who knows art." He kissed the top of her forehead. "I charged five dollars for each portrait."

A portrait that now commanded over a thousand dollars.

"The key to drawing a good portrait is shading and proper proportions." His smile quickened her heart. Art was, first and foremost, a passion for him. "The distance between the nose and mouth is important."

"You sketched in the middle of busy New York?" She visualized him as a young man, alone in a city of eight million people.

"At the intersection of Broadway and West Forty-First Street, just south of Times Square." His answer was matter of fact, though his arm tightened around her. "I displayed the coffee can in a conspicuous spot for tips. I was an emerging artist developing my craft while earning money at the same time."

"Very enterprising."

"The first two dollars I ever earned are in that coffee can." He ran his thumb around the rim of his cup. "A gray-haired grandmother came by on my first day and requested I sketch her granddaughter. When I finished, I thought the grand-daughter's teeth were too white of a contrast, though they seemed pleased. The can is a reminder to celebrate the triumphs, no matter how small."

He'd saved his first tip and carried the money with him all these years. Ashley wrestled with the explosive emotions welling in her chest.

She blinked back tears and searched his face. His expression was carefully aloof.

Be proud, she thought. *Embrace your God-given talent. Never second-guess yourself.*

Lightly, she touched his hand. "That grandmother must've recognized your tremendous ability."

"I doubt it, though I value your compliment." He set down his cup, lifted her hair and nuzzled her nape.

Ashley rested her head on his shoulder and propped her feet on the coffee table. He held her close.

She drew a fortifying breath, reluctant to shatter the intimate mood. Nevertheless, she plunged ahead. "I noticed your vision loss."

He shifted positions. "How can you tell?"

"When you look at me, you favor a certain side. Plus, your reference to a deaf Beethoven the first day we met, coupled with Cherish's rumor mill."

"Am I completely transparent?"

"In times of trouble, we all reach out, whether we realize it or not. You did when you alluded to Beethoven. What happened to you?"

He sighed. "More than enough questions about me."

She almost flinched at the brusqueness in his tone.

His unwarranted flippancy grated on her. How could they not discuss what was so significant to him? Wasn't he the person who had declared not ten minutes earlier that they were virtual strangers?

"Please don't brush off the topic," she replied. "I want to identify with what's important to you. Don't stop painting. You're too talented."

"Thanks for the encouragement." He shoved a throw pillow aside, stood, and reached for her hand. "Let's eat the pizza before it gets cold."

"I thought you preferred cold pizza."

"I changed my mind."

"You're dismissing me."

"I'm dismissing the subject because I refuse to allow an in-depth analysis of my vision loss. Not to anyone except my physician. Not even you." He succeeded in displaying a semblance of a smile. "Come into the kitchen. I prefer to dine with a lovely companion rather than eating alone."

CHAPTER 11

Youth has no age.
– Picasso

*A*s they ate their pizza, sitting across from each other at the kitchen table after she'd whispered a prayer of grace, David was courteous, yet pensive. When they finished, she cleared their dishes, stacked them in the sink, and discarded the paper napkins in the trash.

"No dishwasher?" She tried for an easy-going conversation, hoping he'd bounce back from his contemplative mood.

"I prefer to wash dishes by hand," he replied.

His profile was silhouetted in the glow of the afternoon sun gleaming through the window. His hands were jammed in his pockets, and Pickle relaxed by his feet. A jug of water still sat on the table. She'd sliced lime and lemon into the water for flavor, and two half-filled glasses of water remained.

She started for the living room, intending to pull on her

hiking boots, then ask him to drive her back to the inn. The walk he'd mentioned? Well, they wouldn't be taking a walk anytime soon.

He balled up a napkin she'd missed collecting. "A few months ago," he said softly, "I woke up and discovered I'd lost vision in one eye."

She stopped.

Ignoring the solid beating of her heart, she padded into the kitchen and seated herself at the table again. He sat across from her.

"This subject is difficult for me." He held out his hand. She grasped it and gave a supportive squeeze.

More than a little unnerved, her thoughts spun, one in particular. When she'd studied for her art degree, she happened upon a quote by Pablo Picasso, the renowned Spanish painter and sculptor.

"'Others have seen what is and asked why,'" she quoted. "'I have seen what could be and asked why not.'"

"Picasso," David replied.

With a vague sense of foreboding, she refilled their water glasses. "Maybe I can help you."

"I don't need anyone's help." His dark eyebrows snapped together. "I'm explaining because you pressed me for details."

She hadn't but didn't argue. Stiffening, she shoved her chair back.

Pickle came to his feet and stared up at her.

"Point taken, David," she said. "Loud and clear. I'm leaving and phoning an Uber."

Because the point *was* taken. Now she finally understood.

David enjoyed spending time with her, but she wasn't allowed any closer than a shared pizza. *Virtual strangers.* She'd been an amusing diversion when he was wearied, an excuse for procrastination when he was supposed to be working on a commissioned painting.

He stood, shadowing her. He placed his hands on her shoulders. "Please stay."

Her heartbeat doubled at the despair in his voice, though her tolerance and patience had worn thin. Only a fool would keep listening, conscious of being used as a sounding board because there was no one else.

She swiveled toward the living room.

"Ashley." His voice came from behind her. "Forgive my abruptness."

She whirled. "You drive me away when I want to support you." She seized her tote bag and fished for her cellphone. "I'm a silly art teacher and will never meet your lofty standards to—"

He reached her in two steps and gently caught her wrist. "Don't go."

She jerked from his grip.

"I've got cookies in the freezer." His pleading tone, his grasping for something to keep her near—cookies, of all things—demolished her anger. Undecided whether to laugh or cry, she did both.

He cradled her, kissed her neck, her lips, and wiped the tears from her cheeks. She didn't resist. She couldn't resist. She was falling in love with a man who was creative, enterprising, skeptical, and in many ways reminded her of the enchanting, vulnerable students she taught—all seeking support.

He rested his chin on the top of her head. "I don't deserve someone as sweet and caring as you in my life."

"I'm here," she whispered, and buried her face in his chest. His heart beat fast and solid against her cheek.

He led her into the living room, to the sofa, and circled his arm around her. She sank down beside him, picking up a throw pillow that had fallen to the floor. Pickle took up his usual spot by the fireplace.

"My condition is called NAION, an abbreviation for a lengthy description," David began. "Non-arteritic anterior ischemic optic neuropathy."

"You expect me to remember that?" She smiled, eager to ease a challenging conversation.

Her teasing did the trick, because he chuckled. "In summary, there's a loss of blood flow from my optic nerve leading to the brain."

"Were you in pain when it happened?"

"No. I'm not in pain now, either."

Her smile wavered. "What causes the condition?"

"My doctor in New York referred me to numerous studies citing high blood pressure and/or smoking. Neither applies to me."

"What is your doctor's treatment recommendation?"

"Nothing, except for daily aspirin and a healthy lifestyle. Usually, the condition doesn't get any worse."

She placed a hand on his forearm. "This is encouraging news."

"Nor does it get any better."

She winced. "Will wearing eyeglasses help?"

"No. Eyeglasses aid nearsightedness or farsightedness but won't restore a damaged optic nerve. The doctor assured me that my brain will adjust, and it has."

"Oh, David, I'm sincerely sorry." A thought arose, one she blurted before fully considering. "Is your other eye affected?"

"There's a 30 percent chance. Luckily, my vision is twenty-twenty in that eye."

Thrown off balance, she echoed half to herself, "A 30 percent chance."

"I'm absolutely fine." He gave her a cheerful smile she didn't believe for a minute.

"Really?"

"Really."

"Is your vision loss the reason you aren't painting?" She wavered to steady herself and pace her questions. "You're known for being prolific."

"I can still paint."

"But you're not."

He shrugged. "I'm a realist, and not a very productive one."

"Perhaps you've set impossibly high standards for yourself." *Much like what she'd been accused of doing with her ex-boyfriend.*

"Perhaps." David released a heavy sigh. "Time will tell, though I imagine my painting has changed."

"Change is good."

He rubbed a fist over his jaw. "Sometimes."

"Prayer is better." She kept her hand on his forearm. "Will you pray with me?"

"You pray. I'll listen."

She bowed her head, and David did the same.

"Dear Lord, David is becoming a new creation," she whispered. "Please make way in his mind for fresh prospects and habits. Some of your greatest miracles are created when people are in transition. Encourage David through this difficult period and grant him wisdom and peace. Give him faith to comprehend. Amen."

David lifted his head. "I admit I feel better."

"It's not me. It's God." She raised her palms to heaven. "He promised He will never leave us or forsake us. Take heart in His assurances."

"I'll try."

Unlike the past hour's ups and downs, the next few minutes passed serenely. She relaxed in the comfortable surroundings, a dog by the fireplace, the special man she'd fallen for holding her as if he'd never let go.

A sharp pang of longing went through her. This restful,

contented life was a life she'd never live. She wanted children someday. However, children necessitated marriage and a husband, and neither was part of her future.

David pressed a kiss to her temple. "Now I want to hear more about you."

"Me?" She leaned back.

"Why did Sarah call you Twinkle?"

Something about his engaging smile prodded her to answer. After all, he'd spoken with honesty and openness.

"I've always gotten excited about my students' drawings," she said.

He threw her a speculative grin. "Please continue."

"A few years ago, an adorable autistic boy remarked that my eyes twinkled like sparkly green stars after I'd praised him. He is wonderfully artistic."

"How old is he?"

"Ten." She crossed her feet. "These kids appreciate art. They're my type of people."

"I appreciate art."

She nudged his rib with her elbow. "Therefore, it goes without saying…"

"I'm your type of person. I'm flattered, Twinkle."

She grinned. "Are you making fun of me?"

"Never."

"In summary, the name stuck. My close friends use my nickname often."

"Twinkle, twinkle, you are my shining star."

Heat hastened her pulse at his tender words and heavy-lidded gaze. Surely a man capable of evoking such profound emotions through his paintings wasn't teasing any longer.

Regardless, she wouldn't be drawn in by an artist who was brilliant, funny, and so attractive that her temperature rose ten degrees the moment she set eyes on him.

No, no. Surely, she wouldn't be a pathetic fool a second

time—charmed by a man feigning interest, then dropping her when he found a more appealing woman.

That is, unless that particular man began kissing her with such abandon, cuddling her, his lips caressing hers so urgently her heart responded with intense longing.

Minutes after their kisses ended, he didn't take his gaze from her face as he invited her back into the kitchen.

She lifted a teasing eyebrow. "For cookies?"

"We could eat a box, although I want to paint you first."

"I thought you were using the photograph by the river to paint me."

"You're here in person. What could be better?"

They exchanged smiles.

"I'll take the dog out and grab some special paints I store in my truck," he said.

She perched on the edge of a kitchen chair and waited. He returned carrying an assortment of flamboyant shades of blue and red paint, gold glitter, a brush, and a sea sponge. An old T-shirt cut up as a rag was tucked into the waistband of his shorts.

Her gaze narrowed. "Where's your canvas?"

"Don't need one."

"Aren't you going to paint me?"

And then she realized it. He intended to literally paint *her.*

"Um, nope." She jumped up and backed away. "No dice." It hadn't occurred to her beforehand because the idea was absolutely, utterly insane. "Find someone else to paint."

He looked around. "Who?"

"Call one of your Hollywood models."

"None hold a candle to you." He approached her with the sponge and a pot of cobalt-blue paint. "This is water soluble and will wash off."

"Your assurances are supposed to appease me?" She gazed at the ceiling, searching for a guarantee somewhere, anywhere. "You lured me into the kitchen because I assumed we were eating cookies."

"We can. I have a half box left."

"That's all?"

"I'll spare you a couple."

She lunged for the freezer, pulling open the door, but he was faster. He set down the sponge and paint and snagged the box.

She peered into the freezer. "Where's your frozen pizzas and peanut butter ice cream?"

"I don't eat junk food."

"Yeah, right. What kind of guy doesn't eat Hungry-Man dinners?"

"Me." He held the cookie box over her head. "Shall we eat these now or later?"

She blew out the air stuck in her throat. "Let's wait."

"Wise choice. Body art is fascinating, and you're an inspiration, Ashley."

She cast a sideways glance toward the doorway. "I'll agree under one condition."

"Conditions, now?"

"Absolutely. You paint my face, and I'll paint yours."

"Agreed. Stand still." He tapped the sponge into the paint, then dabbed numerous drops on her cheeks. "Remember, don't sweat."

"On the hottest day of the year?"

"The air-conditioning is on."

"Great. Until I step outside into the eighty-degree heat and humidity."

She curved toward the window, eager to view her reflection in the glass. Her blue cheeks were muted, giving her the appearance of a lopsided clown.

"Ninety-nine percent of people who are body painted say they would do it again." David spoke calmly, his actions focused, as he guided her around to face him. He stood back, then applied a dab of gold glitter on her nose. "Excellent!"

"This calls for retaliation." She flipped him a smile, snatched the sponge, and aimed for his forehead. A blob of gold glitter dripped from his chin when she missed. "Sorry." She reached for the blue paint and knocked over the pot, splattering paint across the stone floor.

"I might need to renovate the kitchen after all." He drew her to him and kissed her. "It's also been noted that face painting unites people."

"Where did you read that?"

"Somewhere."

Yes, he was impossible.

In a lushly renovated cabin in the woods, their laughter rang out.

Pickle barked and raced around them. Frozen cookies were left to thaw.

And all was perfect in Ashley's world.

CHAPTER 12

The chief enemy of creativity is good sense.
- Picasso

*T*he following two days passed in a blur. Ashley notified Nancy at the art gallery, reporting that she'd found David and he was all right. She didn't reveal his eyesight loss. The subject was personal and up to him to explain.

Ashley phoned the leader of the fellowship group at her church that evening. "I'll drive back to my apartment on Saturday, so I'm prepared to teach Sunday School," she told her.

Then she texted her substitute teachers and was assured her students were doing splendidly.

Taking maximum advantage of their days together, David invited her to peruse the boutiques in town, and dine with him at respective restaurants including The Garden Terrace, recognized for their mesquite barbecued ribs and sugar-free lemon cake, both of which delighted Ashley.

She wore light summer dresses, thankfully she'd packed several, as she had the tendency to over-pack. From Sarah, she borrowed flirty straw hats and applied black mascara to bring out her large hazel eyes. Friends had remarked that her eyes were her best feature, so why not accentuate them?

During a shopping trip to Aaron's Art Shop, David insisted on purchasing hundreds of dollars' worth of supplies for her studio. They left the shop with their arms laden with bags, and Pickle walked with them on a secure leash as they crossed the street to David's truck.

Ashley sighed. "I wanted to reach my exercise quota by working out at the inn's gym. Julian told me he recently updated with state-of-the-art equipment."

David deposited their bags into his trunk. "*Wanted* to reach your goals?"

"Yes, that's the key word. I haven't visited the gym once."

"At least your intentions are good." His eyes crinkled at the corners. "I owe you an excursion to Juniper Mountain and the hiking trip I promised the other day."

"You're referring to the day we ate pizza in your cabin?"

He shut the trunk and took hold of Pickle's leash. "The very same."

"And the day you painted me."

"Yup."

She accepted his outstretched hand. "Despite your assurances concerning water-soluble paint, Julian definitely gave me an odd look when I arrived back at the inn."

"You washed the paint off in my bathroom before I drove you to the inn."

She tilted her head. "Yes, I did. Lots of scrubbing and rubbing alcohol helped remove the paint, but the gold glitter insisted on sticking to my nose."

He kissed the tip of her nose. "Lucky for you, all the paint has worn off now."

"Lucky for *you*, or I would've cheerfully thrown you out of a tree."

"If you recall, I don't climb trees anymore."

"There's always a second time."

He chuckled and stopped in midstep. "That's something else I love about you. You always express exactly what's on your mind."

Something else he loved.

Her heart cartwheeled in her chest. David spoke about love.

She stared into his arresting gaze. For a number of seconds, she permitted herself to wonder what it would be like to be loved by this artistic, enigmatic man? They'd spend hours together, conversing about art, wisecracking, and relishing each other's company.

I'll help you confront your vision problem, she thought. *I'll lend support at every crossroad, and you can show my precious students your exquisite canvases and provide expert tips. We'll attend concerts—maybe the music of Percy Grainger. We'll serve in church. We'll pray.*

Where, exactly? In Cherish? In New York City? In Greenwood?

He cupped her chin, smoothing his thumb along her jawline. His woodsy, male scent floated to her nostrils, prompting an intense awareness of the vital man bending his head to kiss her.

Right there. In the middle of the main street.

From the first second she'd met him, her feelings had been overwhelming. No matter how light-hearted their conversations, a kiss invariably followed. Around David, she was comfortable, and everything seemed familiar. With him she felt cared for and safe.

"You're very special, Ashley." His voice lowered to a murmur. "Never forget that."

His deep tone blended with the hum of residents chatting among themselves. A mother chased after a toddler who lifted his shirt over his head as he ran across the sidewalk. On the grassy lawn of the park, children invented a game, legs churning as they ran in circles.

A life worth living. A life with David. A wonderful, fanciful dream.

She recalled the sting of heartbreak, the crushing, biting wound, and she determinedly shoved her dreams aside. She'd been hurt by a man once, her fantasies shattered, and she wouldn't risk it again. Besides, no one fell in love in mere days.

Did they?

They continued their wanderings to Whitney's, the local ice cream parlor. She ordered a chocolate sundae topped with hot fudge and a cherry, and David selected a triple decker coffee cone. Pet-friendly, the owners produced a natural frozen yogurt for dogs served in a bowl. Pickle's eyes grew round, and he lapped up the yogurt.

"We've gone to the dogs," the owner joked, which earned a burst of laughter.

Ashley and David assembled outside on sunny-yellow chairs, leaning their elbows on the wrought-iron table. When they couldn't eat another bite, David offered to walk her to the inn, assuring he'd double back to his truck and deliver her art supplies in the morning.

They resumed their pace, strolling hand in hand. The afternoon sun beat down on them, though a faint breeze stirred and ruffled her hair. Nevertheless, the minutes were sleepy and motionless, the air hot and aromatic. Songbirds chirped from the trees, and joggers passed them at a slow clip.

"About that invite…" David began.

"To Walnut Forest and Juniper Mountain?"

"You're a hiker. Here's your opportunity to show off your expertise." The sparkle in his gaze underscored his sheer enjoyment of joking with her.

"I hike a couple blocks around my apartment, which is on a flat sidewalk." She chuckled. "Primarily, I walk on a treadmill in my living room while I listen to audiobooks."

"What type of books?"

"I gravitate toward adventure thrillers."

They curved onto a quiet, residential lane. "We share many interests, Ashley, beginning with art and audiobooks."

She studied his face, his expressions of tenderness.

By silent agreement, they zeroed in on a park bench. "You're on a roll, David. Please continue."

"Continue what?"

"Listing our interests."

He pressed a kiss on her cheek. "Exercise is another."

She jabbed him with her elbow. "I haven't found the time because I'm spending every waking minute with you. Therefore, it's all your fault I've gained weight this week."

"My fault?" He held a hand over his heart. "I'll willingly accept the blame, honored you'd use me as an excuse."

His good humor erased any reservations for missing her workouts, and she couldn't contain her joking. "As well you should."

"Set aside an hour each day," he said. "Mornings work best for me."

"Your suggestion takes discipline, which I evidently lack."

"You're the most disciplined woman I've ever met. You operate your own studio, you're clearly excellent with children, and your inspirational words shine with conviction."

His observations floored her. She flipped back her thick hair that kept falling over her eyes and studied him. God's purpose was to redeem and rebuild. It wasn't too late for David's faith to be restored.

"The old has gone, the new is here." She referenced a passage from Corinthians.

David grinned. "Make way for the new." His grin widened, his eyes an electric, luminous blue. In its depths, she lost herself in her expectations, her imaginings, her emotions.

She recalled the first day they met at his cabin and formally shook hands. Every part of her senses had fixated on the touch of his calloused fingers linked with hers. He reminded her of the fictional heroes she adored, a resilient, charismatic male. A protagonist straight from a storybook, complete with a happily ever after. The more hours he occupied, the more her initial observations had proved correct. David Fodero could overcome any obstacle, if only his faith and optimism were reinforced.

She pondered a second possibility. Should anything happen and he lost eyesight in his good eye—Well, she couldn't permit her thoughts to go there.

An artist who couldn't see. An artist who couldn't paint.

No.

Nevertheless, uncertainties persisted.

What if?

Her internal response was immediate. *Trust God.*

David shouldn't allow his hardships to prevent him from appreciating what God had planted inside him. Every person was unique and special. Every person had something in them to help press through their adversities and reach the other side.

So deep in thought, she didn't hear David's question at first. "Have you ever gone camping?" he asked again.

She viewed the inn, visible up ahead. "When I was eight years old, I camped overnight with my father and an elderly couple from our church. They'd been married for decades and were schoolteachers. They were reaching retirement age and wanted to serve the Lord by volunteering."

"Did they retire?"

"Yes, and they were excited to offer their unique gifts of support and mentoring children in a remote country. They were Christians and believed giving their lives to God helped to change people."

David picked up his steps and steered her toward a park bench beneath a large magnolia tree. The shade from the fragrant pink blossoms offered a welcome respite from the heat, and Pickle chose a place in the cool grass.

"How did your camping expedition go?" David secured the dog's leash to a tree and grabbed Pickle's striped elephant from his pocket, tossing it to him.

"Camping was an adventure." Ashley settled on the bench, the cool iron pressing against her bare legs. She was grateful she'd worn a casual outfit—cotton shorts, a white eyelet blouse, and sandals. "My father and I prayed with our friends and asked God to mark their journey with safety."

"Sometimes, I miss church."

She touched his wrist, hearing the desire in his deep voice. "Church misses you."

"I'm struggling. You rely on God and never lose faith."

"I've lost faith more often than I can count, beginning with the camping trip."

"Hard to believe."

Seconds ticked.

She expelled a breath, knowing he waited for a reply.

"The married couple was scheduled to devote the upcoming six months to a mountain village overseas, though the wife expressed reservations. There had been recent news reports that the impoverished country was suffering an unanticipated upheaval. I talked them into traveling."

"You?"

"They planned to do so much good and spread the word of the Lord."

Happy remembrances of the tan canvas tents erected side by side, sitting around the campfire toasting marshmallows over a sizzling fire, brought fond memories.

At least initially.

"When did they return from their missionary trip?" David's question pulled her out of her musings and yanked her back to reality. "Are you still in touch with them?"

"No." She choked on the single word.

"Why? What happened?"

"They were killed. Guerillas attacked their village late at night and none of the townspeople and missionaries survived." She swiped at the tears forming at the corner of her eyes. "For months afterwards, I blamed myself."

The warmth of David's reassuring fingers lifted the weight off her chest. "An attack in a foreign country is hardly your fault."

Pickle inched toward them, and she picked him up, allowing him to lick her arms. "I was the person who encouraged them to go on the trip."

"You were eight years old. It's unlikely you influenced their decision."

"I still believed it was all my fault, and my convictions faltered. My father uplifted me, brought me to church, prayed with me at night." She sucked in a lungful of oxygen. "I remember the wife read stories from the Bible that night we were camping. They were righteous, kind Christians."

David leaned closer. "What kind of stories?"

"She spoke about Paul's thorn in the flesh from 2 Corinthians 12:7." While Ashley recited the verse, David trained his gaze on Pickle.

"When I was young, I studied the New Testament and memorized favorite passages," he replied.

"Do you remember the significance of Paul's story?"

"There are many theories." David repositioned himself and faced her. He was so close his legs brushed against hers. "Recollections of Paul's past, former temptations, or perhaps a physical ailment."

"Paul's eyesight, his difficulty seeing, is a possibility often examined." She adjusted Pickle so he wouldn't slide off her lap. "Sometimes God uses our physical weaknesses to humble us."

"I'm hardly a saint, Ashley. You're comparing my eyesight loss to Paul's thorn?"

His question hung in the silence between them. In his tone, she heard defensiveness and despair.

She instructed herself to breathe, and slanted a glance toward him. He didn't meet her gaze.

Who was she to judge him if he was bitter at God? Was she a better Christian?

The sun lowered behind a cloud and softened David's rigid features. She breathed in a bottomless breath, saturated with the scent of fragrant magnolias.

She took his hand. "I'm truly sorry about your vision loss, David."

Absently, he scratched Pickle's head and stared at the empty lot across the road. "I appreciate your concern."

"Remember God's grace and know it is enough. Walk through your season of uncertainty and praise Him. His power is made perfect through our weaknesses."

"Once, I believed. When adolescence kicked in, I questioned everything." He met her gaze for a split-second before refocusing on the lot. "Despite my mother's prodding, I never returned to church."

"How many years has it been?"

"Two decades."

Her lips parted in astonishment. "Yet you're commissioned to paint a church."

"The exterior." He shifted. "Not the interior."

She envisioned him as a young boy, as an adolescent, and her heart fluttered at the image. Fresh-faced, probably skinny with long arms and legs. He craved love and protection and assurance. Quiet and reserved, with a spark of creative mischief. Even when attending elementary school, his artistic ability must have spilled from every pore, although he had recognized his father's displeasure.

She formed her lips into a smile. "Are you sorry you accepted the commission?"

"It brought me to Cherish. It brought me to you."

Her movements never faltered as she placed the dog on the ground, though her emotions spun in a thousand directions. She stared up at David's face, felt the familiar strength of his strong arms as he cuddled her.

Her heart burst with something she could only identify as love.

She longed to vocalize her feelings because she agreed with him. Come what may, their meeting each other had been predestined.

Although no. It had been calculated. By her.

Her throat tightened, and her voice was snatched away.

"Your emotions are written all over your face, Ashley." David seemed unaware of the tears threatening to blur her own vision. "You're an open book."

"Am I?" She drove a hand through her hair, tempted to pat down her rambunctious cowlick, which surely must be sticking straight up in this humidity. She didn't, because David patted it down for her.

"I knew it the moment you showed up at my cabin wearing sandals, searching for a mountain located in another state." A grin tugged at his full mouth. "The expression on your face was a definite giveaway."

A giveaway for her stupidity, she chastised herself. Again, she sent a prayer to God to forgive her for deceiving David.

She shoved to her feet. "I should tell you something."

"No climbing trees, I hope." He stood and unleashed Pickle. "Although I'm accepting options for tomorrow's plans."

"It's not about tomorrow."

And just like that, she lost her nerve, refusing to deflate the shining admiration for her in his gaze.

"What is it?" he asked.

"I can't. I should spend the day packing since I'm planning to leave on Saturday."

His gaze narrowed. He grabbed her hand. "You're leaving so soon?"

"David, I've been in Cherish almost a week."

He stared down at their fingers, firmly entwined. "You can't stay any longer?"

"My students miss me, and I miss them. In addition, I'm in charge of a Sunday school class at my church. I love teaching five-year-old's about God. Besides, I imagine you've neglected your commission because you've invested all your hours with me."

"I've been painting."

"Great! The centennial portrait?"

He paused, forcing her to pause, too. "A subject far more important to me."

His heated gaze robbed her of any ability to form a coherent sentence. She yearned for more, a pledge that he'd phone, a promise to see her, although he hadn't offered any commitment. None at all. Nothing.

Did he even know where she lived? She riffled through their conversations. He'd never asked. She'd never told him.

She didn't press. She didn't wish to become another conquest. Yet the intensity of how much she cared for him already scared her.

She focused on the scattered sunlight dappling through the tree leaves. An artist's eye would be scrutinizing the sun's position, the contour of the spaces where the light shone through, the elevation of the tree canopy.

David looped an arm around her shoulders. "Instead of packing, will you go to the Renaissance Faire with me?"

Taken aback, she gaped. Had she imagined his invitation?

"I have it on excellent authority, specifically yours, that you're not a fan of Renaissance Faires," she said.

"You're a fan, which is all that matters."

"You're not exactly the most sociable guy on the planet."

"I like people."

"Who?"

"You. Very much. It's the silliness involved in dressing up as a character from the fourteenth century that I object to." He held up a hand. "Don't ask, because I won't be wearing any costume."

She eyed him from head to toe. "I envision you as a knight."

He gave a gallant bow. "And you're my lady. We'll eat, drink, and watch a jousting match."

A Renaissance Faire. At last. Her veins hummed with excitement. She steeled herself not to react, but wrapped her hands around his nape, anyway. "I'm so excited, David."

"My pleasure. Let's seal our date."

Happily, she obliged, a treasured kiss beneath a Carolina-blue sky.

Savor every minute, she told herself. Someday, she'd look back upon this wondrous week with joy. A summer to remember. A summer to cherish. Days filled with brilliance and wonder and David. This cynical, witty, artistic, generous man.

She'd miss him terribly after they parted. Nonetheless, she'd provide a clear and simple explanation for why she'd initially come to Cherish. Sure, it was easier to flee than cope with her wrongdoing, but their relationship insisted she push past her fear and risk seeing the disappointment on his face.

Her jaw set, her mind made up. Though her stomach pitched at the thought, she'd tell him the truth tomorrow, at day's end.

And then she would pray, intending to make peace with her failings.

CHAPTER 13

Colors, like features, follow the changes in emotions.
- Picasso

"I refuse to wear a metal helmet." David frowned at himself in the full-length mirror of the Renaissance Faire's costume shop. "What will people think?"

Ashley gazed at him with giggling delight. "They'll think you're ingenious and original."

Considering half the men at the Faire were also dressed as knights, David highly doubted it.

Ashley had dragged him into the first shop she'd spotted and talked him into renting a knight's costume. Of course, she hadn't literally talked him into it. The joy lighting her face was all the convincing he needed. Besides, the Faire was held in a neighboring town. They wouldn't bump into anyone they knew.

As soon as he and Ashley had stepped through the gate-opening, they were hailed by a court jester sporting a three-pointed hat and ringing a tiny bell while being serenaded by an animated group of musicians playing wooden flutes and tambourines.

She brushed a piece of lint off his polo shirt collar, which peeked through the cape. "What's the definition of a brave knight without armor protection?"

"A wise, practical man who can breathe."

There was something about a guy dressed in shorts—David had refused the woolen stockings and metal chest plate—and wearing a red cape that didn't quite match.

Ashley tightened the ties around his neck. "Despite you wearing sneakers instead of pointed boots, you're still the pluckiest, most dashing knight I've ever met."

He peered down at his shoes. "How many knights are plucky?"

"None until now."

She looked adorable, standing in front of him in an emerald-green velveteen gown that brought out the green hues in her hazel eyes. His gaze glided over her figure, lingering on her slim hips.

He placed a roundelet, a headpiece of padded round rings and braided trim, atop her glossy hair. The fake jewels, satin, and gold ribbons flowing from the raised bow enhanced her understated elegance. "You are a classic beauty, Lady Jane."

She grinned at the reference to her costume, fidgeted with the pearl beading along the gown's bodice, then twirled. "You're handsome indeed, Sir Galahad, especially wearing a surcoat."

He fingered the thin cotton fabric. "Surcoat? I thought it was a cape."

"You're confusing the Renaissance era with Batman."

He burst out laughing. "You expect me to walk in this getup? Or take in any air? I'll smother in this mesh metallic hood." He tapped on the hood to emphasize his point.

"Consider yourself lucky. At least the hem of your gown won't drag in the dirt."

He fanned himself before tugging the hood over his head. "I may sweat to death."

"You're wearing shorts. Be brave, Sir Tristan."

"I thought I was Sir Galahad."

"I'm naming all the knights at King Arthur's Round Table."

"There were hundreds of knights."

"I'll list the most memorable, Sir Lancelot."

He produced a gallant bow, then guided her out of the air-conditioned shop. Appetizing aromas of steak and mushroom pies, caramel apples, and roasted turkey legs made his mouth water. "I'm beginning to understand the attraction to these silly Faires."

"Silly?"

"Entertaining," he amended.

She grinned up at him. "Because of the noble knights and elegant ladies parading around?"

"No. Because of the delicious food."

A Renaissance Faire was an elaborate week-long affair, affording a schedule of daily events including royal jousting, comedy improvisation by a swashbuckling trio, and themed weekends such as a pirate invasion.

She tugged at his hand as they walked. "Let's order two glasses of orange soda."

"Does your sweet tooth have no bounds?"

"None at all."

"They didn't serve orange soda in the fourteen hundreds."

"Now you're a purist?" She drew herself up to her full height.

He purchased soda for her, and an iced coffee for himself. While she perused the handmade beeswax candles at an adjoining shop, he debated whether to order roasted almonds sprinkled with cinnamon, or jalapeno.

She skipped back to him. "I'd prefer chocolate-coated."

He ordered the almonds in a cone for each of them—chocolate-coated and cinnamon, respectively. As was her custom, she thanked him, bowed her head, and whispered a prayer of grace. Even here, in the middle of a noisy, bustling crowd, she openly expressed her faith because, as she informed him, "All the food we eat is a result of God's bounty."

He nodded. Her sincere conviction was beginning to rub off on him.

She fished for a handful of chocolate nuts and fed him a couple.

"These nuts are too sweet." He groaned in feigned dismay, smirked impenitently, and snatched another handful. "If I eat any more, I might be sick."

She pushed his hand safely away from her cone. "Uh, huh."

As the afternoon passed, they meandered around the open-air booths hawking items from cloth doll patterns to plush blue dragons, inhaled cheesy French fries and sausage on a stick, and joked about who was brave enough to ride the Whirl and Hurl.

He laughed more than he'd ever laughed in his lifetime.

The reason? He was with Ashley, and she had the ability to bring joy to everyday events.

Children gravitated to her. She applauded enthusiastically while little girls, muffling giggles during a ceremony, extended deep throne curtsies, then were elevated to become ladies of the realm. "By the queen herself," Ashley congratulated the girls, which earned her unreserved smiles. Their smiles included David, which brought an endearing clutch to his heart.

Ashley picked up a pamphlet and noted that the jousting match began at three o'clock. "Let's get there early so we can snag a good seat."

"Is the jousting held outside under the blazing hot sun?" He snatched a last handful of sticky almonds.

"Medieval England didn't offer indoor air-conditioned arenas." She grabbed a few nuts from his cone. "Are you expecting an indoor movie theater with reclining stadium seats?"

"Does that mean no?"

Her shoulders shook with mirth. "An unequivocal no."

As they wandered, munched, and sipped cold drinks, her gaze riveted to a display of handmade jewelry, and she lingered to rhapsodize over a cross pendant suspended from a gold chain. The artisan ran his fingers along the smokey quartz beads, zeroing in on the center green stone.

"Pearls and peridot." He brought the necklace closer so Ashley could examine the quality and craftsmanship. "These necklaces are one of a kind. A set of matching earrings is also available."

"The cross is gorgeous and the design so intricate." She turned it over to view the price tag and pushed it back toward him. "Unfortunately, it's way out of my price range."

David bent and kissed her cheek. "Do you like the necklace?"

"I love it."

"Then it's yours."

She placed her hand on his, her smile shy. "I could never accept such an expensive gift."

"You'd deprive me from buying a special necklace for my fairest lady?"

Before she objected further, he settled up with the vendor and hooked the fine gold chain around her neck. She fingered the cross and grinned into the hand mirror the vendor supplied.

"You're too generous." She kissed David with so much enthusiasm he considered purchasing the entire jewelry display.

"My pleasure." He tripped on the words, his throat welling with emotion.

He was starting to care for her more than he ever dreamed possible.

A rosy tint enhanced her fine cheekbones. "I realize a Renaissance Faire isn't your favorite way to spend the day."

He cradled her, kissed her again. "I'm enjoying every single minute more than I ever imagined." To his astonishment, this was the most pleasant afternoon he ever recalled.

She changed direction, evidently distracted by the scent of leather at a table touting handcrafted leather goods. He grabbed the opportunity to purchase the matching earrings to Ashley's necklace and slipped the gift bag into his shorts pocket.

He pointed to a ride, a swinging suspended barrel. Thrilled screams from the riders blasted whenever the barrel flew into the air. "Are you agreeable to riding the Barrel of Mayhem?"

"Absolutely. It looks a little tamer than the Whirl and Hurl." She set her hand on his outstretched palm. "Human-powered, naturally."

He had turned to a booth to purchase tickets for the ride when a vendor at Robin Hood Archery called out, "How are your abilities with a bow and arrow, sir? Step right up and win your lovely lady a simulated diamond ring. All you have to do is strike the tree stump. If you hit the target six times in a row, you'll win her a cuddly black bear."

David stepped to the booth and scrutinized the bows and arrows laid out on a table. He knew nothing about archery, but how hard could the sport be? No special equipment was required, and his one good eye boasted perfect vision.

Decisively, he dug in his pocket for loose dollar bills.

The vendor focused on David. "All it takes is a steady hand, flexible muscles, and a cool disposition."

Ashley giggled. "David, the man must know you."

He scanned the selection, the sleek curves of the bows, and decided on a recurved design.

Ashley tapped him on the shoulder. "I thought we were riding Mayhem?"

He steered her around and yanked off his metal mesh hood. "Not when I'm presented with the prospect of winning you a diamond ring. The opportunity is practically falling in my lap."

"Only takes one bulls-eye." The vendor's voice lowered as he peered at David. "Haven't I seen you somewhere? You look like that hermit artist guy. My wife showed me a picture in a magazine last year of a famous painting, *Lady by the River*. The article reported you were taking the art world by storm."

A sidelong grin accompanied David's attempt to correct the vendor. "*Woman by the River.*"

"Huh?"

"*Woman by the River,*" David repeated. "Not lady."

The vendor waved a hand. "Woman, lady, something like that."

Ashley met David's grin with a challenging smile. "You realize that no one can find the actual river in your painting."

"My wife said the same thing," the vendor agreed.

"You're kidding. The river is obvious." David shot a stunned look at them both, his eyes narrowing as he took in Ashley's vibrant expression.

Tension filled the air as David secured the arrow, stretched back the bow string, and took aim.

"Rembrandt!" Ashley shouted.

The arrow missed and landed in a mound of dirt.

He lowered the bow, tossed her an offended look, and picked another arrow.

"Not Rembrandt," the vendor corrected. "This hermit painter is supposed to be more avant-garde. My wife claims his paintings are fine art and innovative. Me? I'll take a Michelangelo any day."

While David pondered whether he'd just been complimented or insulted, he granted Ashley a self-assured smirk. He notched his arrow and tried again. On his last attempt, he'd finally gotten the hang of archery and hit the tree stump.

"Hurray! You've won your girlfriend a diamond ring." The vendor fumbled behind the display and planted a plastic case in David's outstretched palm.

David peeled off the cellophane and examined the cheap faux diamond.

"Will you wear my ring?" He gazed at Ashley, delighted by the brilliant smile crossing her face. "I'll buy you something better, something bigger. I promise."

"I don't need anything better." She extended her right hand. "The sentiment is what's meaningful."

He slipped the ring on her fourth finger. "Now it's official."

"What is?"

"We're formally dating." At the realization of how much the moment meant to him, he cleared his throat and noted a banner draped over a gigantic rocking horse. "Like the sign states, I'm a contented fairgoer. I hope you're contented too."

"I am. Thank you." She pressed the ring to her cheek as if it were the most precious item she'd ever worn. "David?"

"Hmm?"

Her lilting voice uttering his name had an odd effect. He felt alive and valued. He trusted her, trusted her enough to be

365

his true self. He felt safe, encouraged by the knowledge he'd found the woman of his dreams.

Here. Not in Manhattan, not at a fancy art gallery in Los Angeles, or on a swanky island in the Caribbean. Here. In this tiny Southern community, that embraced their faith in God.

He smiled as he stuffed the knight's hood into a free pocket.

He was still smiling when they passed a line-up of food stands that led to the jousting arena. At the entrance, he deliberated about ordering an enormous turkey leg and muttered, "A carnivore's dream."

He scanned the gigantic field, humming with merchants, scampering youngsters, and a horde of men clothed in tunics, capes, and plumed feather hats.

Ashley gazed at the scene and sighed. "Sadly, there are no chocolate candy bars sold during the Renaissance, either."

"You eased your sugar fix when you devoured the chocolate-covered almonds."

A frown formed between her delicately arched eyebrows. "You ate half of them."

"Me? Two handfuls at the most."

Good-naturedly, she swatted his forearm. "Your handfuls were more like scoops. The jousting is starting. I don't want to miss it."

"David Fodero!" a familiar male voice called.

David and Ashley turned.

Julian Wilson and his wife, Nora, stood by the fish and chips stand. Julian sported a high-collared hourglass-fit jacket, white ruffled shirt, and matching breeches, every inch the country gentleman. Nora raised a monocle to her eye and waved. She wore a linen sheath and buttercups were braided in her hair.

David looked around. He and Ashley were hopelessly

trapped between a mob and a musician playing the hammered dulcimer.

In the spirit of friendship, Nora extended her hands as she and Julian approached. "How fun to see you two here."

David inclined his head. "What a coincidence."

Julian surveyed David's costume and chuckled. "You're a knight, I gather?"

"I'm a knight if you're a country gentleman."

"Touché."

"I hoped no one would see me except Ashley." David reached for her hand. "I have a reputation to preserve."

"Don't we all." Ever the diplomat, Julian sidetracked the exchange. "Before you ask, Pickle is safe with Samantha. Your dog and ours get along grand."

"Excellent." David had asked Samantha if she could watch his dog, and she'd cheerfully agreed.

"Pickle is so well-behaved, I'll dog-sit whenever I'm free, Mr. Fodero," she'd assured him.

"Did Samantha tell you where Ashley and I were headed?" David inquired.

Julian's smile was one of exaggerated innocence. "As a matter of fact, she did."

"Are you two planning to watch the jousting match?" Nora asked. "We can sit together." With an exclamation of delight, she stared at Ashley's necklace. "Oh my. How lovely!"

Ashley stole a glance at David beneath her long lashes. "David bought it for me at an artisan shop."

"Gorgeous. And your ring." Nora gazed meaningfully at Ashley's right hand. A slow, disbelieving smile bloomed. "Is it new also?"

"David won it for me at the archery game." Ashley tossed her shiny hair over her shoulders. "We're officially dating."

Nora's perceptive eyes met Ashley's. "Congratulations!"

"You're a lucky man." Julian offered his usual clap on David's back. "Aren't you going to kiss her?"

David appraised Ashley's exquisite features. "I believe another kiss is in order."

She displayed a jaunty smile. "Is it?"

"Absolutely." His husky voice betrayed his affection. His lips moved closer, and he kissed her long and thoroughly.

"Remember, our generous Lord will give each of us another day," Julian interrupted.

As the couples picked up their steps to stay with the crowd, Julian joked with David about whether the archery game was fixed, especially when Ashley recapped the vendor's announcement that David had six tries.

David tucked Ashley's fingers in the crook of his arm. "I made a bulls-eye on my last shot."

She flicked a glance at her right hand. "If you had hit the stump all six times, you would've won me a cuddly black bear."

"Which do you prefer? The ring or the bear?"

"The ring."

Her expressive eyes shone with a love he recognized because he felt it, too. The exhilarating promise of a future together beckoned. Ashley was faultless in every sense—goodness, generosity, and a devout faith he felt growing inside himself. A warmth of happiness flowed through him.

The foursome made their way into the arena. In seconds, the space was split with thunderous applause as a juggler appeared near the tent opening.

"It's a shame Ashley is leaving on Saturday." Nora started for a row of empty seats. "Luckily, Greenwood isn't that far away. A little less than two hours, right?"

David grasped Ashley's hand to help her climb the metal steps. "You live in Greenwood?"

She looked at him as if he were unjustly vilifying her. "Yes. Why?"

"We've seen each all week, and I never asked where you lived." His mind raced. "I'm familiar with the town. Do you know a woman named Nancy Trainor? She owns an art gallery there."

"My art studio is connected to her gallery, along with a café."

He stilled. Thoughts came rushing at him, too numerous to comprehend.

Ashley had looked familiar the first day they'd met at his cabin.

As the jousting commenced, the knights paraded out of the tent waving red and blue flags, their magnificent, broad-chested horses flaunting a bard, a glitzy cloth that displayed the knight's emblem. They were introduced and presented to the audience amidst good-natured cheers and boos. A drum roll began, and demonstrations of the knights' skills on horseback ensued as they knocked over progressively smaller targets with their wooden lances.

The announcer lauded unbridled participation, which prompted Julian and Nora to stand and clap. The crowd dissolved in laughter as a jester appeared and cartwheeled across the ground.

David became increasingly aware of the beautiful woman seated next to him, her posture rigid. She didn't stand. She didn't clap. She didn't move. The diamond captured the sun's rays and gleamed.

"Points are awarded for broken lances." Julian pointed to a knight standing by his horse. "No points awarded for broken shields."

What about a broken heart? Any points awarded for that?

Julian and Nora seemed completely unaware of David's

rising tension or Ashley's silence. The rallying roar increased as the knights charged and battled.

For the next fifteen minutes, Nora kept up an animated conversation with Ashley, while Ashley responded in monosyllables.

David carefully considered Ashley's lovely profile. The beaded cross swayed when she shifted.

And during that time, he pondered.

Finally, it dawned on him. She knew he couldn't see out of his right eye and had purposefully moved to his left. In fact, she always did that.

In addition, whenever she rode in his truck, she always sat up straight and turned toward him when she spoke.

She was empathetic and cared about him. She was considerate, often reassuring and loving. *Yes, loving.*

Or so he imagined.

As the jousting continued, his speculations took him further, his recollections in turmoil.

When she'd shown up at his cabin, on a road with no outlet, she'd claimed her convertible had broken down. Once she stepped inside, she spent several minutes fawning over his canvas.

Her friend Sarah had come to the rescue and "fixed" her car.

On another day, Ashley had gifted him with a basket of peaches she'd placed in his cabin, admitting she'd snooped inside. Then she'd appeared at his favorite spot where he painted.

All these coincidences? Maybe. Maybe not.

He shook his head. An idiot could've figured it out sooner. Ashley's studio was linked to the art gallery carrying his paintings, which was the reason why she'd looked so familiar. When he'd visited Nancy several months ago to drop off a painting, he'd glimpsed Ashley on the floor of her studio with a student. She'd smiled and waved.

Nancy must have sent Ashley to Cherish to figure out why he hadn't responded to her messages.

He'd trusted that meeting Ashley in Cherish was circumstantial. Fate. In actuality, it had been planned and calculated. She'd come to Cherish to spy on him.

But why?

He gave a short, bitter laugh, and Ashley glanced at him. He looked away.

Because of money. The stream of revenue from his paintings was obviously an asset for Nancy and the other shop owners.

Ashley wasn't interested in him for himself.

With that knowledge, something inside him splintered apart.

What else had Ashley conveniently forgotten? The fact she was Nancy's spy? The fact she used him, his art, to fill her coffers? All three businesses—the gallery, the café, and Ashley's studio—relied on each other's sales to survive. Nancy had mentioned that to him when he'd commented on the businesses' adjoining doors. Customers walked from one shop to another.

He pondered all this, though, but said nothing. No matter how he tried, he couldn't focus on the match or Julian's jesting commentary.

When the joust finished after an endless sixty minutes, he curtly declined Julian's invitation to watch a glass blower, drawing the other man's piercing gaze. David used Pickle's long day with Samantha as an excuse.

After he and Ashley exchanged their costumes for street clothes, the drive to Cherish was hushed and oppressive.

Sitting in the passenger seat, Ashley tentatively asked, "Is anything wrong?"

"Wrong?" His knuckles tightened on the steering wheel.

She sat straighter. An eternity passed before he realized she was waiting for him to speak.

As they made the final turnoff, he followed the road up a hill, straight as an arrow. He pulled into a lookout point and shut off the engine.

"Ashley Madden." He stared out the window into the fog-shrouded valley. "Who are you?"

"I'm Ashley."

"We've concluded you're not a mountain climber."

"I confessed."

"And you poked around my cabin when you delivered the peaches."

"I confessed to that too."

"You're a Christian woman?"

Her gaze raised to his, glittering with tears. "I try my best."

He swallowed, tasting a heartbreaking defeat. "Maybe your best isn't good enough."

She groped for a handkerchief in her purse and dabbed at her eyes. "If you're concerned about my art studio being located in Greenwood—"

"This has nothing to do with Greenwood." Already, he felt himself separating from her. "I'm trying to deal with your deception."

"I'm not following."

"Aren't you?" A kaleidoscope of distrust emerged. "You should've been up front with me from the beginning. Told me why you landed in Cherish and what you expected to find out."

"David, I didn't intend to deceive you. It's just that you never responded to Nancy's emails and texts and—"

"Let me guess. She was worried."

Her lips trembled. "We all were."

"Worried about me? Or were you concerned about the

372

revenue loss if Nancy wasn't able to secure any more of my paintings? What am I to you, a dollar sign?"

"What am I to you, an excuse to procrastinate?"

"Don't be ridiculous."

A mix of distressing emotions crossed her face. "Likewise."

"You drove fifty miles to Cherish and planned on spending the weekend nosing around. How did you find me?"

"Sarah suggested I contact the state park ranger."

"She was in on this deception too."

"Yes, but—" Ashley tore her gaze from his. "The ranger gave me the name of your road. It was the easiest way to track you down."

"I assume you've reported the news of my eyesight loss to Nancy." David gathered steam to deliver his ace advantage. "Well, tell her this. I'll sell no more paintings in her gallery."

If he ever actually painted again.

Ashley didn't respond at first. Instead, she rested a hand on his arm. "I'm sorry. There were many instances when I—" Tears formed at the corner of her eyes. "I've loved every moment we're together and never wanted to spoil it."

Love. The word brought hope and sadness, snapping his self-control.

"No more of those, I assure you."

"No more of what?"

"We won't spend any more time together." He leaned his head against the seat. In the empty space between them, the distance grew wider. "I'm returning to New York."

"To paint?"

"I'm unsure of my abilities, my career." He rolled down the window. The wind carried the noise of the town below. Cherish. Once, he hoped to belong there. Not anymore.

"You're dealing with your loss the wrong way." Raggedly,

she inhaled. She still had her hand on his forearm. "Keep painting. You can overcome this, the way Sarah did when she confronted her deafness. Her life is full and happy. Rely on God's promise."

"Which is what?"

"God will walk with you through the storm."

He shrugged off her hand. He couldn't forgive deceit. He couldn't forgive God for placing an unfair hardship on him. He'd never forgiven his father. Ashley only proved what David already recognized. Few people could be trusted. Certainly not her.

His motions quick and jerky, he started the engine, rolled up the window, and switched on the air-conditioning. The truck idled. "You're attempting to convert me back to Christianity after learning my religious views?"

"I've always wanted to help you." The tension in her exquisite face gave way to pleading. "Through God's grace, my specialty is fixing problems."

"I'm not a broken car."

"So what if you have a handicap? Don't deny it. Embrace it. Never give up. You're commissioned to paint a portrait of a special church. Memorial Street Church is a building, but the real church is what happens on the inside."

"It's over Ashley." He couldn't trust his voice to say more. To consider the magnificent future he'd once envisioned for them.

"I understand." Ashley didn't falter for a beat. "Now understand this. God will always be there for you."

"What part of *church not being part of my life* don't you comprehend?"

"If there's anything I can do—"

"There isn't." He enunciated the words clearly.

"David, I'm sorry."

"We've already invested a conversation around your apologies. No need for another."

For the remainder of the drive to town, stillness reigned.

As they neared the inn, he slowed, then parked near the curb. "Go home, Ashley. Go back to Greenwood and take the art supplies I bought with you."

She raised her chin. Her face reddened. "You're joking, right? Keep your supplies." Her fingers fumbled with the chain as she unhooked the necklace. "Take this." She placed the necklace on the seat. Her hands shook as she removed the ring and flung it at him. "And don't forget this."

"Those were gifts." He ducked as the ring hit the window. "They're for you."

"I don't want them!" Her shoulders set. Her glorious eyes glittered with unshed tears. She shoved open the door before he could go around and open it.

She stomped from the truck and didn't turn around.

He watched her leave, fighting with himself, wanting to dash after her, but stopping himself from looking more like a fool than he already was. As she flew up the steps and entered the inn, his stomach sank. Somewhere inside, he knew his happiness was slipping away.

He should reach out and grab it. Take the initiative. Life is short.

No. Mission accomplished. He'd broken off their relationship.

It was for the best. They lived miles apart. Long-distance dating seldom worked.

Doubt simmered inside him as he picked up the ring and arranged the necklace with the earrings. He hesitated. He'd placed the ring on her finger. She'd pressed the ring to her cheek as if it were her most precious possession, then kissed him with unabandoned joy.

A faux diamond ring that meant so much.

He stared at the inn in silence. He needed to come to grips with his decision.

The day had held such promise. And just like that, happiness was gone.

Sighing, he briefly closed his eyes. No practical man heeded his heart first. And he was a practical man.

He debated one last time, facing the future without her in his life.

Then he shifted his truck into gear and headed for the Wilsons' home to pick up Pickle.

CHAPTER 14

*Some painters transform the sun into a yellow spot, others
transform the yellow spot into the sun.*
- Picasso

*A*fter a restless night, Ashley got out of bed, groggy
from fragmentary dreams. She showered, phoned
Sarah and left a voice message that she was leaving, then
quickly packed her suitcase. The forecast predicted an unsea-
sonably cool day, and she dressed in tan cotton slacks, a blue
blouse, and a jeans jacket.

She descended the inn's broad staircase on rubbery legs
and scanned the lobby. The pendulum clock rang out the
early hour. The clink of silver coming from the solarium
meant breakfast was ready to be served.

Julian stood at the reception desk and hailed her with a
chipper "Greetings."

She approached with her suitcase in tow. "I'm checking
out today."

He frowned. "I thought you were staying longer."

"No. I'm done here." She wiped an errant tear. "Naturally, I'm happy to pay for the extra nights I reserved."

"There are folks on a waiting list, and your room is easy to fill." As soon as he finished processing her refund, he said, "None of my business, but I assume things didn't work out with David?"

"That's a kind spin."

"You both fairly floated in and out of here. I remarked to Nora that you two have a chemistry people rarely share."

Ashley managed a wan smile. "Did we?"

"You're lucky."

"Coincidental. Circumstance." She shook her head in denial. "We had a falling out, and it was my fault. I apologized."

"Did he accept your apology?"

"Hardly." She pushed up the sleeves of her jacket. "Just the opposite."

"Hopefully you gave him something to think about."

Her face heated. *Yes, had she ever.*

On the mountainous return drive to Greenwood, Ashley blamed herself for handling things so badly. She had an explanation for David on the tip of her tongue more often than not, but in the end, she'd lacked courage. David clearly cared for her. He'd placed her on a pedestal she hadn't deserved.

"Your sincerity is disarming." He'd sealed his declaration with a kiss.

Stunned by her leaking tears, she pulled her convertible over to the side of the road. She'd been hurt before, her heart broken, but never like this.

She recalled his high-handed dismissal. David, the handsome, impossible artist with a sterling character. David, the man she'd come to love.

No. It wasn't possible to fall in love in only a few days. For a second time, she'd been charmed by a man who feigned interest. He probably had already found another woman more to his liking. Sophisticated and alluring and ravishing.

She forced herself to breathe while her heart hammered a heavy beat. There was no sense in denying her emotions. She missed his lazy smile, his wry humor.

She reached for her phone. Perhaps she could text him and apologize again. Her pride would be salvaged if he accepted her apology, even if he was coolly unenthusiastic.

Julian had offered insight into the chemistry between her and David, and she'd denied it. Sadly, her denial wasn't true.

There was interest and magic. Judging by his smiles, David had enjoyed being with her. The memory of his warm lips moving on hers, his murmurings. *"You're beautiful, Ashley."*

Her, the plainest of plain Janes.

Her heart swelled as other memories surfaced.

The first time they officially met at his cabin. Their pillow fight.

The afternoon he declared he was painting *her*, and how she imagined their laughter could be heard for miles.

He cared deeply, which was why he was so hurt by her deception. He'd assumed she cared for him, and then concluded she was after his money.

She slumped in her seat. If he only realized how much she *did* care.

However, he was gone now. Gone forever.

A lump of sadness swelled in her throat, but she vowed not to cry anymore. Unwanted tears trickled, and she brushed them away.

"Show me the way, Lord." She closed her eyes and prayed. "I'm your daughter. You are my friend. I'm sorry for hurting David. I can't control the guilt welling up inside me because of my wrongdoing. I'll rely on your healing grace."

She switched on the ignition and turned the radio to a contemporary Christian station. This drive would mark her last trip from Cherish.

A DAY LATER, in response to Nancy's queries, Ashley explained David's eyesight loss.

"Will he continue to paint?" Worried shadows under-scored Nancy's brown eyes when she'd swept into Ashley's studio and claimed the nearest chair. "I—we, all three of our businesses, need his pieces to survive."

"He refused. I pray he will concentrate on healing and taking care of himself."

Nancy took an overlong time, adjusting her flowing bohemian skirt. "Are you suggesting he can't paint?"

"He *won't* paint, at least not to sell any pieces in your gallery."

Ashley turned to the sound of commotion. Two children in wheelchairs argued over the same brush. She lifted one of the children's wrists, then the other, and clapped their hands together simultaneously. Once they giggled, she encouraged their friendship and asked them to share. Then she swiveled to Nancy.

"Honestly, David can see. For him, it's a struggle to accept his disability."

Nancy stood, staring critically at Ashley. "You look terri-ble, by the way."

Ashley was fully aware her complexion was pale, and that lines of sadness marked her mouth. Wryly, she replied, "Thanks."

"When you extended your stay in Cherish, I assumed you were having a blast."

"Cherish has a storybook quality, and the residents are right-minded and decent." Unwilling to show her regret and heartbreak, Ashley pleaded busyness and excused herself to tend to a curly-haired girl who demanded attention. "I'm grateful to be back."

"My relationships never go over three months," David had told her.

He'd certainly succeeded this time.

THE NEXT MONTH drifted by in a haze of desolation. Ashley continuously checked her phone, hoping to hear from David. Perhaps a text.

Nothing.

Too many times every day, she attempted to shake off the heartbreaking memories that haunted her.

David playing fetch with his dog.

David absorbed in taking photographs of a tree, of a river. David photographing her.

She immersed herself in teaching her precious pupils. When a David Fodero painting was alluded to during a meeting with students and their parents, Ashley couldn't respond. Hiding her face from her students' puzzled glances, she rushed from the studio and into Nancy's gallery, tears streaming down her cheeks.

"What happened?" Nancy grasped Ashley's cold hands.

"David and I were together every day. He was wonderful."

Nancy's fingers tightened. "Will you please tell me more?"

Ashley bent her head. "I deceived him, although it wasn't intentional. I was a coward and never explained my reason for being in Cherish. When he discovered my deception, he was angry."

"You're not deceitful, Ashley. Praying helps. God's got this."

Ashley stared at the blank wall where Nancy had repeatedly hung David's paintings. Once again, she was alone. Once again, she relied on herself and her faith in God.

WHEN THE CALENDAR neared the end of July, Nancy casually mentioned that David had moved back to his penthouse in Manhattan. He'd phoned to inform her he was selling his cabin, and felt he owed her some explanation for his where-abouts because they were old friends.

"If anyone wants to buy the cabin, direct them to my agent in New York," he'd instructed.

Ashley had been thanking a sturdy five-year-old who'd offered her a puffy white hydrangea flower.

Her head jerked up when Nancy relayed the news. She rubbed her palms on her plaid shorts and turned to the half-dozen children staring at her.

"What fun we're going to have today," she declared. "Has anyone ever painted a picture of a tree?"

Smiling at the children's eager, enthusiastic faces, she threw herself into their paint splattering and chortles, giving scrupulous attention to each and every brushstroke.

ON THE FIRST Saturday of August, David stood in the living room of his Manhattan apartment, scrutinizing the painting perched on his easel. He'd painted Ashley, sitting at the top of an oak tree, surrounded by wildflowers—fiery pinks, cardinal reds, and gray-purple violets.

His depiction of her was delicate, resembling a fairy—mischievous and kind, the size of a thumb. He'd captured her profile—small turned-up nose and rounded chin. The luxu-riant mass of honey-blond hair, the full pink lips, the cream-colored complexion. He'd harbored the hope she'd someday see it.

Torn between his internal critic and the lovely portrait, he gave a grim laugh. He only needed to make a few additions beginning with a river … somewhere.

He'd arrived in Manhattan, believing the anonymity of the city would ease the sadness in his gut. He'd painted for hours with an uncontained fervor. Now he stood back and assessed the painting he'd begun in Cherish.

"What's your opinion, Pickle?" He observed his dog snoring by the window. "Ashley is beautiful, isn't she?"

Yes, she was. Only he hadn't captured her genuine beauty, the kindness radiating from her heart.

He stayed where he was, lost in thought.

When he'd retreated to his cabin the day of the Renaissance Faire, he'd devoted himself to his work for weeks. In all that time, he'd produced a few lithographs and sketches, and nearly completed the commissioned painting of Memorial Street Church.

He had never missed a deadline, and the painting was scheduled to be delivered to Marge Addyson by the final week in August. He'd left it in Cherish, assuming he'd add final touches when he returned to pack the last of his boxes.

He'd decided on a two-sided art, two renderings, past and present, of the same church. He'd sketched the older version in charcoal, as he'd mentioned to Ashley. He'd enhanced the painting of the present-day church with a sparkly purple star in the corner and his initials, *D.F.*

Beneath was one letter.

A.

The letter and the star were minuscule.

He hadn't been able to help himself. His dreams were of her. Always of her.

The expansive window of his penthouse faced Central

Park, and rain pounded on the glass. It had rained constantly. Incessant and never-ending, and he'd come to realize he vastly preferred sunshine.

He stared out at the relentless raindrops, the wet pavement far below, pedestrians walking swiftly and carrying umbrellas.

He caught his reflection. His forehead creased with fatigue, and he averted his gaze. He couldn't look at himself anymore. Self-doubt had become his foremost companion.

He sank down on the enormous leather sofa and placed his head in his hands. He hadn't trusted his father after learning of his unfaithfulness. He'd never forgiven him.

David opened the Bible he'd purchased when he'd landed in New York. He leafed to Psalms, reflecting on the passage about God's grace and forgiveness. His mercy was great.

He turned the Bible over, running his thumb along the edges of the sacred book.

David longed to put the past behind him and proceed. But how could he do that when his hopes had abandoned him? Or rather, he'd abandoned his dreams. If people realized his backstory, they'd sympathize. He'd never had any prior health problems. Why an eyesight loss?

Rewind. Remember the exhilarating days with Ashley. The happiest moments of his life had been the hours spent with her.

He'd convinced himself she'd played him for a fool. But hadn't she declared her love for him? Not outright, but in numerous instances.

He straddled two conflicting visions of his future. Him alone in his Manhattan studio, endless months painting in solitude. Or days in Cherish, accompanied by the gorgeous Ashley Madden. Her fresh scent of lemon and sage, wholesome and uplifting, so different from the expensive perfumes of the women he'd escorted to fancy parties.

He could still feel Ashley in his arms, her hand touching his heart. Her gaze had darkened with empathy when he talked about his father.

And there were other times. Pleasurable, joyous times.

Ashley, sitting in a tree:

"I'm an adult, but it doesn't mean I should give up everything I loved to do when I was young," she'd said. *"The view is different up here. Better."*

Better.

Ashley peering in his freezer.

"What kind of guy doesn't eat Hungry-Man dinners?"

Ashley jostling the vending machine:

"Grand idea," she'd said as she inserted his quarters. *"Sadly, it isn't working."*

She was right. Being apart wasn't the answer. He'd presumed self-worth came from his paintings, not himself. That his job defined his existence. The hardest lesson was facing his weakness. But weakness could be turned into strength.

He could paint. He could overcome his impairment by refusing to fixate on it. Instead, he could apply his efforts to helping others and truly appreciate the positive.

With Ashley.

Reach out. It was worth it.

They deserved to be happy.

He recalled the sermon he'd related to her, the sermon he'd heard as a child:

"The blessing ahead of you is bigger than any battle you left behind," the aged pastor had proclaimed.

Those words were appropriate for yesterday and today. David sent a belated acknowledgement to his long-ago pastor, and to his mother for dragging him to church.

"Lord, you must have a plan for me," he prayed. "Ashley

provided inspirational messages every time we were together, and I'm ready to connect the dots."

He came to his feet, his mind made up.

"I'm glad you're a top-notch passenger, Pickle." He scooped up his dog, already deciding to charter a plane to Atlanta, then a car to Cherish. "We're heading back to my cabin tomorrow. You'll sleep in the carry-on. Just think, you might soon get another belly rub from a certain beautiful woman you'll recognize."

David yanked out his phone, then paused. He tried to avoid thinking about his next obstacle, but here it was.

He didn't have the slightest inkling if Ashley would even speak to him. In all these weeks, he hadn't contacted her, hoping she'd contact him.

She hadn't. He hadn't. Two stubborn individuals.

All he knew was that he loved her, and he knew in his heart she loved him.

He wasn't certain of the reaction he'd receive or if she'd agree to his plan.

Never give up.

He was eager to see her. Eager to make things right.

He plugged in the number for an esteemed Manhattan jeweler and requested an early morning appointment. The business didn't open until ten, but for the exorbitant price David was willing to pay, he was confident the jeweler would meet him earlier.

"Tomorrow," David said to Pickle as he set him down in his doggie bed. "We're going home."

CHAPTER 15

Action is the foundational key to all success.
- Picasso

"David Fodero." Nancy Trainor's eyes narrowed as David strode into the Greenwood art gallery carrying an art portfolio case. "I never expected to see you again."

He grinned. "Yet here I am."

"Is that a painting for my gallery?" She zeroed in on the case, and the withering look on her face died. "Can I sell whatever is in there?"

"Sorry." He broke off, nodding casually to the art patrons. "It's not for sale."

People gasped and discreetly gestured toward him. A noticeable silence ensued.

He heard his name whispered but didn't turn. Instead, he quickened his steps and followed the sounds of giggling children behind an adjoining closed door.

He spotted Ashley sitting cross-legged on her studio floor before the door fully shut. She wore a pair of jean shorts and a fitted purple T-shirt. Her hair was secured in a high ponytail.

The room was tidy, and white canvases lay in a pile, along with paper towels. A dizzying array of artwork hung on the wall. A handwashing station was tucked in one corner, and the smell of acrylic paint filled the air.

Surrounded by a group of children wearing imaginative orange smocks, she smiled at a slim little boy dipping his brush in a jar of water.

"Freddie, try to concentrate." Ashley snatched a clean brush from a metal bucket. "Trees aren't hard to draw."

David stepped nearer. His heart hammered in hope, in anticipation.

"Because anyone can paint a tree," he said softly.

Two boys in wheelchairs looked up at him and gaped.

Ashley jumped to her feet. Her fine, pale eyebrows drew together. Her hand touched her throat. "David?"

"Hey, I recognize you." One of the boys wheeled his chair protectively in front of Ashley. His thin shoulders squared. "You're the artist guy Miss Ashley cried about when my mother mentioned your name a few weeks ago."

"I'm here to tell her I'm sorry." David set down the case. His gaze remained on Ashley. Her face lost all color as she continued to stare at him. "I hope she'll forgive me for being a fool."

Tears poured down her cheeks as she picked her way between the children and flew into David's outstretched arms.

"She's crying again," the second boy in a wheelchair remarked accusingly.

"I'm fine." Ashley's shoulders shook with sobbing. "I'm crying tears of joy."

David framed her face and wiped her cheeks with his thumbs. He sheltered her from the children's gazes. "I missed you. I came to tell you I love you."

She slid her hands around his neck. "I love you too."

"Okay, you two." Nancy stepped into the room, unsuccessfully hiding her amusement behind a mask of genteel professionalism. She looked at the children. "Miss Ashley has a substitute teacher filling in for her."

"Who?" The boys chimed.

"Me."

David smiled his appreciation at the keenly perceptive Nancy. She diverted the children by debating color combinations and an abbreviated embellishment of the tree the one boy had begun to paint.

David steered Ashley to a secluded corner. "I couldn't stay away." He kissed her forehead, his fingers drifting up and down her spine. "Please forgive me."

"I'm the one who needs forgiving."

"No." He shook his head, his laugh bitter. "I focused on myself, my pride. In so doing, I overlooked what's most important."

"David, don't feel guilty."

"I have several reasons for being here, but guilt isn't primary."

"What is then?"

"I want to have sons and daughters with hazel eyes and a tender, giving heart. I want to give you my name and all that I have."

She bit back a smile.

He withdrew a jewelry case from his pocket and handed it to her. "Ashley Madden, will you marry me?"

Elation shimmered in her eyes as she opened the case. The ring was larger than the imitation ring he'd won at the Renaissance Faire. This diamond was four carats and exquisitely cut, reflecting the natural light of the sunshine streaming through the window.

"Yes. I'll marry you." Her gaze radiated with love. "Meeting you was a gift from God."

He had hoped she'd recognized the extraordinary hand of fate that had led them to each other. There were no coincidences. He'd met an angel who believed in him and loved him.

He slipped the ring onto the fourth finger of her left hand and kissed her palm. "We're officially engaged."

"You are?" Nancy peered up from the center of a circle surrounded by children. "I didn't mean to eavesdrop but—"

"What's that?" The slight boy named Freddie examined David's carry case. "Aren't you going to show us what's inside?" Freddie inched nearer as the other children gathered round.

"It's a special painting." David reached for Ashley's hand. Her smile radiated with love, and he was certain he'd gotten his first glimpse of heaven.

From the second she'd accepted his hand; he'd recognized the special bond between them. Carefully, because he didn't want to break their connection, he continued, "The decision is totally up to Miss Ashley."

"Why, Mr. Fodero? It's not her painting." Freddie waited for the other children to join him and echo his opinion. "The painting is yours."

"I painted the canvas, but the subject is essential." David focused on Ashley.

She smiled. "Go ahead."

"Yay!" For several seconds, the room filled with laughter from seven children and Nancy, all sharing a collective goal: discovering what was inside David's carrying case.

He pulled the canvas from the case amidst a variety of oohs and ahhs.

"That's Miss Ashley!" Freddie pointed to a whimsical woman sitting in an oak tree. "She's so pretty. Why is she up there?"

"She likes to climb trees," David replied.

Flowers of every color and type surrounded her—gold, silver, and dots of colorful wildflowers. Pickle snoozed beside the tree.

Ashley turned to him. "Where is Pickle today?"

"I left him with Samantha Wilson. When I arrived from New York, I rented a jeep, and drove several treacherous curves on the road connecting Greenwood to Cherish."

She laughed. "The route is challenging."

"Fortunately, it isn't as difficult as climbing Grandfather Mountain."

She took a step back. "Have you ever climbed—?

"Never."

"David, you titled your work," Nancy interrupted, examining the words written at the top of the painting.

Freddie tugged at the bell-shaped sleeve of Nancy's blouse. "What does it say?"

"Mr. Fordero's initials, the letter A, and a sparkly purple star. The painting is titled *My Wife by the River*. My *wife*." Nancy's thick black eyebrows lifted in surprise, though she quickly recovered her diplomatic self. "Congratulations. You took a chance, there, David, didn't you?"

"I prayed."

"Your painting is superb."

"Thank you." He considered the words he'd wanted to write on the canvas.

My dearest Ashley. I vow to fill our days with faith and laughter. Please love me as much as I love you.

He feasted his eyes on her exquisite face. She had the ability to enchant and charm him. "Do you like it, Twinkle?"

"I can't trust my voice." The love in her fathomless hazel

eyes warmed his heart. "Thankfully, you attached my nose to my face."

He laughed. "Where else would I put it?"

"On the tree, on a cloud, floating somewhere in the sky."

"Mr. Fodero?" Freddie was scrutinizing the painting.

"Hmm?"

"Where's the river?"

Stunned, David sobered. "Can't you find it?"

"No." Freddie, along with Nancy and Ashley, murmured agreement.

"Mr. Fodero?"

David shifted. "Yes, Freddie?"

"What's the pointy gold thing growing out of the grass?"

Unable to suppress his amusement, David pulled Ashley nearer and kissed her hair. "Miss Ashley's cowlick."

EPILOGUE

 *ne Year Later*

"ASHLEY, we won't be able to do much more of this." David gazed at his beautiful wife, precariously balanced on a tree branch beside him.

"Why not?" Ashley popped a frozen chocolate cookie into her mouth and chewed. "The obstetrician advised sweets in moderation and claimed they're safe for the baby."

"I'm not referring to cookies." He gazed out at the lawn, the garden overflowing with zucchini. *What would they do with all that zucchini? Was there such a thing as zucchini bread?* "I'm discussing your penchant for climbing trees and dragging me up here alongside you."

"You won't let me climb alone anymore."

He patted her stomach. "With excellent reason, considering you're two months pregnant."

"Thank you for getting over your fear of tree climbing."

He chuckled. "I didn't have a choice. My heart was in my throat at the thought of you climbing up here alone."

She planted a sweet kiss on his lips, immediately appeasing him.

From below, Pickle romped across the lawn carrying a Frisbee, Ashley's mixed breed chihuahua racing at his heels. She'd adopted the five-pound dog with solid red fur and an angelic face from an animal rescue center in Greenwood, before relocating to Cherish. David affectionately named the puppy Dogzilla because of his feisty personality.

"Next month when I see the doctor, we should be able to hear the baby's heartbeat."

"I can't wait," he said in a husky voice he hardly recognized. "Together, my beautiful wife, we are complete."

He sipped his energy drink, then balanced it gingerly on a tray secured to a sturdy branch. He was trying to quit caffeine altogether and had weaned himself down to only one drink per day, which he savored.

He gazed at the Just Married sign they'd attached to his pickup a year earlier, for they'd gotten married not long after their engagement. He didn't own a vintage turquoise convertible. Instead, he'd opted for the sign embossed in bold turquoise letters. The sign now hung as a banner draped over the railing of his front porch. A reminder of a wonderful life, an exquisite marriage.

He'd wanted to give Ashley a lavish wedding in New York City with hundreds of guests, an orchestra providing entertainment, and a honeymoon in the Caribbean. She'd declined, requesting an intimate wedding and a quiet cabin in the Carolina mountains.

Two nights before their wedding, he'd sensed something was on her mind.

"I have one special request," she said, her smile dazzling.

She'd been typing last-minute notes on her laptop, and he adored her for handling all the pressure she'd been under so well—planning their wedding, moving to Cherish, and delivering a tearful goodbye to her students with a vow to visit often. Nancy had graciously offered to teach several classes, and Ashley's substitute teachers became full-time employees.

Before he had time to respond to her, a knock sounded on his cabin door. He opened it and stared at his two older brothers and his sister, Quinn. Ashley disappeared out the back door with Pickle and Dogzilla.

"Thanks for the piano books," Quinn began.

He hadn't heard from her since he'd sent the books, but Ashley had taught him about God's love and forgiveness. His doubts could die so that his faith could live.

"And congratulations on your wedding, David."

He shook hands with his brothers, embraced his sister, and invited them inside.

He hadn't imagined a way to forgive, especially when his eyesight loss still hung heavy on his mind. Ashley kept assuring him the hand of God was on his life.

On a sultry day at the end of August, he'd entered Memorial Street Church and presented Marge Addyson with the commissioned painting. Ashley had stood by his side. The first Sunday he'd attended church in over two decades, he had sung praises along to an amazing selection of worship music.

He had held Ashley's hand as they slid into a front pew and was encouraged by an inspiring sermon. All the while, he remembered her words: *"Memorial Street Church is a building, but the real church is what happens on the inside."*

Since their engagement, and then marriage, he'd worked on a new collection of six avant-garde paintings, each with a theme centering on stars. The collection was scheduled to be exhibited at an exclusive auction house in New York. His return to the art world after nearly a year's absence assured widespread publicity and demand.

For now, he enveloped his wife in his arms.

"Thank you, David, for buying that empty lot in town," she said.

"It's not empty anymore. The art studio should be finished within the month."

"Special needs children and adults can enjoy the facilities." She smiled. "I love the name Starlight Vision."

He buried his face in her fragrant, lemon-scented hair. "Art should be nurtured. Creative expression and all that."

She laughed. "Typical artist."

"I hope every student, no matter their disability, will express themselves freely." He slid a hand around her waist, drawing her close. He kissed her stomach. "A miracle to cherish."

"Any plans after your art collection is sold?"

"I might consider purchasing a television for my study."

"You? The minimalist?" She didn't seem the least bit deceived by his nonchalance. "What will you watch? Another documentary?"

In between nuzzles, he murmured, "I'll begin with a certain black and white sitcom."

She began whistling the theme from *The Andy Griffith show.*

From high in a treetop, near a lushly designed cabin set in the woods, laughter rang out.

Pickle and Dogzilla barked and played tug-of-war with a plush striped elephant beneath a large oak tree.

Frozen cookies were left to thaw.

And all was right in a summer to cherish.

THE END

RECIPE FOR MELISSA'S SWEET & SOUR MEATBALLS

Ingredients:
   1 lb ground beef
   1 lb ground sausage
   Spices such as pepper, salt, garlic powder, onion powder (whatever spices you enjoy in your meatballs)
   1 bottle of chili sauce
   1 large jar of orange marmalade

Directions:
   Mix ground beef, sausage, and spices to taste. Form small meatballs, a little larger than a marble. Fry or bake meatballs until almost cooked through. Set aside and drain.

In a Crock-Pot or large saucepan, mix the bottle of chili sauce and jar of marmalade. Over medium heat on the stove or high heat in the Crock-Pot, let the chili sauce and marmalade melt together. Once mixed, lower the heat and add the meatballs.

Mix the meatballs into the sauce. Allow to simmer for about 30 minutes. Lower the heat to keep warm.

Serve with toothpicks for guests to pick them up.

Or serve with rice or on a bun if wanting more of a dinner item.

Enjoy!

A NOTE FROM JOSIE

Dear Reader,

Thank you for reading my sweet inspirational romance, *A Summer To Cherish*. I hope you enjoyed this heartwarming story, featuring Ashley and David. This is the sixth book in my contemporary "Cherish" series.

Faith is fragile. Faith takes time. And the best solutions are always painted with love.

This story is set in the charming fictional small town of Cherish, South Carolina. Here, I introduce two new characters to our beloved mix of familiar heroes and heroines. I loved writing the spunky, fun heroine, and David was a swoon-worthy hero.

I also researched the hero's profession—painting—and his heartbreaking eyesight loss.

If you loved this story as much as I loved writing it, please help other people find it by posting your review.

A Summer To Cherish is available in ebook, paperback, Large Print paperback, audiobook, and Hardcover.

Love music?

My Spotify List for A Summer To Cherish is here.

Love the inspirational Cherish series? Be sure to grab
Cherished Hearts.
Six Books in one giant boxed set.

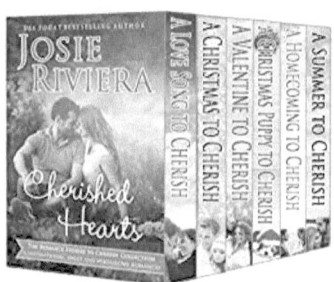

ABOUT THE AUTHOR

Josie Riviera is a *USA TODAY* bestselling author of contemporary, inspirational, and historical sweet romances that read like Hallmark movies. She lives in the Charlotte, NC, area with her wonderfully supportive husband. They share their home with an adorable shih tzu, who constantly needs grooming, and live in an old house forever needing renovations.

Become a member of my Read and Review VIP Facebook group for exclusive giveaways and ARCs.

To connect with Josie, visit her webpage and subscribe to her newsletter. As a thank-you, she'll send you a free sweet romance novella directly to your inbox.

ALSO BY JOSIE RIVIERA

Valentine Hearts Boxed Set

1-800-CUPID

1-800-CHRISTMAS

1-800-IRELAND

1-800-SUMMER

1-800-NEW YEAR

The 1-800-Series Sweet Contemporary Romance Bundle

Irish Hearts Sweet Romance Bundle

Holly's Gift

A Chocolate-Box Valentine

A Chocolate-Box Christmas

A Chocolate-Box New Years

A Chocolate-Box Summer Breeze

A Chocolate-Box Christmas Wish

A Chocolate-Box Irish Wedding

Chocolate-Box Hearts

Chocolate-Box Hearts Volume Two

Chocolate-Box Double Hearts

Recipes from the Heart

Leading Hearts

New Year Hearts

SENIOR HEARTS

A Summer To Cherish

Summer Hearts

Romance Stories To Cherish Volume Two

Cherished Hearts

Christmas in the Air

A Very Christian Christmas

The 1-800-Series Volume Two

The 1-800-Series Complete

Christmas Tails of the Heart

Pawfect Christmas Hearts

Most books are available in ebook, audiobook, paperback, Large Print paperback and Hardcover.

Many are FREE on Kindle Unlimited!